GLADYS MITCHELL

Death and the Maiden

VINTAGE BOOKS

London

Published by Vintage 2010

2 4 6 8 10 9 7 5 3 1

First published in Great Britain in 1947 by Michael Joseph

Vintage
Random House, 20 Vauxhall Bridge Road,
London SW1V 2SA

www.vintage-books.co.uk

Addresses for companies within The Random House Group Limited
can be found at: www.randomhouse.co.uk/offices.htm

The Random House Group Limited Reg. No. 954009

A CIP catalogue record for this book
is available from the British Library

ISBN 9780099546832

The Random House Group Limited supports The Forest Stewardship
Council (FSC), the leading international forest certification
organisation. All our titles that are printed on Greenpeace approved
FSC certified paper carry the FSC logo. Our paper procurement
policy can be found at www.rbooks.co.uk/environment

Typeset in Sabon by Palimpsest Book Production Limited,
Grangemouth, Stirlingshire

Printed and bound in Great Britain by
CPI Cox & Wyman, Reading RG1 8EX

To
WINIFRED BLAZEY

'But howsoever it be (gentle reader), I pray thee take it in good part, considering that for thee I have taken this pain, to the intent that thou mayst read the same with pleasure' WILLIAM ADLINGTON—*To the Reader of the Golden Ass of Lucius Apuleius*

*

and to the
RIVER ITCHEN

'From all diseases that arise,
From all disposed crudities;
From too much study, too much pain,
From laziness and from a strain;
From any humour doing harm,
Be it dry, or moist, or cold, or warm.
    Then come to me, whate'er you feel,
    Within, without, from head to heel.'

Anonymous (*Early 17th century*)—from the later editions of SIR THOMAS OVERBURY'S MISCELLANY

Chapter One

*'Nothing happened till nearly half-past eight,
and then pale watery began to trickle down,
followed by tall blue-winged olives, and a fish
or two rose tentatively. As I worked my way
up, I saw, round a corner through the long
grasses, such a commotion as must assuredly
be a rat or a waterhen: but, no, it was not . . .'*

J. W. HILLS (*A Summer on the Test*)

'IT BEARS investigation,' said Mr Tidson. 'It bears investigation, my dear Prissie.'

'Very well, Edris. Investigate by all means, as long as it isn't too expensive,' said Miss Carmody; and she smiled at the eager little man.

Among the numerous persons washed into her life by the irresponsible tides of consanguinity, Mr Tidson was a late but interesting piece of flotsam. He was the elderly Miss Carmody's second cousin, and had been living in Tenerife since his marriage. The fortunes of war had put off until late his retirement from his business, which was that of a banana grower, but he and his wife had at last come to England to live. It had transpired that they purposed to live with Miss Carmody, an arrangement which, she had confided to Connie Carmody, her niece and ward, she hoped would be readjusted.

Connie concurred in this hope. She had watched, with growing jealousy and alarm, the gradual settling-down of her Uncle Edris and his wife and the consequent disruption of the quiet life which she and her aunt had been leading, and she was becoming accustomed to think of Mr Tidson as an interloper and a nuisance.

'What is it that bears investigation, though?' Miss Carmody enquired. She and her ward were seated in the window of her eighteenth-century drawing-room in South-West London. The drawing-room was discreetly, comfortably but not expensively furnished, and formed part of a four-roomed flat which had housed Miss Carmody and her niece admirably, but which provided such close quarters for four people that Connie had been obliged, since the invasion (as she savagely but excusably termed it) to share a bedroom with her aunt, an arrangement which she, naturally, disliked.

Mr Tidson, who was occupying most of the settee, straightened himself and looked with exasperating benevolence upon Connie before replying to Miss Carmody's question.

'There is a newspaper report of something singular in the River Itchen,' he said. 'It seems, from this report, that a man has alleged that he saw a naiad or water-sprite below one of the bridges not very far from Winchester. Very interesting, if true. I should like to go and look into it.'

He went on to describe some extraordinary experiences of his own in connection with the folk-lore of the Canary Islands, and stated that these had caused him to become a keen student of primitive survivals and manifestations. Connie listened impatiently, and Miss Carmody with a blend of kindly but obvious incredulity mingled with slight disapproval, for some of Mr Tidson's recollections seemed unsuited to the ears of his niece.

By the time he had concluded his remarks, the fact that he should show excitement at a silly-season report of a water-sprite in a Hampshire chalk stream which ordinarily offered a *habitat* to nothing more sinister than a pike, more beautiful than the grayling or more intelligent than the brown trout, occasioned the disdainful Connie no surprise; neither was she surprised by Mr Tidson's experiences. He was, she knew already, rather a salacious little man.

'Let me see the paragraph,' said Miss Carmody; for she could scarcely believe that the newspapers, short as they were of newsprint, would devote space to a report upon anything quite so unlikely as the classic visitant. It was true that, the war being over and the Loch Ness monster having made no peace-time reappearance, even that single sheet of newsprint which formed the daily paper had somehow to be filled, but it seemed to her quite ridiculous that space should be devoted to the naiad.

Connie appeared to share her views.

'You must have misread it,' she said, 'or else it's rot!'

Miss Carmody took the paper which Mr Tidson handed her and read the marked column without comment. She observed, however, that it was not a newspaper report but merely a letter to the editor, and was clearly from the kind of person who claims to have heard the first cuckoo in Spring. Connie remarked upon this. Mr Tidson ignored her. She smiled, then, and asked to see the paper.

'Crete would accompany me if you did,' Mr Tidson observed, looking at Miss Carmody expectantly. Miss Carmody, having seen nothing of him for almost thirty-five years, had not found it difficult to revive her previous interest in the earnest and persistent little man, and it was with a certain degree of sympathy that she had begun to realize that time was already hanging on his hands, and that his young wife, Greek by extraction and extremely beautiful, was not proving the ideal companion of his leisure.

'Very well, Edris,' she said. 'There is nothing I need attend to until early September except my Working Men's Eldest Daughters, and I shall be glad to gather strength for them. Let us go and investigate. It will make as good a summer holiday as any other. Tell me your plans whilst I put these flowers in water, and then you shall teach Elsie how to make a Madras curry in place of the Ceylon one which you did not care for yesterday.'

'A summer holiday in quest of a naiad?' said Mr Tidson. 'Charming, my dear Prissie! Quite delightful! And we shall go to Winchester – when? I mean, how soon? Could you manage Monday? I do not want the scent to grow cold, and, besides, I want to hear the Cathedral choir doing Gray in A. Do you think it is likely that they will?'

'Monday? Admirable. Toogood is using the last of the petrol to take two of my Mothers to the seaside to-morrow, but by Monday he can get the next allowance,' responded Miss Carmody, ignoring Gray in A, a key she did not care for very much, preferring Church music in E flat. 'On Monday, then. Very pleasant.'

'Good,' said Mr Tidson. 'Or, of course, we could go by train this afternoon. What do you think?'

Perceiving that he was impatient to be upon the scene and obtain first-hand information of the naiad, Miss Carmody agreed to lose no time, but (rather to her relief, for it was inconvenient to arrange to leave home at not more than four hours' notice, and she knew that Connie, who did the packing, would not like it, and, in any case, disliked Mr Tidson) this decision was overridden, for at that moment Crete came in, and, catching the last remarks of the parties concerned, vetoed the notion that they could go without preparations.

'We have to arrange at Winchester to stay somewhere,' Crete pointed out, 'and I have to get my hair done, and you have to find enough coupons (I suppose from my book) for at least two shirts before you can go anywhere. Do be reasonable, Edris. You are a very foolish old man.'

She turned away from him contemptuously and looked at herself in the glass.

Crete Tidson was twenty years younger than her husband. She was a slender woman with greenish-gold hair, large dark eyes like those shown in early seventeenth-century portraits, the curling mouth and proudly-carried head of her race, and a rounded, wilful chin. She erred on the side of severity towards her husband, but encouraged him in the free expression of his tastes. She had a well-founded although critical respect for his ability to get his own way, and seldom trusted him out of her sight, for Mr Tidson had developed to a marked degree the foible (noted by St Paul in the Athenians) of desiring always some new thing, and in pursuit of these novelties he was inclined to get into mischief.

'At any rate,' said Mr Tidson, 'I can and will send for a local newspaper, which should contain a fuller account than the one I have just shown Connie.' He beamed amiably upon his niece, who scowled in return. 'And I will also go to the public library for information about Winchester, the River Itchen, naiads, fishing, and the folk-lore of Hampshire. I do so love anything new, and this will be delightfully new. I could do the preliminary research this afternoon, before we leave London, couldn't I?'

Glad for him to have something to do which would innocently dispose of his time, his wife and Miss Carmody immediately agreed that he could, although Connie remained aloof, and (considering that he had introduced her to the naiad at her own request) unreasonably scornful.

'I will wire for the rooms,' said Miss Carmody. 'We will stay at the *Domus*. Connie and I always do. An excellent hotel in every way, although, of course, not cheap.'

'But what is it really all about?' asked Crete, who had not been present when Mr Tidson had looked up from the newspaper and announced the great discovery. 'What could we do in Winchester? It is a mare's nest, is it not?'

'It is a naiad in Hampshire, my dear Crete,' said Mr Tidson.

'Nonsense, Uncle Edris,' said Connie, annoyed to think of any more of her aunt's money being thrown away on the Tidsons. 'There are no naiads in Hampshire. There never have been, and there never will be. Hampshire was part of Wessex. You know that as well as I do!'

'King Alfred,' agreed Miss Carmody, 'not to speak of his pious father, Aethelwulf, would not have permitted naiads in country already menaced by the Danes.'

'Red-haired, horrid people,' said Crete, who had known two modern Danes on Tenerife, and had found that they rivalled her in beauty. 'I do not like the Danes.'

'There were Roman settlements in Hampshire, though,' went on Miss Carmody pacifically. 'May not the Romans, with their *flair* for appropriations, have introduced a stolen Greek naiad into the waters of Venta Belgarum?'

'It is possible,' Crete admitted, losing interest. 'In any case, Edris seems determined to take a holiday, and he might as well pursue a naiad as butterflies or tit-mice – or the daughter of Señor Don Alvarez Pedilla y Lampada, as happened last time,' she added darkly. 'He has immoral itches.'

'How soon do we go?' demanded Connie, who disliked Crete almost as much as she disliked Mr Tidson, and was jealous of her beauty and charm.

'On Monday, if we can have the rooms. They are likely to be full at this time of year, however,' said her aunt. 'I have been before, and I know.'

The fear expressed in the last sentences proved to be unfounded. By the evening, accommodation for the party had been arranged, and Mr Tidson, deep in the chronicles of Winchester College, seemed certain of a fortnight's pleasurable nymph-hunting (in the classical and not the piscatorial sense) and the rest of the party of a peaceful and interesting holiday. Connie studied the Ordnance map, Miss Carmody revived her recollections of Winchester Cathedral, the *Domus* hotel, and the walks which could be taken from the city, and Crete arranged a personal orgy of embroidery, for it was her practice, it seemed, to remain within doors in a climate she neither liked nor trusted, and she therefore would need something to do.

The few days soon passed. On the Saturday morning preceding the Monday on which the party were to motor down to Winchester, Mr Tidson put into his notebook a passage which pleased him mightily. It was, he explained, an extract from a diary of the time of the Civil War, and, read in the evening by his wife and by Miss Carmody, ran thus:

'He wase by perswation of my ffather-in-lawe then putt to schoole at Winchestor and stayed 6 yeres and wase beten for the trwe reason that he tawlked lewdely and with littell discretion of a nakid mayd wett in the feldes where shee doe lye abedd, and hee not aschamed even att such tinder edge to saye itt.'

'You see?' said Mr Tidson triumphantly. 'Even in the seventeenth century she was known. What do you say now to my naiad?'

'Amazing,' said Miss Carmody. 'May I have another look at that?' She took the notebook from Crete's hands and perused the passage again. 'The spelling puts me in mind of something, although I can't remember quite what.'

'I think you should share your knowledge,' said Mr Tidson. 'Think, my dear Prissie, think! We must learn to control our verbal memories.'

Connie leaned over and took the book from her aunt. She flicked over the pages contemptuously. Mr Tidson looked at Miss Carmody and smiled.

'Women have very inaccurate notions of history, I believe,' he remarked with conversational inoffensiveness. 'Except you, of course, my dear Prissie.'

'I don't know about inaccurate,' said Connie, tossing the book at him so that a sharp edge hit him on his little round paunch, 'but I do know that there's a book of seventeenth-century memoirs in auntie's bureau bookcase in which you could find all these words.'

'Is there indeed?' said Mr Tidson. 'And is it your custom to peer into your aunt's bureau bookcase?'

'Really, Edris!' remonstrated Crete. 'You must not speak to Connie like that. It is not kind. Perhaps she does not know that she should not peer. What is it – peering? It is an offensive word, I think. Snoop, do you say?'

Connie crimsoned and got up. She looked so threatening that Mr Tidson actually drew his knees up a little as though to protect his stomach from further assault. Miss Carmody seemed to suffer fears on his behalf, too, for she held on to Connie's arm, said that she detested the word 'snooping,' and added with unwonted sharpness that Connie had had the run of her bureau bookcase for years, ever since she had been old enough to be trusted with her aunt's favourite volumes, and that no question of prying, peering or snooping entered into the matter.

Mr Tidson smiled sweetly, and observed that Connie ought not to be touchy, and that she knew as well as he did that he had been joking. He also upheld Miss Carmody's pronouncement that snooping was a vulgar synonym.

'I don't like his ways,' said Connie, when he and Crete had gone. 'Half the time he says nasty, spiteful things, and the other half he's trying to paw me about. I think him a disgusting old man.'

'Not so very old,' said Miss Carmody.

'He's old enough to know better than to go chasing nymphs in rivers,' said Connie stoutly, 'although, of course, it's only on a par with his other activities, I suppose.'

Miss Carmody, in the day or two that followed, confessed herself worried by Mr Tidson's enthusiasm for the naiad. He was alternately in high spirits at the thought (or so he said) of adding to his repertory of folk-lore, or cast down because the naiad might have left Hampshire before he had an opportunity to see her. The possibility that the letter to the paper might be either a practical joke or the gibberings of a maniac he appeared to disregard.

'I can't make him out,' said Connie. 'His business life, I expect, was a mixture of cadging, sharp practice and double-dealing, and I should think he was a menace to his employees and unpopular with the other banana growers.'

There was something frightening, she went on, in the fact that Mr Tidson should suddenly leap at this ridiculous newspaper communication as an excuse to go to Winchester. Why Winchester, she wanted to know; and held her aunt's gaze.

Miss Carmody said nothing, but she was sufficiently perturbed, it appeared, to go to the telephone next morning, before her uninvited guests were astir, and call up a psychiatrist, a sound and talented old lady whose name was Bradley. She gave the facts, and added that she thought it would do no harm to obtain an expert opinion upon Mr Tidson's mental condition before he went down to Winchester in search of his naiad.

'You understand that I don't want him to suspect that we think there might be anything *odd* about him,' she said anxiously, 'because, of course, there probably isn't. His interest may be quite genuine, and probably is. I just thought that, if you could spare the time ... Well, look here! I mustn't thwart him. Could you possibly come to Winchester? I – we have met, you know – a mutual friend, Miss Carroll, at Cartaret College—'

'I quite understand,' said Mrs Bradley, 'and I am most intrigued. I shall be in Winchester and at the *Domus* by Monday lunch-time. Your naiad may be full of possibilities.'

'Yes, that is what I fear,' said Miss Carmody. Very much cheered, however, by Mrs Bradley's comforting promise, she expressed her gratitude and rang off. She then sent Connie to the bank for a Statement, and knit her brows over this when it came. Mr and Mrs Tidson were costing her rather dear. They had already spent six weeks at her house, and the *Domus,* as she herself had advertised, was not a cheap hotel. However, it was where she had always stayed, particularly during the blitz on London, and she had always said that she could not contemplate staying anywhere else. Connie reminded her of this almost snappishly when she put forward a tentative suggestion that, to save expense, the party might take furnished lodgings for the holiday. Connie disliked furnished lodgings, and said so roundly.

'And, in the end, what with one thing and another, you won't be a bit better off,' she added ill-temperedly.

Miss Carmody sighed; but she reminded herself that Connie had been accustomed to better things than she could offer her, and also that the *Domus* was indeed a most comfortable and kindly hotel, and not even actually in the city.

Mr Tidson enjoyed his drive to Winchester, and, by the time the car was passing Basingstoke on road A30 to rejoin A33 *en route* for the string of villages on the somewhat uninteresting journey past Micheldever and Kingsworthy to the lane on the north side of Winchester, where the *Domus* hotel is to be found, he had remembered and remarked upon a nephew of his who, he believed, went to school in Winchester but would now be on holiday, he supposed.

'What nephew would that be, Uncle Edris?' enquired Connie, who had been bidden privately by Miss Carmody to be civil to Mr Tidson, although not to countenance or encourage his oddities.

'Why, Polly's girl's boy,' replied Mr Tidson unhelpfully. 'What's the name, now?'

'Preece-Harvard,' said Connie, through her teeth. 'I ought to know!'

'Preece-Harvard is the name,' agreed Miss Carmody, 'and it is nothing to do with Polly, as you very well know. They live not very far from Winchester. We had better look them up while we are there.'

'Don't ask *me* to go!' said Connie.

'I must look up the address,' said Mr Tidson.

'You will hardly have time to look the boy up, though,' observed Crete, not without malice. 'You will be too busy looking up your nymph.'

Mr Tidson became silent, and looked out of the car window at College Wood, distant half a mile from the road.

'We should be passing Bradley Farm about now,' said Connie, who had the map open on her knees. She was seated between her aunt and Crete Tidson on the back seat of the car. Mr Tidson was in front, beside Toogood.

'Bradley? Ah, that reminds me,' said Miss Carmody. 'My friend Mrs Bradley is also proposing to stay at the *Domus* with us. Miss Carroll took her place at Cartaret College, Connie, you remember, when she relinquished the post of Warden of Athelstan Hall.'

'Yes, I remember,' said Connie. 'That terrifying, black old lady who always wore dreadful colours and did indescribable knitting. We heard her lecture. I should hardly have thought you could call her a friend of yours, though. We only knew Miss Carroll very slightly, and although you spoke to Mrs Bradley—'

'*Black?*' said Mr Tidson, turning his head.

'She has black hair and black eyes,' Miss Carmody sharply replied. 'There is nothing else black about her, of course. Connie is given to wilful and misleading exaggeration at times.'

'Exaggeration is always misleading,' said Crete. Mr Tidson, who did not believe this, resumed his contemplation of the landscape, and the car swept smoothly past Dodsley Wood and a couple of *tumuli*, and then along a stretch of what had once been a Roman road, and so past Abbots Barton towards Winchester.

'And although you spoke to Mrs Bradley after her lecture on hereditary tendencies,' said Connie, who disliked to be cut off in the middle of a sentence, 'I don't see that that could exactly make her a friend of yours, Aunt Prissie, and I don't want to meet her again! I didn't like her.'

'Put that rug back, dear,' replied her aunt. 'You won't need that in the hotel. Well, here we are, Crete,' she added, turning to the slightly more bearable of her parasitic guests. 'I wonder how you will like it now we're here?'

'Oh, I shall like it,' said Crete. 'Edris will have his nymph, you will have your friend the black woman, Connie will walk and go early, very early, to bed, and I shall enjoy myself alone. But how is this the hotel? We are not yet in Winchester.'

──────────── Chapter Two ────────────

*'... which is to inform such Housekeepers as
are not in the Higher Rank of Fortune, how to
Eat, or Entertain Company, in the most elegant
Manner, at a reasonable Expence.'*
   MRS SARAH HARRISON OF DEVONSHIRE (*The
   House-Keeper's Pocket Book and Complete
                           Family Cook, 1760*)

THE *Domus* hotel was in a side-turning and free of the
   main road traffic. It was approached by way of a lane
south-west of the broad arterial road from which A33
debouched before appearing, out of a maze of tributary
meanderings, as the main Southampton Road beyond St
Cross.

The *Domus* had been in turn a monastery, an Elizabethan
mansion devoted to the cause and hiding of Jesuit priests,
an eighteenth-century town house, a nineteenth-century
nunnery, and, lastly, a hotel, and it showed traces of all
these adventures. The car had been driven past a long garden
whose wall still carried stigmata in the form of a small Cross
and the date 1872, relics of the nunnery, and was now
drawn up before a glassed-in entrance-lounge containing a
wicker-chair, an iron shoe-scraper, two plants in pots, a fibre
mat, a model of Winchester Cathedral, and the hotel cat.

Further doors led into the hall, and a door to the right
showed the reception desk. A tall, cadaverous porter of
Scottish extraction jerked a Wee Free thumb towards the
office and took charge of the smallest piece of luggage which
Toogood had dumped on the tiled floor. Miss Carmody,
followed by Mr Tidson, went to the reception desk, and the

porter put down the smallest piece of luggage, glanced about him as though in deep suspicion of the whole party, and asked lugubriously of Connie:

'You'll be staying long, no doubt?'

'Oh, not so long as all that,' said Connie, glancing uncertainly at Crete.

'For a fortnight,' said Crete.

'Ou, ay,' said the porter, as though this confirmed his worst fears. A voice from the desk said:

'Twenty-nine, thirty-three and seven, Thomas.'

'Twenty-nine, therrty-three and seven,' repeated the porter. 'You'll follow me. *Fifteen*, therrty-three and seven is what I was tellt this morning, but ye'll suit yoursel's, nae doubt!'

Twenty-nine, a pleasant little room in the oldest part of the house, was assigned by Miss Carmody to Connie. Thirty-three, containing twin beds and a double wardrobe, was for the Tidsons, and was on the same floor. Number seven was on the ground-floor of the annexe, and was gained by going through the sun-lounge into a bungalow building, very modern and pleasant. Seven was Miss Carmody's room, and when she found that it was exactly what she had asked for – for she suffered slightly from pyromania and disliked to sleep above ground level in strange houses – she was extremely pleased. Crete was *not* pleased. She demanded a separate room.

The four met in the cocktail lounge and were served by the severe Thomas with excellent sherry, except for Connie, who preferred gin and Vermouth. They had not been there long when Miss Carmody, putting down her glass, said that they must find out whether her friend Mrs Bradley was expected for lunch. She asked Connie to go and see.

'They won't know,' said Connie, 'and, if they did, I wouldn't dare to ask. This place always did terrify me, and Thomas makes me feel as though I'd jam on my face. I call him an awful sort of man.'

'Oh, nonsense,' said Miss Carmody. 'I will send for him and enquire.' She summoned Thomas, to the admiration of her niece, by pressing the bell. Thomas, who had added to his first impressiveness by putting their drinks before

them as though he knew full well that they were jeopard-
izing the safety of their immortal souls with every sip they
took, acceded civilly, with an inclination of the head and
a 'Verra guid' uttered like a curse, to Miss Carmody's request
that he would find out whether Mrs Bradley was expected
for lunch, and returned in due course with the information that she was.

'And a verra clever body,' he added, looking pontifical
as he gazed over Mr Tidson's head at the red geraniums
in the garden. 'A verra clever body. Just that.'

It sounded like an epitaph, and all found themselves gravely
inclining their heads. The rite was interrupted by the entrance
of a small, black-haired, black-eyed woman in a hairy
heliotrope tweed costume and a green felt hat. She was of
witch-like aspect, and heralded her coming with a harsh cackle
which sounded oddly from her beaky little mouth.

'Mrs Bradley!' exclaimed Miss Carmody, getting up.
Thomas made way respectfully for the new arrival, and,
without being asked, went out and shortly returned with
another glass of sherry.

'Your Amontillado, madam,' he said. As this title had
not, so far, been bestowed upon the other ladies of the
party, it was particularly impressive, and when Thomas
went away (which he did without taking notice of being
yelled at as 'Waiter!' by a young officer in the uniform of
the Royal Air Force), Crete Tidson, having, with her
husband and Connie, been introduced to the witch, enquired
whether Mrs Bradley had often stayed at the *Domus*.

'Once, some time before the war,' Mrs Bradley replied.
'Are you familiar with the country in and around the New
Forest?'

The gong for lunch interrupted the flow of conversation
which followed these last magic words, and the party of four
were allotted an excellent table at the garden end of the
dining-room and were provided with copies of the menu.
Mrs Bradley was conducted to a table for one by a window.

'Pig's face!' said Mr Tidson, enraptured, when he had
read the menu. 'I haven't eaten pig's face since I was a little
tiny boy.'

He began to hum under his breath until his wife prodded him sharply. The waitress, a nice girl, perceiving his excitement, saw to it that he received a generous portion. She took his order for bottled beer, and decided, in the security of her small alcove between the sideboard and the serving-table, that the little man had picked the wrong wife and was henpecked. She made up her mind to make his stay as pleasant as she could. He reminded her of her uncle from America.

'I like it here,' said Connie, looking favourably upon a plate of excellent cold beef and the salad and boiled potatoes which came with it. 'What are we going to do this afternoon?'

'What you like,' replied her aunt. 'Crete? Edris? What are your suggestions?'

'I shall explore the city,' said Mr Tidson, 'and possibly I shall seek an interview with the editor of the local paper. I shall be happiest alone.'

'I shall sit in the sun lounge, which appears to be warm and pleasant, and get on with my embroidery,' said Crete.

'Then you and I will walk to St Cross,' said Miss Carmody, 'if you would like that, Connie.'

Connie said that she would like it very much, and Crete asked what there was to see at St Cross. Whilst Miss Carmody (interrupted often by Mr Tidson, who had read up St Cross in a guide book before he had left London) was answering this question, the plates were changed and the party received jam roll and custard, or, if they preferred it, plum tart.

Mr Tidson finished his beer, and, before anyone could prevent it, he had crossed over to Mrs Bradley's table and was soon in a deep discussion upon cheese, for she had chosen cheese and biscuit rather than the sweet course. Mr Tidson was inclined to reproach her for declining the excellent jam roll, and they had a pleasant and inspiring conversation before he returned to his place.

After lunch Mrs Bradley accepted an invitation from Miss Carmody to accompany herself and her niece to St Cross, and none of them saw any more of the Tidsons until dinner.

'I hope you are staying a good long time,' said Connie, to the great surprise of her aunt.

'I hope to stay as long as you all do,' Mrs Bradley replied. 'I am very fond of Winchester, and, besides, Miss Carmody and I have much to talk about.'

'You'll have more still if Uncle Edris finds his water-nymph,' said Connie. Mrs Bradley looked interested and asked for an explanation, although she had already, on the telephone, received tidings of the water-nymph from Miss Carmody. She could perceive, however, that Connie was even more in need of help than Mr Tidson.

'Ah,' she said, when Connie, who had some wit and a gift of mimicry, had given a lively picture of Mr Tidson's raptures, 'that explains the expression in his eye. He looks gleeful, a sign I have learned to dread in my patients. But all is now made clear. Clear as the waters of the Itchen,' she added, regarding the crystal river with great favour, for they had made short work of the distance between the *Domus* and College Walk.

'You don't think Edris is mad?' asked Miss Carmody anxiously. 'I shouldn't mind in the ordinary way, but I don't much want him mad in an hotel.'

'No, it is not the place,' Mrs Bradley gravely agreed. 'But, indeed, no such thought had crossed my mind. I remarked upon my patients because, with the exception of very small children engaged upon very dark deeds, I do not see gleeful persons unless they are in some degree abnormal.'

'But Uncle Edris *is* a small child engaged upon dark deeds,' observed Connie. Mrs Bradley disregarded this, and looked expectantly at Miss Carmody.

'Yes, I am afraid that Edris *is* abnormal. He has lived thirty-five years surrounded by nothing but bananas,' Miss Carmody explained with great simplicity.

'I see,' Mrs Bradley replied. She looked thoughtful. 'No doubt that would make a great impression, especially on a sensitive spirit. Has Mr Tidson a sensitive spirit?'

Connie glanced at her to find out whether she could be laughing, but Mrs Bradley was gazing benignly upon the prospect of St Catherine's Hill, which could be seen half a mile away on the further side of the river. Her expression gave no clue to her thoughts, but, whatever these may have been, it hardly seemed likely, judging from her profile, that they were of a humorous nature.

The conversation turned to earthworks, and then to thirteenth-century architecture, and the subject of Mr Tidson's peculiarities was not resumed. The three ladies had an interesting hour at the medieval hospital, over which they were conducted by one of the brothers, and then they returned to the city by the way they had come, and, at Connie's request, had tea not at the hotel but at tea-rooms which were partly supported by the only remaining pillar of William the Conqueror's Norman palace, a relic which Connie found romantic.

It was half-past five before they returned to the *Domus*. Crete Tidson had given up her embroidery and was reading an evening paper brought to her by a young man who had already fallen in love with her greenish hair, slim body and (as he said) fathomless eyes. Of Mr Tidson there was no sign.

'You might be the naiad yourself, Crete,' said Miss Carmody, greeting her. 'Has Edris come in yet from his walk?'

Crete, who had looked startled by the reference to the naiad, resumed her expression of remoteness and slight boredom, and replied that Edris had come in to tea at half-past four and had eaten everything on the tray except the one piece of brown bread and butter which had fallen to his wife's portion. She added that he had then gone out again.

'He is as pleased as a child with Winchester,' she remarked at the conclusion of this narrative.

'I should not have supposed that a child would have been particularly pleased with Winchester. I should have thought it was an adult person's heaven,' Mrs Bradley thoughtfully observed. Crete gave her the same kind of sharp and startled glance as she had bestowed upon Miss Carmody at mention of the naiad, but Mrs Bradley remained in bland contemplation of the scarlet geraniums which, apart from smooth lawn, brown earth, a gravel path, a disused chicken coop and an aristocratic mound which covered the out-of-date air-raid shelter, formed the chief attraction of the somewhat unimaginative garden.

'Well, Edris is rather like a child, in many ways, when he is pleased. That was what I meant,' said Crete. 'Have you all had tea? And is there a bookshop near? I cannot embroider all the time.'

Connie told her where to find a bookshop, and said that there was a lending library at the back of it.

'You go through the shop,' she added helpfully.

'No, thank you!' said Crete. 'I only like new books. By that I mean books which have not been handled by others.'

'But I expect they have. The new ones, I mean,' said Miss Carmody. 'People handle the new books to see what they want in exchange for their book tokens. No one ever knows what to do with a book token. I've noticed it.'

'Oh, I do!' cried Connie. 'All my friends give me book tokens, and I give them book tokens, too. It saves all the bother of presents.'

'But it isn't the same fun,' said Miss Carmody, who had certain old-fashioned ideas, although not very many.

'Well, I must have a book, and it must be a new one. Edris will have to find me something,' said Crete. 'He will know what to get, no doubt. I am not hard to please.'

Confronted upon his return with the task of finding her a book which should be both light and sensible, Mr Tidson, who seemed to be in great good humour, promised to attend to it in the morning, as the shop would most certainly be shut at that time of the evening.

'I will get you a guide book,' he said. 'It will save you the trouble of visiting the places of interest, and will last you longer than a novel.'

Miss Carmody, to whom these uses of a guide book had not previously occurred, looked somewhat surprised. Mrs Bradley cackled, and Crete observed that Edris sometimes had very good ideas. She added that she had had no intention whatsoever of visiting the places of interest, but that one should be informed upon matters of cultural and historic importance, and that a guide book would be most welcome.

Upon this note of conjugal understanding and felicity, husband and wife went up to dress for dinner, and Connie, who did not think much of the walk she had had that afternoon, went out, as she said, to stretch her legs. Miss Carmody, with a grateful sigh, sat down beside Mrs Bradley.

'Well, what do you make of Edris and Crete?' she enquired.

'They seem well matched,' replied Mrs Bradley thoughtfully. This comment seemed to cause Miss Carmody some surprise. 'Will they enjoy their stay in England, do you think?' Mrs Bradley went on.

'It is not a stay. It is permanent,' Miss Carmody replied. She hesitated, and then added, 'Edris has retired from his banana plantation, although not as comfortably, I believe, as he had hoped. He has had losses, I understand, and then I suppose trade must have suffered somewhat during the war. I believe they have not much to live on, and as I believe they propose to live on me, that will not be much for them, either.'

Politeness forbade Mrs Bradley to ask more, and she turned the conversation on to Connie, who seemed, she said, an interesting child. Certainly Connie's ill-humour, which had been most marked since the advent of the Tidsons, seemed to have disappeared. Miss Carmody commented on this, and added that she was very fond of Connie.

'She is my cousin's child. I took her for his sake, but I keep her now for my own,' she said with apparent sincerity.

Mrs Bradley understood from this that Miss Carmody supported Connie, and she was surprised that so independent-seeming a girl should be content to live on an aunt past middle age.

'She is technically illegitimate,' said Miss Carmody, as though she were explaining away Mrs Bradley's uncharitable thoughts. 'A very sad case. My cousin – Arthur Preece-Harvard, you know – was very deeply in love with Connie's mother. There was no dishonour attached. They intended to marry. Connie is the first-fruits of impatience.'

'And the mother?' Mrs Bradley enquired, perceiving that Miss Carmody wished to develop the conversation.

'A sweet, sweet girl,' said Miss Carmody. 'She died, I am sorry to say, in giving birth to Connie. Arthur was broken-hearted for a time, and, of course, the whole thing has made life hard for the child. I wish she got on with Edris better. They dislike one another very much. It *is* so awkward at times. Of course, Connie has suffered great hardship and some injustice. It has made her rather bitter, I'm afraid. I do what I can, but, of course, it isn't what she was used to. It is very wrong to treat a child unfairly.'

'I see,' said Mrs Bradley; and the thoughts engendered by this conversation lasted her all the time that she was dressing.

The party met for cocktails at half-past six, and spent a pleasant time until dinner, which was at seven. Mr Tidson, who, from his own account, had spent a delightful afternoon in roving all over the town from the Westgate to the river bridge, and from Hyde Abbey gateway to the farthest boundary of St Mary's College, invited Mrs Bradley to sit at their table for the meal, but she pleaded that there were papers she proposed to study during dinner, and produced an impressive brief-case which did, indeed, contain papers of a sort, although not anything of immediate or first-rate importance.

Mr Tidson led the way into the dining-room, made a pleasant remark to the waitress, pulled Mrs Bradley's chair out for her and even, rather officiously, cleared a space beside her plate for her documents. Then he saw his own party seated, flipped open his table napkin, said 'Ha! Oxtail soup!' and called boisterously for the wine list. There was no doubt that he was in great holiday spirits, and there was no doubt, either, thought Mrs Bradley, that the wine would appear in due course on Miss Carmody's bill.

'You are enjoying Winchester, sir?' asked the waitress, when she came to bring the bottle and change the plates.

'Winchester,' declared Mr Tidson, 'is the queen of cities. And you, my dear, are the queen of Winchester.'

'My home's in Southampton,' said the girl, registering a theory that Mr Tidson was an old sport but would bear watching. Anecdotes about Southampton, Liverpool and

Bristol, from all of which his banana boats had sailed, then lasted Mr Tidson until coffee, and the waitress decided that she was wrong, and that the poor old bloke was harmless after all, thus confirming her first impression of him.

'I shall hope,' he said, changing the conversation when all five of them were seated in the lounge after dinner, 'to have your company, Mrs Bradley, in my exploration of the city and its environs. I am, as you may imagine, a little out of touch with details of English architecture after so long a sojourn abroad. Would you care to accompany me to-morrow, perhaps, or the next day?'

'It would give me great pleasure,' Mrs Bradley replied. 'Shall we say to-morrow afternoon? And where would you like to go?'

'I should like to go to Alresford,' Mr Tidson replied, 'but as my nymph is not there I shall postpone my visit in her honour, and we will walk as far as Shawford, if you are willing.'

'Alresford?' said Connie, startled. 'Oh, but you can't go there!'

'That is what I said,' replied Mr Tidson. 'Moreover, I did not address the remark to you!'

Chapter Three

'Dr Thorne promised to come also but was prevented by being obliged to attend some Patients.'

*   *   *

'Soon after breakfast I went out a fishing by myself, into Wilmots Orchard as it is called and stayed there till Dinner time near 3 o'clock had very good sport, caught 3 fine Trout, the largest about 1pd and 1/4, and 4 fine Eels . . .'
Diary of a Country Parson: the REVEREND
JAMES WOODFORDE, Vol. 3, 1788–1792.
Edited by JOHN BERESFORD.

As it happened, Mrs Bradley spent only two days in Winchester, or, rather, two parts of days, for she was recalled by telegram on the Tuesday afternoon to attend an ex-seaman who had been ordered psychiatric treatment for shock following some bad burns.

Mr Tidson, therefore, continued his tour of Winchester and the neighbourhood alone, for his wife still declared that she preferred a chair in the sun-lounge to walking or sightseeing, and Miss Carmody and Connie refused to have anything to do with fishing.

Mr Tidson had announced himself to be a devoted and persistent angler, and argued that, besides this, the trout-rod in his hand would cloak the gravity of his true quest, his search for the naiad, for it gave a screen, and seemed to provide a reason, for his wadings and mud-larkings across water-meadows intersected by ditches, brooks, tributary streams and carriers, and for his getting dirty and wet.

A wet and muddy angler was almost an object of nature, he observed, but a naiad-hunter in similar plight might have been regarded askance, particularly as the quickest way back to the hotel lay across the Cathedral Close. He therefore purchased a green-heart rod and some tackle, and set about acquiring tickets for the local waters.

His first action after lunch was to see Mrs Bradley off. His second was to walk to the offices of the County newspaper and enquire whether anything more had been added to the first report of the naiad. Rather to his annoyance, Miss Carmody insisted upon going there with him. Connie, whom he had attempted to persuade, refused to be seen about with him, an announcement which she made in the most offensive tone of which she was capable. She then went off to the bus station and left Mr Tidson and Miss Carmody to walk to the office of the newspaper.

The staff could tell them no more. They cast polite doubts upon the authenticity of the letter and also declared that it was unusual for ladies to bathe in the open river so near the Cathedral precincts. The story of the naiad, they thought, had been invented to provide a silly-season sensation, or possibly to provoke a newspaper correspondence. It had not appeared in any of the local papers, although a local resident had sent them a cutting.

They had not, however, troubled to get in touch with the sender of the letter. They thought that he must have been someone staying in Winchester on holiday who had found the place quiet – some people did – and had tried to create a diversion in the form of a stupid hoax.

Miss Carmody listened with critical attention, putting in a word here and there. She confided to Connie, upon her return to the *Domus*, that she still found herself slightly worried. She could not forget that Mr Tidson had been out of England for a great many years, and, in any case, had no sense of humour, and she feared lest his researches should lead him into difficulties. She referred afresh to the instinct which had caused her to ask Mrs Bradley to come to Winchester, and said soberly that she would have been glad of the continued support and comfort of her presence.

Connie, who meant to go to Andover, where she had friends, listened with considerable impatience, for she knew she would miss the bus if she stayed too long. She did, in fact, miss it, much to her annoyance, for there was no other which fitted in with the hotel meals, and this fact caused her to postpone her outing and behave rather sulkily in consequence.

Miss Carmody, still perturbed, got up at six the next morning and went out by herself for a walk. She crossed the High Street and stood for a moment beside the Butter Cross before she passed beneath an archway which led across the green to the Cathedral.

Except for a postman she saw nobody as she left the flying buttresses of the south wall of the Cathedral behind her and crossed the silent and beautiful Close. She paused, as she had paused in years gone by, to admire the sixteenth-century houses near Kings Gate, and then she walked under the arches of the gate itself, with the Church of St Swithun athwart it, and turned down College Street towards the river.

She passed the College booksellers' and the house in which Jane Austen died, and admired, on the other side of the road, the grass-plot and rambler roses of the outside wall of the Close. The beautiful little garden was denuded now of its railings, which had all gone for wartime scrap and had not been replaced, but it retained its ancient well, and its tall and brilliant flowers almost hid the stone wall from view.

At the bottom of the street a loose, broad path, a white-painted wicket gate and an avenue of limes led on to the open water-meadows through which ran the main stream of Itchen and those other clear chalk-streams, occasionally green with weed and in places deceptively deep, beside which she, Connie and Mrs Bradley had walked to St Cross on the first afternoon of their stay; and as she walked between streams in that fresh, cold, early morning air, and crossed a two-plank bridge above a six-foot pool, and lingered awhile to look southwards towards Saint Cross and then up at the grove of trees on Saint Catherine's brow, it began to seem, she confessed to Crete and Connie when she returned, as though there might be something in the letter after all, and that the surprising thing might be, not the sight of the naiad, but the failure to be able to see her. The time, the place and the loved one could so easily be in confluence, she thought.

She added, in exalted mood, that, although no more willing to believe the writer of the letter than she had been when she was in London, she was now prepared to extend to him the freedom of poets' licence, this for the excellent reason that Truth, as Tagore has said, in her dress of fiction moves with ease.

Crete, obviously bored with all these rhapsodies, went on with her embroidery and said nothing. Connie had not quite forgiven her aunt for the loss of the Andover outing, and would not encourage the conversation by taking part in it. In fact, to her aunt's disappointment, she remained sulky, and was rather disagreeable.

The rest of the day passed calmly, but immediately after dinner Mr Tidson left his wife in the lounge with the guide book and some coffee, saw that Miss Carmody and Connie were playing two-handed whist, and went forth, rod in hand, at eight o'clock, ostensibly to try his luck at the evening rise of the trout, but really, he told the others, to lie in wait for his shyer quarry, the naiad.

At just after half-past ten he returned, wet through – in fact, soaked to the skin – and in high excitement. His wife, who was inclined to be cross with him for spoiling his suit and shoes, listened with more than her usual attentiveness. Miss Carmody, who had soon given up the whist and gone out to look at the Cathedral by moonlight, had just returned, but Connie, who had decided that the West Front was rather ugly, had left her aunt and gone off for an evening stroll.

Mr Tidson, stuttering a little, declared that he thought he might have caught a glimpse of the naiad. He had been as far as the St Cross water, and, observing that, so far as he could make out in the fading light, spinners were falling on the water, although he could not see what kind, he had tried the evening rise with a fisherman's curse, but had had no luck at all.

Returning, he had walked to the plank bridge on which Miss Carmody, it transpired, had stood that very morning, and was aware of something glimmering. The stream bent, and as he leaned over the rail of the bridge to try to see round the bend, he lost his balance and fell into the swift-running water. Thence, garlanded with cresses and embellished by a scrased arm and hand (from the gravel at the bottom of the river), he had scrambled on to the bank, where, fortunately, he had left his rod and tackle. He believed himself to have suffered no ill effects except the inconvenience of having to squeeze the water out of his clothes and empty it out of his shoes, and he described, with some gusto, his return in waterlogged discomfort to the hotel.

'Fortunately,' he concluded, 'no one saw me fall in, otherwise I should have felt extremely foolish. But I might very easily have been drowned. I am safe, so there is no need to worry. Unfortunately, if it *was* the naiad I saw, I am afraid I may have frightened her away.'

'And a good thing, too!' said Connie, who had appeared in the vestibule whilst he was talking, and had heard him with growing irritation. 'For goodness' sake! You and your naiad, Uncle Edris! I hope you've said goodnight to her, that's all! If not, you had better go and do it!'

'I shall not go out again this evening. I shall go first thing in the morning,' said Mr Tidson. 'To-night I should hardly descry her, but to-morrow I can look for any traces she leaves on the bank.'

'The only things that leave traces on the bank are cows and rabbits,' said Connie, with vulgar impatience. 'You'd much better stay in bed. Don't you think so, Aunt Prissie? Still, I'm getting up early myself. Do you want me to call you?'

Mr Tidson did get up early and go out. He went out at just before five and returned to an eight o'clock breakfast.

'Ah, porridge!' said he, in great good-humour. He certainly seemed none the worse for his ducking of the previous night.

'And coffee! Splendid! Well, I saw nothing more of my naiad, and nothing of Connie, who very kindly knocked on my door, but, all the same—'

'Bacon and fried potatoes to follow, sir,' said the waitress, who was still taking a protective interest in him, an attitude to which he was accustomed. 'Or scrambled egg on toast.'

'*Dried* egg?' demanded Mr Tidson.

'Yes, sir, I am afraid so.'

'Awful stuff,' said Connie, who had just come in.

'Excellent!' said Mr Tidson. 'I *like* these scientists' tricks! Scrambled egg on toast by all means, my dear. Prissie,' he added, as the waitress went away, 'it was almost certainly the naiad. You must accompany me at some convenient time. I will point out to you where I saw her!'

He made a hearty breakfast, and, after it, he suggested that Crete might like to go with him to the Cathedral.

'Whatever for?' asked his wife, who kept her church-goings for Sundays and not always then.

'They are doing Stanford in F, dear.'

'Oh, well, if you really want to go, I suppose we could. I imagine one should see the Cathedral.'

'Thank you, my dear. I really do want to go. I must not miss Stanford in F. An amusing key.' He began a contented humming.

It was extraordinary, thought Miss Carmody, putting on a suitable hat and picking up her gloves, how often the meek little man had his own way, even with Crete, who was selfish and hard. Possibly Crete mothered him, she thought. He was, in some matters, very childish. He might also have a child's capacity for lying, she decided, turning over in her mind his account of his evening's adventure, and his reiteration that he had actually seen the naiad.

Mr Tidson skipped up the stairs as soon as breakfast was over, and came down with a sandal in his already gloved hand. He said the naiad had left it on the bank. Connie refused to touch it, and remarked that if he supposed that the muddy and battered object he was offering for commendation had ever been on any except a human foot

– and a boy's at that – he was an even sillier old man than she had supposed. She added that, supposing there might be such a pagan creature as a naiad, she would certainly not wear a leather sandal. To Miss Carmody's consternation, she sounded both angry and frightened, and continued, after all necessity to do so was over, to scold her uncle pettishly.

Mr Tidson, who disliked to be called a silly old man, stopped listening, stuck out his bottom lip, refused to speak to them, and, on his way to the High Street, wedged the sandal among the rubbish already on a dustman's cart. Then he wiped his gloved hands on his handkerchief, and went on to hear Stanford in F.

---Chapter Four---

'*All this while, therefore, we are but upon a*
defensive warre, *and that is but a* doubtful state.'
                    JOHN DONNE (*Devotions XIX*)

MRS BRADLEY was both pleasantly and unpleasantly
preoccupied during the drive back to London. Her
thoughts were engaged by Mr Tidson, Crete and Connie,
and, to an even greater degree, perhaps, by the somewhat
unfortunate Miss Carmody. Life, she reflected, is rich in
situations which even the talking-picture world would
regard with superstitious mistrust, and the Carmody household, comprising, as it did, the fantastic Mr Tidson, the
astoundingly beautiful Crete, the discontented Connie and
her troubled, respectable aunt, appeared to have something
more in common with the surreal than with the real.

Connie at first filled her mind, because of her youth and
the vague and anomalous position which she filled in Miss
Carmody's apparently ill-assorted household. There was
something rotten in the state of Denmark so far as Connie
was concerned. For one thing – the most obvious, perhaps
– Miss Carmody, a mild maiden lady of more than middle
age, was probably a trying companion for a girl of nineteen,
and Mrs Bradley felt sure that Connie had immortal long-
ings in her, if only for a young man or a job.

Thus speculating, idly enough, as the car travelled
rapidly towards London, Mrs Bradley came to the conclusion that as Miss Carmody was not rich enough, possessive
enough and invalid enough to require the constant
companionship of a young girl, the most probable explanation of Connie's dependent position was that the girl

29

might be Miss Carmody's own illegitimate daughter, difficult though it was to envisage that respectable spinster in the rôle of unmarried mother.

Miss Carmody, in fact, Mrs Bradley thought, seemed (at any rate at first sight) an object of sympathetic pity. Her limited income, her apparently unwanted and parasitic guests, and her doubts about Mr Tidson's mental health, all marked her out as a member of the Bessie Mundy, Miss Barrow, Camille Holland class. She seemed a natural victim, one born to be the prey of the unscrupulous. In common with her historic counterparts, however, was she not also rather foolish, Mrs Bradley wondered? The expensive hotel, the wine-bills, the diurnal cocktails all seemed to indicate this. Besides, if she really suspected that Mr Tidson was mad, why had she brought him to Winchester?

Then there was Mr Tidson himself. Mrs Bradley wondered how serious Mr Tidson's banana losses had been, and how long he proposed to support himself and his wife by living in Miss Carmody's flat and on her money. Before the war, land on Tenerife had been worth a thousand pounds an acre, and yielded (so Mrs Bradley had always understood) a reasonable if not a substantial profit. Nevertheless, bananas, she supposed, although a fairly hardy, were still a perishable product. If Mr Tidson had been unlucky in bananas he might have lost a good deal of money, and he might not be altogether nice in the means he would choose to replace it.

There was something pathetic about Mr Tidson, however, no less than about Miss Carmody. If she were the unprotected spinster, he, surely, was the 'little man' of the advertisements, the comic strips, and the music-hall stage. It was tempting, and, somehow, easy to think of Mr Tidson as the victim of unfortunate circumstances. It was tempting to think of him as the dupe of trade rivals; as the victim of siroccos, monsoons and tornados; as the plaything of gods and half-gods; as the man on whom camels and asses died, and around whom bananas blackened and perished; a rather less picturesque and, of course, a childless Job.

Mrs Bradley cackled at this mental image, but she

realized, too, that, whatever one thought of Mr Tidson, no picture of him could now be either satisfactory or complete without reference to his new toy, the naiad. Mr Tidson and the naiad were indissolubly wed; not less so than he and the green-haired, inscrutable Crete: and the latter marriage might be a good deal less pleasing to Mr Tidson than the former: there was that to consider, too.

The more Mrs Bradley thought about the naiad the less she liked her. A middle-aged gentleman of slightly eccentric mentality could cause a naiad to cover a progressive multiplicity of actions, including quite a number of sins. It was a fascinating field of surmise, in fact, to work out what sins in particular the naiad could help to screen.

On the subject of Mr Tidson's mental condition Mrs Bradley was not depressed. He was sane. Even his frantic interest in the naiad was not necessarily evidence of mental collapse, although it might indicate some abnormal preoccupations. Wishful thinking, as Mrs Bradley's patients had often made abundantly clear to her, could take a variety of forms. Escapism was not a vice; it was often the only means the mind could formulate of retaining a hold on sanity. The naiad, however, although a charming conception, was one sufficiently bizarre to arouse suspicion. She was probably an unconsciously-formed image – a kind of mirror-picture – of Crete, Mrs Bradley thought.

Was Mr Tidson a jealous husband, then? – a cuckolded one? – a disillusioned, disappointed, cruelly-treated one? The possibilities were endless and all were interesting. One thing, however, was certain. If Mr Tidson had decided to create the nymph for his own amusement or to fill an emotional hiatus, he was not to be blamed because he intended to believe in her and wanted to see her. That he would certainly see her in the end (whether subjectively or objectively was a matter of little moment) Mrs Bradley most confidently anticipated.

She dismissed the naiad and turned her thoughts on Crete. Crete's dresses and jewels had certainly not been bought with Miss Carmody's money. It was an open question, Mrs Bradley decided, whether Mr Tidson's banana losses had not, perhaps, been debts. She wondered whether the Tidsons might not have fled from Tenerife in a welter of unpaid bills!

It was good to get back to the clinic. She put in four hours' work before she drove back to her house in Kensington to have dinner with Laura Menzies, her young, large, lively secretary, and to hear the news of the town.

'How's Herbert?' Laura enquired, referring to the sailor, Mrs Bradley's new patient. Laura was, in her own expression, 'no mere hireling,' but took a deep and (she was pleased to think) a constructive interest in all Mrs Bradley's work.

'Better than I expected,' Mrs Bradley replied. 'In fact, he is going to his service clinic almost at once. He's making an amazing recovery. He certainly hasn't been difficult. There is something else on my mind, child. I want to know all about a Mr Tidson, until recently of Tenerife in the Canary Islands. Liverpool might be a happy hunting ground. Will you see what you can find out about him? I don't know whether it's really important, I'm sure, but he seems a rather odd little man.'

'Shall I go to Liverpool, then?' enquired Laura promptly. 'And what sort of things do you mean? *All* about him seems a slightly tall order, but, of course, if you mean it, that goes!'

'I do mean it. You must find out all you can. His Christian name is Edris; he has a semi-Greek wife, cold and beautiful, named Crete, and, so far as I can tell, no children. They lived in Santa Cruz, on the Canary island of Tenerife, where he had a banana plantation. He's come home to England to live. He seems to have no money of his own, and he and his wife are living on a not-too-prosperous elderly spinster named Carmody. I want to know why. I want a picture of his financial position, his tastes, hobbies, extravagances, sins; whether he was popular or unpopular; whether he left any debts; and everything else you can think of.'

'Sounds a George Joseph Smith to me,' said Laura. 'May I team up with Kitty? I had a letter from her this morning to say she's on three months' leave to think up some new ideas for post-victory coiffures or something. It would be rather good if we pigged it together for a bit. How soon do you want me back?'

'Not until you've found out all about Mr Tidson. It is an excellent idea to have Kitty with you, I think. Make a holiday of it if you can. Why shouldn't you?'

'Because I'm having another one in September,' said Laura promptly. 'By the way, may I stay at the *Algo*?'

'Of course, if you want to, dear child. Why, have you stayed there before?'

'No. But it's got a Turkish bath, so my spies inform me, and old Kitty in a Turkish bath will be a sight for sore eyes, I fancy. She's got fattish, you know, since College.'

She went out, neighing loudly, to find out from the Encyclopædia Britannica all that she could about bananas, as the first approach to Mr Tidson and the Canaries. Mrs Bradley wrote up her case notes and then put through a call to the editor of the *Vanguard*, whom she knew. The *Vanguard* was the paper (this she had learned from Miss Carmody) which had published the 'naiad' letter that had sent Mr Tidson down to Winchester.

'Who handles the newspaper correspondence?' she enquired. 'I want to know all about a letter sent to you a few days ago about a naiad in the River Itchen near St Cross, Winchester.'

'You do? Then you shall,' said the *Vanguard*. 'A naiad, eh? Girls will bathe anywhere nowadays. There's no glamour left for us boys. Hang on. I'll put through young Hyland.'

Young Hyland in due course came through, and Mrs Bradley held with him a brief but valuable conversation whose real importance did not emerge until later. The letter about the naiad had been signed by a certain John Brown who had given an address in the Great West Road, it appeared. The address was forthcoming and Mrs Bradley noted it down, and handed it over to Laura.

'Strange. More than strange,' said Mrs Bradley, putting down the receiver. Laura, who was seated at the table, deep in the statistics and the cult of the banana, asked why. Mrs Bradley cackled, but did not answer. 'As to the Great West Road, there are several miles of it,' she said, 'between Chiswick and Hounslow, aren't there? – so perhaps we had better tackle it in the morning. Would you care to come for the drive?'

'You bet,' said Laura. 'Anything rather than work!'

The drive was not a long one. Once past Hammersmith and through Chiswick, the car gathered itself together and was very soon speeding down the Great West Road, past factories and various side-turnings, until it had crossed the canal. Beyond this, George drove slowly, in search of the flats.

These, not at all to Mrs Bradley's surprise, did not produce the writer of the letter, nor had anyone of the name of John Brown ever lived there, so far as was known by the porter. One of the tenants, however, a lady, had not yet moved in.

'Now, what?' asked Laura, returning from making these enquiries. But Mrs Bradley seemed strangely satisfied, and nodded like a mandarin as she listened to Laura's recital.

'Why should the writer have decided to remain anonymous?' she enquired, as they drove soberly back to Kensington.

'I can't imagine,' answered Laura, 'except that there ain't goin' to be no water-nymph. But that was a foregone conclusion.'

'Yes,' said Mrs Bradley absently. 'But I wish I were certain about that. I wonder who the missing tenant is, and whether she sent the letter? Anyhow, child, I am very glad that you're going to Liverpool on Saturday.'

'I'd far rather come and chase naiads in Winchester with you.'

'I daresay you would, and perhaps you shall do that, too.'

'When are you going back to Winchester?'

'I'm not sure, child. Probably some time next week. It depends upon the news you get in Liverpool. Mr Tidson is certainly sane, and that is what Miss Carmody wanted to know. My mission to Winchester is concluded. It is only curiosity – probably idle – that takes me back there at all.'

'In other words, you've smelt a second rat,' said Laura.

At this point the telephone rang. The message was from the *Vanguard*, which had a correspondent, it stated, in Santa Cruz de Tenerife. According to this correspondent there had been no gossip about the Tidsons, so far as he could find out, except on the score of Crete's beauty and Mr Tidson's extravagance on her behalf. He had heard of no debts, however. Trade had dropped during the war, and it was known that the Tidsons wanted to get back to England. Mrs Bradley wondered whether to cancel Laura's trip to Liverpool. There seemed little more to find out. However, on the evening following the visit to the flats in the Great West Road, Laura came in with the evening paper. She looked solemn.

'What has happened, child?' Mrs Bradley enquired. 'You've been reading the paper? What is in it?'

'The water-nymph has sprung into fame,' said Laura. 'Or sprung a leak. Which you like. Look, here it is. What do you make of her now? Is this what you were expecting?'

The paragraph was a short one, less than a quarter column. A boy of twelve had been found drowned in a little stream near Paneworth Level. This was a broad stretch of water-meadow to the north of the city and on its eastern boundary. The reference to the naiad came at the end of the paragraph.

'There is a local rumour,' said the paper, 'of a water-nymph which brings ill-luck to anyone who sees her. It is not suggested, however, that any such fantastic interpretation can be placed upon the accident to Bobby Grier, who was said to have been warned by his parents to be careful.'

'You don't think the boy was chasing the water-nymph, do you?' asked Laura, when Mrs Bradley had taken in the main statements made by the newspaper.

'Time will disentangle what I think, child, but I am going back to Winchester for the inquest.'

'And that's your last word,' said Laura, recognizing this

to be the case and not in the least attempting to argue the point. 'All right. I still wish I could come with you.'

'You shall come to Winchester the moment it is possible,' said Mrs Bradley, to comfort her. 'But I do want to know a little more about the Tidsons and, of course, Miss Carmody and Connie. It is none of my business, in one sense, I suppose, but Miss Carmody did call me in, and she does seem to be victimized by that rather terrible little man and his cold and beautiful wife. And I'm worried about the girl. And now this incongruous reference to the naiad ...'

'I do hope I get back from Liverpool pretty soon,' said Laura. 'I think that end of the stick will be a wash-out.' She paused, and then added, 'Coldness and beauty ought not to go together, do you think?'

'No, I don't think they ought, child.'

'They don't, in Deb's case,' said Laura, referring to a very lovely girl who had married one of Mrs Bradley's picturesque and fortunate nephews.

Mrs Bradley paused to consider Deborah, of whom she was fond and proud. Then Laura said:

'Don't mind biting my head off if I'm wildly beside the mark, but do you think this Mr Tidson had anything to do with the murder? Is that what this Miss Carmody expected when she lugged you into her affairs?'

'The murder?' said Mrs Bradley. 'Nobody mentioned murder! The newspaper certainly does not; and, so far as I can see, there is no reason in the world why Mr Tidson should have had anything to do with the boy's death, if that's what you mean, or that we should in any way suspect him, even if murder were proved.'

'Ticked off soundly! Yet this Mr Tidson came into your mind as the *deus ex machina*, didn't he?' said Laura shrewdly. 'Is that because the paper mentions the naiad? And why should they call it a local rumour? I thought that was just what it wasn't!'

'True, child, it was not a local rumour, and I see no reason why the naiad should have been mentioned, but I'm not going further than that until after the inquest, so please don't leap to conclusions or put ideas into my head!'

'Do you think,' asked Laura, not at all abashed, 'that Mr Tidson himself wrote that first letter to the *Vanguard*?'

'It is strangely probable, child, although there is at least one other equal probability, especially as we are told that the tenant of the flat is a woman.'

'Why should anyone write it, anyway?'

'I have the glimmerings of a notion about that.'

'You mean Mr Tidson wanted an excuse to go to Winchester?'

'You are too intelligent, child,' said Mrs Bradley. 'That is one theory, certainly.'

'But why invent something as impossible as a water-nymph?' argued Laura. 'If I wanted to go to Winchester – or anywhere else, come to that! – I could invent a dozen better excuses! Let's not talk rot about this!' She eyed her employer with a good deal of solemn reproachfulness. 'See here, we know perfectly well that water-nymphs are all moonshine, and can be dismissed as such, so why a water-nymph? Why not invent a monster trout? A monster trout in the Itchen would be sheer Isaak Walton, but a naiad—! This Mr Tidson *must* be bats, and you could write him off as such, I should have said. Of course, a murderer – that's another matter.'

'Well and bravely spoken,' said Mrs Bradley. 'But Mr Tidson, if I have summed him up at all successfully, is perfectly capable not only of inventing but of producing a water-nymph, and of wishing her on to sceptics like yourself. So, if you do come to Winchester, don't you press him too far, or I won't be answerable for the consequences.'

'As though you haven't foreseen the consequences, weighed them up, and decided how to deal with them!' said Laura, hooting rudely to rob this speech of its otherwise complimentary aspect. 'I'm not getting anywhere with all this banana stuff, dash it! We must go and get ready for dinner. Grub omnia vincit, don't you think?'

Chapter Five

*'Take the Leaves of Rue, pick'd from the Stalks,
and bruise them . . .'*
'N.B. *You may occasionally change the Con-
serve of Rue for that of Roman Wormwood,
which is rather more agreeable, and nearly as
efficacious.'*
Mrs SARAH HARRISON OF DEVONSHIRE
(*The Housekeeper's Pocket Book, etc.*)

───────────────────────────────────

THE reference to the naiad would have taken Mrs Bradley back to Winchester without the telegram from Miss Carmody which arrived whilst she and Laura were at dinner, but, as the telegram did come, Mrs Bradley's decision was confirmed.

'Return at once fear worst frantic,' the telegram ran. A prepaid reply form accompanied the message. Mrs Bradley filled it in and returned to Winchester early enough on the Friday morning to attend the inquest on the drowned boy. Miss Carmody insisted upon going with her, and whispered, just before the inquest opened, that she did not expect there to be any hope at all.

'Hope of what?' Mrs Bradley enquired. Miss Carmody did not reply, and Mrs Bradley wondered whether she had connected Mr Tidson with the boy's death because of the reference to the naiad, and whether, in making the connection, she had jumped to the same unreasonable conclusion as Laura.

The proceedings soon came to an end. There was little to be learned from them except the age of the boy which, given in the newspaper as thirteen, turned out to be only twelve. This discrepancy was explained, amid tears of contrition, by the boy's mother – or, rather, foster-mother – who confessed that the family had moved to Winchester just before the war, and that the boy was the child of some friends who had sent him away from Southampton. They themselves had been killed, six months later, during a raid. She confessed that she had given the boy's age as a year more than it was, so that he could go to work a year sooner than the law allowed. Her tears, Mrs Bradley thought, were from the mainspring of greed rather than grief, for the family, although humble, were comfortably circumstanced enough, and the woman's only regret was for the money now never to be earned. Apart from that, it seemed more than likely that she was glad to be rid of the boy, for the billeting money, she declared, was insufficient for his keep.

'Not much love lost in that household!' said Miss Carmody, as she and Mrs Bradley walked back towards the *Domus* for lunch.

'And not much explanation as to how the boy came to be drowned,' said Mrs Bradley. 'I wonder whether I could get permission to see the body? Not, I imagine, that that would tell me much. But it seems rather odd—'

'I will find out when the funeral is to be,' said Miss Carmody readily. 'One thing, I shall scarcely feel, after what that unpleasant woman said, that I am intruding on the sanctity of grief! By the way, I ought to tell you about the sandal.'

'Did the dead boy wear sandals?' Mrs Bradley immediately enquired. 'I thought we were told it was boots.'

'Yes, yes. He had boots. This was just something very peculiar that Edris did. You remember I warned you he was given to odd ideas . . .' She recounted how Mr Tidson had shown them the sandal, told of the way he had disposed of it, and mentioned Connie's reactions.

'And, of course, he was out that night, and got very, very wet, and he was out very early next morning,' she said in conclusion, and explained how she knew all this. 'His arm and hand had abrasions,' she added, 'which seems strange in a six-foot pool.'

The family on whom the dead child had been billeted occupied a small house, one of a compact, uninteresting row, in a street alongside a stream on the north side of the city. Far from experiencing any difficulty in getting in to see the dead child, Miss Carmody and Mrs Bradley discovered that his home was open from front to back so that the whole neighbourhood, if it wished, could file past to look at the body.

Mrs Bradley and Miss Carmody, stared at with unresentful curiosity by the neighbourhood, had only to join the small single-file queue of morbid sightseers in the street outside, to find themselves at the end of an hour at the bedside of the dead boy. He had been laid out in the sitting-room, and a collecting-box for money to be spent on wreaths and (if the appearance of the foster-father gave any guide) upon alcoholic comfort for the relatives, was displayed at the foot of the bed.

Death had given to the child the strange and awful beauty of the departed. His eyes were closed, his fair hair, now carefully dried and combed, was long and curled slightly on his brow, and his arms had been crossed upon his narrow and bony chest. Mrs Bradley drew back the covers to see this. The people in front of her had done the same thing, and had muttered, 'Don't he look peaceful,' before they drew the covers back again, so she knew that she would be violating none of the customs if she followed their example. She even passed a claw gently over the top of his head, on which was an unexplained lump – referred to by the doctor at the inquest – which indicated that the lad had been struck before he was drowned, or had fallen on something hard before he tumbled into the extremely shallow water where he was found.

Mrs Bradley's bright eyes and beaky mouth did not betray her thoughts. She put money in the collecting-box, gave a last look round, and, followed by Miss Carmody, went out at the back door of the house. They found themselves in a narrow alley, beyond the fencing of which they could see a bend of the river. Mrs Bradley collared a little girl who was playing with a skipping-rope nearby.

'I want to see where Bobby was drowned,' she said. The child, who was only too willing to display to strangers what had become the site of a nine days' wonder, nodded intelligently and said with emphasis:

'I'm going to the pictures after the funeral, if I can get the money.'

'But do you think that is right?' demanded Miss Carmody, shocked by this juxtaposition of entertainment.

'It's a sad picture,' said the child defensively. She turned from the unsympathetic Miss Carmody, and said importantly to Mrs Bradley:

'It's over the bridge and down along 'ere it was. My father found 'im.'

Mrs Bradley had already heard the evidence of the man who had found the body. He had come upon it at just after five in the morning, on the way to his work. The medical evidence – the doctor had seen the body at six o'clock – showed that the lad had been dead for less than twelve hours. Mrs Bradley looked at the shallow water. It was wide and sedgy, but one would scarcely have thought it could be fatal, especially to a twelve-year-old boy. (Still, the bump on the head explained all.)

'When will your father be home from work?' Mrs Bradley asked the little girl. It appeared that he was expected within half an hour, and, the gift of sufficient money for the pictures having established their right to her services, the child led the way to a house in the same row as that in which the dead child lay. The village, an offshoot of Winchester proper, consisted of a single long main street in which the houses were almost all alike. The child turned the handle of the front door, invited the two ladies into the parlour, left them just inside the room, and went through to the kitchen for her mother.

'Mum, they've come about Bobby Grier,' she called out.

The mother, an anxious soul, came in looking thoroughly frightened.

'Are you sociable ladies?' she enquired.

'Yes,' said Miss Carmody, who felt that she could claim this description for herself. 'We came to find out whether there was anything we could do. The poor little laddie, you know . . .'

'For the Griers?' enquired their hostess, with a sniff. 'I daresay they'll *let* you, but, although I wouldn't talk against *any* of the neighbours, because that don't do, and things gets around so quick, I don't say it 'ud be *necessary*. Not what sociable ladies wouldn't call necessary, any'ow. Very grabbing she is, although I'd take it a favour you didn't tell 'er I said so. We've got reasons to 'ave our differences.'

She spoke breathlessly, Mrs Bradley noticed. This was explained a moment later.

'Ted – that's my 'usband – the police haven't been very nice to 'im about poor Bobby Grier. Don't leave you a chance to tell the honest truth. I feel frightened every knock at the door, and so I tell you. It's 'ard not to be believed. Ted couldn't 'elp it if 'e found 'im. You'd think the poor child 'ad been murdered and Ted 'ad done it, the way they've kept all on. It's been really cruel. And, of course—'

The pause was awkward. Mrs Bradley filled it.

'And, of course, the police want such full explanations,' she said, 'that our lives become scarcely our own.'

The woman agreed, and seemed about to enlarge on the point, but at this moment Mr Potter, the husband, was heard. He scraped his feet beside the front door of the house, and then walked into the parlour, which opened directly off the street.

He looked a little shy, and not particularly gratified, when he saw that there was company in the house. He said, 'Servant, ladies,' in what Miss Carmody referred to afterwards as a delightfully old-fashioned way, went through to the kitchen, and dumped his bag of tools on the floor. He looked a good deal younger than the woman, and was well-set-up and good-looking.

'You got to go back, Ted,' said his wife, who had followed

him out. There was a lengthy and muttered colloquy, and then the wife added loudly, 'It's some sociable ladies come to see you about the Griers. There ain't nothing for you to be afraid of. Not as you deserve I should say it, but there it is.'

Mr Potter observed that he had better clean himself, then, and proceeded, from the sounds, to sluice himself vigorously under the kitchen tap. He reappeared at the end of ten minutes with damp front hair and wearing, to Miss Carmody's gratification, a rather tight collar.

'A mark of *real* respect,' she muttered to Mrs Bradley.

'Not newspapers, I suppose?' he said nervously as he sat down and put his large hands on his knees. 'You wouldn't come from the newspapers, I suppose?'

'I don't know but what it will come to that,' said Mrs Bradley, before Miss Carmody could speak. 'I'm worried about the death of that boy, Mr Potter. Why was it such a long time before he was found?'

'Ah!' said Mr Potter, lifting one hand and bringing it back into place with a fearful whack. 'What did I tell you, Lizzie? "Funny I'd have looked," I said, "if that boy 'ad 'appened to be murdered," I said. Didn't I say that, Lizzie? You're my witness to that, my gal. I said it the minute I come in when I'd fetched the police. Now didn't I?' He looked at his wife with a kind of hang-dog defiance not very pretty to see.

'Yes, you did say it, Ted, but I dunno as you ought to repeat it in front of strangers,' said Mrs Potter, glancing at the strangers to see the effect of his words. Relations between the Potters were not too good, Mrs Bradley noticed. She wondered what the woman suspected, or, possibly, knew.

'What made you think of murder, Mr Potter?' asked Miss Carmody keenly, leaning forward, her hands on her knees.

'Why, nothing,' he replied, a trifle confused, 'except – well, you know 'ow it is, mum. It struck me comical, like, as a biggish lad like Bob should a-got hisself drownded in about six inches of water, as you might say, for 'e laid very near the edge, half into some plants. And another thing—' He lowered his voice and gave a furtive glance at his wife. The two of them were certainly on the defensive with one another, almost as though they had quarrelled but did not want strangers to know it.

'You be careful, Ted!' said the woman. He shrugged his wide shoulders, but seemed disposed to obey her.

'Yes, Mr Potter?' said Mrs Bradley, with hypnotic effect. Miss Carmody sat straighter in her chair.

'Oh nothing, excepting a soft straw hat laid underneath him. I didn't tell the police. They'd 'a thought I was making it up. You see, mum, it wasn't there when I went to work after taking of 'im home and making Ma Grier call the doctor.'

'Ma Grier!' said Mrs Potter scornfully. 'That's a new name for 'er, ain't it? And you shouldn't of mentioned that 'at! Very likely your fancy, I reckon. And as for 'im not being drownded, you know very well that 'is poor little head was right under! You said so yourself to the coroner! Don't you remember? Bob was drowned. His head was right under. That's what you said, and you can't go back on it now.'

'Well, right enough, so it was right under,' Mr Potter admitted hastily. 'But if these 'ere ladies 'ave seen the place, I'll back they know what I'm a-gettin' at. Not deep enough to drown in, not for a lad of his sense.'

'The same thought struck *me*,' said Mrs Bradley. 'But the boy might have fallen and stunned himself, as the doctor suggested at the inquest, and have tumbled into the water. He had a bad bruise on his head.'

'But the bump was on *top* of 'is head, and he was laying face downward in the water,' said Mr Potter. 'That's why the coroner *would* give an open verdict. Quite right, too, in my opinion. There's been too many murders since the war.'

After a slight pause, Mrs Bradley again asked whether the parents had not missed the boy on the Wednesday evening, and repeated her observation that a very long time had passed before he was found. Had not the parents looked for him, she enquired.

'Foster-parents. He wasn't theirs,' said Mrs Potter. 'But

miss the boy? Not them! Down at the *Bull and Bushell*, same as usual. Wednesdays and Saturdays was their nights, and that's where they was, chance what! What do you say, Ted? *You* ought to know where old man Grier spends his time!'

Mr Potter confirmed this view, and said he had seen them in there. He had popped in for half a pint, he added (with an appealing glance at his wife), and there they both were.

'Was that generally known?' asked Mrs Bradley. 'That they frequented this public house on Wednesdays and Saturdays?'

'Known all along 'ere, at any rate.'

'And in the city?'

'Us takes no truck in the city. Nought but ecclesiastical that don't be.'

'I see.'

'Till late years, been a separate village, us 'ave. Worked in the city, maybe, some of us 'ave, but nothing to do with their affairs. Don't know nothing about 'em, anyhow. The Dean, he see to Winchester. Us keep ourselves to ourselves.'

'Yes, I see. Then – don't the children go and play along the river past Winchester? Do they never go into the water-meadows towards St Cross?' demanded Miss Carmody, the nymph and Mr Tidson foremost in her thoughts.

'Why should 'em?' asked Mr Potter in surprise. 'Got our own river, 'aven't us, 'ere in the village? Why *should* 'em go? If they think to go further, they goes over to the reck, like, or to that there bit of a brook by King Alfred's gate.'

'Yes, I see,' said Mrs Bradley. 'What kind of boy was Bobby Grier? Did the other boys like him?'

'That I couldn't tell you, mum. Little enough I knowed of him. My little un, now, her could tell you. But he wasn't Mrs Grier's own, as I daresay you 'eard us say a minute ago.'

Mrs Bradley nodded. The little girl Potter was not visible when the two elderly ladies left the house, and Mrs Bradley was about to suggest that they should return to the *Domus* when Miss Carmody said surprisingly and suddenly:

'I think we ought to tax that Grier woman with Edris.'

'Tax her?' Mrs Bradley enquired.

'Certainly. Edris must be the man the police will want for the murder. There! It is out! I've said it!'

'But why should you say it?' Mrs Bradley enquired. 'What makes you connect your Mr Tidson with the death of this boy?'

'Little enough, in one sense, but a very great deal in another,' Miss Carmody mysteriously replied; and they walked back to Mrs Grier's house. The house was quiet now. The curiosity of the villagers was sated, the front door was shut and the family had settled down to tea.

After Mrs Bradley had knocked twice, the door opened to about one-seventh of its possible semi-circumference, and a suspicious eye peered forth.

'When did you first miss Bobby?' enquired Mrs Bradley, deeming that surprise tactics would be the best method of approach.

'We never,' said the owner of the eye. 'And we don't want no more bothering. We got the funeral to see to.' The door slammed. Mrs Bradley took Miss Carmody by the hand and hurried her up the street, and they came back to Winchester by way of Water Lane into Bridge Street. All the way Miss Carmody asked only one question, but it was one which Mrs Bradley found herself unable to answer satisfactorily.

'Don't *you* think the little boy was murdered?'

'Only by the pricking of my thumbs, and that will hardly impress the police,' Mrs Bradley replied. 'It is the bump on top of his head that interests me most. I felt for it, as, no doubt, you noticed. It was a bad enough blow to have stunned him, and I have no doubt it did, but it certainly did not kill him. The question, of course, is how he came by it.'

'Well,' said Miss Carmody, with a certain amount of hesitation, 'he *might* have knocked his head accidentally and then felt faint or confused and fallen forward into the water. But there *was* that sandal which Edris put on the dust-cart. Crete mentioned it to me last night, and then, I think, wished she had not, and, certainly, I would never have dreamed of reminding *her* about it. Of course, she might be very glad to get rid of Edris, and if he were proved to be a murderer . . . You know, I'm afraid of Edris. He is really a very strange man . . .'

Mrs Bradley said nothing. She was too much astonished to speak. There were various ways in which a wife could have reminded Miss Carmody about the sandal, and Mrs Bradley could not help wondering whether Miss Carmody's remark was not uncomfortably disingenuous. After all, it was rather more likely, considering all the circumstances, that Miss Carmody, rather than Crete, should be anxious to be rid of Mr Tidson.

Another picture rose unbidden before Mrs Bradley's inward eye – the picture of a tall, mild-mannered spinster visiting the Cathedral by moonlight. By moonlight, Mrs Bradley reflected, glancing sidelong at her companion, almost everyone takes on a personality not entirely righteous or his own. 'Ill met by moonlight, proud Titania,' . . . She suddenly cackled, startling a baby and a dog.

'Why do you laugh?' Miss Carmody nervously enquired.

'I laugh at my thoughts,' Mrs Bradley replied,' although they are not really much of a laughing matter. How steeply the High Street mounts to the West Gate, does it not?'

'Well, and what do you think of my naiad now?' enquired Mr Tidson, when the party met for cocktails before dinner. 'I have a theory that the boy was drowned in pursuit of her, you know. She may even have beckoned him in.'

'Yes, you said so before,' said Crete. 'But we do not see what you have to go on.'

'He was a fine little boy. I've seen him,' said Miss Carmody. She described the afternoon visits which she and Mrs Bradley had paid, but did not reconstruct their conversation.

'These parents who go off in the evening and leave their children to fend for themselves are incurring a very serious responsibility,' said Mr Tidson, beaming upon Thomas as he beckoned him to come to where they sat. 'Champagne cocktails, I think, this evening, Thomas.'

'Verra guid,' said Thomas, indicating by his tone that it was very far from that. 'And for the young leddy?'

'Gin and Italian,' said Connie, 'and get an evening paper, Thomas, will you?'

'There'll be nae mair peppers the night, but ye may borrow mine if ye'll promise no to do the crossword,' said Thomas. 'Ye filled in *victors* for *lictors* on Wednesday, and put me out terrible.'

'But "victors" was right! I looked at the answers next day!' said Connie indignantly.

'I dinna work out the crossword to get it *right*,' said Thomas withering her. 'Ony fule can dae that! But if ye pit *lictor* where it should hae been *victor*, ye get *mallet* in place of *velvet* and that gives ye *antimony* instead of *enticing*. *Enticing!* Well, well!' He laughed shortly. '*Enticing*, where he could hae pit *antimony*!'

'That's a very odd sort of man,' said Mr Tidson, gazing with nervous interest at Thomas' retreating form and at the two dragon's eyes of silver buttons on the back of the old man's livery; for Thomas acted both as porter and cocktail waiter in the same greenish uniform. It had silver-braided cuffs and silver buttons, and he had worn it for years past. It was almost threadbare, but nothing would induce him to take to the new and smart blue-and-gold suit which the manageress had been anxious to provide. He had confided to Connie when she had come down early one morning and had discovered him, with the coat off, going over the buttons with plate powder, that he liked fine to gie his wee lozenges a bit of a shine, for, between themselves, (meaning himself and Connie), they minded him on a kiltie suit he had had as a wee laddie in Kilmarnock.

'He is not only an odd sort of man; he is a very intelligent fellow,' said Miss Carmody. 'And he serves very good sherry,' she added, 'although perhaps that is more to the credit of the hotel than to his own personal credit.'

'We are not having sherry to-day, though,' said Crete, 'and Thomas does not approve of champagne cocktails.'

She smiled at Thomas when he returned with the glasses. Thomas inclined his head in acknowledgement of the smile, but did not move a muscle of his Covenanting face as he set the cocktails down on the polished table.

'I think,' said Mrs Bradley suddenly, 'that Connie ought to take me up all the hills to-morrow. Will you?' she added, turning to the girl. 'I believe you walk fast and far, and I feel the need of exercise.'

'I'd love to go with you,' replied Connie. 'But what about you, Aunt Prissie?' she added, turning towards Miss Carmody.

'You and Mrs Bradley would walk my legs off,' Miss Carmody comfortably replied. 'I shall write up my Mothers. It is a task much overdue. I will sit with Crete whilst she does her embroidery. What do you say, Crete, to that?'

'She says nothing,' said Mr Tidson, raising his glass. 'What can she say, my dear Prissie? Convention does not permit her to say that she prefers her own company, and if she does pretend to welcome your presence you are not to be blamed if you think her protestations sincere.'

He sipped his cocktail thoughtfully after this rather rude speech, then suddenly started, and called excitedly for Thomas. The factotum appeared, and gazed with disapproval at the party.

'What will ye?' he enquired, looming like a minor prophet with a major message, uncompromisingly beside the tiny table.

'This cocktail! Where's the brandy?' Mr Tidson demanded. Thomas picked up the glass, bent bristling brows upon the complainant, walked to the window, held the innocent drink to the light, and then replied in justly withering tones:

'I will be speiring.'

'Oh, dear!' said Miss Carmody, taking up her drink. 'You've annoyed him! Next time we shall get no brandy in them at all! You are rather provoking, Edris!'

'I am a connoisseur,' Mr Tidson replied. 'And when a connoisseur finds that what should be a masterpiece is nothing of the kind, honour compels him to say so. I suggest, my dear Crete, that you put your cocktail down.'

'Just what she *is* doing,' said Connie vulgarly, watching Crete's tasting of the mixture. Thomas returned at this juncture with the glass on a silver salver.

'Your drink, sir – *laced*,' he observed.

'Splendid!' said Mr Tidson, sipping his drink. He waited until Thomas had gone, and then remarked, 'It is amazing, my dear Connie, what a display of firmness will do.'

'You must try it some time, Uncle Edris,' said Connie angrily. Mr Tidson looked at her with an expression of concern, gulped his drink hastily, and choked.

'It's a verra great peety ye wouldn't be content with the proper mixture,' said Thomas, coming back with a table napkin and mopping up the cocktail that was spilt on Mr Tidson's light-grey suit. 'Maybe anither time ye'll admit that this hoose kens whit's *guid* for ye.'

This classic setting down of Mr Tidson struck everybody dumb except Connie, who, to the consternation of the guests at another table, suddenly put down her glass and went into hysterical laughter.

'Dear, do control yourself,' said her aunt. Connie wiped her eyes, apologized, gulped down her drink, and fled out into the garden.

'I can't *think* why Connie is quite so ill-mannered,' said Miss Carmody. 'I do apologize for her. She has made us the cynosure of all eyes, and that, in a public place, is unforgivable. I will go and call her in. She shall at least say she is sorry.'

Connie, it proved, was ready enough to do this, and she sat down very meekly and waited for lunch to be announced.

'Talking of plans, I must say I had hoped that some one or two of you would come and sit on the bank and watch me fish,' observed Mr Tidson, in an attempt to recover his poise.

'Not to-morrow, Edris,' said Miss Carmody. 'I really must do up my Mothers.'

'Perhaps I will come,' said Crete amiably. 'That is, I will come if it is not too far to walk.'

'No, no. I shall try the St Cross water again,' said Mr Tidson. 'I should like to fish the stretch by Itchen Abbas, but, alas! – it is privately owned and I have no acquaintance whatever, so far as I know, with the owner. Never mind! I must work out my ticket.'

'I thought most of the water was privately owned,' said Connie. 'Do they allow you to take trout?'

'He is not fishing for trout, but only for water-nymphs,' said Crete, 'and, as he says, he has his ticket.'

'Could one be had up for murder if one caught a water-nymph?' asked Connie.

'Probably only for cruelty to animals, I should say,' Crete replied. 'Perhaps, Edris, you would rather be alone?'

'No, no,' said Mr Tidson. 'Do come with me, my dear. The naiad might recognize in you a fellow-countrywoman.'

'Half a fellow-countrywoman,' said Connie. Crete looked at her with lazy hostility.

'You ought to be more agreeable to Crete,' said Miss Carmody, getting her niece to herself after lunch, although Mrs Bradley, writing a letter to Laura, was seated at a desk in the window. 'And to Edris, too.'

'I am as agreeable as I can bear to be,' said Connie. 'I don't like Uncle Edris, and I don't like Crete, and I wish we hadn't come to Winchester with them. And I do my best to please you, Aunt Prissie, you know I do, but I think it's time I lived my own life, and I'm going to, as soon as we go home. I am sorry about the cocktails, but I can't go on like this. You can't expect it. I know you think I'm rude to Uncle Edris, but it's the way I keep him from frightening me, that's all.'

'Now, what does that mean?' asked Miss Carmody. 'It sounds like nonsense again.'

'I'm going to get a job. In fact, I've got one. It is at four pounds ten shillings a week, and I have already been interviewed. It's time I had my own money. I don't intend to live on charity, and I shan't!' cried Connie, ending up with a gasp.

'Charity?' said Miss Carmody, disguising, she hoped, her real feelings. 'But, Connie dear, there was never any question of that. I've been only too glad to have you. You *must* know what an interest and comfort you've been, and I always thought—'

'Well, you need not think it any more! I'm off!' said Connie crudely. Miss Carmody was deeply upset. She swallowed, looked with compassionate horror at her niece, and then walked out of the room.

'Well, well,' said Mrs Bradley, getting up, 'and how old are you now?'

'Nineteen,' replied Connie, ashamed of her tender age.

'So much? Perhaps you are right. No, I'm sure you are right. Will you live with your aunt, or are you going into lodgings, I wonder?'

'I intend to go into a flat,' replied Connie, betraying by her tear-filled eyes her sense of her own bad behaviour. 'You know, about Aunt Prissie, I don't really mean to be nasty, but I feel I *must* get away! It's all too much for me. Sometimes I think I'm going mad! And you don't know how unfairly I've been treated!'

'Oh, dear!' said Miss Carmody, coming back with slightly pink eyelids. 'But you *will* be polite to Crete and Edris? I wouldn't like them to think that you had left me because of them, you know. It would hurt their feelings, and I should not like to do that.'

'I don't see why they should live on you,' said Connie. 'And I don't mind whose feelings I hurt, except, perhaps, yours, Aunt Prissie.' She looked helplessly at her aunt, and then burst into tears. Miss Carmody took her hurriedly out of the room, but her anguished sobs could be heard all the way up the stairs.

Chapter Six

'I put the fly well to my side of him, showing him no gut: he turned out to take it, but before doing so, he swam round it to see if there was gut on the other side. He saw it and sheered off. I can never get anyone to believe this simple and truthful tale.'

J. W. HILLS (*A Summer on the Test*)

Mrs BRADLEY, who had spent much thought upon the results of her expedition with Miss Carmody, spent some time on the following day discussing the circumstances of the boy's death with the Tidsons. Mr Tidson clung to his theory that the boy had been enticed into the water by the naiad.

'I knew it would happen,' he said. Mrs Bradley watched him with her sharp black eyes; summed him up, pursing her beaky little mouth; assessed him against a background of extravagance, ill-luck, hot sunshine and green bananas; and had to give him up, or, rather, to pigeon-hole him. She had done the same with the conversation between Connie and Miss Carmody in the lounge. There was something hidden in that talk which she meant to bring to light when she could.

Meanwhile Laura had written entertainingly from Liverpool, where she and her friend Kitty were contriving to combine bananas with pleasure. They had managed, wrote Laura dashingly, to contact a man who had known something of the Tidsons in Santa Cruz de Tenerife.

The Tidsons, it appeared, had been well known at the Sporting Club, the English Club and the Yacht Club, chiefly because of Crete's unusual and striking beauty. There had been some scandal of the domestic kind in which Mr Tidson, having stepped out of his own and into the Lothario class, had been involved, and there was a rumour that it had taken most of his money to hush it up. It was an old story, however; eight years old at least. There was a better-substantiated tale that Crete was an incurably extravagant wife.

This bore out what Mrs Bradley had already learned from the editor of the *Vanguard*, and she found nothing surprising nor particularly disquieting about it.

She would write direct to Santa Cruz, Laura continued, if Mrs Bradley thought it worth while. Mrs Bradley did think it worth while, but decided that the time had not arrived for this, since she had nothing against Mr Tidson so far except a surmise that his water-nymph was a cloak and an excuse for activities he did not want known. Whether the death of the boy Grier could be included among these activities she did not know, although it was impossible to shake off an uncomfortable impression that it could. However, there was nothing to connect Mr Tidson with the drowned boy beyond the fact that he had spent most of his time near the river since the party had come to Winchester, and that on the one significant occasion he had fallen into the water.

Miss Carmody, pressed for evidence in support of her apparently outrageous theory that the boy had been murdered by her relative, instanced Mr Tidson's mishap, and emphasized the fact that it coincided, nearly enough, with the time of the boy's death. She also referred again to the sandal which Mr Tidson had got rid of on to the dust-cart.

'I *know* that sandal was worrying him,' she said.

Mrs Bradley and Connie did not get their walk on the day following the champagne cocktails, for the weather turned wet, and so everybody except Crete went to afternoon service at the Cathedral, to hear Noble in B minor.

'A very good key for the *Nunc Dimittis*, but I am not

so sure about the *Magnificat*,' said Mr Tidson, as they dodged a stream of traffic across the narrow High Street.

Mr Tidson did not revise his opinion of the key of B minor, but talked intelligently upon Stanford in A and Wood in F as he walked beside Mrs Bradley across the Close and out of the gate by Saint Swithun's Church at the termination of the service.

'I used to be a choirboy,' he said.

Mrs Bradley found herself more and more interested in the strange little man. His potentialities, she felt, were infinite. She longed to ask him, point-blank, whether or not he were a murderer, but she felt that this would ruin their friendly relationship and defeat the object of the question, which was, quite simply and unequivocally, to find out the answer.

The evening passed pleasantly and sociably, and gained from the absence of Connie, who went to bed immediately after dinner upon plea of a headache. It was left to Connie, however, to provide the next line of excitement. This she did in the manner beloved of adolescents (whether consciously or unconsciously) by introducing the subject of ghosts. She began by contacting Thomas on the following day, and, to bolster up a weak approach to the matter, adopted a belligerent tone in demanding of the dignified old man whether the hotel was haunted.

'I have heard it is,' she asserted, 'and I certainly think it might be true. What about it, Thomas? "Ghaists nor bogles shall ye fear," and all that, you know.'

'Likewise,' said Mrs Bradley, '"By the noise of dead men's bones in charnel houses rattling."'

'Oh, don't!' said Connie anxiously. 'Please don't!'

'And,' said Miss Carmody, innocently adding her quota to what she believed to be an intellectual game, '"powers above in clouds do sit," you remember.'

'"Wee, sleekit, cow'rin', tim'rous beastie,"' said Mr Tidson, giggling at Connie and avoiding Thomas' eye as he adapted Robert Burns to the trend of the conversation. The others looked at Thomas expectantly.

'There's a wee hoose on the ither side o' the town, so I

have haird,' began Thomas gravely, 'that is said to contain a *footstep*.'

'I shouldn't care to hear it,' said Connie. 'But I'm not talking about a house across the town. I'm talking about this hotel. You ought to know whether the hotel is haunted or not. You've lived here long enough, Thomas.'

'Hotels are not made to be haunted. The guests, maybe, couldna thole it,' said Thomas, picking up his little round tray. 'Ghaisties wadna come whaur they werena welcome.'

Connie felt herself snubbed by this original* thought upon the subject, and did not ask any more questions; but Mrs Bradley, who had her own reasons for being interested, said to her after lunch on the following day:

'Will you come with me to the top of St Catherine's Hill? It is fine to-day, and *we* shall not mind if it's slippery. I think I'd like you to tell me about your ghost.'

'I suppose you think it sounds ridiculous?' said Connie, on the defensive.

'Oh, I don't see why the hotel shouldn't be haunted. It has had a long and troubled history. Have you discovered the priest's hole yet? Perhaps you have seen it on a previous visit? I know you have stayed here before,' said Mrs Bradley, taking no notice of the protest.

'Not that long linen-cupboard place down two or three steps at the top of the main staircase?'

'I understand so. There is a story that a Jesuit was in hiding there when the mistress of the house was taken before the Council to be questioned. He wanted to give himself up, but the servants would not let him. They said that the honour of the house was involved, which, one must admit, was true.'

'My ghost was a nun,' said Connie. 'Nothing *happened* exactly, but I don't think I want to sleep in my bedroom any more. Do you think they would change it if I asked them? I don't want to be laughed at by that sneering Crete Tidson, though. I wish I could make a change without her

---

* Doubtful. It is probably a widely-held theory, but does not, of course, apply to Poltergeists.

knowing. Better still, I wish I could start my job a bit sooner, and leave the hotel altogether!'

'You had better change with me if you feel like that,' said Mrs Bradley, 'and we will say nothing to any of them. Now come along, and we'll see how many miles we can walk.'

'Oh, dear! I suppose I've *got* to come with you,' said Connie, very ungratefully. Miss Carmody had gone into Alresford, Crete had decided to lie down, and Mr Tidson was off on his own affairs as usual.

The route they followed led them past the Cathedral and across its Close, down College Street and along College Walk, and then, by the river footpath, to the path across the water-meadows. This brought them to the main stream of the Itchen, for this walk was one way – and by far the most delightful – to reach St Catherine's Hill.

There was a choice of paths, for a bridge spanned the river and led to the towing-path; on the right bank, which Connie chose, was a narrow path alongside the water. They passed forget-me-not and meadow rue, and, on a pool beside the stream, the yellow water-lily. There was water-cress in abundance on all the streams, and the ragged-robin stood two feet high in the water-meadows.

Mrs Bradley and Connie walked for the most part in single file and in silence. At last they crossed the by-pass and began to climb the hill.

They mounted some chalk-cut steps to the first of the pre-Roman earthworks which crowned the top of the hill. From a kind of circular plateau covered with short springy grass a fine view could be had of the river, the city, and the water-meadows. There was an open prospect across the river to the hills around Oliver's Battery, and away to the south-west were the barrows on Compton Down.

'Well, now,' said Mrs Bradley, when she and Connie had seated themselves on the turf and were gazing across to the hills on the opposite side, 'go ahead, and please don't leave out anything.'

'The ghost?'

'The ghost, child.'

'And would you really change rooms with me? Really?'

'Certainly. I confess I should like to see a ghost. One reads so much and experiences so little of these things. This hotel – who knows? – may be a place of first-rate psychic interest and importance.' She cackled, but Connie remained serious.

'Well, if you really wouldn't mind, I'd be terribly glad. It's a nun, you know. I told you, didn't I?'

'Yes? A nun?'

'In a white habit. She's fairly small and she – and she squeaks.'

'Squeaks?'

'Yes. I don't know how else to describe it. She frightened me horribly. I hid my face under the bedclothes, and *prayed* for her to go away, and when I peeped next time she was gone.'

'Whereabouts in the room did she appear?'

'Close by the dressing-table, I think. But I couldn't say for certain. It seemed between there and the fireplace.'

'Have you any idea of the time when she appeared?'

'Yes, but it isn't exact. I heard a clock strike three very soon after she had gone.'

'You know it was striking the hour?'

'Oh, yes. It had done all its chimes, and then it struck three clear notes. I expect you've heard the clock I mean. I think it's somewhere near, but in the town, not in the hotel.'

'Well, child, we shall see what luck I have. If you are ready, let us climb to the grove of trees.'

'You go,' said Connie. 'I'd sooner look at the view.'

Mrs Bradley got up, and climbed, by a broad turf path closely worn to the chalk of the hill, to a grove of trees on the summit. Here she poked inquisitively about among the tree-trunks and discovered what looked like a tramp's lair in a hole in the ground where, at some time, possibly, a tree had been uprooted. There were the remains of a fire, a couple of rusty tins which had not been opened but were dented all over as though they had been flung against the trees, two great hunks of badly mildewed bread, and a heap of dead leaves which might have been used as a bed.

Although an ancient British track was believed to have run up and over the hill, it was not very likely, Mrs Bradley thought, that a modern tramp would have troubled to take the same route when roads went in every direction around the base of the hill. She was interested in these evidences of human occupation, therefore, particularly as they did not look like the remains of a picnic.

She poked into the hole with her foot, and turned up an old leather sandal. She was sufficiently interested in this to continue poking. She felt that Connie was watching her, so she thoughtfully pushed the heap of leaves over the sandal and strolled towards the bushes as Connie came into view.

'Thought I'd come up after all!' said Connie, panting. 'Anything to see up here?'

There was a miz-maze cut in the turf nearby. Mrs Bradley referred to this fact, and they left the trees and came out into the open. There were legends to account for the miz-maze. Mrs Bradley detailed these, and the time passed pleasantly.

'You'll remember not to mention the exchange of rooms,' said Mrs Bradley, as they descended by a path on the other side of the hill. They came out upon Twyford Down and crossed the golf course.

'*I* shan't say anything! They'd all think I was crazy,' Connie replied. 'I suppose we'd better let the chambermaid know, but she isn't likely to mention it, and, if she did, it would only be to Aunt Prissie, and I don't much mind her knowing. It's the other two, especially Uncle Edris. I am really afraid of that man.'

'I wouldn't let anyone know, and I'm sure we can square the chambermaid. Let's keep the whole thing to ourselves,' said Mrs Bradley. 'But why should you fear Mr Tidson?' She neither expected nor received an answer to this question.

'I don't know,' said Connie, 'but I do.'

They followed a footpath across the golf course, and

came out on to the by-pass road, which they crossed. Then they took the towing-path, beside what was part of the old canal, on the other side of the railway, Connie leading the way. Suddenly, as they came in sight of the weir, she turned and said:

'You said you wanted exercise! Do let's run!' And, on the words, she fled like Atlanta, but what she was running away from Mrs Bradley could not determine.

Mrs Bradley was intrigued by Connie's story of the ghost. Not altogether to her surprise, the next news of the visitant came from Crete Tidson, who said at tea, when the party were all assembled at a table in the garden:

'I hear that this house is haunted. I do not think I should come here any more.'

'Why ever not?' enquired Miss Carmody abruptly. 'A ghost never harmed anyone yet. Personally, I should rather like to see one. What do *you* say, Connie?'

Connie laughed without mirth, and said that she supposed it might be interesting.

'Very interesting indeed,' said Mr Tidson, waving a piece of bread and butter. 'Extremely so. But I don't know what you mean when you say that a ghost never harmed anyone yet! What about the one in Berkeley Square? And on the Canaries we heard rumours of volcanic entities – enormous, nebulous creatures that come out of the mountains, you know – which are supposed to be capable of driving people insane.'

'Really?' said Mrs Bradley. 'I have stayed in the Canaries several times, but I never heard such a story.'

'Possibly not,' said Mr Tidson. 'But *living* there is a different matter entirely from merely *staying*. I could tell you, out of my own experiences—'

'Eat your bread and butter, Edris, or, at least, stop waving it about,' said Crete. 'Your experiences are in no way unique, and I don't suppose for one moment that anybody wants to hear about them.'

'I'll tell you what somebody *does* want,' said Connie,

who desired above all things to have the subject changed, 'and that somebody is myself. I do want to visit the College.'

'Why, of course,' said Miss Carmody. 'We must remember that we have young Arthur Preece-Harvard at school there. And although he is on holiday at present—'

'By Jove, yes!' Mr Tidson cried loudly, putting down his cup at a warning exclamation from his wife. 'Arthur Preece-Harvard! I had forgotten all about him! I must certainly visit the College. But not to-morrow, Connie, my dear. I am hot on the track of my nymph, and all else must wait, for fear lest the scent should grow cold.'

'I think I must come nymphing with you one day,' said Mrs Bradley, soberly. 'One should not miss these excitements.' To her surprise, Mr Tidson assented with great enthusiasm.

'Nothing I should like better! Nothing! Nothing!' he cried. 'Oh, yes, do come! These sceptics—' he waved towards his wife, Connie and Miss Carmody – 'are most discouraging. If I were a sensitive man I should have become depressed.'

'Well, thank heaven you're not, then, a sensitive man,' said Crete. 'It is very kind of Mrs Bradley, don't you think, to take interest in your silly old nymph?'

'I know it is kind of her,' Mr Tidson retorted. 'It is also intelligent and enlightened of her. It is good to find someone else among the prophets, and I greatly look forward to her company.'

Mrs Bradley, extremely puzzled by his reactions, since she had deduced that the very last thing Mr Tidson desired was that anyone should accompany him upon his expeditions, looked forward keenly to the outing.

At Mr Tidson's request, they set out directly after tea, at a time when there were numbers of people everywhere in the city, and a procession of visitors between Winchester and St Cross along the river.

'Where do you expect to find her to-day?' Mrs Bradley briskly enquired, as though the expedition were of the most ordinary nature.

'That remains to be seen,' said Mr Tidson. 'I have not

yet discovered where she hides, but I think I ought to take cover to-day and give her a chance to appear.'

'Is the late afternoon a good time? I should have thought that all these people – the little boys particularly – would most certainly have frightened her away.'

'Oh, I think she likes little boys,' said Mr Tidson. 'These, for instance; dear little chaps. Perhaps they are hardly safe. One never knows.' He smiled at the boys as they passed.

Once past the Winchester playing fields, the stream ran past the wall of a garden, and, after that, it crossed the end of a road in a wide, deep opening rather like a small pond. Boys were paddling, sailing their boats, poking into the river bed with willow sticks, collecting minnows in jam-jars and in other ways enjoying themselves while the sun shone and the long summer daylight lasted.

'Of course, Crete and I have no children,' said Mr Tidson.

'Then you are fond of children?' Mrs Bradley enquired, as she fell into step beside him, and they walked on past the end of the row of small houses.

'Everyone is fond of children; I am, perhaps, more attached to them than most are,' he replied.

'How do you suppose Bobby Grier came to drown himself like that?' asked Mrs Bradley, full of Miss Carmody's dreadful theories and greatly desirous of putting them to the test.

'I do not suppose he did.'

'The water-nymph?' She glanced at him sharply. 'I don't believe a word of that, you know.'

'I do not believe it, either, in this particular case,' said Mr Tidson. He kicked a stone out of his path. 'I think some villainy was at work there. Don't ask me what. I have nothing to go on, of course, but my opinion is (I think) the same as yours, and I have my reasons for holding it. The nymph may be here. I think she is. She may drown little boys. I think she does. But I don't think she drowned little Grier.'

'Really? What do you think, then?'

'It is what I think *of*,' said Mr Tidson, somewhat myster-iously. 'Repressed spinsters, monomaniacs, sex-maniacs, mass murderers ... lorry-drivers ... curates ... kindly persons with nasty little bags of sweets and horrid little pockets full of gooseberries. Goblin market, you know. I think of them all, but mostly, of course, of the spinsters.'

'Really?' Mrs Bradley looked astounded.

'Very, very sad,' Mr Tidson continued. 'When one lives side by side with one of them, one gets to see their point of view, you know. Very odd things, repressions. Charlotte Corday, and so on.' He shook his head, stopped suddenly, looked at the sky, and then said with some abruptness, 'I am not in the mood for my nymph. I am going home.'

Chapter Seven

'Take two Oounces of Jesuit's Bark, infuse it in
Spring-water . . .'
Mrs SARAH HARRISON OF DEVONSHIRE
(*The Housekeeper's Pocket Book, etc.*)

Mrs BRADLEY was as interested in Mr Tidson's unexpected views as, if he had intended to interest her,
he could have wished. She did not betray her feelings further,
however, but startled Mr Tidson by giving a short, harsh
cackle.

'It seems a pity to go home straightway,' she said. 'Why
shouldn't we do a little sightseeing? What about the
Cathedral?'

'Not that, if you have no objection. If we are going to
stay out, let us take a good long walk to give us time to
forget what I have said. I think you know that I intended
nothing definite. It is just that one sees what one sees, one
hears what one hears, and one understands with whatever
understanding one has been granted by omnipotent
Providence.'

'And what do you mean by that?' asked Mrs Bradley.
Mr Tidson waved a plump hand.

'Live and let live!' he replied. 'And now for a really long
walk. Emotion shall be dissipated in action.'

Mrs Bradley was astonished by this change of plan, and
she wondered what, in Mr Tidson's opinion, constituted
a long walk. He turned left along the road and they walked
on to the by-pass and then began to climb Saint Catherine's
Hill.

Mrs Bradley made no comment. She merely lengthened

her stride and had the satisfaction, very soon, of hearing her companion begin to puff and blow. She smiled, and went almost at a run up the short turf mound as it rose ever more steeply to the earthworks.

Soon she had outdistanced Mr Tidson. She stopped when she reached the fringe of the grove of trees, and waited for him to join her. He was pouting and scowling like a bad-tempered little boy, but Mrs Bradley, unperturbed by this emotional display, raised a skinny arm and pointed downwards towards the water-meadows and over the plotted landscape with its intersecting carriers and brooks.

'I suppose you have brought your field-glasses?' she enquired. 'Otherwise you will scarcely see her from here.'

'See whom? Not the nymph?' Mr Tidson's ill-temper vanished. 'I believe,' he added, taking out his handkerchief and wiping his face, 'you are as interested in her as I am! Confess, now, if you are not!'

'I am quite as interested,' said Mrs Bradley emphatically. 'But I'm still not sure that I believe in her, in spite of all you can say.'

'Don't you?' asked Mr Tidson anxiously. 'I do think you'd better, you know. You must try to forget what I've said this afternoon. I believe in my nymph fully, and you would be well advised to do the same.'

'Perhaps it would make things simpler,' Mrs Bradley agreed. 'But what do I see down there by the old canal?'

'Where? Where?'

'That way, look! To your left. Isn't some kind of disturbance going on? There, by the railway signal. Look!'

'I don't see anything,' said Mr Tidson peevishly. But she noticed he had turned very pale and his plump cheeks shook. 'We can go back that way, if you like, but I think you must be mistaken. That is – those are – the grounds of a private house. We can't get in, even if we do go down there. I know it well.'

'I should like to go back that way,' said Mrs Bradley. She started off at the same tremendous pace as she had set in coming up-hill. Mr Tidson grunted, slipped and slithered, and then swore in the bastard Spanish he affected when something did not please him. At last he gave up any attempt to keep level with her, and found her waiting for him on the rough and muddy path which led under the railway arch at the foot of the hill.

They returned alongside the water, but whatever Mrs Bradley had seen from the top of the hill had left no trace, and their homeward walk was uninteresting. 'I shall come out alone this evening,' said Mr Tidson.

'I'm afraid your relative doesn't like me very much,' Mrs Bradley said later to Miss Carmody. 'I think I shall go upstairs early, out of his way.' She and Connie had already changed rooms, and Mrs Bradley, who had spent some time in examining number twenty-nine, thought that it had, as it were, some ghostly possibilities.

A squarish Tudor window looked on to the side entrance of the hotel, and a large open fireplace seemed to speak of logs, priest-holes and a chimney with a long and interesting history. A low window-seat concealed a box, and the room also contained a massive and gloomy cupboard.

Mrs Bradley shut the window, locked the door, took off her skirt and shoes, and, putting her head up the wide aperture and shining her torch upon the blackened brickwork, soon discovered footholds in the chimney.

She put the torch in the fender, but where she would not tread on it when she came down again, listened at the door, wedged an armchair against the cupboard, put her heaviest suitcase, fully packed, on the window-seat, and then climbed into the chimney.

About halfway up she discovered, as she had expected, that there was easy access to the roof, for the chimney terminated squarely and had no pot.

The roof here was flat, and facing her was another chimney, broad-breasted and nearly three feet thick. She walked over to it, or, rather, almost crawled, hoping that she would not be detected from the garden below. She was also in mortal fear of being spotted from somebody's bedroom window. It was by this time almost dark, however

– the chimney had been like the Pit – so she hoped to remain undetected.

It took her ten minutes to find the concealed door on the outside surface of the second chimney. The doorway had been painted to look like the brickwork, and she had to explore the whole side of the chimney, as soon as she discovered which face was of iron, before she could swing the door open.

She managed it at last. The door was on a pivot, and, as it swung, it showed a dark flight of very narrow steps. Mrs Bradley descended into the hotel and soon found herself in a small square room. There were six feet of headroom, and the floor space, roughly, was eight feet by seven. It remained to discover how to get from this elaborate priest's hole into one of the bedrooms or on to the main staircase.

She listened again, but could not hear a sound. She had closed the top door behind her and now, by carefully testing the walls, she discovered that a hidden spring gave admittance not to a bedroom or to the main staircase, but to that other priest's hole, the present, prosaic linen-cupboard passage which she had pointed out to Connie soon after their arrival at the hotel. To construct a priest's hole to conceal another priest's hole seemed to Mrs Bradley an intelligent thought, and she wished she could have shared her discovery.

However, as the ghost had taken to walking, it would be as well, Mrs Bradley thought, to keep to herself the means by which it could make its entrances. She would wait, she decided, upon the order of events before she took anyone into her confidence.

She did not undress, but sat for some time at the window, gazing out and with ears alert for sounds. There were plenty of these to be heard. Conversation, laughter, and what seemed, at one point, rather like a quarrel between Crete and Edris Tidson, came floating up out of the garden. There was the hum of traffic from the High Street, not so very far away; and, half an hour later, raucous singing from men turned out of the public house at the top of the quiet street.

Gradually all sound was hushed, but Mrs Bradley sat on in the quiet darkness. It was a warm night, and she had raised her window halfway up at the bottom as soon as she had entered the room. She knew when the lights in the public rooms went out, for they cast no more reflections on the lawn. She saw the lights in the glassed-in corridor which led to the annexe flick out one by one as a distant clock struck a quarter past eleven, and Thomas made his solemn nocturnal rounds – a Presbyterian elder sentencing the household to slumber.

Mrs Bradley sat on. All was silent and dark. She strained her ears. At last came the sound that she was waiting for. She got up noiselessly, tip-toed over to the towel rail, which she had moved out a few inches from the wall, and squeezed herself quietly behind it. She was wearing a black dress which was wide and easy-fitting. She bent and crouched so that only her eyes and the top of her head appeared above the screen she had selected, and then, with grim patience, waited, watching the chimney.

The ghost, however, came gliding in from the built-in cupboard which served the room as a wardrobe. It had to open the door of the cupboard, Mrs Bradley noted, a human trait which gave her confidence. Having entered the room, it went unhesitatingly up to the bed, which it leaned over, making a very faint mewing noise, more like a kitten than a cat. It was white and tall, but the movements it made were not menacing. Mrs Bradley started forward. The towel rail fell with a muffled sound owing to its smothering of towels. It made just sufficient noise to frighten the ghost, which turned, with a flourish of draperies.

Mrs Bradley picked up a piece of soap from the side of the bedroom basin, and flung it hard, but it was slightly wet, and slipped as she let it go. She picked up the nailbrush and let fly. There was a muffled yelp as the nailbrush got home, and the next instant the ghost had disappeared, apparently through the bedroom wall.

Mrs Bradley came out from behind the towel rail. She partly closed the window and drew the blind. Then she switched on the light and spent the next two hours in searching and sounding every part of the room. She gave it up in the end, as being a task more suitable to daylight than to the unequal lighting given to the room by the dressing-table and bedhead switches. She then went to bed and slept soundly.

Next morning she sought out Miss Carmody.

'Let us leave Mr Tidson to hunt alone,' she said, 'and take Connie with us to visit Bournemouth. Why not?'

'I shall look rather odd at Bournemouth,' said Miss Carmody. 'I knocked into the edge of my bedroom door last night whilst I was groping for the switch in the dark. Just look at my eye! People will think I have been fighting!'

Mrs Bradley had been unable to keep a fascinated and glittering eye off Miss Carmody's contused face ever since she had first encountered her, and she welcomed this frank reference to a large and interesting bruise.

'I wondered what you had been doing,' she said. 'But it isn't really your eye. It is more to the side. I don't think it would notice any more at Bournemouth than it does here. But just as you like.'

'Oh, I should like above all things to visit Bournemouth,' exclaimed Miss Carmody. 'Do let us find Connie and tell her. I expect she is still in her room. As a matter of fact, I think Bournemouth a most restful idea! No one will question me there!'

The two ladies were in the garden. Breakfast had been in progress for an hour, and Mrs Bradley had already had toast and coffee. Miss Carmody usually waited for Crete and Mr Tidson, and sometimes for Connie, who, like nearly all girls of her age, was either out of bed before six or fast asleep until ten unless somebody woke her.

Not at all anxious that Miss Carmody should discover so soon that she and Connie had changed rooms, Mrs Bradley began to frame an excuse for keeping Miss Carmody with her, and was pleased to see Crete coming out of the sun-parlour towards them. As she drew nearer, the two ladies raised a questioning cry, for Crete, like Miss Carmody, had an interestingly-tinted contusion just between the eyebrow and the temple.

'Oh, yes,' she said. 'I did a stupid thing. I tripped on the bath mat and caught my head against the edge of that silly little shelf below the mirror. You know the one I mean?'

'Ah?' said Mrs Bradley, immensely intrigued by this revelation. But further matter for speculation was in store when they encountered Mr Tidson in the hall.

'Good heavens!' Miss Carmody exclaimed. 'Have *you* got a black eye, too?'

Mr Tidson warily touched the bruise at the edge of his cheek-bone.

'Crete gave me this,' he said, with some natural annoyance. 'I asked her to pass some cold-cream from her room to mine. Instead of handing it to me, she flung it – positively hurled it – in the direction in which I was standing, supposing, she said, that I should catch it.'

'I hope she apologized,' said Mrs Bradley solemnly. She went close up to Mr Tidson and examined his wound minutely.

'Well?' he said, resentfully backing away. Mrs Bradley cackled. Mr Tidson was about to add to this one tart observation when it dawned on him that Miss Carmody and his wife were both adorned with facial bruises not remarkably different from his own. The expression on his face as he made this discovery gave Mrs Bradley great pleasure. She watched the Tidsons go into breakfast, followed by Miss Carmody and Connie, and then glanced at the letters on the hall table, for the *Domus* had no letter-rack.

'Naething for ye,' said Thomas, coming to rest beside her.

'I am not sorry,' she said. 'Tell me, have you had any complaints about people slipping and hurting themselves in this hotel?'

Thomas took time to consider this question.

'Weel,' he said cautiously, 'there was Sir William, wha

slippit on the soap in 1925, and there was a wee shrappit body by the name of Wemyss, I mind, in 1932, who was knockit over on the staircase by a professor from Harvard Univairsity. I dinna recollect ony mair.'

'Strange! Miss Carmody and Mr and Mrs Tidson have all been injured either last night or this morning. Have you not noticed their bruises?'

Thomas clicked his tongue, but more in wordless condemnation of their carelessness than for regret at the accidents, Mrs Bradley decided. She went out to find George, her chauffeur, and, upon re-entering the hotel, she came face to face with Connie Carmody, who was just descending the stairs. Connie had her hand to her eye. She took it away to disclose an already purple swelling. Mrs Bradley could have cried 'Eureka,' but restrained herself.

By ten Miss Carmody and Connie were ready, and at lunchtime the party found themselves at a hotel on the front at Bournemouth and in full enjoyment of the yellow sand, the sparkling sea, the combes, the cliffs, the balmy air and all else that the queen of watering places has to offer.

When lunch was over, Connie took herself off to Christchurch Priory with the remark that she would be back in Bournemouth in time for a bathe before tea, and the two elderly ladies, left alone, sat in deck-chairs on the sand. They indulged in some lazy conversation and some even lazier knitting, and thoroughly enjoyed their time beside the sea. It was an ideal afternoon. The front was crowded, the air was warm, a band was playing, and there were plenty of people to look at; there was even time, if they cared for it, to sleep.

Mrs Bradley, who cared nothing for an afternoon nap, and minded the immoderate heat not a bit more than a lizard does, gazed out to sea and thought deeply and constructively on the subject of the ghost and the bruises. Miss Carmody, giving up both knitting and conversation, soon dozed off, and was no liability to anyone.

Connie came back at a quarter to four and woke Miss

Carmody up by searching for her bathing things in Miss Carmody's bag. When she had entered the water and could not be distinguished, except by the eye of love and faith, from the dozens of other swimmers, Mrs Bradley said to Miss Carmody:

'Does Connie inherit anything under your will?'

'Oh, yes, of course, dear girl!' said Miss Carmody, opening her eyes.

'And what about Mr Tidson?'

'Edris?'

'Yes. I have reasons for asking.'

'Oh, Edris gets nothing from me.'

'Does he know that?'

'Yes. I made it clear soon after they came. As a matter of fact, he asked me. You would scarcely believe that, would you?'

Mrs Bradley, who was beginning to think that she would believe anything, either good or bad, of Mr Tidson, did not answer this question. She said:

'I'd like to get it quite clear. Do I understand that under no circumstances whatever does Mr Tidson come into your will?'

'You mean if Connie – if anything happened to Connie?'

'That's what I mean.'

'If anything happens to Connie, either before or after my death, the money goes to charity. In any case, it isn't much, you know. But why—?'

'Yes, I know these blunt enquiries must be puzzling,' said Mrs Bradley, 'but, after all, you did bring me down to Winchester, didn't you? And upon a special mission.'

'And how thankful I am that I did!' said Miss Carmody roundly. 'You don't mean that Edris is dangerous to Connie, I hope?'

'Well, no, I don't say I mean that. But I thought it as well to inform myself of what he might have to expect from you, that is all.'

'I *wish* I could get rid of them both!' cried Miss Carmody. 'It is really too much of a strain on my resources to keep them all this time! But I don't know how to make them

go! And for Connie's sake . . . Oh, dear! I would love to
be rid of them!'

'Perhaps we shall find a way,' said Mrs Bradley. 'By
"both of them" you refer, of course, to Mr and Mrs Tidson,
and not to Mr Tidson and Connie.'

'Oh, Connie will soon be quit of me, anyhow,' said Miss
Carmody, with a hard and hurt little laugh. 'Connie has
made up her mind, as you surely must have heard her
saying, to leave me as soon as she can. I really do *not*
understand her.'

'Well, children will be children,' said Mrs Bradley indul-
gently, 'and part of being children is that they have to
pretend to grow up. You are not going to let that worry
you? What about when she gets married? You'd lose her,
in any case, then.'

'I don't know that she would find it so easy as all that
to get married,' said Miss Carmody. 'Do you call her
attractive? I hardly think I should if I had not become
her foster-parent, you know.'

'I don't know whether she is attractive,' said Mrs Bradley.
'She is very young. I am interested in all young things, and
feel very sorry for most of them.'

'There is good reason to be sorry for Connie, I suppose,'
said Miss Carmody. 'She has had some disappointments
which have gone very deep, I am afraid. They have spoilt
her nature. She is rather irritable and selfish. Still, I should
not like to be without her, and I am hoping she will soon
tire of this adventure of launching out on her own, and
come back to live at my flat. Of course, Edris and Crete
are the trouble. One cannot expect her to like them, and,
as I say, I don't know how to get rid of them. Edris has
really no scruples, and secrets are not secrets to him.'

Mrs Bradley volunteered no advice, except to say:

'If I had to choose between them and Connie, I think I
know what I would do, and, if you will forgive me for
saying so, I think you should have made it clear before.'

'Yes,' agreed Miss Carmody. 'It sounds very simple, put
like that, but, you know, Mrs Bradley, it is not at all easy
to dislodge people, particularly when they are one's own

relations and have made up their minds to stay. And I'm rather afraid of Edris. He is a strange person – this business of the naiad, for example – and, of course, he drowned that little boy. I have no doubt whatever about that. But, then, he has lived abroad for so long that his ideas are not quite ours.'

'His ideas of morality, you mean?' asked Mrs Bradley.

'Yes, I do not understand him. And Crete, as you know, is half Greek – the wrong half.'

'The wrong half?'

'Her father was Greek. That counts for a good deal with me. One can smother up a foreign mother, I always think, but not a foreign father.'

Mrs Bradley professed interest in this view, and they discussed it at some length. In the animated talk on heredity which followed, Connie and the Tidsons were forgotten, and it was with surprise that Miss Carmody, upon noticing that Connie had come out of the water and was walking up the beach towards them, glanced at her watch and saw that they had been sitting there for more than an hour.

'Ought you to have stayed in the water so long, dear?' she enquired, as Connie, in a two-piece bathing suit of which her aunt almost violently disapproved but in whose defence Connie had long ago been victorious, came up to them shell-pink from the sea.

'Oh, I've been in and out several times,' said Connie. 'I'll dress now. What about tea?'

'As soon as you're ready, dear. Wipe yourself quite dry, for fear of rheumatism.'

'She certainly does not look unattractive now,' remarked Mrs Bradley, as Connie, tall and well-made, walked back to her dressing cubicle and disappeared into its interior.

'No, indeed,' Miss Carmody, agreed. 'I see why Venus was, perhaps, well-advised to rise from the waves.'

Mrs Bradley disguised her reactions to this remark, but she could not help remembering Mr Tidson's extraordinary outburst against spinsters, monomaniacs and curates. The ivory tower might be delicately constructed and to a mild,

Edwardian pattern, but its secret inventory remained the same, it appeared.

George picked them up at just after six. They spent half an hour at Wimborne Minster, and the drive home through the New Forest was a delightful ending to the day. They came back through Ringwood to Fordingbridge, thence by way of Romsey to Winchester.

The Tidsons, it seemed, had finished dinner by the time the travellers returned, and were found – Mr Tidson behind an evening paper, Crete with her embroidery – enjoying their coffee in the lounge in that polite dissociation from one another which, as Mrs Bradley pointed out when Connie, indiscreetly, made a rather loud remark on it, is the hall-mark of a well-matched, middle-aged couple.

That her explanation, also loud, was not one whit more tactful than Connie's remark was shown very clearly by Crete, who, upon hearing herself referred to as middle-aged (an obvious libel) turned upon both of them a dark, bleak stare of intense loathing before proceeding with her embroidery. Between her temple and her left eyebrow was still an inch of black and yellow bruise, a mild edition of Mr Tidson's now very impressive black eye. Withdrawing from all four of the mysteriously ill-starred group, Mrs Bradley escaped to her room. She had locked it that morning and had unlocked it only to wash her hands before dinner. She now unlocked it again, and, once inside, she re-locked the door behind her.

She then made sure that the window was fastened before she began to go over the interior of the wardrobe cupboard.

She soon found a button to press; the wall at the back of the cupboard swung away, and a passage opened before her.

She scarcely needed to explore it. She could deduce where it led. Still, to assure herself of all the possibilities, she followed it. It led into the air-raid shelter, and it was a fair piece of deduction that both Connie and Miss Carmody could have known of it, but the Tidsons probably did not. There was one more passage to find. She tapped and pressed for twenty minutes or more. She guessed that the passage opened somewhere between the dressing-table and that end of the fireplace wall which was nearest the window. This part of the room formed a wide recess the depth of the chimney-breast, and the wall area measured at least a hundred square feet, half of which could be discounted as being too high. Almost another quarter could also be disregarded because of the position of the dressing-table.

About thirty square feet of the lower half of the wall were therefore to be explored. Mrs Bradley tried every dodge which she knew of, or of which she had ever read, but for a long time all was in vain. Then, in the way things often are brought about, she leaned against the wall to take the crick out of her back, and immediately precipitated herself into the secret – or not so secret – passage.

It led into the air-raid shelter, and was parallel with the passage from the wardrobe cupboard. It was an old passage reconditioned. Mrs Bradley kept watch that night but was not disturbed. Next morning, after she had had an interview with the management, workmen sealed off both the passages which led from the air-raid shelter to her room.

'Who comes now, comes down the chimney,' thought Mrs Bradley. The idea gave her great satisfaction. She thought it extremely unlikely that the Tidsons or Carmodys knew of the way in by the chimney.

'Yes, we used to notify our guests of a passage through one of the principal bedrooms on every floor if they did not want to run across the lawn to reach the shelter,' the manageress had said. 'Of course, we have had no raids to speak of in this neighbourhood, but we did get the warning sometimes, and in winter, I must say, the guests were very thankful that they did not need to come outside the house to reach the shelter. We are most anxious, however, that no one should be disturbed now the war is over. We really ought to have blocked up the passages before this.'

Mrs Bradley agreed that the comfort of the guests was the first and last consideration in any well-managed hotel, and slept remarkably soundly that night, for a complicated booby trap was in the hearth to discourage ghostly invasions. Before she slept she mused again upon the Carmody and Tidson bruises. She had come to a very definite conclusion about them.

Chapter Eight

*'If any soft or perished Place appear on the
Outside, try how deep it goes, for the greater
Part may be hid within.'*
      Mrs SARAH HARRISON (*The Housekeeper's
                              Pocket Book, etc.*)

THE second seaport of England and the greatest cotton
market of Europe seemed at first to Laura Menzies dirty,
congested, dull and inextricably confused. She had set out,
however, in the spirit of adventure which characterized her
outlook, and the hotel and Kitty, between them, reconciled
her to the greyness of an atmosphere which seemed to be
compounded in equal parts of drizzle and soot.

'Well, Dog,' said Kitty with candour, 'I don't know why
on earth you brought me here.'

'As I told you, young K., to improve your education and
give you food for thought,' replied Laura, summing up the
sandwiches with which she had provided herself before
retiring to rest, and then selecting the largest. 'Anyway, the
grub's all right. What are you beefing about? Don't you
want to help your Auntie Laura?'

'Yes, if I knew what you were up to. But I don't. What's
all this about water nymphs? It sounds a bit Picasso to
me.'

'Oh, Lord! Did you see that show?'

'Yes, I did. And I'll tell you what, Dog. I got a new hair-
style out of it.'

'Not off Pop-Eye?'

'Off one of the Ladies in Grey. And that Fish-Hat, Dog.
An idea.'

'Maybe. You're welcome to it, if so. But the water-nymph, K., is Mrs Croc's latest murderer. It's killed someone already, she thinks, and repercussions are expected hourly.'

'But that was at Winchester, you said. What's Liverpool got to do with it?'

'Have patience, duck, and I'll explain. It seems that the water-nymph is sponsored by a rather odd, Mr Pym Passes By sort of bloke by the name of – Oh, well, that doesn't matter.'

'Name of what?' asked Kitty, who preferred her friend's narrative complete and the characters labelled.

'Name of Tidson, then.'

'I used to know someone named Tidson,' said Kitty. 'Or was it McCallahan? Anyway, he married a Chinese girl and inherited an opium den.'

'Oh, do dry up!'

'Sorry. Go on, then. But, you know, Dog, my word-associations are very free. That's why I get on in my job.'

'I'll bet they are, if Tidson reminds you of McCallahan. Well, this Tidson read in the paper about the water-nymph, swallowed the story whole, and insisted on going down to Winchester to see whether he could spot the bally thing.'

'How does Mrs Croc. come into it?'

'Well, this Tidson's relations were worried, and Mrs Croc. was drawn in to find out whether he was quite right in the head, and, if not, whether dangerous or only goofy.'

'Oh, I see. Go on. What about Liverpool, then? – And when you've done turning over all the sandwiches and taking the tops off I think I'll have one.'

'Eh? – Oh, sorry! Here you are. Yes, well, this Tidson used to grow bananas, and as his boats sometimes came to Liverpool, Mrs Croc. sent me down to consort with any of his pals who might happen to hang out in the vicinity of the docks or elsewhere to find out whether he's likely to have murdered this boy.'

'Oh, heavens, Dog! Don't be such an ass! I don't see any point in what you're saying.'

'To tell the truth, duck, I don't either. But let that pass. Shall I order another plate of sandwiches?'

'Not for me. I'm going to bed.'

'Not an unsound scheme,' said Laura, getting up. '"To-morrow to fresh woods and pastures new." In other words, I shall take a ride on the overhead electric railway, which, my spies inform me, is the best if not the only way of getting a birds-eye view of the docks. During our tour I shall formulate my plans for obtaining the low-down on this Tidson.'

They enjoyed their ride next morning, and were given a free pass to visit a Cunarder, then in dock. It was on board this ship that Laura experienced a stroke of that luck which, as she modestly explained in a letter to Mrs Bradley, was always apt to dog her footsteps.

She was standing on the port side of the orlop deck and was talking in her usual confident, hearty tones when a young man near by came up and raised his hat.

'I beg your pardon,' he said, 'but I think I heard you mention the name Tidson.'

'Yes, I did,' said Laura, scanning him frankly. 'A man who used to keep a banana plantation on Tenerife.'

'Yes. One of our managers. Just retired. He had charge of San Sábado, on Puerta de Orotava, hadn't he?'

'I don't think so. My Tidson was a banana grower in his own right.'

'Scarcely likely, if you don't mind my saying so. The banana plantations belong to us, you know. He managed San Sábado for us until this last year. I wondered what had happened to the old chap. We used to think him unlucky.'

'Unlucky? Why?'

'Well, his men used to die on him, you know. They got so superstitious, in the end, that he couldn't get enough labour to keep San Sábado going. Everybody said he had the evil eye. Personally, I think it was the wife.'

'The wife?'

'Crete Tidson. Beautiful woman. Half Greek.'

'Tell me,' said Laura, earnestly. 'Was there ever any suspicion of *foul play?* Among the labourers, you know.'

'Good Lord, no! The chaps died naturally enough. Girls, too. We employ a lot of female labour. It's an amazing thing to see what some of these Island girls can carry. Make some of your Covent Garden porters open their eyes, I can tell you.'

'Is your Mr Tidson *queer* at all?' enquired Laura. 'He's in the care, more or less, of an alienist at present, and we wondered – I'm her secretary – whether he'd ever shown any signs of anything (so to speak) peculiar.'

'Oh, the old bloke was as mad as a hatter,' said the young man cheerfully. 'Ask anybody on Tenerife or Orotava. Used to climb the mountains to look for the boogie-woogies jumping out of the volcanoes. Harmless as a child, of course, but definitely bughouse. No doubt whatever about that.'

'But nothing sinister?' persisted Laura.

'Not a thing. Used to borrow and not pay back, which didn't make for popularity exactly, but people soon got wise to that, and simply didn't lend him anything. He spent a fortune on his wife. That's where the money went, all right. Can't think, for my part, why she married him. Quite staggeringly beautiful, you know. The Spaniards used to call her Doña Alba.'

'Well, talk about pennies from heaven!' said Laura, when she and Kitty were on shore again. She spoke regretfully. 'That's the end of our holiday, duck. I shall embody what I've just learnt in an official letter to Mrs Croc. this afternoon, and she'll probably reply with a telegram recalling me at once to her side.'

Mrs Bradley, however, had far too much right feeling to do this. She told Laura to go on to the Lakes or to Blackpool with Kitty if she liked, and to be sure to enjoy herself. She would expect her when she saw her, she added, and expense need not be spared.

'So what!' said Laura, handing over the message.

'So nothing,' said Kitty firmly. 'You'd better forget the Lakes, Dog. As I see it, we've got work to do here.'

'Such as?'

'Track down this banana person again, and make him produce his affidavits.'

'His what?'

'His affidavits. A business precaution. You know, like

making people pay a deposit when they book their permanent wave.'

'Lord, K., don't be such an ass! We're off to the Lakes
as soon as we can book a couple of rooms.'

'Oh, Dog, don't please be awkward. You can't leave this
in the air. Either you've got to get evidence that this man
knew what he was talking about, or else you're here under
false pretences. Besides, there's an American woman in the
lounge who's got a hair-style I've never seen before, and I
want to find out how it's done.'

'Oh, Lord!' said Laura. 'All right. As it happens, I know
where he's staying. He tried to date me up for dinner, and
told me the name of his hotel.'

'Well, of all the cheek!' said Kitty wrathfully. 'I look
tons nicer than you, and, besides, I'm more the right size.'

'Right size be sugared,' said Laura, who stood a brawny
and solid five-foot ten. 'Small men often like large women.
Besides, I *told* you you were getting too fat, you lazy rotter.
This proves me right. It's time you took some exercise, and
laid off the starchy foods.'

'Chance would be a fine thing,' said Kitty, good-
temperedly. 'Well, when do we call upon this Mormon?'

'To-morrow, if you say the word. But I can't see what
we can ask him. Dash it, he's told us all he knows. I can't
go along there and pump him. It isn't decent.'

'Be yourself, Dog. Surely you can think of something!
You've got to make him *prove* he knew this Tidson.'

'Well, he knew Crete. That's obvious. And—'

'She was probably the talk of the town. He'd be sure
to have heard of *her*. I expect all the Dagos fell for her,
for one thing. If she's really as good-looking as he says,
you could hardly *not* hear of her if you'd been to the
Canaries at all. Doesn't prove he knew *Mr* Tidson, does
it?'

'All right, all right! I'll think of something during the night.'

As Kitty knew that Laura would most certainly think
of something during the night, she felt that the matter
could be left safely in her friend's hands, and was not disappointed, for Laura, at breakfast, produced a simple and

workable plan. She conducted the docile Kitty to the young man's hotel and proceeded, over cocktails in the lounge, to canvas his views on the desirability of visiting the Canary Islands for a holiday.

He was immediately and deeply interested, and gave them a vivid and attractive picture of life in the Islands to which Laura listened with close and earnest attention. Then she suddenly said:

'Ah! But what proof have we that you've ever *lived* in the Canaries? Still less that you ever knew the Tidsons!'

'Proof? Oh, but, surely, after all that I've said—' He looked astounded and somewhat hurt, and then began to laugh. 'Look here,' he said, 'I don't know what you're after, but I can assure you that poor little Tidson isn't wanted by the police, or anything of that sort. As for having known the Tidsons, I'll tell you what I'll do, if you like. I'll give you the address of a fellow in Las Palmas who knew them well when he was on Tenerife.'

He wrote out this address, which Laura later sent on to Mrs Bradley.

'And now,' said Laura, with great satisfaction, when she and Kitty had left the young man, 'what about the Lakes, after all? Or, of course, Blackpool, as Mrs Croc. suggests. There's nothing to keep us here, once we've returned the hospitality of this spy of ours, and that we can do to-morrow morning.'

'I'd like to go to Winchester,' said Kitty, 'if we shouldn't be in the way. Write and ask Mrs Bradley, will you? I should think she might be rather glad of two intelligent sort of females like us on the trail without anyone being the wiser.'

'Golly!' said Laura reverently, struck by the extraordinary intelligence (as she saw it) of this suggestion. 'Not your own idea? I'm dying to get to Winchester, but I thought you'd loathe it.'

'Of course it's my own idea! I'm dashed if I see, Dog, why you always think nobody gets ideas but yourself! You'd sound conceited if people didn't already know you were!'

*   *   *

Mrs Bradley, not at all displeased at the thought of some lively company for Connie, and delighted, in any case, at the thought of seeing Laura and Kitty, answered Laura's telegram by another, inviting them forthwith to Winchester.

They arrived before tea, for they had left Liverpool very early in the morning and had had a whirlwind journey from which Laura emerged fresh as paint, and Kitty as though she had spent the afternoon in her bedroom making up her face and doing her hair. Of fatigue, or the rigours of travel, neither of the young women showed a trace in appearance or bearing.

Mrs Bradley was careful not to greet them. It had been agreed that they should contrive to make Connie's acquaintance, and, through her, meet Miss Carmody and the Tidsons. Kitty, who was sometimes gifted with ideas so brilliantly simple that she left Laura gaping with that insulting amazement with which genius is often greeted by its friends, suggested that their best plan might be to go to the place where the body had been found and make some independent enquiries among the dead child's playfellows.

'Kids always talk to me,' she said, with a confidence which Laura had reason to know was not in the least misplaced. 'They'd probably run a mile, and screaming at that, at the sight of Mrs Croc., but they always seem to think I'm harmless.'

This statement did Mrs Bradley considerable injustice, as Laura immediately pointed out, but there was certainly something attractive in Kitty's suggestion. It could not be carried out, however, until the following day, so they had tea at the *Domus*, arranged to stay for a fortnight at the hotel, took a short walk, had dinner, and then took coffee in the sun-lounge, in order, as Laura observed, to 'get an angle on the Tidsons and the other impedimenta of Mrs Croc., and decide which way the cat jumped'.

Mrs Bradley came into the sun-lounge with Miss Carmody's party at just after eight, and Kitty and Laura, from a table which was modestly in the background between a fig-tree and a fifteenth-century holy-water stoup (a relic of the monastery, not of the later nunnery which had existed on the site of the hotel), obtained what Kitty termed 'an eyeful' of Edris and Crete Tidson, Connie and Miss Carmody, for they had not quite liked to study them too closely in the dining-room. Then Laura sauntered over to Mrs Bradley.

'I *do* know you, don't I?' she enquired. 'If not, I've seen your photograph in the papers. Am I wrong in thinking that you are Mrs Lestrange Bradley, of Cartaret?'

'Sure you're not wrong, Dog,' said Kitty, backing her up. 'What's more, I feel pretty certain Mrs Bradley remembers that we were at Athelstan Hall.'

'Of course!' said Mrs Bradley. 'Cartaret? You must, I think, be Miss Menzies. And you—?'

'Trevelyan is the name, Warden,' said Kitty, with a face of brass, using the title which Mrs Bradley, as head of a hostel, had had bestowed on her at the college.

'Yes, yes, of course! How stupid of me,' said Mrs Bradley. 'Miss Carmody, do let me introduce two of my former students. Are you staying in Winchester?' she continued, when the introductions had been made, and Connie warily, Mr Tidson enthusiastically, Crete languidly and Miss Carmody gushingly, had acknowledged the new acquaintance.

'Oh, here to-day and gone to-morrow, more or less, I expect, you know,' said Laura. 'Thought we'd barge round the Cathedral and all that sort of thing. Never seen Winchester and thought perhaps we ought to. See Naples and die,' she added vaguely.

'An excellent idea,' said Mr Tidson, eyeing the buxom Kitty with almost as much approval as if she had been his nymph. Kitty smiled brilliantly upon him, and observed to Laura, when they were clear of the sun-lounge, that she thought him a horrid old man, and one perfectly capable of murder.

'Would you say that?' asked Laura. 'Off here to the left, I imagine, from what I remember of our passage downstairs before dinner. Can't say I see it, quite. Childish and rather spoilt, I should have thought.'

'Well, that's what I mean. It's all the same thing,' said Kitty. 'You know, irresponsible and pink and a bit bald-headed.'

'Don't babble,' observed her friend. 'Now, then, where's this room of ours? You'd think our forefathers were descended from rabbits, wouldn't you, to build these complicated domiciles!'

'What shall we do about the sightseeing?' demanded Kitty. 'Do we *have* to barge round the Cathedral?'

'Sure,' replied Laura. 'I'll show you.'

They spent the following morning in ecstatic exploration of the Cathedral. Nothing escaped their fascinated contemplation, and Kitty enjoyed herself more than she had expected to do. Conversation was brisk, although they had to carry it on in low tones.

'Look, Dog! Fancy having your skeleton for a memorial!'

'They're called rebuses. The guide book says they are quaint. After all, there's nothing like understatement.'

'The Communion rails are quite the nicest thing here, Dog. Don't you think so?'

'Late seventeenth-century. Yes, but what about the choir stalls? And those wall-paintings in the chapel of the Holy Sepulchre?'

'The thing is that people *couldn't* have looked like that. Let's go and see whether the verger is going to open the crypt. Then perhaps we could go up the tower and look at the view. Cathedrals give me a headache.'

Laura, after an hour or so of this, took her friend back to lunch, and announced, on the way, that she had found out where the boy Grier had been drowned, and that they would go in search of information directly the meal was over.

Accordingly, they lunched, and then went down the High Street to the bridge and the mill, and took a side-turning. After five minutes' walking, Laura suddenly observed:

'I was told there was a Youth Hostel somewhere about. Do you see one?'

'We passed it. It's the old mill. You should use your eyes, Dog,' said Kitty, with the triumph of the down-trodden.

'I did – on the lie of the land. Oh, well, if we've passed the Youth Hostel, we're on the right track, and that's something. I imagine, then, these are the houses.'

They soon encountered some children. In fact, there seemed to be a considerable number.

'It's the boys we want,' muttered Kitty, 'not the girls. Boys will know what took that other poor kid to the river late at night. Girls wouldn't know anything like that.'

'Late at night? Lord, K.! You remembered that?'

'You're not the only person who can take an interest, Dog,' said Kitty with great complacence. 'Wait till someone asks us the time, and we'll make our grab. Kids always ask strangers the time. I believe it's an obscure form of cheek.'

As they came to the bridge, they were stopped by three little boys who were playing with an orange box on perambulator wheels.

'Please can you tell me the right time, missis?' asked the leader. Kitty consulted her watch. It was very tiny, and excited immediate interest.

'The right time?' said Kitty, squinting down at it. 'Oh, Lord! I must get my glasses.' She did not wear glasses. Her sight was remarkably good.

'I'll tell it, missis! Let me 'ave a look!' urged one of the children at once. Kitty let him look. She even took the watch off and let the three boys handle it. Laura looked on, expecting every moment that one of them would let the watch fall, and smash it, but it was passed from one pair of dirty paws to another without disaster. At the end, the leader strapped it on to Kitty's wrist. It was not very hard after this to ask the boys the necessary questions.

'The boys all made a raft out of pieces of packing case, and hid it in the reeds, and this drowned kid, they think, went and sneaked it away,' said Laura thoughtfully, as they turned back over the bridge to gain the long lane and the hotel. 'Well, that's quite a likely reason for a kid to be prowling about late at night. Pity there's no evidence as to how he was hit on the head.'

'If there were, we'd know who murdered him, wouldn't we?' Kitty enquired. 'Still, the raft says something, doesn't it?'

Both of them, Kitty in particular, received Mrs Bradley's compliments as soon as Laura imparted the facts after tea.

'And they are your due, too,' said Laura cordially, sitting on the end of Kitty's bed before she went to her own room for the night. 'The way you handled those kids was masterly. The profession lost a promising recruit in you when you took up this hairdressing business.'

'Oh, rot, Dog! I'd never have made a teacher. Kids never behave themselves with me, and I never think of ticking 'em off or telling 'em not to until it's too late and they've done it.'

'Yes, there is that,' agreed Laura. 'What do you make of the infant who tags about after that Carmody woman, and calls her Aunt Prissie or something? The one whose closer acquaintance we're scheduled to make. Not such a pill as she looks.'

'Connie Carmody? I suppose she's all right.'

'Ah, but you ought to attune yourself, K., to her reactions. Ask me, that girl's scared for her life.'

'Literally, Dog, do you mean?'

'Pretty nearly literally, I should say. Didn't you notice she made some excuse not to go upstairs by herself, and that in broad daylight? Not normal, K., in a wench of nineteen summers. And didn't you notice how quickly Mrs Croc. took the hint and went up with her? There's something got on the girl's nerves, and Mrs Croc. guesses what, I think, and believes there's something in it.'

'Oh, I don't know. Some people are fearfully nervous. I know I was when I was eight. Nothing on earth would induce me—'

'Eight ain't nineteen, duck. Besides, this Connie is scared of something definite. And do you know what I think?'

'Yes, of course. Tidson,' said Kitty.

'Tidson?' said Laura, the wind taken out of her sails.

'Yes. He's a nasty old thing. I expect he's made an improper advance, or what-not.'

'You haven't gone all nymphomaniac, have you?' asked Laura, eyeing her friend with keen interest. Kitty was about to deal with this libellous enquiry when Laura got up off the bed and went softly to the door. Twisting the handle suddenly, she pulled the door open with a jerk. Connie Carmody stood there, a suitcase on the floor beside her.

'I say, I've got to get up to Town,' she whispered. 'Can either of you lend me any money?'

──────Chapter Nine──────

'Break off the dirty Ends, put Salt to them.'
Mrs SARAH HARRISON (*The Housekeeper's
Pocket Book, etc.*)

'Y OU could have knocked me down with a feather,' said
Kitty vehemently. Laura surveyed her friend's comely
proportions with amusement, Mrs Bradley with courteous
interest.

'Honest?' asked Laura, with much more point than kindness.

'I'm not talking to you, Dog,' said Kitty with splendid
dignity. 'Don't butt in.'

'The floor's yours,' agreed Laura, taking out a cigarette
and regarding it thoughtfully before she put it into her
mouth. 'Say on; but be brief. I smell Tidson, so we'd better
pipe down.'

It proved to be Crete, who came dispiritedly into the
lounge, her embroidery frame in one hand and a handbag
dangling from the other. She had a cigarette in her mouth,
and when she put down her things and took it out, its
lipsticked extremity might have been covered in blood.

'You know,' said Kitty abruptly, addressing her sternly,
'it's quite the wrong colour on you. Come up to my room
and I'll show you. That lipstick is three shades too dark.'

Crete looked taken aback.

'You see?' said Kitty, inspired, as always, by the tactless
zeal of the artist. She took a little mirror from her handbag.
'Look in this and smile. Wider. Why, you don't even know
where to stop, or how far you ought to take the colour.
For goodness' sake let me get at you! You've got—'

Her voice faded away as she thrust the astonished Crete outside the door. Laura grinned at Mrs Bradley and gave her a chair.

'Alone at last,' she observed. 'Now what's all this about Connie? Lost, stolen or strayed, should you suppose? Judging from last night's encounter—'

'The last, for choice,' said Mrs Bradley. 'I'm rather worried about Connie. I want to put the police on her track, but, so far, Miss Carmody won't hear of it.'

'I shouldn't have given her any money, I suppose,' said Laura. 'But she came and asked for it, and I had it, and old K. also subbed up, and off she went. We thought she had a date, as a matter of fact, and, after all—' she squinted solemnly down at her shoes – 'we've all been young once.' She glanced at the door and then added, 'What do you think is happening hereabouts, and what did you make of the raft?'

'To answer the second question first, I make nothing of the raft except what you do, child,' Mrs Bradley replied with a shrug. 'It may well explain what the boy was doing down by the river, and if it does – and I think it does – it disposes of one of our problems. The question is where is the raft?'

'I suppose,' said Laura, 'there's no question of his having been – I mean, of his having met with an accident anywhere but where he was found?'

'The point did not arise at the inquest,' Mrs Bradley replied. 'But what—?'

'I just wondered. Lots of places round here where a kid could be drowned, I take it.'

'I saw him, you know. The water is very shallow and muddy where he was found, and there were no abrasions on the face or hands, and not on the knees, according to the doctor who examined him. Still, if the boy had been knocked on the head and somebody laid him down gently, no matter how stony it was—'

'Pity the whole thing happened while you were in London,' said Laura, 'except, I suppose, that's the point.'

'Of course, the most extraordinary accidents can happen,'

Mrs Bradley observed. 'Now, what can we do about Connie?'

'Well, isn't she entitled to run off on her own if she wants to?'

'She is under certain obligations to her aunt.'

'Yes, I see what you mean. Has she met any earnest young men since she's been in Winchester?'

'Who can tell? Girls are fairly good at keeping that kind of thing from their guardians. I shouldn't have thought she'd have had much opportunity to make contacts, but, of course, these things can be managed, and she's often been out on her own.'

'You surprise me,' said Laura, grinning. 'Have you sounded Thomas? These *factota* – is that the right word? – very often have inside dope on the clients, don't you know. They notice things, and can usually put two and two together. It's a matter of experience, I fancy. They must get to know hundreds of people, and be able to sum them up.'

'I *have* sounded Thomas,' Mrs Bradley replied, 'and I think he knows something, but his remarks were laconic and obscure. Further, they were couched in the Doric, which, like all dialects, is rich, dark and fruity, but, to me, a trifle indigestible.'

'Tell me. I can translate.'

'Very well, child. This was it.' She repeated the observation as accurately as though she had written it down.

'So she's awa,' Thomas had said. 'Weel, weel! There's a chiel the noo wull be speiring tae ken whit way the wind blaws tae fill toom pooch, I'll be thinking.'

'Had Connie any money of her own?' enquired Laura, at once. 'Doesn't sound like it if she had to borrow ours, but, of course, her cash might be held in trust until she's twenty-one or something, I suppose. Thomas' remarks, in translation, are: "So she's gone! Well, well! There's somebody now who wishes to know which way the wind blows to fill empty pockets." Does that make any sense, either?'

Mrs Bradley cackled. It was not a mirthful sound, and Laura, who had learnt to regard it as a war-cry, looked at her rather in the manner of stout Cortez regarding the Pacific.

'It begins to add up?' she asked. 'One thing, I thought, stuck out a mile. This Connie's been scared since we've been here. I should say that something must have happened almost as soon as we came, or just before. We wondered whether perhaps she suspects Mr Tidson of base designs, or whether she thinks somebody has the goods on her, somehow. Or does she think that the mermaid Crete might stick her with an embroidery stiletto or something? And I still think there's always the aunt. Suppose Miss Carmody stood to gain something by getting rid of this Connie – Oh, no, that wouldn't work out. Talking of getting rid, I suppose it's the Tidsons Miss Carmody wants to get rid of. Oh, Lord, it's like groping in the dark. What do you think we ought to do? I mean, why should Connie disappear?'

'Well, there's just one thing which might be useful,' said Mrs Bradley, ignoring the question of Connie's disappearance, and confining herself to what they ought to do.

'I know! Keep tabs on the Tidsons and Miss Carmody to make sure they don't put in some dirty work. We ought to dog their footsteps! We ought to pop out from unexpected corners and get in their hair and on their nerves. They're bound to give themselves away if we get them thoroughly rattled. What do you say?'

'You could try it,' said Mrs Bradley, 'but I think a less picturesque but equally useful task would be to find Connie before she gets into any more mischief.'

'Bother this Connie! Bags I watch the Tidsons!' said Laura.

'You could try it,' said Mrs Bradley again. 'But don't be annoying, will you? There is no more reason to connect them with Connie's disappearance than with the death of the boy.'

Laura grinned and promised, and went off to break the news to Kitty. That heroine was still in conference with Crete Tidson, but she came out at last, looking pleased, and was promptly waylaid by Laura, who took her off to her bedroom and spoke in a whisper.

'Oh, Lord, Dog, speak up!' said Kitty. 'I can't hear a word you're saying.'

Laura, cursing her briefly, outlined the plan of campaign.

'Yes, but it's gaga,' said Kitty. 'It isn't the Tidsons or Miss Carmody. It's some awful man at the lower end of the town. He's been arrested.'

'What?'

'Fact. Name of Potter. Thomas told me when I sent him out for some setting combs.'

'You – what?'

'He said he knew a shop where they had some. His daughter bought some yesterday,' said Kitty serenely. 'Don't look so moon-struck. You've heard of setting combs before.'

'Yes, but not of Thomas being sent out to buy some,' said Laura. She wasted no time in discussing this phenomenon, however, but sought the earliest opportunity of acquainting Mrs Bradley with what had happened.

'Potter?' said Mrs Bradley, deeply interested. 'Hm! The man who found the body, of course. I wonder what else they have against him?'

The arrest was reported in the evening papers, but there was nothing else to be learned. The papers gave a résumé of the circumstances of the boy's death, so far as they were known, but gave no hint of the ground the police had covered before they arrested Potter.

That evening Mrs Bradley left Laura and Kitty to their self-imposed, and, she thought, unproductive task of keeping an eye on the Tidsons and Miss Carmody, and went to the lower end of the town and along the narrow street to Potter's house.

The small front parlour was as neat, dead and frowsty as before. Mrs Potter was in. Mrs Bradley had ascertained this before she knocked at the door. The village women were gossiping at their front doors, for none of the houses along the village street had front gardens.

'Is Mrs Potter at home?' she had asked the next-door neighbour, interrupting her in what seemed to be the already twice-told tale of Potter's villainy and of how the neighbours had always expected that he would be found out some fine day.

'Ah, she's home,' the woman had replied, giving her a stare out of a curiosity more bovine than offensive.

'What is she doing? Is she busy?'

'No. Just sitting.'

It was upon receipt of this information that Mrs Bradley had knocked at the door. The woman who stood there looked twenty years older than the wife and mother whom Mrs Bradley and Miss Carmody had met such a short time before.

'I got nothing to say,' said the woman.

'Don't put me off,' said Mrs Bradley, promptly walking past her into the house. 'You know he didn't do it, so why do you worry?' Mrs Potter dusted a chair, automatically it seemed. Mrs Bradley sat down.

'Don't you reckon so?' asked Mrs Potter. She seemed to have no interest in the subject.

'I feel fairly certain about it. He isn't that kind of man.'

'That's what I would have said,' said poor Mrs Potter, looking at her now in puzzled misery. 'But neither wouldn't he have been the kind to go along of that trollopsing Gert Grier. If he could do that, and me all in the dark, and thinking I'd got a good husband and my little Dorrie a good father, he could do any dreadful thing, I reckon.'

'So you think he killed Bobby Grier?'

'I do, too and all.'

'But—'

'He went with Gert Grier. That's the reason for all this trouble – all of it,' said the woman. She still intoned her words as though for her they had no meaning. 'Bobby Grier knowed, and Potter, he knowed Bobby knowed. Gert Grier let it all out as soon as the police took her up.'

'So you believe Mrs Grier? What does your husband say?'

'I don't know, and I don't much trouble.'

'Does he know you think like that?'

'I don't care what he thinks. And I don't know for why you've come 'ere.'

'No,' said Mrs Bradley, getting up. 'I ought to be with Mrs Grier, I suppose. Where is your little girl?'

'Gone to stay with her auntie in Andover.'

'She doesn't know that her father has been arrested?'

'No, she doesn't know. I wouldn't 'ave her know for anything.'

'Good. Well, goodbye, Mrs Potter. Don't believe all that Mrs Grier says. I think she's lying.'

The woman's face did not change.

'Her wouldn't tell lies without there was something in 'em,' she said obstinately. 'And the police wouldn't have come 'ere if there 'adn't been nothing to come for. Good-day to you. Mean well, you do, but I don't take no truck in sociable ladies no more. I don't take no truck in nothing never no more.'

With these heavy and lack-lustre negatives she opened the door and Mrs Bradley walked out. She went straight to the Griers' house. Here her reception was cordial, suspiciously so, she felt, considering the way she had last been received. She came to the point without going into the house.

'What put the police on to Potter?' she demanded.

'Ah,' said Mrs Grier, with an arch smile, 'his own doing that was, but it ain't no business of anybody's 'cepting me. Still, of course, I'm ready to answer questions. Nothing to 'ide, I 'aven't.'

'I see. The police, no doubt, have asked you a good many questions?'

'As may be,' responded Mrs Grier. 'I said what I'm going to hold to, and Potter, 'e 'asn't got an alibi, that's what I say.'

'That's what you think,' said Mrs Bradley. 'Tell me, have you seen anything more of the little man in the panama hat? It isn't safe to have too much to do with *him*, you know.'

She bestowed on Mrs Grier a grin which caused the woman to retreat a step, but the door remained open.

'I don't know what you mean,' said Mrs Grier, indicating clearly that she did not want the conversation to terminate.

'Don't you? Well, *he* knows *you*, even if *you* don't know *him*. How did Bobby come to be out so late that night?'

'You better come in,' said the woman. Mrs Bradley went inside the dark little parlour.

'Why do you keep the blinds drawn?' she enquired. It was the room in which Bobby had been laid out, and it retained a funereal air.

'Getting dark, ain't it?' said the woman. 'And people stare in as soon as you've got the light on.'

'Do you use this room much, then?'

'On and off we do.'

'You know,' said Mrs Bradley, 'I think you would do much better to tell me the truth. You *must* know that Potter didn't do it.'

At this Mrs Grier became shrill. Mrs Bradley listened patiently to the spate of blasphemy, protest, vituperation and self-vindication which ensued, and then walked composedly to the door. The woman watched her go, but, before the door was pulled open, she had started forward.

'What you going to do?' she demanded, trying to insert her bulk between Mrs Bradley and the opening.

'I am going to wait and see what happens,' said Mrs Bradley in her calm and beautiful voice. 'The question is, what are *you* going to do, I should have thought. You are a very vindictive woman. Have you heard of Potiphar's wife?'

The woman gave way before Mrs Bradley's black eyes and triumphantly beaky little mouth. Mrs Bradley went back to Mrs Potter.

'Why did you believe her?' she asked.

'That Grier?'

'Yes, of course. She was lying. You ought to have known.'

'Then where *was* Ted that night the boy was drownded?'

'So you don't believe your husband murdered the boy? You only believe Mrs Grier's foul slanders, do you?'

'What *can* I believe? He were out – and it weren't for the first time, neither.'

'Didn't you ask him to explain?'

'He said he was kept late at work. Work, at after eleven o'clock at night!'

'Not very convincing, I agree.' She took her leave. The woman accompanied her to the door.

'You don't think he was with that Grier?' she asked, showing the first sign of softening that Mrs Bradley had detected.

'I don't think he's a murderer,' Mrs Bradley replied. 'Sleep on it, Mrs Potter, and, if I were you, I shouldn't worry.'

It was easy enough to talk, she reflected, as she walked up the mean village street towards Winchester and King Alfred's imposing statue. Infidelity was uncommon enough to be unforgivable among the respectable Mrs Potter and her associates. She wondered, all the same, what Potter had been doing on the night of the boy's death, although she thought she had found out why Mrs Grier hated him sufficiently to wish to see him hanged. 'Hell hath no fury like a woman scorned,' and Mrs Grier was personable enough in her way.

'I wonder who the woman is that he *does* go to?' thought Mrs Bradley, turning north-east towards the *Domus*. 'She'll have to be found.'

Chapter Ten

*'Our little Spark runs better and better and is
full of his gibberish.'*

RALPH PALMER TO RALPH VERNEY
(*The Verney Letters*)

BY THE morning post a letter arrived from Connie. She
had put no address at the top, but the postmark was
London, W.4.

'Chiswick,' said Mrs Bradley, to whom the letter was
addressed. Laura looked interested but said nothing. Mrs
Bradley cocked a bird-bright eye at her.

'Great West Road,' said Laura, in response to this glance.
Mrs Bradley nodded.

'Interesting; whether significant or not we shall know,
perhaps, when we have tracked Connie down.'

'Do you propose to do that?'

'Yes, child. Or, rather, I propose to allow you to do it.'

'And Kitty?'

'Well, if you wouldn't mind, I would sooner keep Kitty
here. I only wish Alice were at liberty, too. I think we might
be glad of her help.'

'I should think she must be free by now. The schools
round here have broken up. I'll wire the old scout. She'd
love to come along and join the party.'

'She may have fixed up her summer holiday, though,'
said Mrs Bradley.

'She can unfix it, then,' said Laura. 'Dash it all, it's a
time for all good men to come to the aid of the party. I'll
wire to her home address.'

She did this, and prepaid the reply.

'And now,' said Mrs Bradley, 'off with you. I don't say bring Connie back, but you must find out why she went, and whether she is short of money. You know the kind of thing.'

'Sure,' said Laura, with great cordiality.

'You have gone to London on business for me,' said Mrs Bradley. 'That is our official story, and true enough, too, in its way. It gives a reason for your departure. As one of my former students it will seem quite natural for you to be sent off on my affairs. Get back as soon as you can, and good luck, child.'

'I may need it! Talk about a needle in a bundle of hay!'

Laura caught a morning train and had lunch in town. Then she went on the local line to Chiswick station, and, having decided upon her line of approach, she went first to the Public Library and consulted the Directory.

Connie's name was Carmody, the same as that of her aunt, and it appeared in the Directory at several addresses. Laura copied out all these, and spent the afternoon and early evening in trying them all. She had no success whatsoever. None of the Chiswick Carmodys were connected with Connie or her aunt.

Laura went for dinner to Mrs Bradley's Kensington house, was welcomed by Henri and Célestine, who liked her, spent the night in her own bed, and had breakfast at seven the next morning.

She needed very little sleep, and during the night had turned over in her mind the next move towards finding Connie. The bizarre and the adventurous always appealed to Laura, and she was never short of ideas.

She went out after breakfast and, visiting various shops, she purchased a couple of dozen pairs of boot and shoe laces. She returned to the house, begged a light tray with handles from Célestine, put on an old beret and her shabbiest gardening clothes, including a pair of shoes which received dubbin from time to time but never any polish, and set off for Chiswick Empire.

Here she sat on the steps until the cleaners moved her away, and then loitered up the broad alley between the side of the music-hall and the line of shops, and, with the tray on a length of webbing and the bootlaces prominently displayed, she watched the Turnham Green bus stops on either side of the high road, prudently retiring into a side doorway whenever she saw a policeman.

She had some time to wait, but, as the clock on the church showed eleven, Connie came strolling from the Hammersmith direction and stood in the queue for buses travelling westwards.

'Got you!' said Laura to herself. She thrust the bootlaces into her pockets, unshipped the tray, and, going into the booking office of Chiswick Empire, thrust it at the astonished clerks, and said:

'Mind it until I get back!'

She then crossed the road and joined the bus queue, to find herself conveniently separated from Connie by three stout women carrying shopping baskets. Connie went on top and Laura sat just inside the bus, ready to get out the moment the quarry appeared on the conductor's platform. She did not know what fare to pay, so compromised on a twopenny ticket, and had the satisfaction of seeing Connie get off at the stop which was nearest to the Great West Road.

'The boy guessed right the very first time!' muttered Laura, flattening herself against a telephone box as Connie, who seemed in a hurry, glanced about her before crossing the road. Laura let her cross, and then sauntered after her, avoiding by an inch or two a car which came swiftly along the high road.

At the bus stop Connie hesitated, and for a moment Laura thought that she was going to wait for a bus. There was no cover available, and Laura believed she would have to declare herself and demand to be told why Connie had run away. After a pause lasting less than a second, however, Connie walked on again. Laura followed behind, but did not close up.

Connie quickened her pace. Laura increased hers so that the distance between the two of them remained approximately the same. They crossed a narrow turning and then came to one still narrower. Connie dived up this turning and walked still faster. Laura, afraid that she might lose her in a maze of side-streets, hastened her steps. They crossed a narrow bridge over a railway, and then Connie dived to the left into a long lane paved with stone which led alongside the line. Three wide, rough steps led down to it. Connie galloped down these, and then went on running.

Laura continued to walk until Connie had turned a slight bend, then she flew like the wind and almost caught her.

'I say!' she called; for she was sure by this time that Connie had intended to follow the Great West Road, and had altered course when she discovered that Laura was trailing her. There seemed no further need for taking cover.

By way of response to the shout from Laura, Connie sprinted again. Laura, seriously handicapped for running by her gardening shoes, lost ground at first, and, by the time they had passed another bend in the lane, Connie was no longer to be seen.

Laura was not long deceived. A footbridge crossed the railway. Connie must have used it. Laura spurted, and saw Connie disappearing down a twisting path which reason informed her must come out somewhere along that part of the Great West Road which the two girls had already traversed.

She soon found herself in a small park or pleasure ground where children were playing. Of Connie there was still no sign, and it took Laura several minutes to find the gate. She came on to the Great West Road again, but still could see nothing of Connie.

She cursed herself briefly for not having closed up on her sooner, but wasted little time in regrets. She walked to the bus stop and waited. Less than a quarter of an hour later she was again at the block of flats she had visited with Mrs Bradley, and was ringing the bell marked *Brown*.

Connie opened the door. Laura thrust her way in, although Connie tried hard to keep her out. She might as well have tried to stop a tank as Laura's ten-stone-nine of bone and muscle. She had to give way, tall and strong though she was, and Laura stood in the hall and closed the front door behind her with her heel.

'It's all right,' she said, aware of Connie's terrified eyes. 'I've come from Mrs Bradley. She's worried about you. Why did you run off like that?'

'You lent me the money. You can't stop me now,' said Connie.

'Who wants to stop you, you little fathead? I want to know what you think you're doing, that's all.'

'I'm running away from Uncle Edris.'

'*Uncle?* That's a new one, isn't it?'

'No. Of course he's my uncle. He's a nearer relation, actually, than Aunt Prissie. He wants me to live with him and Crete, and I won't. That's all there is to it.'

'Look here,' said Laura, who felt certain that Connie was lying, 'what is behind all this? Let's go inside somewhere, and sit down, and then you can tell me all about it. It sounds a lot of boloney to me. You don't have to live with Mr Tidson and his wife if you don't want to. Anyway, Miss Carmody doesn't want you to, does she? I thought you were starting a job?'

She took Connie by the arm and bundled her into the room which opened on the left of the hall.

'It began with the ghost,' said Connie. 'Well, actually, I suppose, it began a lot before that. But don't fuss me! I'm not going to tell you!'

Alice Boorman, Laura's and Kitty's friend and Mrs Bradley's third Musketeer, arrived in Winchester in response to the telegram from Laura, and appeared at the *Domus*, whose obliging management contrived to accommodate her with a top-floor single bedroom, almost immediately Laura had set out for London. She invited Kitty to her room for a council of war.

'Now what's it all about?' asked Alice. In contrast to the plump Kitty and the Amazonian Laura, this third member of their trio was small, thin and wiry, and was the only one of the triumvirate who had taken up the work for which she had been trained. She was the Physical Training specialist at a large school in north London and was, as Laura was fond of pointing out, equally compounded of guts, indiarubber, and the sort of innocent, practical disposition which Jezebel may have had before she encountered the theory of Jehovah and learned to sin.

'Well, to tell you the truth, I haven't the foggiest,' Kitty frankly replied. 'There's been a murder of sorts, and I gather we're expecting another, but what it's all about is more than I can say. You know me – Dopey's little sister. I am completely befogged. Pity old Dog isn't here. She pushed off just before you came, and we don't know when she'll get back. She'd have told you all about it in no time. But she's off on a toot for the Old Lizard. Chiswick, or some-where. Ever been to Chiswick, young Alice? Famous for a house and the boat-race and all that. Dog says—'

'I see,' said Alice, following her usual custom of discounting Kitty's vapourings. 'But what's all this about the Tidsons, and what do you want me to do?'

'Ah, there you have me,' said Kitty. 'According to old Dog – who, of course, may be talking through her hat; she often is – we have to stalk these Tidsons like leopards, report upon what they're up to if it's nefarious, and stop them committing any murders if they seem to be so inclined.'

'Ah, stalk the Tidsons,' said Alice, with quiet satisfac-tion. 'Do the Tidsons go about together?'

'No, they don't. Would you rather go into the nice fresh air and keep an eye on *him*, or stay in the sun-lounge and watch *her*?'

'Him, for choice. But you choose.'

'Me for the sun-lounge. I'd much rather. I'm not one for the wide-open spaces. I'd far sooner stay behind glass or in the garden. Don't you really mind doing the field work?'

Alice, who very much preferred it, said that she did not.

'I hope you'll get back in time for tea, but I rather doubt it,' said Kitty. 'Still, he always comes in for his dinner, that's one good thing about him. About the only one, I should think.' She shuddered with feminine distaste.

Alice, who had enjoyed the discreet and satisfying meal

the hotel had provided at lunch-time, said that she thought so too, and did not mind missing her tea. She went up to her room, changed her costume for a shirt, a skirt and a blazer, and her stockings for a pair of tennis socks, came down to the hall, and, standing modestly behind a couple of men who were gossiping just inside the smoking-room doorway, she waited for Mr Tidson, hoping desperately that he would choose this afternoon to go out.

At half-past two he came down the stairs, his fishing rod in his hand and his other appurtenances festooned adroitly about him. Alice followed him out of the hotel, soon lost him in the crowded High Street, picked him up again in the Square, followed him past the west entrance of the Cathedral and then saw him trotting under Kings Gate. She stood beneath Kings Gate arches to make sure that he went down College Street, and then again she followed.

When he reached College Walk she dropped behind. She could pick him up, she thought, anywhere over the water-meadows. She had not been introduced to either of the Tidsons and only to Miss Carmody off-handedly as 'Miss Boorman, who was at College with us,' by Kitty. She had sat at a separate table for lunch, and the inference was that the acquaintanceship between Kitty and herself was slight and cool. Moreover, Mr Tidson had not shown himself attracted by her slight, wiry, muscular physique, thin face and observant eyes. Her clothes were what Kitty called 'tweedy,' her shoes were stout and sensible, and already she bore the hall-mark of a profession as individual as that of a sailor, a pugilist or a horse-coper, (all of whom it resembled in some measure), and which had the merit, as she saw it in this instance, of discouraging the opposite sex.

When she came through the wicket-gate on to the meadow she could not at first see Mr Tidson. Numbers of children and other holiday-makers were on the foot-path and by the water, and the small figure of Mr Tidson was not to be discerned. Alice quickened her steps. She had a long, lithe stride and she covered the ground very quickly.

She had a fair knowledge of the environs of Winchester because she had taken a party of children there on a school journey earlier in the summer. She knew that Mr Tidson might have swung to the left at the bridge over the stream called Logie, and taken the College path across the water-meadows, so she glanced in that direction when she came near the wooden bridge, but there was still no sign of Mr Tidson.

Alice began to feel baffled. The people had thinned out considerably, for many of them, the small children with their parents, particularly, had not come so far along the path, but had remained near the trees on the grassy sloping bank at the edge of the river where the two streams separated.

Alice hurried on, for she decided that Mr Tidson had increased his pace whilst she had sauntered, and that he must by now have reached the road. A modern bridge carried the road over the river. One end of the road joined the Winchester by-pass and the other the St Cross and Southampton Road.

On the other side of the bridge the path alongside the water was very much narrower, and, until she came to the children's paddling pool, Alice met only two people. It occurred to her that Mr Tidson must have been in hiding somewhere along the route, and she must have passed him without knowing it. Perhaps even now he was in cover preparing to fish. There were tall reeds in plenty which might have screened him, both from her and from the brown trout of Itchen.

She retraced her steps, and scanned the river banks, but no trace of Mr Tidson or his fishing rod was to be seen. Patiently she went back to the bridge, crossed the road, and, breaking into a trot, soon covered the distance between the bridge and St Cross Hospital.

Here she met with unexpected good fortune – or so she thought at the time. Against the only seat was set a fishing rod. Two urchins were examining without touching it. Alice went up to them.

'Is it yours?' she asked.

'No, missis. An old man left it here, and give us fourpence to keep our eye on it,' responded one of the boys.

'Which way did he go?'

'Over there. Most of 'em goes in through the gate, and then round to the archway.' Obligingly they pointed out the wicket-gate in a short piece of railing. Alice went through, saw the gatehouse of St Cross, turned in under the archway, paid her sixpence, received a ticket, and, directed by the custodian, walked across a large courtyard to the splendid twelfth-century transitional Norman church which is the greatest glory of the Hospital.

She entered the church with a silk scarf tied Polish peasant fashion over her head, and received a smile from the cleaner, who jerked her black hat towards the east and said:

'He's through there. You'll catch him before he gets telling about the lectern, miss, I shouldn't wonder. He hasn't hardly started. He's done the tiles and the circumference and heighth of these yere pillars, but that's about all. You haven't missed much.'

Alice thanked her. She could hear the voice of the guide, and found that he and his party of docile visitors were standing before a triptych in one of the side chapels. Hastily she cast her eye over the party. There were the guide, a kindly, respectable old fellow in the black habit and silver cross of the Brethren, a lady with two children, a Naval officer and his wife, and a couple of elderly women. Of Mr Tidson there was no sign. Genuflecting profoundly as she came in front of the high altar, Alice made for the door by which she had entered. The voice of the guide became more audible.

'You can't get into the dining 'all without me, you know, missie, so it's no use you being so impatient,' he called out after her. 'You best come and listen to me 'ere.'

Alice realized from this that Mr Tidson could not be in the dining hall unless there was a second guide. Ignoring the black-gowned pensioner, she went back to the cleaner and said:

'I've lost track of my uncle. Is there another party going round? I made certain I should find him in the church.'

'No; this is the only party this afternoon,' the woman replied. Alice thanked her again, dropped some money into the box near the door, and went into the open again. The custodian called out blithely from the gatehouse:

'Don't you want the wayfarer's dole, then, young lady? Pity to go away without it. It's historical, you know. You'd like to go home and say you've had it. I didn't ought to offer it to you really. You'd ought to ask. But here you are.'

Alice felt compelled to accept the gift of bread and ale, and to pass some observations upon the beauty of the church. She got away as quickly as she could, went back to the seat, and found the boys and the fishing rod still there.

She sat down on the seat to think. Then she looked around. There was only one conclusion she could come to about Mr Tidson. He must have known he was being followed, and she had been tricked deliberately. She worked out how it had been done. Mr Tidson, she thought, must have taken to the road at the bridge, sprinted along it, come round to St Cross from the Southampton Road, planted the fishing rod and had his word with the boys, and then he must have hidden in the entrance to the private house which was opposite the St Cross gatehouse. From there, he had watched her go in, and then had gone off about his own business, intending to come back later for the rod.

'Missis,' said one of the boys plaintively, 'we reckon we done our fourpence-worth minding the rod, and we want to go now.'

'Cut along, then,' said Alice absently. She glanced at her watch. She had lost a great deal of time. Whatever his business might have been, Mr Tidson had obtained, either by accident or cunning – and Alice was inclined to think it had been the latter – just over twenty minutes' grace. Alice got up and began to run. She ran well, and was soon at the bridge. She turned to the right and crossed the water, and then, still running, she followed the road towards the Winchester by-pass.

Having gained the railway bridge she was uncertain which way to turn. There were five or six possible routes. Some children were paddling, and one or two were splashing and swimming, in a wide, shallow bend of the river beside the further bridge. Hoping that one of them had noticed him, she spoke of Mr Tidson to two girls who were seated on the bank in charge of the younger children's clothes.

'Did you see a rather small gentleman in a grey tweed suit and without a hat go by here?'

'There's been a lot of people go by,' replied one of the girls.

'I seen a man in them baggy knickerbockers,' said the other.

Alice had to decide for herself which way to go. Then she was blessed with an idea. She passed under the railway arch and crossed the by-pass; then she began to climb Saint Catherine's Hill. She went up by the most direct way, regardless of the steepness of the slope by which she had chosen to ascend, and, in a remarkably short space of time, from the earthworks where Mrs Bradley had stood beside Mr Tidson not so many days before, she was able to survey the scene below her, and search the landscape for the small, plump, hurrying figure of her quarry.

Her eyes were exceptionally keen, but there was no one in the least like Mr Tidson. In any case, from that height and with the very slight knowledge she had of his appearance and the way in which he moved, she was not at all sure that she would have been able to recognize him. There was, however, something else which interested her.

While she had been scanning the landscape around and below her, a man had mounted to the small square platform of a railway signal which lay a hundred yards down the line. She could see his gesticulating figure. Something had attracted his attention, for, having pointed downwards, away towards the farther side of the track, he scrambled down from his platform and Alice immediately lost sight of him.

She trotted upon the short turf which had been worn into a path above the ditch of the earthworks, and then, when she was opposite the signal (as nearly as she could judge), she descended the sharp slope, came under another railway arch and soon found herself again beside the water.

This stream, however, was very different from the clear and beautiful river which flowed through the flowering meadows, for it was shallow, neglected and unsavoury.

A little further downstream from where Alice was standing was a roughly-constructed weir. Wooden sluice-gates controlled the flow of the water, and below them the river dropped six feet. Below the sluice was a concrete plat-form, and beyond this again was a waterfall to a depth of about three feet to the continuance of the stream. It was the place past which Connie Carmody had run on the day that she had gone walking with Mrs Bradley.

On the same side as the path and the railway line was a kind of ledge made of brick, and as it was a drop of nearly ten feet from the edge of this to the lowest level of the water, and about six or seven to the concrete platform (over which the water had a depth of inches only before it cascaded over the broken stone edge of the waterfall), a wooden railing had been erected, presumably for the safety of those passing by along the bank.

Alice climbed this fence, and the next moment the horrid presentiment she had had since she had first lost sight of Mr Tidson, and which had gradually become stronger when she failed to catch up with him or to find him, came back again in full force.

Lying on the slab of concrete was a body. Instinct told her that it was a dead body, and the horribly unnatural position in which it was lying seemed to confirm this atavistic guess. Habit, however, was all-compelling. She took off her shoes, socks and blazer, and climbed down the brickwork to see whether there was anything she could do in the way of First Aid or artificial respiration.

She bent over the body, which was that of a barefoot lad of about fifteen, but that same sub-reasoning power which had caused her to know at once that the boy was dead now refused to permit her to touch him. He was sprawled on his face with the left leg so curiously bent that it was obvious it must be broken, and his arms were flung out, one sideways and the other one close to the head, as though, having fallen, he had not moved his limbs or his head.

As Alice stood up – with some difficulty, for the stone was slippery and the water, although it was extremely shallow, poured rapidly over the concrete towards the fall – she saw that two men in railway uniform were standing on the brickwork above, and were looking down. A young policeman was with them.

'What be up to down there?' asked the policeman.

'Give me a hand, please,' said Alice. They hauled her to the top of the brickwork. The policeman had his notebook out and was moistening the lead of his pencil.

'Get down there first and see whether he's really dead,' said Alice peremptorily. 'I shan't run away. You can ask me all the questions afterwards.'

The policeman nodded, and, the official boots scraping purposefully on the brickwork, he lowered himself to the concrete, and, regardless of the water, knelt on one knee beside the corpse.

'Nothing to do for *him*,' he announced at once. 'I've sent for the doctor. He'll be here in a minute. Haul me up.' The railwaymen hauled him up. 'And now, miss,' he said, 'to your account. Name and address, please, first. And then you can say how you come to be finding this corpse.'

'You can have my name and address, of course,' said Alice, 'but I wasn't the first person to find the body, you know. One of these gentlemen did that. He saw it from that little platform on the signal.'

'Right enough,' agreed the constable. 'I've had his story, which is the corpse came slithering down the bank. Poor kid must have had a heart attack, shouldn't wonder. Now, miss, what about you?'

Alice gave her name and that of the *Domus*, and explained how she had seen the signalman waving.

'I don't know whether you're right about a heart attack, though,' she added. 'This boy has been dead some time, and I think there's a lump on his head. And where are his shoes?'

'Ah, I noticed them bare feet,' replied the policeman. 'That's why I say it's Heart. Been paddling, and the cold water done for him. Like ice, that water is. Well, thank you, miss. Perhaps I'd better have your home address as well, just in case.' His tone had become less official and much more friendly. Alice gave her home address. She was impatient to be gone. There was no time to be lost, she felt, in acquainting Mrs Bradley with the results of her afternoon's hunting.

Tea was still being served at the *Domus* when she arrived. She went straight into the sun-lounge and had the great good luck to find Mrs Bradley alone. She seated herself at a separate table, ordered tea, scribbled a note, walked casually towards the double doors which led on to the garden, dropped the note in Mrs Bradley's lap as she passed, and opened the double doors.

It was neatly, adroitly and unobtrusively done, but Alice was a neat, adroit and unobtrusive young woman. Mrs Bradley took no more notice of the note than she would have done of a flower-petal blown, as Tagore has said, upon the breeze, and Alice, satisfied that the manœuvre had not been observed by any one of the few remaining guests, went into the garden. There she saw Thomas coming out of the dining-room French doors. She grinned at him and went back again to the sun-lounge and her table.

Mrs Bradley had read the note. She grimaced at Alice, and then invited her in a loud tone to come and sit at her table and give her opinion of a crossword puzzle which Mrs Bradley had almost completed.

Alice moved over, and Mrs Bradley showed her the newspaper. They discussed the crossword until Alice's tea arrived. The sun-lounge emptied. The waiter disappeared.

'Tell me,' said Mrs Bradley. Alice gave a brief, accurate and lucid account of the afternoon she had spent in pursuit of Mr Tidson.

'He came back at four,' said Mrs Bradley. 'I saw him come in.'

'But that means he left his fishing rod at St Cross and came back here by road!'

'It seems so.'

'Ah, then he couldn't have had anything to do with the affair at the weir,' said Alice, with great relief.

'Why should he have had anything to do with it? You have not been told how long the body had been there, and the death, in any case, was most probably the result of an accident. You don't even know yet who the boy was. How old a boy, should you say?'

'I don't know. Sixteen, or perhaps even younger. I think, really, not more than fifteen. And his leg was broken.'

'How was he dressed?'

'Oh, he had on flannel trousers and a shirt and a tweed jacket. No shoes. He couldn't have been there for more than a matter of minutes. Somebody would have seen him long before the signalman spotted him. The man said he slithered down the bank, but I don't see how he could have done. He hadn't – he hadn't just died. He'd been hit on the head. That's certain.'

'But why should the signalman invent the story of the corpse sliding down the bank? I must take a look at the place. Don't you think what he said must have been the truth?'

'I don't see how a corpse *could* suddenly slide down the bank. Well, not at that spot. If you saw it you'd know what I mean.'

'I do know what you mean,' said Mrs Bradley. 'But I believe the signalman, too. If it didn't *slide* down it was *pushed* down, and that might bring Mr Tidson into the picture, don't you think? He'd have had time to give it a push before coming on here.'

'I don't know what to think. Please, where is Kitty?'

'I don't know. She's out.'

'I thought she was guarding Mrs Tidson?'

'Yes, but Miss Carmody altered those plans by inviting Kitty to accompany her to Andover on the bus.'

'Andover? Why Andover?'

'Miss Carmody pointed out that there was charming scenery along the bus route, which happens to be true, and that Andover is a typical Hampshire country town and well worth visiting,' said Mrs Bradley, with no expression in her tone.

'I see,' said Alice, registering the idea that Mrs Bradley believed Miss Carmody to be not less villainous than the Tidsons.

'Do you?' Mrs Bradley looked interested and felt slightly amused, for Alice's mental processes were artless.

'I mean,' said Alice, with her usual gravity, 'that I see – at least, I think I see – why Kitty had to go with her. One thing, she couldn't have had anything to do with it, either – Miss Carmody, I mean. *You* know – the body at the weir.'

'But why *should* she have had anything to do with it? I repeat that we do not know who the boy was, or how he met his death. He may have stumbled on the brickwork you have described, and fallen on to his head, and his companions may have hidden the body, afraid of being blamed for the death. Such cases, although uncommon, have been known. But do boys of that age usually fall on their heads from a height of six feet, you will ask – and I don't know the answer. Even if he were pushed—'

'Yes,' said Alice. 'It's difficult. His leg was broken, you know, as I said before.'

'So you did. Ah, well, no doubt the inquest will tell us more about it, and perhaps whether the signalman was the first person to see the body. Was Mr Tidson wearing a hat?'

'No, he wasn't. Does he usually wear a hat, then?'

'Well, he used to, and thereby, we think, may hang a tale. If you see him in a hat you might let me know. Our next task, as I see it, is to find out where he went and what he did. His behaviour may or may not have been suspicious. We cannot tell in the present state of our knowledge.'

'No,' said Alice, who felt (although incorrectly) that she was being blamed. 'I'm awfully sorry I lost track, but I did lose all trace of him so completely that I think he must have known he was being followed, and I think he dodged me deliberately, which doesn't really look too good.'

'The majority of people resent being followed, child, and most of them are nervous about it, I believe. I'll tell you what. You and I must take an early morning walk, and see whether we can find out where he went. Would you care to come with me? – If so, when?'

'First thing to-morrow, I should think,' said Alice, gaining heart again in the undertaking.

'To-morrow? Right. I wonder when Laura will get back, and with what tidings?' said Mrs Bradley. 'Something very strange must have happened for Connie to have run off like that. I think I can guess what it was, but time will show. And now this boy ... I wonder how long he has been dead?'

───────────Chapter Eleven───────────

'On my word, Master, this is a gallant Trout,
what shall we do with him?'
Sir Izaak Walton (*The Compleat Angler*)

───────────────────────────────────

L AURA returned at six next day with a very unwilling
Connie. They had read in the early editions of the
evening paper of the discovery of the body at the weir.
Mrs Bradley had been on the telephone to Scotland Yard,
the Tidsons were in their room, and the only person to
see the two girls arrive was Thomas, who met them in the
vestibule.

'Where's everybody, Thomas?' enquired Laura.

Thomas gave her a brief theory of his own:

'I'll be thinking they are all getting through the time,
Miss Menzies; just getting through the time, as ye might say.'

'That's his delicate way of saying they're all in a queue
for the bathrooms, I suppose,' said Laura. 'Come on. We'd
better follow suit. There isn't too much time if you're going
to unpack as well.'

'I'm not going to unpack. I'm not going to stay,' said
Connie. 'I can't spend another night here. It isn't safe. I
keep telling you. Why won't you believe me?'

'Bless you, duck, I believe every syllable you utter. But
you don't avoid peril by running away and being followed.
Face it, and have it out, that's my idea. Besides, Mrs Croc.
will want to talk to you.'

'Who?'

'Mrs Bradley. So come on up, and I'll find out whether
she can see us.' She collared the reluctant Connie and
bundled her up the stairs.

Mrs Bradley invited them in. She was combing her hair, and saw them first in the mirror.

'Ah,' she said, turning round. 'Chiswick?'

'Not quite. That Brown address on the Great West Road,' said Laura. 'She says – here, *you* go on,' she added, turning to Connie. Connie gave way before two pairs of anxious eyes.

'We let it,' said Connie. 'The flat, I mean. My aunt does. The name of the tenant is Brown, but he's in Manchester part of the time. He's in Manchester now, and I knew I could hide in the flat until he came back. That's why I went. I knew he wouldn't mind, and when he comes back—'

'Nonsense!' said Mrs Bradley. 'Don't tell me lies. There is no tenant named Brown. Whose *is* the flat?'

'It belongs to Uncle Edris, I think,' said Connie. 'He wrote the letter about the naiad from there. I thought I could hide there for the time. I knew he'd be staying on here, and I begin my new job next month, and then I—'

'Where did you spend last night?' asked Mrs Bradley. 'And what made you leave this place so late at night?'

Connie looked frightened and did not answer.

'Ah,' said Mrs Bradley. 'Well, never mind. We shall find these things out in good time. How long did you propose to remain in Chiswick?'

'Hardly any time,' said Connie quickly. 'I've been asked to live in at my job. I – if it weren't for Uncle Edris I should have lived in the West End in a mews.'

'Expensive, in these days, surely?'

'I was going to share with three friends.'

'A commodious sort of mews,' said Laura, grinning. 'How many rooms? – Oh, sorry! Not my cue.'

'Well, that explains all that,' said Mrs Bradley, speaking, her acute and intelligent secretary thought, in some haste. 'Laura, go off and get ready for dinner. Now, child,' she added kindly to Connie when Laura had gone, 'suppose you sit down in that armchair whilst I finish my hair, and explain to me why you ran away.'

'I was afraid of the Tidsons,' said Connie with simplicity.

'Both of them?'

'Yes. They pumped me about my parents. I didn't like it.'

'What did they want to know?'

'The usual things. Whether my father had been rich, and who my mother's people were, and whether I was related to auntie's nephew Arthur, and how long I had been living with auntie, and whether she had adopted me legally – that sort of thing. I thought it was beastly cheek. It certainly was no concern of theirs.'

'I can see why it annoyed, but not why it frightened you, child.'

'Perhaps I've been silly over that, but, ever since the ghost, I've felt them conspiring against me. Oh, I know you're a psychiatrist, and that you've got all sort of weird names for people who think they're being followed and persecuted and all that, but it isn't my being crazy, honestly it isn't! They're dead against me, I know they are! And they're sponging on poor Aunt Prissie all the time! They're beasts! I hate and loathe them! *I* had Aunt Prissie first, and I mean to keep her, and I'm not going to stay any longer to play second fiddle to Crete Tidson, so nobody need expect it!'

'I shouldn't think anybody does expect it, though,' said Mrs Bradley, her voice dropping like honey after this wild oration. Connie sat humped in the armchair, and stared miserably and resentfully out of the window.

'That's all *you* know!' she rather rudely retorted.

'No, it isn't, quite,' said Mrs Bradley. 'Come and do up these fasteners for me, there's a good child.'

Connie got up and slouched over to where Mrs Bradley was standing. She looked sulky, but, as Mrs Bradley realized with pity, she was almost at the end of her nerves.

'And now,' said Mrs Bradley, kindly, but with the utmost decision, 'I'll tell you what you're going to do. You're going to stay at my house, in the village of Wandles Parva, until you begin your new job. No one can get at you there. Would you like to go there to-night? If so, I will order a car. It is not above twenty miles from here, and no one except Laura Menzies – and I think you'll agree that she can be trusted – knows anything about it or where it is.'

'Oh, if only I *could* get away! Would there be people there? I mean, I couldn't bear to be alone,' said Connie, whose mind was as much (or as little) confused as this speech suggested.

'There are my servants, and my chauffeur will be there. You'll like George. A most sturdy fellow. Come downstairs with me, and we'll send for him. That will be very much better than hiring a car.'

'But I don't want to stay here another minute! I don't want to meet the Tidsons ever again! You don't understand – I could never tell you the things he's said to me!'

'You shall not meet them again,' said Mrs Bradley. 'You can wait in here instead of coming downstairs. When the car arrives – we shall all be at dinner, I should think – all you have to do is to answer Laura's knock – three quick raps on your door – and take yourself off as fast as ever you can go. And you'd better not come back without sending me word.'

'And you'll let Aunt Prissie know? You won't let her worry, will you? You'll let her know I'm safe, but not where I've gone!'

'I'll reassure her. Don't worry. George will bring the car to the hotel entrance at about a quarter to eight. We never finish dinner before eight, so that should allow you to be well away from here before we come out of the dining-room.'

'It's decent of you,' said Connie. She hesitated, flushed, and then added, 'I only wish I could tell you everything, but you wouldn't want to know it, and, anyway, it wouldn't be fair. I've got to sweat it out by myself.'

'No, you haven't, child. And why wouldn't it be fair?'

'It's too much responsibility,' said Connie, looking completely miserable. 'But don't worry! I'll get by all right. I mean to.'

'You haven't told me the truth about your behaviour, have you?' said Mrs Bradley. Connie looked at her and then answered:

'No, not quite. But you can always pump Uncle Edris.'

Mrs Bradley laughed, but Connie did not join in this response. After another silence, she said abruptly:

'I suppose you've never thought of killing a person?'

'Oh, yes, I have,' Mrs Bradley equably replied.

'A harmless person?'

'No – not exactly harmless. Can anyone we have the urge to kill be considered harmless, do you think?'

'Oh, you couldn't understand how I feel!'

'Oh, yes, I think I can,' said Mrs Bradley gently. 'But before I made any definite confessions, I'd think them over if I were you. You might be sorry you'd trusted me, you know. Did you think about finger-prints, I wonder?'

'Oh, I haven't done anything terrible! Well, not so *very* terrible,' said Connie hastily. She gave a half-glance at Mrs Bradley's face and then broke down. 'I didn't mean to! I didn't mean to! Truly I didn't mean to! I must have been mad! It was all Uncle Edris! I hate him! You say "Don't confess," but you want me to confess, and I will! I'll kill him, I'll kill him! I'm going to get rid of him somehow! I won't let him live to kill Arthur!'

'That's what I'm afraid of,' said Mrs Bradley, looking at her sternly but with compassion. 'Therefore you'll do as I say.'

'And suppose I wont'?'

'"Then I'll huff and I'll puff, and I'll blow your house down!"'

'Yes, I believe you would,' said Connie, with a look half-beseeching, half-terrified. 'All right, then, I'll go.'

'And now for our walk,' said Alice. It was barely six o'clock and the morning was pale, fair and misty, with the promise of heat to come. The water-meadows, faintly shrouded, were as beautiful as the fields of the cloths of heaven, and the sound of waters was everywhere. The waters themselves, blue-grey, full-flood, deep-pooled, clear, swirling and haunted with deep weed, furtive fish and the legendary freshness of cresses, divided yet held the landscape.

Mrs Bradley and Alice walked for some time without speaking. Alice, young, slightly inhibited, impressionable, a pace ahead of the older woman, was far more in tune with the beauty and coldness of the morning than with the object of the walk itself, and showed this by her silence and the distance she remained ahead.

By the time they reached the wooden bridge, however, her grey eyes were searching the immediate landscape, and the morning, now rapidly widening to red and gold, showed her eager, alert and intense, still leading Mrs Bradley along the narrowing path towards St Cross, but now the person of action more than of contemplation.

There were no clues to Mr Tidson's activities of the previous afternoon. Whatever he had done, or wherever he had gone, he seemed to have left no traces of his actions and no sort of signposts to indicate which direction he had taken.

'It's no good,' said Alice. 'There's nothing to give him away.'

'Then we had better stop using our eyes and try using our brains, I suppose,' said Mrs Bradley. 'How far along here do you know he came? I mean, which is approximately the point at which you last saw him?'

'Oh, much further back: before you get to the bridge from the College playing-fields.'

'Right. Let's get back, then, and start from there.'

'Good heavens!' cried Alice. 'Do you really think so? That is, if I see what you mean!'

'What has occurred to you, child?'

'Why, that he could have crossed into the school playing-fields! I didn't think of looking for him there. Don't you see? If he'd done that, all he had to do then was to go along the river, still at the edge of the playing-fields, until he got to that little track by which you can leave the playing-fields and get on to the road! That's what he did, I feel certain! Then he hurried along to St Cross – he could have outdistanced me easily while I searched the river banks to find him – left his fishing rod with those boys to make me think he'd gone into the St Cross grounds, hidden in the entrance to one of the private houses opposite St Cross gatehouse, and gone off to commit a murder or push the boy's body down the bank, or anything else he pleased, without my knowing a thing! It would have given him plenty of time, and time, I imagine, was the thing of most importance.'

'There's something in that,' said Mrs Bradley. 'Good for you! I think there isn't much doubt that you've worked out how he dodged you. There is just one more thing, though, that we ought to look out for, and—'

Alice stood still.

'Good heavens! Do you see what I see?' she exclaimed. 'Do look! The water-nymph!'

Mrs Bradley glanced, stared, looked at the surrounding reeds and willow trees, and then again at the water. A splendid, naked figure, firm, buxom and rosy, had just dived over a great clump of flowering rushes and, entering the water like a spear-thrust, had left nothing but the widening ripples and the half-echo of a splash to convince the watchers that they had not been mistaken.

Alice had clasped her strong and biting fingers on Mrs Bradley's wrist. She now disengaged them, and, bending low, began to stalk the water-nymph, losing sight of the river in her anxiety to remain unseen.

Left alone, with fifty feet of long, wet grass between herself and the nymph, Mrs Bradley suddenly cackled, and, leaving Alice to her Boy Scout devices, she picked up her skirts and ran, with surprising speed and agility, in the direction of the path which led from the College bridge to the plank and handrail structure which carried the College path across the Itchen. Here she leaned on the rail and had the felicity to find, in the six-foot pool below the bridge, her handsome and graceless secretary.

'Rather an outsize in grayling or trout,' said Mrs Bradley.

'Hullo,' said Laura. 'Lucky it was you, and not the bishop or someone!'

'The bishop might not object,' said Mrs Bradley, 'but I would not care to answer for the dean. Why do you introduce your handsome, heathen form into the waters sacred to Saint Swithun?'

Laura paddled to the bank and climbed out. She had a piece of green waterweed dripping from the top of her head and a long streak of mud from the bank on one rosy and muscular thigh. It occurred to Mrs Bradley that Mr Tidson might have looked further for his naiad and fared worse.

'Ah, well,' she said, observing Laura's lovely lines with detachment and admiration, '"a rainbow and a cuckoo's song may never come together again; may never come, this side the tomb." Get into the water again, child. You'll turn cold.'

Laura squelched in soft mud to the shallows, walked deeper, leaned confidently forward, and gently re-entered the pool. Then she climbed to the rail of the bridge, balanced, first precariously and then with confidence there, drew breath and filled her deep lungs, flattened an already flat belly, soared like the sail of a yacht and took off with the flight of a swallow.

Meanwhile the over-sensitive Alice had abandoned her writhings through mint, forget-me-not, moon-daisies, purple loostrife and fools' parsley, and now came on to the path and up to the bridge.

'Well, I'm dashed!' she said, at sight of the naked Laura. 'Here, Dog, wait for me!' In a wriggle, a squirm and a couple of heaving thrusts she was out of her clothes, and two seconds later she had entered the six-foot pool, an arrow of thin, pale light, like a willow wand newly-peeled or the sound of a silver trumpet.

Mrs Bradley sighed, and, as though in echo of her nostalgia, from far away on the other side of the meadows a cow lowed, only once, and sadly, and she thought of the Border ballads, and Apuleius' *Eros and Psyche*, and Hans Anderson's little mermaid, and Frederick Ashton's *Leda and the Swan*.

The risen sun flung gold upon the shallows of the water, but the deep pool kept its shadow and greenish gloom. Larks ascended. The sky began to deepen and grow nearer. It was by this time intensely blue, and gave promise of the finest day of the summer. A breeze, very soon to die away and give place to intense and vital warmth, began to stir among the leaves of the willows, and the world was again composed of water, the air and the sun, as it had been at the time of Creation.

Mrs Bradley cheered up. The nymphs emerged, and shared Laura's towel beneath a pollarded willow, and then they trotted fast – Mrs Bradley retained an old-fashioned faith in the benefits of blood-stirring exercise after bathing – in the direction of the road bridge a couple of hundred yards off. They crossed the bridge and Mrs Bradley, who had been walking rapidly behind them, found them leaning over the second bridge, east of the first, and watching the water dividing itself between a tiny lock, and a culvert on the opposite side of the road.

She joined them for the next ten minutes, for rushing water has the fascination of its own apparent endlessness, and then the three walked on together. They turned alongside the railway path below Saint Catherine's Hill, and soon reached the spot where Alice had seen the boy lying on his face on the concrete below the weir. Laura and Alice poked about, and Mrs Bradley, seated on her waterproof coat on the brickwork, watched them with benign indifference until Laura, who had gone down stream a little, came running back.

'I think I've found the raft!' she said. 'Come and see! Those kids could identify it, couldn't they?'

──────────── Chapter Twelve ────────────

*'More and more each year does nymph fishing
become a part of the modern angler's equip-
ment, and he who does not possess the art is
gravely handicapped.'*

J. W. HILLS (*A Summer on the Test*)

'IT IS curious and instructive,' said Mrs Bradley, regarding
Mr Tidson benignly, 'how loth I was to believe you when
you said you had seen the naiad.'

'I don't know that I ever went so far as to say that I
had actually *seen* her,' Mr Tidson replied, regarding her
with a cautious, propitiatory smile. 'Ah, thank you, my
dear.' He turned with some relief to the waitress who had
brought him, at his request, a box of matches.

'Ah, then I must claim to be further on in my researches
than you are with yours,' said Mrs Bradley. She continued
to look at him thoughtfully and with the kindliness of a
gourmet giving eye to a dish which presently he knows he
will devour. Her manner appeared to disconcert Mr Tidson,
for he pulled the matchbox open so suddenly and clumsily
that half the contents were spilt on to the cloth.

'I don't understand you,' he said feebly. 'You are not
trying to tell me—?'

'Oh, but I am,' said Mrs Bradley earnestly. 'That is
just what I am trying to tell you. I saw the water-nymph,
and not longer ago than this morning. At least, to be
accurate—'

'Ah!' said Mr Tidson, giving up rescuing his matches
and bestowing on her a look in which artfulness, innocence and triumph were nicely blended. 'You propose to

be accurate? I see.' His manner was less offensive than his words.

'Yes. I saw the naiad when she was pointed out to me,' said Mrs Bradley. 'I was not the first to see her.'

'You really mean— But what did she look like?' There was no doubt that he was badly startled at last.

'Oh,' replied Mrs Bradley, waving a yellow claw, 'she looked exactly like the poem, you know. Sabrina fair, the green, pellucid wave, and all the rest of it.'

Mr Tidson spilt the rest of his matches, deliberately this time, and began to make patterns with them, moving them about on the cloth.

'I don't quite follow you,' he said. 'Are you telling me you actually *saw* her?'

'You mean you don't believe me,' said Mrs Bradley serenely. 'Perhaps you don't think me the kind of person to whom a naiad would think it worth while to appear?'

'I – I don't think so at all,' said Mr Tidson, frowning in concentration upon the matches. 'I can't understand, as I say, but, then, one doesn't pretend to understand miracles. I – Where did you say you saw her?'

'Come with me whenever you like, and I will show you the exact spot. You must often have passed it, I am sure.'

She rose from her table, and, followed by the enquiring gaze of those guests who had been fortunate enough to overhear the conversation, she went out of the dining-room followed by Mr Tidson. Crete had not come in to dinner. She had pleaded a headache. Miss Carmody, who owned to considerable anxiety on Connie's behalf, had caught the mid-morning train to Waterloo and had not yet come back to the *Domus*, and Alice, who had now joined forces openly with Laura and Kitty, had, in their company, left the dining-room some ten minutes before Mrs Bradley's conversation with Mr Tidson. The two of them were therefore alone.

'Would you like coffee?' Mr Tidson enquired. 'Perhaps we'd better have it in the lounge.'

'I should like coffee very much,' Mrs Bradley replied, 'and I should also like some brandy. I wonder what Thomas can do? We had better find out. What about this walk? Would to-night be the best time? Perhaps not. The naiad might be resting. What do you think?'

'Not brandy for me,' said Mr Tidson. 'And I think, on the whole, that coffee so near my bedtime would not be the wisest thing. Some other time, perhaps. And the naiad—? Perhaps to-morrow – I don't think to-night. No, I really do *not* think to-night!'

He rose, and almost fled from her presence. Mrs Bradley ordered coffee and brandy, and when Thomas brought the tray she looked up to see Miss Carmody come into the room.

'You will be in time for dinner, I think, if you go straight in,' said Mrs Bradley. Miss Carmody shook her head and dropped wearily into a chair. The weariness was exaggerated, Mrs Bradley thought, but, without doubt, Miss Carmody showed signs of pessimism.

'I don't want any dinner. Connie has gone for good!' Miss Carmody said tragically. 'I've looked in at my flat. I've looked everywhere! I've questioned or rung up her friends. She was always a thoughtless, selfish girl, but I really can't understand her going off like this without a word. I am worried and displeased. I feel very tired after my long, fruitless day. I shall go to bed. I think she must have caught a touch of the sun. Nothing else would excuse her!'

'Are you still determined not to consult the police?'

'Oh, she can't be in any *danger*, wherever she is. But I will still think that over. It is not a step that one takes lightly. There is something degrading in going to the police to find one's relatives. I do not like the idea of it at all.'

Mrs Bradley agreed that it was not a very pleasant idea, and again suggested that Miss Carmody would be much better off if she dined. Miss Carmody allowed herself to be persuaded of this, and went off to the dining-room. Mrs Bradley was about to go to her bedroom when Thomas came into the lounge to say that she was wanted on the telephone.

The telephone was in a little kiosk in the hall. Mrs Bradley discovered herself to be in communication with Scotland Yard.

'That naiad of yours,' said the voice from the other end. 'We don't think we like her much, and the local police seem to think she comes from London. Whom would you suggest we sent down? You know our bright young men.'

'It had better be someone who knows all about dry-fly fishing,' said Mrs Bradley.

'And nymph-fishing, surely?' said the voice at the other end with a happy chuckle. 'I'd like to come down myself. I'm due for some furlough. What do you say? Shall I come?'

'Well, if you think you will be of any use,' said Mrs Bradley. The voice replied with further laughter, and said that if Mrs Bradley felt like that, it would send young Gavin, and not risk its own reputation.

'Seriously, though,' it added, 'two boys in a fortnight is overdoing it. We'll send Gavin in time for the inquest. It's all right. As I said, the local people have asked for us. The bishop or the precentor, or, maybe, the dean and chapter, have been a bit terse with them, it seems. Why couldn't both the deaths have been accidents?'

'How do you know they were not?'

'The bumps on the heads had nothing to do with phrenology. Don't be naughty! Oh, and please speak kindly to young Gavin. He's apt to burst into tears if roughly handled. I had dinner with Ferdinand last night. What on earth induced you to give your only son such a name? A bit tempestuous, surely?'

'He isn't my only son,' said Mrs Bradley. 'And his father named him, not I. He was *his* only son, but that's not what you said. I remember Detective-Inspector Gavin, bless his heart, and shall be very glad, and very much relieved, to see him. Is he going to stay at the *Domus*?'

'No. At a pub nearby. He hasn't chosen it yet. No doubt he'll go round and take samples. We hope you'll be nice to the boy. And whatever he does, don't shoot him. Remember, he's doing his best.'

That night Mrs Bradley had another visit from the ghost. It had long since been discovered that she and Connie had changed rooms. The management had been discreetly reticent, but not secretive, when various guests had enquired the reason for the blocking-up of the entrances to the air-raid shelter, but the real reason did not come out. Argument, therefore, was brisk, for the *Domus* had several residents, elderly invalids for the most part, whose subjects of controversy and conversation were strictly limited by a narrow environment. These had held some exhaustive and lengthy discussions upon the subject of the air-raid shelter entrances, and several schools of thought had their adherents. Mrs Bradley told nobody the facts, but the change of rooms became known by the time that Connie went away.

For some days prior to her second visit from the ghost, Mrs Bradley had removed all obstacles to its ingress, and had waited patiently for its reappearance, for, although its easiest bolt-holes were now filled in, there remained the original priest-holes by which it could reach and leave the bedroom. She had deduced that the ghost she had hit with the hard edge of the nail-brush might possibly have been Crete Tidson, but it might equally well have been Miss Carmody. Both had shown bruises in the morning. Mrs Bradley dismissed Mr Tidson from her thoughts because she was almost certain that the intruder had been a woman (although she was also of the opinion that Connie's own squeaking nun might have been a man), and because his black eye, she decided, was a far more serious injury than any the small, light nail-brush might have inflicted.

Of course, the nail-brush might have left no mark on the person who had been struck, but, in that case, the arm of coincidence which had blacked the eyes of Miss Carmody, Connie, Crete and Mr Tidson would seem to have been ungainly long. The notion that the ghost had been entirely spirit, and not flesh at all, Mrs Bradley dismissed. There had been something definitely tangible about the figure struck by the flying nail-brush, and she was not a believer in ghosts when these made noises. The spirit world, she felt, should be silent unless it could produce sounds in keeping with its own mysterious dimension. Gasps and squeaks were, to her mind, automatically excluded from the list of sounds which any genuine spirit ought to be able to make. She would not have found it at all easy to defend this theory, but she held to it very firmly. Poltergeists, of course, came outside her argument.

The ghost paid its third visit at, in Mrs Bradley's view, an inopportune time, for its arrival must have corresponded with Mrs Bradley's trip downstairs to answer the telephone call of which a sleepy, dressing-gowned, slightly reproachful chambermaid apprised her at just before midnight.

Mrs Bradley had not gone to bed. She was seated at the small table she had asked to have in the room, and was writing an article for the Psycho-Antiquarian Society on the probable neuroses of Saint Simon Stylites, an unprofitable and idiotic task which gave her considerable enjoyment, for contemplation of the extraordinary and complicated psychological make-up of the more anti-social of the saints had always been to her a most fascinating way of wasting time.

When the call came through, she answered it in good faith, although this faith was considerably shaken when a voice at the other end said:

'I am speaking for Miss Constance Carmody. Will you hold on, please? I have to let her know you are on the line.'

The message perturbed Mrs Bradley, but she held on dutifully. In due course the voice continued:

'Are you there?'

'Yes,' replied Mrs Bradley. 'Who is speaking?'

'The janitor at the flats. Hold on, please. Miss Connie is just coming down.'

Mrs Bradley put down the receiver, and went thought-fully back to the staircase. Her faithful servants, she knew well, would not have permitted Connie to return to the flats without at once communicating to Mrs Bradley the fact that she had left the Stone House at Wandles Parva. The call, therefore, was bogus. She wondered idly what message would have come through if she had not replaced the receiver.

She went back to the little telephone booth in the hall, and rang up the Exchange. The call, it appeared, had come from a public telephone booth in Southampton.

'Very odd,' said Mrs Bradley to Thomas, who, in a respectable brown dressing-gown so long that it concealed all but the last three inches of his pyjamas, had appeared like an archiepiscopal wraith in the hotel vestibule. 'Very odd indeed, it seems to me.'

'Ay,' replied Thomas, shaking his head. 'Ye'll hae feenished wi' the light the noo? Then I'll just switch it off. There's mair things queer than a wee telephone ca' in the deid o' the night, maybe, madam. There's folk that dinna sleep in their beds. Ay, and no in ither folks' beds, either, gin that's what ye're after speiring.'

'I never said a word,' said Mrs Bradley. She regarded the intelligent man with trustful gravity. 'But something lies behind that speech of yours, and something, I can see, of peculiar moment. What is your news?'

'I was takin' the wee draught to yon Tidson for his cough, the way ye were saying I should, but he isna in his room,' said Thomas, lowering his voice so that its tone should be in keeping with Mr Tidson's mysterious activities. 'His bed hasna been slept in the night! Onyway, no yet! Ye'll ken, maybe, he changed tae a single when he came? And Henry – ye'll mind Henry, the knife and boots? – Henry was saying the wee mon was awa' oot o' here the minute before I came by to lock up the hoose. He gave Henry a shilling tae keep his mouth shut, but a shilling's no muckle tae laddies these days, and Henry thought I should ken he was awa'. I am refairing tae this Mr Tidson. Weel, Henry ca'd Mr Tidson a name I wadna repeat in the lug o' a leddy the like o' yoursel', and I ran after him tae bring him tae a sense o' decency and his duty, but ye ken what lads are – he was just too supple for me. I'll hae mair tae say tae Henry the morn's morn, the wee haverin' skelpie, but there is that which wis in it, as I telt ye!'

'But what did Henry call Mr Tidson?' Mrs Bradley felt compelled to enquire. 'My lug is hardened, Thomas. Tell me the worst.'

'Na, na,' said Thomas, with a high, free giggle. 'We'll just say he ca'd him a dirty auld mon, and leave it at that the noo.'

'I see,' said Mrs Bradley. She went thoughtfully back to her room and unlocked the door with the key which she had carried away with her. There was no doubt that during her absence the room had received a visitor; one, moreover, who had provided his own entertainment. The room had been ransacked. All the contents of her chest-of-drawers and her wardrobe had been flung on to the bed, and her suitcases were open on the floor. 'Somebody would like to know Connie's address, I should think,' she said to herself with a shrug.

She put the room to rights, put the barricades across the fireplace and the wardrobe as she had had them the previous week, and placed the bedroom utensils underneath the window. Then she got into bed and slept her usual light but infinitely refreshing sleep until seven o'clock the next morning.

Detective-Inspector Gavin, a light-haired young man in a tweed suit, brogues and heather-mixture socks of a colour-scheme so uncompromising that it could be assumed that his easiest way of disguising himself would be to leave them off in favour of more sober-hued hose, dropped into the cocktail lounge of the *Domus* at the following mid-day and asked for beer.

Mrs Bradley had no difficulty in recognizing him, although she had met him only once before. They took no notice of one another, however, and, when he had finished his beer, Gavin lit a pipe and sauntered into the vestibule of the hotel. When the Tidsons went in to lunch, Mrs Bradley strolled to the front entrance as though to look at the weather.

Gavin joined her in a very casual manner, smoked for a moment, and then said:

'Inquest to-morrow morning. Important developments. Boy had been dead some days when he was found. How do you like that, Mrs Bradley?'

'What beautiful weather we're having,' said Mrs Bradley. She had become aware of the approach of Crete Tidson. She smiled at the dark-eyed, greenish-haired and very beautiful woman.

'Edris is having champagne. He wants to know whether you'll join us,' said Crete at once. She did not appear to include the inspector in the invitation, but he promptly said:

'Why, thanks very much, I think I will. Very good of you. I think I know your husband. Wasn't he in bananas?'

Mrs Bradley, who had witnessed some entertaining incidents in her time, was now entertained by this one, and she helped matters (to her own satisfaction, at least) by exclaiming with great cordiality:

'Oh, good! Yes, of course, Mrs Tidson, you know Mr Gavin, don't you?'

'Gavin? Oh – *Gavin!*' said Crete. She smiled winningly upon the young man.

'Mr Gavin,' said Mrs Bradley, with a peculiarly evil grin, 'is an old Etonian. You understand what that implies?'

'Please?' said Crete, looking bleak. Mrs Bradley cackled.

'There is something about your stockings, Mr Gavin,' she added, as she eyed those Hebridean horrors with great respect and liking, 'which suggests the complete angler, and that fact, I know, will fascinate Mr Tidson even more than the now rather shameful disclosure that you paid for your education.'

'I *do* do a little fishing,' Gavin admitted. Crete's smile returned.

'Then you will please drink champagne with Edris!' she exclaimed. 'Edris will fall on your neck, do you say? I think he will. Why not?'

'And so will Crete, if she can make the grade,' said Laura rudely, when the gist of this conversation came to her ears in Mrs Bradley's rich and beautiful voice a little later in the day. 'We must wait and see. Is this Gavin susceptible, do you think, to nymphomaniacs?'

'To what?' enquired Mrs Bradley, very much startled. Laura shrugged, and then laughed.

'Well, granted that Crete Tidson is, in any case, a bit of a leper,' she said, 'it would, after all, explain a good deal if she were a nymphomaniac. Mr Tidson's banana profits would all have been needed for hush-money, very likely.'

'You ought to be careful, Dog,' said Kitty soberly, when she heard these outrageous remarks. 'You could be had up and fined for saying such things as that.'

'I shouldn't wonder,' said Laura languidly. 'The greater the truth, the greater the libel, don't they say? Illogical, but the law's often that. Anyway, this Gavin has gone off fishing for tiddlers, and old Tidson's gone off with him. I wonder what they will catch?'

'The flying hours,' said Mrs Bradley absently. 'That boy you found had been dead for some time, as you thought,' she added, with apparent inconsequence, to Alice. 'He certainly could not have been killed on Mr Tidson's afternoon outing, which may bring us back to that raft.'

'Have they found out who he was?' demanded Alice.

'Yes. His name was Hugh Biggin, and his home was in Southampton. He came to Winchester about a fortnight ago, but although his parents were worried at having no news of him, they did not inform the police because the boy had run away from a Borstal institution and they were afraid they would get into trouble because they had given him shelter.'

'Then when *did* the parents tell the police he was missing?'

'That has not been made public. I doubt whether they told the police anything. I think the police themselves have found out who the boy was. The verdict at the inquest this time was murder by persons unknown.'

'It's all so horrible! Two boys for no reason! What are your own ideas? You've got some theory, haven't you? I mean, apart from the fact that you think Mr Tidson did it!'

'But I have never said that I thought Mr Tidson did it!' Mrs Bradley protested. 'I have never said anyone did it! I have three theories, child, and one complete conviction, but I cannot prove anything. The deaths, if they *are* murders, seem motiveless, unless Potter murdered the first boy for the reason that Potter's wife gave me, and I'm perfectly certain he did not.'

'This second boy had been knocked on the head and killed.'

'He had been struck dead, yes. There was no doubt, in this case, about that. Further, the lump on his skull was approximately in the same position as that on Bobby Grier's head. Further, his leg, as you know, and two of his fingers were broken. He was a weakly boy, and did not look as old as his age, which was nearly eighteen. The police searched the place where he was found, and have concluded that someone (who may or may not have been the murderer) thrust the body on to the concrete after it had been dead for some days. The boy Biggin must have been killed only a very short time after little Grier – possibly on the same night—'

'Possibly to shut his mouth,' said Alice, 'and that Tidson—'

'I am not, as I tell you, accusing Mr Tidson, although much of his behaviour has been suspicious,' said Mrs Bradley. 'You see—'

'Don't bother about me,' said Alice. 'I'm not at all squeamish; you can tell me anything. And I've read all the morbid psychology books, you know. Umbrellas and things,' she added helpfully. Mrs Bradley cackled, but refused to be drawn by this remark.

'It is all a question of motive,' she said. 'No-one except Potter can be shown to have had any motive for killing either of the boys, and at present the death of this second boy has not predisposed the police in Potter's favour. They think, like you, that the second murder was an attempt to screen the first, but they cannot, of course, at present, show any connection whatever between little Grier and this boy Biggin. Still, that may not be necessary. Another task awaits us, and ought to be dealt with soon. I want to find out what Connie Carmody is doing. I had a telephone message which mentioned her name, and the caller apparently thought I could be persuaded to believe that she could be in two places at once.'

Alice looked intelligent, and said, 'Really?'

'Yes,' Mrs Bradley responded. 'You wouldn't care to go down with Miss Trevelyan to my house in the country, and find out whether Connie has escaped from the clutches of my servants, and, if so, where she's gone, and, if not, how she is feeling, I suppose?'

'Leaving Laura here?'

'Well, yes, I have work for Laura.'

'Oh, well, I'd like to go, of course.'

'Of course,' said Mrs Bradley, with a sudden screech of laughter. 'Of course! Of course! Your enthusiasm overwhelms me.'

'No, really,' said Alice, bewildered. 'I only meant—'

'Off with you, then. You know the address, and so does Kitty Trevelyan. Don't say a word to the Tidsons or to Miss Carmody, and don't write letters to me here. When (or if) you see Connie, give her my regards and ask whether there is anything she needs. We must try to make plans to amuse her, and help her to pass the time. Whatever you find out you must tell me over the telephone, but only if it seems of any importance. The pass-word,' Mrs Bradley added, 'is Buttercup, but if you forget, and say Daisy, we shall manage.'

Alice looked at her wildly, received a poke in the ribs for encouragement, and went off to find Kitty and acquaint her in private of their errand.

Chapter Thirteen

'God speed you good woman, I have been a fishing.'
SIR IZAAK WALTON (*The Compleat Angler*)

WHEREVER he had been during the previous night, whether to put through a bogus telephone call or on some other private business, perhaps of an amorous kind, Mr Tidson had appeared at breakfast, Mrs Bradley had been interested to note, in very good time, in a light grey suit, with a cheerful morning countenance, and certainly with the appearance of one who had taken his usual night's rest in a guileless bed.

It was not until the following breakfast time, however, that Mrs Bradley recounted to him, across the short distance which separated her table from that of Miss Carmody and the Tidsons, the tale of the telephone and the ghost. Mr Tidson expressed surprise and Crete amusement. Miss Carmody showed deep and obvious concern. No one gave any indication that it was known that Mr Tidson had left the hotel after dark on the night in question, but, as soon as the meal was over, Mr Tidson earnestly requested Mrs Bradley to show him the spot along the river from which she had seen the nymph.

There was a solitary fisherman on the bank as they made their way across the water-meadows. It was Detective-Inspector Gavin. He was in cover behind high reeds from which he made a very pretty cast just as they approached along the path.

'Don't let us go too close,' said Mr Tidson. 'There is a man who knows what he is doing. Let us leave him in peace to do it.'

Mrs Bradley was only too willing to do this. She had an appointment with Laura at the pool below the little wooden bridge, and she did not want her secretary to catch cold. The morning, although well advanced, was fairly chilly.

Cresses at the mouths of the drains lay close and thick, but not sufficiently so to check the bubbling flow of the water. There were startwort, dropwort and water crows-foot to be recognized by those who knew them; the grass, hiding boggy holes and the plashy flats and marshes, gave place to the stiff, thick reeds at the edge of the river. Beyond the bridge a line of dark woods hid the road. The river wound and turned. There were cattle along its banks, and the rough yellow flowers of the fleaban were thrusting up between cowpats and soggy hoof-marks. Every stream was marked by its line of willows, and, as the fisherman cast, a kingfisher swooped like a jewel.

There were slow swans stately on the main stream, and a very old willow tree leaned out over the water. The current distorted the green and silver reflections, and carried the image of hawthorn bushes as shadows under the bank. Beyond this dusk the grey-green waters were bright, and those in the fullest light were iridescent, like crystal, or solidly flowing like clear, green, moulded glass.

'A morning for gods and maidens,' said Mr Tidson, rapturously sniffing the air. 'She cannot resist such a day! You really believe you saw her?'

'I know I did,' said Mrs Bradley positively. 'What's more, I can see her again.'

She pointed. They had almost gained the bridge. There was the flash of a white body followed by the sound of a splash.

'Somebody bathing,' said Mr Tidson uneasily. 'That was no nymph, dear lady.'

'I wonder?' said Mrs Bradley. They took the narrow path which led to the bridge, but, by the time they got to the broad wooden planks, there was nobody anywhere to be seen.

Mr Tidson stood in the middle of the bridge and gazed

downstream. Mrs Bradley crossed to the opposite bank of the river, and, disregarding the mud, the cowpats and the grey-spined thistles around her, walked in the direction of some willows from whose shade she could keep Mr Tidson and the whole of the plank bridge in view.

There was a short but dramatic sequence of events. From the brimming blue-grey carrier, which cut the meadows with a beautiful, swift-running arc of clearest water, came Laura Menzies like an otter. She was wearing a brief green bathing suit, and she moved with barefoot noiselessness, crouching behind the stiff reeds. She crossed a slip of the meadow behind Mr Tidson and the bridge, waded into the river, walked to the wooden supports, climbed up, and, just as the little man turned to see her (for the bridge shook under her antics), she came behind him, seized him by the leg, and, with the heave of a coalman emptying a two-hundred-weight sack, she tipped him with strength and celerity into the six-foot pool.

The ripples round Mr Tidson widened and shimmered. They gurgled in eddies under the holes in the bank. They slapped with shivering ecstasy into the tree-roots, and danced among the stems of the reeds.

Laura leaned over the rail and studied the patterns on the water. Then, finding that Mr Tidson, when he came to the surface, merely submerged himself again, and was, moreover, choking and in distress, she ducked under the rail, grinned evilly, gave him a last, pleased glance, dropped carelessly into the pool and scooped him out.

She dragged him up the bank through the mud, and laid him face downward on the grass. She then raised his head and turned it sideways, and set to work to pump the water out of him, displaying a horrid skill and unfeeling aptness. She propped open his little mouth with a hard piece of stick, and seemed to be doing her best to break his ribs. She got up at last, grimaced at Mrs Bradley (who had come near enough to obtain a close view of the proceedings), tossed the back of a rosy heel at Mr Tidson, took a gentle run, and dived deeply into the pool.

By the time Mr Tidson had managed to scramble to his

feet, she had come up out of the stream and was dressing behind a willow tree near by. Mrs Bradley assisted Mr Tidson to wring the water out of his suit. A moment later there lay on the path, tossed out from behind Laura's willow, a dry suit of clothing, some shoes and socks, and a towel.

'Ah!' said Mrs Bradley, pouncing upon this gift. She dried her hands on the towel, handed it over, indicated another clump of willows, gave him the dry clothes, and made her way back to the hotel. Laura, coming up at a gentle trot, joined her at the mill near College Walk.

'Barbaric but effective, child,' said Mrs Bradley comfortably, referring to the ducking of Mr Tidson. 'I think we may conclude, from this morning's demonstration, that, whatever Mr Tidson's other gifts, he certainly cannot swim.'

'I hope all his past came before him,' said Laura roundly. 'I regard that little man with great dislike.'

Mr Tidson reappeared at the *Domus* in a very bad temper for his mid-morning glass of whisky, and to Thomas' tactlessly blunt enquiry as to what he had been doing to fall into the river again, he returned a squeak of rage as he handed him over the bundle of sodden clothes.

'Dried and pressed, and as soon as possible,' he said.

'A word with you,' said Mrs Bradley, waylaying Mr Tidson at the door of the cocktail lounge. 'Come back, and I will order another whisky.'

Mr Tidson went back, and, as soon as the whisky was ordered, he began a long and querulous complaint against Laura Menzies, citing instances of cramps and sudden heart-failure. Mrs Bradley listened sympathetically, nodding her head and observing that girls would be girls, and that she was sure that the boisterous Laura intended no harm, and that the bridge had a rickety handrail, although this last was not strictly the truth and had had nothing to do with the affair.

A couple of whiskies improved Mr Tidson's outlook. He modified his reasonably peevish point of view. Finding him mellowed, Mrs Bradley suddenly demanded, with almost wifely menace, and with no leading up to the subject:

'And what have you done with your hat?'

'My panama?' said Mr Tidson, who did not seem to be taken aback by the question but might have prepared an answer to it. 'It *is* so annoying! I lost it fishing, you know. I cast very badly – oh, *very* badly. It really was quite a disgraceful cast, I am afraid; and, before I realized what had happened, I had struck! – but in my hat and not in a fish! Off came the hat, and into the river it went, and that was the end of the hat, for it was not well hooked and the current soon floated it away.

'I pursued it, needless to say, but—' he spread his little plump hands – 'to no avail. I was obliged to abandon it to Peneas, and write it off a dead loss. A pity! I was much attached to it.'

'You carried your flies in its band?'

'Yes,' said Mr Tidson, looking suspiciously at her, 'of course I did.'

'Especially your hackle caperers,' pursued Mrs Bradley, 'not to mention your fisherman's curses.'

Mr Tidson permitted himself to cackle.

'What a wit you are!' he said in sycophantic admiration. He patted her yellow claw. It was like a toad patting a raven, thought Laura, who had entered the smoke-room in quest of a half-pint of beer. Seeing the room thus occupied, and fearful of breaking in upon Mrs Bradley's interrogation of Mr Tidson, she tip-toed out again.

'I don't wonder she's ashamed to come near me,' said Mr Tidson, thankful to return to his complaints. Mrs Bradley smiled gently, like a crocodile contemplating food, and Mr Tidson, to his own surprise, gave a sudden gulp as though he had bitten his tongue, and forbore to enlarge upon his grievance.

'And I have found out Connie's address,' said Mrs Bradley. 'Her aunt will be so much relieved. The only trouble is that I'm asked to keep it a secret.'

If Mr Tidson had any particular reaction to this last statement he did not show it. He merely replied:

'You will relieve Prissie's mind. I know she has been most anxious about the girl.' Then he added, in the tones of a mourner, 'I suppose you have not given further consideration to what I said about the death of that boy, Bobby Grier?'

'Oh, yes, I have thought about it often,' Mrs Bradley truthfully replied.

'Ah, well, it appears I was mistaken. I'm glad they've got the man who did it,' said Mr Tidson. 'What a scoundrel to have deceived his wife like that! And with such a woman!'

Mrs Bradley wished with all her heart that there could have been witnesses to Mr Tidson's last sentence. She wondered how he came to remark upon Mrs Grier so understandingly. He might, of course, have been fishing for information. If so, he had put the fly to a very wily trout who refused to take it.

Kitty and Alice came back to Winchester with the welcome news that Connie was still at the Stone House and was prepared to stay there quietly until she received further orders.

'Well, that's something,' Mrs Bradley observed. She told Miss Carmody that Connie was safe and well, but that she preferred to keep her whereabouts a secret.

'She seems,' said Mrs Bradley in explanation, 'to have formed a poor opinion of Mr Tidson.'

'Ah!' said Miss Carmody. It was a sigh of acquiescence; a reproachful verdict of Guilty; Mrs Bradley very much admired it. She liked economy in words, and felt that Miss Carmody had achieved this.

'It is good of you to take it so sensibly,' she said.

Matters were thus in a state of comparative suspension and remained very quiet and uneventful for nearly another week, during which the party contrived to re-book their rooms. At the end of that time Miss Carmody announced that her expenses at the *Domus* had already mounted to more than she had been prepared to pay, and that, nymph or no nymph, she and the Tidsons must return to London. They had stayed, she added, a good deal longer than she had ever, in her wildest estimates, intended. She spoke with sorrowful severity, as though it were Mrs Bradley's fault that she had stayed so long.

Mr Tidson was almost broken-hearted. This fact he confided to Laura, with whom he was soon on speaking terms again. Laura regarded with suspicion this sudden and kindly forgiveness of her high-handed action in pushing him into the river, but she kept her thoughts to herself and returned Mr Tidson smile for smile.

On Thursday morning of the week in which Miss Carmody had announced that they must take their departure, her party decided to go to Dorchester for the day. Mrs Bradley went to see them off, and the last that she and Laura saw of them was the flash of the August sunshine on the spare wheel at the back of their car as they turned at the top of the street.

Miss Carmody had made no further mention of Connie, and the moment the car was round the bend Mrs Bradley was at the telephone booth in the hotel vestibule, and was putting through a call to Wandles Parva. Connie Carmody, driven by the faithful George, Mrs Bradley's chauffeur, was at the *Domus* in time for lunch.

'And now,' said Mrs Bradley, 'where is your job?'

'In Lewes,' Connie replied, 'and I have to go in on Monday. I must dodge Uncle Edris until then.'

It turned out that Connie had not been nearer Lewes than Brighton, and had been to Brighton only for the day. Mrs Bradley rang up Miss Carmody's London flat to make certain that she and the Tidsons had not deceived her, but really had gone out for the day, and, receiving no reply, thought that all would be well.

Immediately lunch at the *Domus* was over, she bundled Connie into the car and on to the back seat, climbed in beside her, waved a skinny claw to the Three Musketeers who were collected at the front door of the hotel, sat back and ordered George to drive on.

The car took the route through Petersfield and Midhurst to Lewes, and Mrs Bradley and Connie went to an hotel in the High Street. After coffee they walked, at Mrs Bradley's suggestion, down the steep hill through the lower part of the town, and then crossed the main road at the foot of the slope and climbed up the rough path past the memorial, and on to the golf course, and beyond it.

In a field of stubble they sat down, and, after a period of silence during which they took in the view, Mrs Bradley remarked:

'And now to business. I want you to tell me all you know.'

'About what?' Connie naturally enquired.

'First, about your parents; secondly, about yourself; thirdly, about Mr Tidson; fourthly, about your aunt; fifthly, about the ghost; sixthly—'

'Oh, dear!' cried Connie, flushing and then becoming pale. 'I can't remember all those!'

'Oh, yes, you can. They are named in a logical sequence which you ought to be the first to appreciate. You could even, if you wished, tell me what the sixth account is to be.'

'Yes,' said Connie, 'I suppose so. You mean Ronald.'

'Very well, then, I mean Ronald, although I should have thought that I meant the Preece-Harvards. Isn't that the name I've heard mentioned?'

Connie, with a scared expression, agreed that it was, but muttered that she was going to live with Ronald, whatever anyone might say, and that her relatives (and, she inferred, Mrs Bradley) could mind their own business.

'I see,' said Mrs Bradley. 'This young man is of independent means, I perceive.'

'He's an artist,' said Connie defiantly. 'I went to a show he had in Town.'

'I'm sure it was most successful,' said Mrs Bradley.

'Well, yes,' Connie doubtfully replied. 'I suppose it was. It was held in Pimlico. Wasn't there a Pimlico Mystery? I seem to remember hearing something about it, although—' she attempted an unsuccessful giggle – 'I'm afraid it only makes me think of sausages. Was there a Pimlico Mystery?'

'Yes, a very atrocious murder,' said Mrs Bradley. 'Were you, by any chance, born in Pimlico, I wonder?'

'Of course not!' said Connie, surprised into sudden confession. 'I thought you knew I was born down here, near Alresford.'

'I had guessed as much. Go on.'

Chapter Fourteen

'It happened one day, about noon, going towards my boat, I was exceedingly surprised with the print of a man's naked foot on the shore ...'
DANIEL DEFOE (*Robinson Crusoe*)

'MY FATHER and mother died,' said Connie, without betraying emotion, 'when I was six years old, and until I was thirteen I lived with the Preece-Harvards. Of course, they are quite rich, but so was my father, until the smash in 1931. I was only four then. At the Preece-Harvards' I had a governess, and my little cousin Arthur shared her with me until I had to come and live with Aunt Prissie and he was sent to his prep. school.'

'He's a good deal younger than you, then?'

'Not so very much younger, really. Three years, that's all. But, of course, he was rather spoilt, and that made him precocious, and even older than he was.'

'An only child, I imagine?'

'Oh, yes, and I was treated as his sister until Colonel Preece-Harvard died. It was then that Aunt Prissie gave me a home with her, for Mrs Preece-Harvard turned me out. She said that, after all, I was no relation of hers, and she did not feel that she could be responsible for me. It was a dreadful shock to me. I felt I should never get over it.'

'You minded the change very much, then?' said Mrs Bradley, noting with interest the featurelessness of the narrative.

'I was heartbroken. You see, I missed Arthur so terribly. That was one thing. In fact, I think it was the worst.

I was fond of Arthur. We meant a great deal to one another.'

'But he was going to be sent to school in any case, I thought you said.'

'Oh, yes, but only because I was leaving to live with Aunt Prissie. I – you see—' She began to flounder. Mrs Bradley was glad of the change to an unrehearsed effort.

'But surely a boy of ten would have been sent to school whether you were staying with his mother or not?' she enquired.

'Oh, well, perhaps. If so, I didn't know. I wasn't told. The whole thing was a really dreadful shock. I was a sensitive child, I suppose,' said Connie, returning to her first lifeless voice, and looking to see the effect.

'No doubt. Lots of children are sensitive, particularly where their convenience is involved,' said Mrs Bradley sharply and in very unsympathetic tones. There was a pause, for Connie, after giving her a surprised and resentful glance, gazed over the distant hills and preserved an offended silence.

'And your aunt has had you with her for the past six years,' said Mrs Bradley, changing her tone to one of casual interest. 'You must feel that you owe her a good deal.'

Connie turned her head sharply as though to repudiate this theory, but she must have thought better of it, for she turned her face away again, pulled at a few stalks of the stubble, and said, in quiet tones:

'I suppose I do. Poor Aunt Prissie! But it did mean a very great change.'

'No doubt. But now that change has given place to another. You are about to live your life in your own way, I believe, during the time that must elapse before your marriage.'

'Well, as soon as you let me *go* my own way,' said Connie, with a certain amount of justifiable resentment. 'I mean, I know you intend it for the best, and want me to be safe, and all that, but, after all, who would harm me, so long as I keep away from Uncle Edris? And even that doesn't matter now.'

'Mr Brown might harm you,' said Mrs Bradley. Connie gave a gasp, almost as though she had been stabbed, and Mrs Bradley saw her stiffen as though to resist another blow.

'So that's what you think?' she said. 'I tell you you're wrong! I know nothing of any Mr Brown!'

Facing her, and keeping her alert black eyes on the girl's perspiring forehead, Mrs Bradley began a slow and rhythmic nodding.

'But you can't prove anything!' said Connie, breaking away with difficulty from the hypnotic effect of this performance. Mrs Bradley stopped nodding, and gazed at her with mild interest.

'No,' she agreed, 'I cannot prove anything, at present. Perhaps I never shall. But I suggest that you stay here as long as you can, and on no account write any letters. It is a pity you cannot bring yourself to tell me the truth, but I think I understand your point of view.'

'You don't agree with it, though,' retorted Connie. 'But I wouldn't be safe for a day if I told you everything.'

'Bless you, child, I *know* everything!' said Mrs Bradley.

'Are you going straight back to Winchester?' asked Connie.

'Or London,' said Mrs Bradley. 'I have not made up my mind.'

They walked down the rough turf path at the side of the rutted track towards Cliffe High Street and the shops and houses of Lewes.

'Suppose,' said Connie, 'you could prove anything? What then? You see, it's the absence of motive that makes the difficulty, isn't it? You'd find it almost impossible to pin a murder on anybody if you couldn't show a motive, wouldn't you? That's what I've always understood.'

'Your understanding was well-founded,' Mrs Bradley admitted. 'But there *is* such a motive as that practice makes perfect, don't you think? I believe that might hold good in law, although I've never had occasion to test it.'

Connie looked startled, and almost missed her footing. Mrs Bradley grasped her elbow as she stumbled. Her yellow fingers were steel on the girl's plump arm, and she hitched her roughly sideways, for there was a drop of two hundred feet to the houses below.

'A suicide complex,' thought Mrs Bradley, with interest.

'I see you've got something to go on,' Connie said as they reached Cliffe High Street. 'Do you think – does psychology tell you – whether anything more will happen?'

'More murders, do you mean?' asked Mrs Bradley. 'It depends on the murderer's commonsense, I imagine.'

'Then psychology doesn't really help?'

'I don't know. I only find that few murderers seem to be blessed with commonsense.'

'Suppose there were no more murders—'

'The police would continue to investigate the Winchester deaths. There is no doubt at all about that.'

'They would? Ah, but they'll never be able to get any further with those, and neither will you. As I see it, if nobody else gets murdered, it will be impossible to show a motive for the deaths of those two boys.'

'And a very well-reasoned conclusion,' said Mrs Bradley.

'In other words,' said Connie, 'the reason for those boys being killed is so far-fetched that nobody would believe it, and I am the only person to have worked it out.'

'What is the reason? Let us see whether I can believe it.'

'That wouldn't help. Besides, once you knew, I don't believe I'd be safe.'

'Safety is a comparative term, I feel. "Safe where all safety's lost; safe where men fall." You can finish the quotation, I presume?' said Mrs Bradley.

In spite of the warmth of the sun and the effort of walking uphill, for there was a steep ascent through Cliffe to Lewes High Street, Connie gave a shudder.

'Somebody walking over your grave,' said Mrs Bradley absently. 'I shall say good-bye for the present, as soon as we reach your hotel. If you find you must communicate with me, write to the Stone House and not to the *Domus*. And here we are.'

'*Sauve qui peut*,' said Connie. 'And *honi soit qui mal y pense*. Good-bye.' She managed to smile.

'Winchester, madam?' asked George, who had brought the car round to the front of the hotel.

'No. London. The will, the will. We will see Cæsar's will.'

'Very good, madam.' He paused. 'I could do that for you, madam, if you wished. There is no need to put yourself to fatigue.'

'Very well, George. To Winchester, then, and, as we go, I will tell you what I want to know. Preece-Harvard is the name of the testator. He died in 1933, if the information at my command is correct and my faculty of simple arithmetic not at fault. Anyhow, I'm fairly sure of the name. However, since all men are liars, if no Preece-Harvard is available, try Carmody and also Tidson. One never knows.'

'They are not uncommon names, madam. Could I have the address to assist my researches? The county, perhaps?'

'Hampshire. The town might be Alresford and it might be Andover. Alresford is the more likely.'

'Thank you, madam. I will do my very best.'

'Yes, George, I'm certain you will.'

George drove Mrs Bradley back through Havant and Fareham, and then turned north for Bishop's Waltham. They reached Winchester at just after five. Most of the guests at the *Domus* were finishing tea. Mr Tidson was not among them. Crete, at a table between two young men (strangers to Mrs Bradley), and Kitty, Alice and Laura, who were sharing a table, greeted Mrs Bradley as she entered the sun-lounge, and the Three Musketeers made room for her at their table.

'How's Connie?' Laura enquired.

'Not in an optimistic frame of mind,' replied Mrs Bradley. 'What have you done with Miss Carmody and Mr Tidson?'

'They've gone to see a man about a dog,' responded Laura. 'No, honestly! Mr Tidson conceived this idea of purchasing a hound, and Miss Carmody went with him to choose it. It appears that he saw an advertisement in the local paper, and has gone off to take his pick.'

'What sort of a dog?' enquired Mrs Bradley, interested.

'I don't know. He didn't show us the advertisement. Will the management let him keep a dog?'

'Oh, yes,' Mrs Bradley replied. 'There are kennels out in the yard in front of the lock-up garages.'

Mr Tidson came back at six accompanied by Miss Carmody and a half-grown dog of mixed ancestry. Mrs Bradley who, although not in the strict sense a dog-lover, was knowledgeable about breeds, could not help wondering why anyone with quite such a curate's egg to dispose of should have spent money on an advertisement.

The mystery was soon solved.

'Oh, I didn't care for the Sealyhams,' said Mr Tidson. 'I really want a watch-dog, you know.'

'And *I* didn't care for the price!' Miss Carmody added. Mr Tidson hastily continued his remarks.

'So we went to Oliver's Battery, as I remembered hearing somebody in the bus talking about puppies for sale at one of the new houses up there. The puppies were golden retrievers, very beautiful, but this was the little chap which took my fancy! He is the son of the yard-dog, and as soon as I saw him I said to Prissie here, "That is the fellow for me!" Did I not say that, Prissie?'

'Yes, you did,' Miss Carmody replied.

'And for five shillings, including the collar and a piece of string, he was mine,' said Mr Tidson, in triumph. 'I shall, of course, buy him another collar and a lead. And now to obtain a kennel in which he can be left for the night.'

'You will never be able to go fishing with a dog like that!' said Crete, regarding the animal with contempt and a certain amount of dislike.

'He will not disturb the fish,' said Mr Tidson. 'Some dogs learn to retrieve fish.'* He took the dog under his arm and rang the bell.

* Mr Anthony Buxton's fox-terrier. Chapter 4 of *Fisherman Naturalist*.

'Thomas,' he said, when the old man appeared in the doorway, 'what about a kennel for – what shall I call him?' he added, turning to Mrs Bradley.

'Pedigree Kelvin Grove,' she responded at once. Mr Tidson pulled at his lower lip and looked like a little boy who knows he is being teased but does not see the point of the joke. 'The song,' Mrs Bradley kindly explained. '"Through its mazes let us rove," you remember.'

Thomas gave vent to a high giggle, took the dog from Mr Tidson and said, with unusual heartiness:

'I'll tak' him tae Henry mysel', and bring ye the number of his kennel.'

'No, no,' said Mr Tidson, retrieving the dog. 'No, I thank you, Thomas. I will speak to Henry myself. Come, Kelvin.' And he carried the dog through the french doors of the sun-lounge into the garden and took the narrow path beside the air-raid shelter which led round into the yard.

Mrs Bradley rang up Connie from the inn at which Gavin was staying, told her of Mr Tidson's dog, and observed that Miss Carmody seemed easier in her mind. Connie, who had been anxious about her aunt, replied with great cordiality, said that she looked forward to taking up her new post, and added that she had hired a horse in Lewes and had had some good gallops on the Downs.

'Doesn't sound as though she were short of money,' said Laura. 'I say, I don't like that tyke of Tidson's. It's a nasty, snappy, yappy little beast.'

Mrs Bradley expressed her concern, and invited Laura to walk to the bus station with her to catch a bus for Oliver's Battery.

'Don't tell me you're inquiring into the antecedents of Tidson's hound,' said Laura, grinning.

'No, no, child. I want nothing except a walk. The air is good up there, and there is a barrow I would like to inspect.'

The ride to Oliver's Battery was a short one, and th
walk from the bus stop fulfilled Mrs Bradley's promise, for
the air was fresh and keen, and the walking, although
rough, was rewarding. Laura smoked a couple of cigarettes
whilst Mrs Bradley poked around in a declivity which might
have been an accident of nature, the opening to a Neolithic
flint mine, the burial chamber of a badly excavated round
barrow, or a partly-worked modern chalk-pit, and they
returned to the *Domus* satisfied, pleasantly tired and very
hungry.

The week-end passed, and Mr Tidson, to his great
pleasure, heard Bach at the Cathedral and spent nearly all
Saturday afternoon watching nymphs at the local swimming pool. It was not until after dinner on Sunday evening
that, wishing to take his dog for a stroll, he found that
Kelvin was missing.

Henry, the knife, boots and kennel boy, questioned
closely, revealed that the dog had slipped his collar whilst
Henry was finishing serving teas in the lounge – for the
Wee Free Thomas served nothing after two o'clock on
Sundays – and that nothing more had been heard or seen
of him. The Inspector had happened to come round, and
Henry had let him take away the collar.

'Don't tell Mr Tidson that! He will think the worst!'
said Mrs Bradley; but she did not explain what she
meant.

Mr Tidson, after broadcasting his loss to those who
seemed interested, and after being the recipient of
advice from such of the guests as cared whether his dog
were lost or not (a surprisingly high number), gave up
the enquiry and reported his loss at the police station
to a lack-lustre sergeant on duty who already knew all
about it.

Time passed again. The dog did not return, and Mr
Tidson continued to fret for him and looked each day for
the naiad. Miss Carmody, consulting Crete as a matter of
form and Mrs Bradley as a matter of inclination, again
announced her intention of leaving Winchester.

'A pity Arthur's term does not begin earlier,' she said, 'but I am really afraid we must go.'

Mr Tidson, subdued since the loss of his dog, offered no objection, and the party ordered their car and set off for London.

Mrs Bradley and Laura watched them go. Mrs Bradley noticed, divided between interest and amusement, that they did not appear to have taken any luggage. She ordered her own car, and drove off to Lewes to visit Connie. Laura's inference that Connie could not be short of money had not escaped Mrs Bradley's notice, but, whether Connie were short of money or not, Mrs Bradley had made herself responsible for Connie's hotel bills, and this gave her all the excuse she needed for looking the girl up and finding out what she was doing. The job Connie spoke of had been regarded by Mrs Bradley from the first as purely mythical.

After Mrs Bradley had left again for Lewes, Laura sought out her friends and laid before them a plan of campaign. The coast, she pointed out, was clear of Tidsons, and no time ought to be wasted.

'Look here, though, young Alice,' she remarked compassionately, 'don't you stay in on this if you'd rather be elsewhere. It seems a bit too thick to expect you to put your summer holiday in the bag. You hop off to the moors and mountains, if you'd rather. Old K. and I can manage, can't we, K.? And I know Mrs Croc. won't mind. She didn't expect you to stop.'

'Thank you,' said the trim Alice sedately. 'Keep all your pity for yourself, Dog, and don't butt in on my pleasures. You need not think you're going to get rid of me and have all the fun of hunting Mr Tidson by yourself. If you do think that you can think again! He dodged me once, but he's not going to dodge me a second time!'

'But we ain't hunting Tidson! We're hunting a nymph, duck. Don't you know the difference?'

'I don't believe in the nymph, and I'm positive Mr

Tidson knows something about that poor boy,' said Alice stoutly.

'We ought to challenge him, and see,' suggested Kitty.

'Be your age,' said Laura. 'All the same, I'd like to get hold of something, if we could. Sort of confront Mrs Croc., when she returns, with the evidence we've collected. Come on, both of you! Any ideas, young Alice?'

'I have one,' said Crete Tidson, from the doorway. 'May I come in? I wasn't eavesdropping, but I couldn't help hearing your voices. I was just going along to have a bath, but someone forestalled me, so, if you've no objection, I'll wait in here. It's a long way back to my room.'

'Good Lord!' exclaimed Laura. 'I thought you three had gone to London!'

'Oh, we came back,' said Crete, carelessly. 'Edris doesn't like London in August.' She came into the bedroom, dropped her sponge bag and towel on the floor, took a seat on the bed, and surveyed the three girls maliciously, resting on each in turn her large dark eyes.

'Well, what makes you think my husband knows anything about a poor boy? – and what poor boy does he know about?' she demanded.

'Well, it was very funny,' said Alice. 'You see, on that afternoon when the boy's body was found – the one by the railway signal box, you know—'

'It was you who found it,' said Crete. 'What has that to do with my husband?'

'He was known to have been in the neighbourhood,' Alice replied. 'In fact, I was trying to catch up with him. He dodged me, I'm almost certain, and then he deceived me into thinking he'd visited the Hospital at St Cross—'

'Oh, he had been fishing, as usual,' Crete replied. She allowed her sardonic eyes to rest on Alice's thin, hard arms and freckled, plain, honest little face. 'He cannot always be bothered with young girls. You must make some allowance for a man accustomed to cosmopolitan society.'

Alice grinned – an English reaction which appeared to

ruffle Crete. She stooped to gather up her sponge bag and towel.

'Do you swim?' asked Laura suddenly, as Crete straightened herself and stood up, her face rather flushed.

'I was swimming a good deal at Santa Cruz,' replied Crete sitting down again and pulling her dressing-gown together. 'Deep water, and very warm. We could bathe for hours.'

'From rafts, or just from the beach?'

'We bathed in every way that one can. Once I swam five miles for a bet.'

'Hm! Not bad,' said Laura carelessly. 'Talking of young girls, did you know I went all girlish myself the other morning, and shoved Mr Tidson off the bridge?'

'He told me – yes. It is a habit of yours, this rough play? – this practical joking?'

'Well, it was like your own stunt, a bet,' said Laura, eyeing her. 'I bet old K. here that Mr Tidson couldn't swim. Didn't he swim with you off Tenerife?'

'I swim with *young* men,' said Crete.

'Well, didn't Mr Tidson swim with young women, then?' asked Kitty.

'I don't know.' Crete got up again, but paused at the door. Her brown eyes lingered a moment on Laura's blue ones. 'I saw very little of my husband on Tenerife. He was, of course, very busy.'

'The bananas?' enquired Kitty, with sorrowful sympathy. Crete looked at her as though she suspected the question of having two meanings, but Kitty's bland gaze gave nothing away, and Crete, in the end, retreated on the excuse that she had heard the bathroom door being opened and shut, and did not want to lose her turn.

'A bit funny, her using the bathroom on this floor,' said Alice dispassionately. 'How much had she heard when she came in?'

'Everything, of course,' said Laura, 'and a good thing, too, I rather think. Soon we shall know where we stand, and that's always worth something, even if it only means getting a black eye to be going on with. It's all very well for Alice to trail old Tidson along to St Cross, and for me to push him into six feet of water, and for you, K., to exercise his libido or whatever it is that Mrs Croc. sets store by, but we haven't rumbled him yet, and it's my belief we never shall, except by more drastic methods. What about trying to make the little horror confess, as you suggested yourself a while ago?'

'But he wouldn't, except from fright, and what's the good of that?' demanded Kitty. 'If you ask me, Dog, we'd do better to let well alone until we get further orders. You'll only muck things up if you try to proceed on your own. Where did you get with that drowning stuff? Simply nowhere.'

'I don't know so much,' said Laura. 'According to old Tidson, that's the bridge he fell off trying to see his nymph on the night little Grier got drowned. Well, it couldn't have been! And now Crete—'

'What's she got to do with it, Dog?'

'Well, she doesn't want me trying the same stunt on her. Not that she'd make a bad nymph. I *will* say that for her. She's got classical lines all right. Wonder why she married old Tidson?'

'Oh, nymphs and satyrs,' said Kitty. 'But it isn't the nymph who drowns the boys, or is it? Could be, you mean, if Crete can swim.'

'It could be. And we don't always know what Crete does while we've all been out.'

'Still—'

'Oh, I admit it's unlikely. I can't see her bothering herself, and that's a fact. Still, she *is* a bit unaccountable. Why did she marry old Tidson, I still demand. I should think she could have had her pick, shouldn't you?'

'Perhaps he was rich when she married him,' Alice deferentially suggested. 'Rich husbands can always get wives, whatever you may say to the contrary.'

'But I don't say anything to the contrary, duck,' said Laura. 'I'm with you every time, especially in statements of fact, of which that undoubtedly was one. Only, you see, from what K. and I could learn on our visit to Liverpool, it didn't sound as though Tidson had ever been fabulously wealthy. Certainly not wealthy enough to tempt a female who could have married the man who broke the bank at Monte Carlo, or anyone else she pleased. She's a woman who'd make a painter scream with joy.'

'Perhaps she wanted British nationality. Some foreigners will do anything to get it. She'd have got it by marrying Tidson,' suggested Alice.

'The fate worse than death, I should have thought, to marry Tidson. Still, something, perhaps, in what you say. It doesn't account for the murders of two perfectly ordinary boys.'

'You don't know whether it does or not,' said Alice. 'And were they such ordinary boys? The second one was a delinquent. I don't call that frightfully ordinary.'

Laura picked up the soap from the washstand and threw it.

'Good Lord!' she said, starting up. 'I'm awfully sorry, young Alice! Did it hurt?'

'Nothing to signify,' said Alice, tidily retrieving the soap and replacing it in the soap-dish before putting a hand to her head.

'Where did it catch you? In the eyeball?'

'Not quite. Don't fuss. I've had far worse knocks from people's elbows in netball.'

'You'll have a black eye to-morrow, I shouldn't wonder. The others did, according to Mrs Croc.'

'What others?'

Laura explained.

'Wish I'd been here to see,' she regretfully added. 'It appears the bruises soon wore off, but they must have been fun while they lasted. Do you bruise easily, young Alice?'

'Fairly easily. Don't keep on. I've no beauty to spoil, thank goodness.'

'A Christian attitude,' said Laura. 'Nevertheless, accept our sincere apologies.'

'Rather funny if she *didn't* bruise,' said Kitty, thoughtfully. Laura looked at her in surprise, but Kitty's bland expression betrayed no detective faculties, and Laura, who had been in close association with her friend from their early school days, knew better than to suspect her of having any. It was a chance and frothy remark, made merely on the spur of the moment, but it put such a wild idea into Laura's head that she felt she could scarcely wait until Mrs Bradley's return to confide it, nor for the next morning to prove whether Kitty could possibly be right. If she *were* right, such vistas of crime and counter-crime rose before Laura's inward eye that she felt staggered at the implications which they evoked.

'Let's go out and chase naiads,' she suggested. 'Crete will be out of that bathroom in two or three minutes. Let's not be here when she comes back.'

'Let's go to the place where the body was found,' said Kitty. 'I might get an idea. Who knows?'

'*I* do,' said Laura rudely. 'Sherlock Holmes might, but I'm pretty sure *you* won't, duck. It's a mistake to go out of your age-group.'

The thought of a walk was welcome, and an objective seemed desirable. Laura put her head in at the doorways of all three lounges and into the smoking-room, too, and Alice went into the garden. Miss Carmody was in the garden with some crochet and the hotel bore who had engaged her as audience, and so was safe, thought Alice, for at least another hour. Of Mr Tidson there was no sign anywhere. Alice joined the others without having been seen by Miss Carmody, and Laura waylaid Thomas in the vestibule and asked for Mr Tidson.

'He was awa' wi' his fishin' rod,' said Thomas. 'Mabel was speirin' wad he be in tae his dinner, and he said he thought he wad, and for his tea, too. He was verra, very pleased wi' himsel', was yon wee mannie, although whit way he would be so, I dinna ken.'

'I thought Mr and Mrs Tidson and Miss Carmody had left the hotel,' said Laura.

'We didna think tae see them syne,' said Thomas, 'although they didna tak' their luggage. Bad bawbees aye turn up again, I'll be thinking!' He went off to the kitchen, and the girls went up the marble steps to the hotel entrance, and were soon in the street.

'I wish I knew where to 'phone Mrs Croc.,' said Laura. 'I feel she ought to know about the Tidsons and Miss Carmody coming straight back. I wonder how long she'll be away? They could never have intended to leave. It was some sort of blind. I wonder what the scheme is, anyway? Well, never mind! Come on.'

─────────Chapter Fifteen─────────

*'He will have had much experience: and this is
necessary if you are to describe so varied a
pursuit as angling, where the possibilities are so
many that some incidents only repeat themselves
once or twice in a life-time.'*

J. W. HILLS (*A Summer on the Test*)

───────────────────────────

A LONG the edges of the carriers the water-mint and the
loosestrife were in flower. Meadow-sweet, with its large,
dense cymes; the meadow-rue, with its spreading stamens
and smooth, tripartite leaves; the lance-leaved Ragged Robin;
the watercress; the hollow-stemmed angelica; the fertile water
dropwort, and, in a tiny pond, the yellow water-lily, clothed
the fields and the river banks and tinged the streams with
red, white, purple, green and gold.

The sun was hot, but thunder hung in the air. Laura
glanced at the sky and then at the hills.

'We'll probably get wet,' she observed. 'It's going to
rain.'

'Oh, rot!' said the urban Kitty. 'There isn't a cloud!'

'It will rain,' said Laura, with conviction, 'and you
haven't a hat. Will that coiffure of yours come unstuck if
we get a downpour?'

'Lord, no, Dog. It's a perm. Besides, it won't rain. You'll
see. And, talking of hats, we could have a look for old
Tidson's.'

Alice made no remark. The three, sauntering and
loitering, took nearly an hour to reach the brickwork
banking on the weir. Laura, astride on the verge, surveyed
the concrete platform.

'Nasty sort of place,' she said. 'Why have we come?'

'To watch Mr Tidson fishing,' Alice replied. She indicated a lone fisherman occupied with what seemed a heavy line.

'In *this* water? Has he gone crazy?' Laura demanded.

'I don't know. That's a boot on his line,' said Alice simply.

They watched, from the cover of some bushes. Suddenly Alice touched Laura's arm. Crete Tidson was coming along the railway path. She walked with a long, free stride and was softly whistling the Soldier's Chorus from *Faust*.

'Now what?' muttered Laura, drawing her companions deeper into the bushes. 'Look out, Kitty! Don't fall backwards down the bank. The water's filthy down there.'

The unsuspecting Crete soon joined her husband, and then they walked towards the girls and stood on the brickwork. Their antics were instructive and peculiar. First one and then the other would toss the boot into the water. It was retrieved every time with the fishing line, on the end of which was a meat-hook. As soon as this hook took hold of a piece of bent wire which had been fastened between the eyelet-holes of the boot to form an arch, the line was reeled in and the catch removed from the hook. Each partner did this in turn.

A group of little boys came along and inspected the strange proceedings. At one time there must have been a dozen of them or more. They were difficult to count because they were hardly ever still, for they followed the adventures of the boot, and occasionally waded into the stream to retrieve it for the Tidsons when it fell over the edge of the concrete slab and into the rapids below.

On the approach of some grown-up people, Mr Tidson, whose turn it was to fish, and who had just hooked the boot for the fourth time since the girls and the audience of children had been watching, took the trophy and flung it into a clump of bushes on the other side of the stream. Then he put up the rod, and, accompanied by his wife (after he had distributed some coppers among the children), walked under the railway arch, so that the girls lost sight of both of them.

The children followed him. Very soon some of them returned. They seemed half-inclined to paddle across the stream in search of the boot. This scheme was abandoned, however, and after about ten minutes the children went away again.

'So that's how it *could* have been done,' said Alice thoughtfully.

'What could?' Kitty enquired.

'Enticement, duck,' said Laura. 'You could collect fifty kids as easy as winking, and look them over and decide upon the victim. You could bet kids would fall for a silly stunt like that boot business. They're like sheep when there's something daft or dangerous to look at.'

'Doesn't sound to *me* like sheep,' objected Kitty.

'Well, you know what I mean. I'm going to nab the Inspector if Mrs Croc. isn't back, and put him wise to this. Otherwise there may be another murder before we know where we are. I can't understand why Tidson shows his hand like this, though, and, unless he'a a homicidal maniac, I can't see the point in what he's doing.'

'What a wicked old man!' cried Kitty. 'How *dare* he murder little boys!'

'Of course, we don't know that he does, duck. Alice only said that's how the victim could have been chosen, and I agreed with her. I *do* think he might be the murderer, but we've still to prove it.'

'Yes,' said Alice. 'If he's the murderer he's a fool to show his hand so openly, but, all the same, as I say, it just proves how easy it is to get hold of children, and I think Mrs Bradley ought to know about it.'

'And the Inspector,' reiterated Laura. 'Goodness knows when Mrs Croc. will be back, and now we have these suspicions I don't think we ought to hold our horses. Even one more day might may make a difference.'

'Before we leave the place,' said Kitty, 'what about retrieving the boot?'

'Not a bad idea. What about fingerprints, though? We don't

want to superimpose ours on Mr Tidson's,' said Alice. To her astonishment and discomfort, Laura suddenly slapped her on the back.

'That's it! Of course!' she cried. 'Oh, no, though, it isn't, at that, unless they knew we were watching, and I don't think they did.'

'What on earth are you babbling about, Dog?' asked Kitty resentfully.

'Be prepared for a great thought, duck,' Laura responded. 'Supposing there were some reason – some subtle and horrible reason – why Tidson's or Crete's fingerprints were on that boot *before* this afternoon – that second boy was barefoot, you know, when he was found – it would be to their advantage to have witnesses to this afternoon's little game. Well, they've got their witnesses, although the audience was mostly a gang of kids. All the same, our first idea may be right – you know, a way of deciding which kid to pick out for the next little bump on the head.'

'With a half-brick,' said Kitty, without foreseeing the result of these words. Laura gazed at her spellbound, then spoke in reverent tones:

'Not your own unaided thought? Attababy! We'll go after that boot! The half-brick may be over there, too. By the way, we think this boy was wearing sandals, but never mind that. Go on, young Alice! Watch your step. There are old tin cans below the weir, or my eyes deceive me.'

'We'll all go,' said Alice firmly. 'I'm not going alone to a bank where bodies slide out of the bushes!'

'*I* shan't go,' said Kitty, with a shudder. 'You'll need someone on this side to look after your shoes and stockings. Go with her, Dog. Don't be so lazy. And both of you mind how you go. There might be something horrid again in those bushes. I'm sure there's a nasty smell.'

Laura sniffed the air.

'You're about right at that,' she agreed. 'I thought at first it was merely the "unforgettable, unforgotten" mentioned by R. Brooke, but I don't believe it's the river, after all. It's a much worse stink than any river could manage. I thought something put those kids off. Kids are apt to have delicate noses. Of course, the local council's rubbish dump isn't so far away, but, all the same—'

'I'm not going to be made responsible for finding another body,' said Alice, with a shudder. 'One is enough. I'm not going over there, Dog. You had better go and fetch the police.'

'Fie, fie upon thee!' replied Laura, sitting down upon the brickwork and removing her shoes and stockings. 'Here goes. It's probably a dead rabbit the stoats have had, that's all.'

Without another word Alice sat down beside her, and, stony-eyed but loyal, immediately followed her example, and removed her stockings and shoes.

'Now don't go to sleep, K.,' said the leader of the expedition, lowering herself to the concrete with its inch or two of swiftly-running water. 'We may want help, and we may want a message taken. Come on, young Alice, and look out, because it's hellishly slippery on this stone stuff, and if you fall you may easily crack a bone.'

'Don't worry. I feel like a dog on a tight-rope,' said Alice. This striking simile caused Laura to choke with surprise and she missed her footing. Slipping wildly on the slimy concrete, she flung herself at the opposite bank, determined not to fall down.

'Oh, gosh!' she cried, as a cloud of flies, of a green-winged nauseating kind, rose up in a cloud like bees from an overturned hive. 'It's a – I think it's a dead animal of some sort. No, definitely nothing human, but I should go back, if I were you. It isn't terribly nice, and there's not more than half of it left!'

'Phew!' said Alice. 'I hope we shan't be poisoned! How long do you think it's been dead?'

'Days, Days *and* days, I should say. Come on. Let's go.'

They retreated, and, at Alice's suggestion, took the long way home.

'I feel I need a breath of fresh air,' she explained. The consequence was that they reached the hotel at five, and dead-heated with Mrs Bradley, who had returned to the *Domus* from Lewes.

'A dead animal?' she said very thoughtfully. 'And the Tidsons and Miss Carmody are back? Very interesting, all of it. What have you done with Inspector Gavin, by the way?'

'I expect he's fishing,' said Laura. 'Have you had tea?'

'No. Let us have it together.'

'I don't know that I feel like tea,' said Laura mournfully. 'My stomach's been turned, that's what.'

'You said it would rain,' said Alice, to change the subject. She looked up at the sky above the square white Georgian house on the opposite side of the street. 'See? Here it comes.'

Great drops, proving her assertion, fell on the pavement and splashed on the roof of the car. The party went into the hotel and through to the lounge, and in a very few minutes the episcopal Thomas appeared with a laden tray, followed by one of his myrmidons, a small, black-trousered individual called Pollen, with another, larger tray.

'It's guid tae see ye,' Thomas announced as he set the tray down. 'Pit the tray dune, mon,' he added to Pollen, 'and bring over the wee table. The night's settin' in real weet. I'll just pit a light tae the fire.'

Brushing aside such guests as were in his way, he did this, and the fire, recognizing the master-touch, crackled cheerily.

'And very nice, too,' observed Laura. 'I feel hungry now, after all, and a fire's always jolly when it's wet. How's Connie?'

'Still in the land of the living,' Mrs Bradley cautiously replied. She greeted the Tidsons and Miss Carmody with a very nice blend of surprise and pleasure when she saw them come in from the garden. Miss Carmody explained that London was dusty and hot, and that Edris feared for his asthma.

'So here we are, back again,' she concluded, 'and now, of course, it's going to set in wet. If the rain continues over to-morrow, we shall go back to London after all. Strange, was it not, that we all forgot to have the luggage put into the car when we left!'

'Not so very strange,' replied Mrs Bradley. 'It is a Freudian symbol.'

'It is?' said Mr Tidson, joining in the discussion with frankness, benevolence, and curiosity. 'Pray explain, my dear Mrs Bradley. I am afraid it only seems to me like carelessness, both on our own part and on the part of the hotel. But, of course, I thought Prissie had looked to it, and she thought I had. But Freud—?'

'It is very simple,' said Mrs Bradley. 'Freud thinks—'

'Thought,' said Miss Carmody, 'surely?'

'Thinks,' Mrs Bradley firmly but courteously reiterated. 'There is no past tense in the conjugation of genius, especially when it has left us whatever of itself can be conveyed by the printed page; and there is no past tense in heaven, which Freud undoubtedly inherits.' She eyed her cowed audience benignly, and then continued, 'Freud thinks that we leave objects necessary or dear to us in the place where we leave our hearts. You desired to be in Winchester, not in London (and I admire and applaud your choice), and so you left your luggage here. That is all.'

This speech left all her female hearers with nothing to say. Mr Tidson, however, was not so handicapped.

'Allow me to point out,' he began; but he was interrupted by the entrance of Thomas, who bore in his arms a fine log of wood, and was followed by Pollen carrying a bucket of coal.

'Ye'll pardon me, madam,' said Thomas, pausing in his stride and holding the log in the experienced but slightly absent-minded and off-hand manner of the officiating clergyman with a baby at its baptism, 'but there is a kind of a body wishing tae speak wi' ye in the smoke-room. I wad hae shown him in here, but he isna fit for the lounge carpets. That yin in the smoke-room is no great matter.'

'Has he been fishing, Thomas?'

'I dinna ken. He has nae rod. He is after fa'ing into the burn, mair like, frae the look o' him. But ye'd better gae and speir at him yoursel' whit way he's as weet as he is.'

'It sounds like you, Mr Tidson,' said Mrs Bradley, preparing to take her departure. 'Didn't *you* fall into the river? I had better see him at once. One figures to oneself that he MUST HAVE SEEN THE NAIAD!'

She suddenly bellowed these words into the unfortunate Mr Tidson's right ear, so that he jumped like a gaffed salmon and had the same expression on his face as one sometimes sees on a dead fish – at once surprised and peevish.

'Really!' he said, when Mrs Bradley had gone. He rubbed his ear and then stared angrily at the door through which she had passed, and then more angrily at Alice, who was struggling with a sudden fit of hiccups, with her a nervous reaction which was apt to appear at awkward moments. 'Really! You know, Prissie,' he added, turning round on Miss Carmody, 'I don't understand Mrs Bradley! I don't understand her at all.'

The visitor, of course, was Detective-Inspector Gavin, as Mrs Bradley had supposed.

'I've got something, I think,' he said.

'Yes, so have I,' said Mrs Bradley.

'Swop?'

'Swop.'

'Well, then, you know this second boy's home was in Southampton? I've been there and interviewed the parents. They swear they had no idea that the kid had gone to Winchester. He'd run away from an Approved School the night he was killed. That all came out at the inquest, of course, as you know. But that isn't all. I've also found out that the parents were very glad to be quit of the boy. He was always a difficult kid, and it also appears that his grandfather left him a bit of money. Not much – forty-five pounds, to be exact. Curiously enough, the father was in debt, and the forty-five pounds, which he took from under the floorboards in the boy's room, will clear him nicely, and give him twenty pounds to spare. I had to bounce the information out of him, but there it is. What do you think about that?'

'I don't know,' said Mrs Bradley. 'I can't see why he didn't steal the boy's money before. Is there any evidence that the creditors were pressing him to pay?'

'Well, he owed it to a bookie at Brighton, and there had been some loose conversation about a razor-slashing gang. It all adds up, you know, doesn't it? The whole family are rather bad hats. The father's been in quod twice for house-breaking, and it seems that the boy was taking after him.'

'I'm still more surprised that the father left the money under the floor, and did not steal it sooner.'

'He may have been scared of the kid. You never know. But it *does* all add up, don't you think?'

'I don't think it adds up with the unopened tins I found on Saint Catherine's Hill, but, of course, it might,' said Mrs Bradley, without much enthusiasm. 'And housebreaking isn't murder, although I know there have been cases of violence lately. Still, the money, no doubt, was very useful if the father was mixed up with a race-gang, and apart from any question of foul play, may be one of the reasons for not reporting the death. My own news is rather different.' She referred to the strange behaviour of the Tidsons and Miss Carmody in affecting to leave the hotel and coming back to it next day, and then mentioned the discovery of the dead animal among the bushes beside the weir, and the Tidsons' fishing with the boot.

'But you haven't told me yet how you come to be half-drowned,' she added. 'I do hope you won't catch cold.'

'I never do, thanks, and that bit of news isn't very important, I'm afraid. It's interesting, though, in its way. I saw the nymph, and went in after her. No, please don't laugh! I really did think it was she. It couldn't have been, of course, but it gives some colour to old Tidson's raptures, doesn't it?'

'But what *did* you see? – And how do you account for having seen it, and been deceived?'

'Oh, I hardly know how to describe it. Just some trick

of the light and shade upon the river, and somebody talking near by. I'd like to tell you more about it later. Now, I should think this dead animal must be a coincidence, shouldn't you? Still, it wouldn't hurt to go and take a look. What animal was it – a dog?'

'I haven't been told. I don't think the girls stayed to see. They didn't like the smell, I imagine. But there's one other thing. I am wondering whether it could possibly be the dog Mr Tidson lost some days ago.'

'Really? Well, if you're game, let's go and investigate. It would be interesting to find out why the animal died so near to where Biggin's body was found, whether it's Tidson's dog or not.' He glanced at the rain. 'At seven to-morrow?' He glanced at his clothes. 'And now I'd better go and get changed.'

They were descending the High Street next morning at seven o'clock, and, crossing it, they walked past the west door of the Cathedral and were soon in the Close. After the rain the day was flawless, although there were pools and puddles everywhere, for the night had been very wet.

'So Miss Menzies tried ducking Tidson?' said the Inspector. He chuckled in an unpolicemanlike way. 'What exactly was the object of that?'

'To give him due warning,' Mrs Bradley replied, 'and to persuade him that we know he's a liar. All pure kindness really. Unfortunately, he seems disinclined to profit by it, and at present we should find it embarrassing to be more explicit, I fear.'

'A nod and a wink to a blind horse?'

'Exactly. Well, he should have resisted the temptation to come here and look for his naiad. Trouble was bound to follow, either for himself or the nymph. But possibly I wound you? You, too, have sighted the naiad.' She cackled harshly. They turned at the end of College Street and were soon beside the water. The Inspector suddenly laughed.

'I may see her again! This seems the place for naiads. It certainly isn't the spot for two murders, is it? I do think

Cathedral cities, and these water-meadows, ought to be immune from horrors, and policemen, and nasty little brutes like Tidson.'

'Not every policeman would confess to having glimpsed a naiad,' said Mrs Bradley. 'And these murders are not native to the place. They have been planted here by the devil, or some of his agents.'

'By the power of witchcraft, more likely. Strange, when you come to think of it, how many people must have believed in witches.'

'I had a remote ancestress who was a witch,' said Mrs Bradley with great complacence. The inspector, stealing a glance at her black eyes, and at the yellow countenance whose bones had been the architecture of a beauty now fallen into decay, felt very much inclined to believe it.

'She was tried in Scotland in the time of James I,' Mrs Bradley continued, 'but was let off by the favour of the presiding magistrate, whose paramour she was said to be when the devil was occupied elsewhere and her incubus not in the mood. It's a very odd story. Rather well documented, too.'

'Was she young?' the inspector enquired.

'Oh, yes. At the time of her trial she was barely nineteen, it is said. One day I ought to get someone to write her story.'*

'I shall look forward to reading the book,' said the inspector. He looked abroad upon the lovely waters, their sedgy meadows, the hill beyond the meadows, the Winchester College playing-fields, the wet long grass and the willows. He sighed deeply. Mrs Bradley said no more, and very soon, crossing the bridge from which Mr Tidson had been translated into something new and strange, an animal scarcely aquatic and certainly terrified, they reached the further stream and took the narrow path beside it to the road-bridge nearer the hill.

They dropped down on the other side of the road-bridge and walked, rapidly still, along an asphalt path to the weir.

* A suggestion made recently by Mr Jeremy Scott.

The inspector, regardless of his natty shoes, lowered himself to the concrete platform and crossed the swiftly-rushing but shallow water.

'It's a dog all right!' he called back from the bushes amongst which he had plunged after scrambling up the bank on the opposite side of the stream. 'He's not very nice. The rats have been at him, I think.'

'Has he been knocked on the head?' asked Mrs Bradley.

'Difficult to say. I shouldn't come, if I were you. He isn't any sight for a lady, and the smell is enough to make you ill!'

But Mrs Bradley was already halfway across.

'Yes, I could smell him some distance away,' she said calmly.

'A post-mortem on a dog, ma'am?' said the local superintendent dubiously. 'Well, yes, I daresay he would, if you thought it necessary.'

'I do think it necessary. I want him to check my findings.'

'And those, ma'am, are—'

'I prefer not to say until the police doctor has examined him.'

'Very good, ma'am. I'll have him come along. We can't take the dog to the mortuary, though, I'm afraid. Was Inspector Gavin having a joke when he suggested it?'

'Oh, yes. He'll do very well here. We shall want a deal table, of course, and, for your own sakes, you had better spray some disinfectant about.'

'Practice makes perfect,' said Gavin. 'That's what was said, I believe. I don't know how you could stick that post-mortem! I'm thankful to get away from that dog, and that's a fact. Knocked on the head like the boys? I wonder what the murderer uses?'

'I don't think there's very much doubt. It must be a fairly heavy stone. We can't tell whether the same hand killed the dog and the boys, you know, but a stone was used in both cases.'

'Thanks for the information, which had occurred to
as a probability after the earlier reports. The local peopl\
have made a preliminary search, and they'll find that stone
eventually if they have to examine every pebble between
here and Southampton. They're particularly keen to have
an end to this beastly business. And when they do find it?
What then?' And he shrugged his shoulders.

They parted, and on the way back to the hotel Mrs
Bradley met her chauffeur in Jewry Street, where he was
gazing in at the window of a confectioner's shop.

'Yes, the chocolates are excellent here,' said Mrs Bradley.
'You are well advised to consider parting with your personal
points, George. I also have a few left. Let us go inside, and,
in the shop, you can give me what I would not take from
you yesterday at the hotel.'

The document changed hands whilst the shop-assistant
was weighing out the sweets.

'I sometimes feel I am dogged by Mr Tidson,' Mrs Bradley
continued, as they left the shop and began to walk back
to the hotel. 'For a short time I have shaken him off. I
would not like him to know what I have in my possession.
It might look to him a little odd, and to Miss Carmody,
too, that I should possess the facts of the Preece-Harvard
will. I shall want the car after lunch, George. We must go
to Alresford and then, very likely, we shall need to go on
to Andover. Do you think we could make a détour, as
though we were going somewhere entirely different? I am
pretty certain to be watched, and we must not give too
much away.'

'Certainly, madam,' said George. 'And there is Mr Tidson
coming along the street. I think he has been buying himself
a hat. And the boys have identified that raft.'

'Excellent,' said Mrs Bradley. She greeted Mr Tidson
warmly, and walked back with him after offering him one
of her chocolates.

George took her to Alresford by the unusual route of
the Botley Road and through Bishop's Waltham,
Corhampton and the crossroads north of West Meon. They
did not need to go to Andover. The first person they met

on the road between New and Old Alresford – it happened
to be a greengrocer's lad on a bicycle – told them where
the Preece-Harvards lived and exactly how to find the
house. It was more than two miles outside the village, and
along a lane, but the car could find a track and went
bumpily towards its destination.

────────── Chapter Sixteen ──────────

*'Wormwood, Rosemary and Lavender, of each
a like quantity, and Charity, two Handfuls.'*
   Mrs SARAH HARRISON (*The Housekeeper's
                    Pocket Book, etc.*)
*'An occasional fish rose, one, indeed, at an arti-
ficial mayfly, but was not hooked.'*
       J. W. HILLS (*A Summer on the Test*)

T HE PREECE-HARVARDS, as Mrs Bradley had expected, were
away from home. The housekeeper, impressed by the car
and also by the staid respectability of the uniformed George,
readily supplied their address as soon as Miss Carmody's
name was mentioned. She remembered Miss Carmody well.
Miss Carmody had called there not so long ago, and had
been told that the Preece-Harvards were in Bournemouth.

'I suppose you remember Miss Connie Carmody, too?'
Mrs Bradley enquired. 'Although no doubt it is some time
since you saw her?'

'Oh, I remember Miss Connie clearly,' the housekeeper
answered; and then closed her lips in the manner of her
kind when they intend to indicate that they could add
to their replies if they chose, and hope to be asked to
do so.

'A dear girl,' said Mrs Bradley carelessly.

'Handsome is that handsome does,' replied the housekeeper; and, with this sidelight upon the relationship
between Connie and the housekeeper, Mrs Bradley went
back to the car.

'How long will it take us to get to Bournemouth, George?'
she demanded.

'A matter of an hour and a quarter, if I am to push along ordinary, madam. I could do it in less, but—'

'That will do charmingly, George. We shall get there in time for tea at the hotel. I have a feeling that a widow with a schoolboy son will go in to tea at her hotel, especially in Bournemouth, where the teas are often so good. Very convenient indeed.'

Mrs Bradley's deductions proved to be correct. It was a quarter to four when she went into the lounge of Mrs Preece-Harvard's hotel, and at five minutes to four a tall, thin woman accompanied by a tall, fair boy of the required age came and sat at a table near by. Mrs Bradley immediately joined them, a proceeding which, much to her surprise, was welcomed and not resented.

'Ah!' said the woman. 'So nice of you. Hotels are rather lonely places, aren't they? Are you staying here long? I do hope so.'

'I have only just arrived,' said Mrs Bradley with truth. 'I have been staying in Winchester at the *Domus*.'

'Good gracious! You must know Priscilla Carmody! My late husband's cousin. A dear person. Hasn't she been staying there too?'

'Yes, with a Mr and Mrs Tidson, I believe.'

'Quite a nest of my husband's relations! My late husband, I should, of course, say. This is my son, as no doubt you can see by his expression. It's no good looking daggers at me, darling. I must have a little gossip sometimes with people you don't think you care for.'

'Oh, but, mother!' said the boy, scandalized, as well he might be, by this tactless and crude piece of thought-reading.

'You are at school in Winchester, I believe?' said Mrs Bradley. 'Tell me, do you go in for cross-country running?'

'Oh, yes, sometimes.'

'I think these games they play make them too thin,' said Mrs Preece-Harvard, with a bold disregard for the effects of heredity on her son. 'Football, cricket, hare-and-hounds, or whatever they call it – why can't they go fishing, like their fathers? I'm sure my poor Arthur doted upon the little trout and things he used to catch with his rod. And the Itchen is quite a nice river. Lord Grey of Falloden liked it, so why shouldn't you?' She addressed the last sentence to her son.

'But I do like it, mother,' said the boy. He turned to a waiter and ordered tea for three. 'Please excuse me. I want to go out for an evening paper.'

He escaped. His mother gazed after him and sighed.

'It isn't easy for a widow to bring up a boy,' she remarked. 'He misses his friends. He wanted to go on a walking tour. Imagine! They are very clever boys at Winchester, and I think they overtax their brains. It was much better for Arthur to come here, just the two of us, for a rest, but you would scarcely believe the trouble I went through to persuade him. It's really tiresome, the same trouble every year. Children are very selfish.'

'I suppose he missed Connie Carmody at first,' said Mrs Bradley. 'They were brought up together, I believe.'

'I suppose he did miss her at first. But that was a long time ago. I should think he has forgotten her by now. Not a nice little girl. Very spiteful and rather bad-tempered. A nervous type, I suppose.'

'Do they never meet?'

'Oh, no. Priscilla doesn't want it; and, as she took on Connie, I quite see what she means. Besides, I don't know that it would be a good thing for us to see any more of Connie. It would bring back painful memories.'

'To your son and Connie?'

'I am afraid that, for once, I was thinking only of myself. You know who Connie is? Priscilla, no doubt, will have told you?'

'You mean that Connie is your son's half-sister?' said Mrs Bradley.

'Yes, of course,' said Mrs Preece-Harvard. 'My late husband's conscience troubled him about the girl. He thought he ought to provide for her – a deed of gift, you know – before he died. But I thought – and said – that an illegitimate child has no right to steal from a legitimate one, and my son had to come first. It would have been very wrong to deplete Arthur's inheritance by a deed of gift, even had his solicitors sanctioned it, which, as the estate is strictly entailed in the male line, I do not think they would have done. You will realize, naturally, that this infatuation – I refer to my late husband's passion for Connie's mother – was two years prior to our marriage. I should not like anyone to think—'

'Of course not,' said Mrs Bradley.

'Arthur was a most devoted husband,' Mrs Preece-Harvard went on. 'Priscilla, I believe, expected that there would be something, but, as it happens, she is well enough paid.'

'You mean by Connie's companionship and affection, no doubt?'

'I mean by the gift of a hundred a year, which comes from my late husband's private fortune, and has nothing to do with the estate,' said Mrs Preece-Harvard sharply. 'And if anything happens to my son, I shall be left without even this wretched hundred a year for myself, and this Tidson man, whom I have never met, will inherit everything that is Arthur's. This wretched Tidson, or his descendants (if he has any) are likely to inherit, anyway, for Arthur has told me that he has thought about his future and is going into the Church. He believes in the celibacy of the clergy, and will never marry. Such a very curious thought for a boy of his age!'

Mrs Bradley decided that it was, on the whole, and in the particular circumstances in which Arthur found himself, quite a natural thought for a boy of his age, but she did not say so. Tea arrived, Arthur returned, and the talk turned to other subjects. Mrs Bradley returned to the main theme, however, as soon as opportunity offered. This occurred when Mrs Preece-Harvard sent her son upstairs for her library book, which she wanted him to go out and change for her after tea.

'I'd better go now,' said Arthur, affecting a humorous resignation, but obviously not sorry to escape.

'Very well, dear. Don't be long. The girl has my list,' said his mother, 'but look inside the book first to make certain that it is quite clean.'

Arthur consented to do this, and took himself off. Mrs Bradley gazed after his tall, thin figure, and then said abruptly:

'It must have been hard on Connie to know the truth.'

'The truth about what?'

'Her birth. Her illegitimacy.'

'Oh, but she doesn't know a thing about *that!*' exclaimed Mrs Preece-Harvard in genuine consternation. 'Surely no one would be so unkind! I mean, I didn't like Connie, and she was always a thorn in my flesh, but there was never any question of anyone *telling* her about herself, you know.'

'Miss Carmody?'

'Most certainly not! Priscilla has far too much nice feeling. What good would it do to tell Connie? She knew she was not my daughter, and Arthur never told her that he was her father. Of that I am perfectly certain. He said to me just before he died: "I suppose you will have to tell Connie. Keep it dark as long as you can, and, when you tell her, take care you let her down lightly. It isn't the fault of the child." An idea, of course, which I share with all sensible people,' Mrs Preece-Harvard concluded.

Mrs Bradley bowed her head.

'And there was no way in which Connie could have found out by accident?' she asked.

'That she was my husband's daughter? Oh, dear, no!'

'How many people knew she was illegitimate?'

'Well, apart from our tiny circle, hardly anyone knew, I imagine. This Tidson person had to know, of course. His lawyers wrote to our solicitors. Not that it made any difference to *his* position, detestable little man!'

'Oh, do you know Mr Tidson?' asked Mrs Bradley.

'No. I have never met him, but I know I should not like him if I did.'

'"Nothing can clear Mr Collins from the guilt of inheriting Longbourn,"' said Mrs Bradley under her breath.

'Oh, you mustn't think that!' said Mrs Preece-Harvard at once. 'There is certainly no guilt about it! I am not as prejudiced as that! But one hears things, and I have always been glad that the Canary Islands are quite a long way off. Didn't he marry a native girl or something?'

'No. His wife is of Greek extraction, and a very beautiful woman,' said Mrs Bradley. 'So far as you know, then, this Mr Tidson is the only person outside your immediate circle (who are all pledged to silence on the subject) to be aware of the fact that Connie is your late husband's daughter?'

'Certainly. Connie was always known as Carmody, even before Priscilla took her on. That was Priscilla's idea, and a very convenient one for us. But really—!'

'You are wondering why I am interested,' said Mrs Bradley, interpreting Mrs Preece-Harvard's obvious thought. 'The fact is that Miss Carmody has reason to think (from Connie's peculiar behaviour) that someone has told the girl the truth.'

'Then it must be that Tidson person, or his wife. Most likely the wife. These people have no sense of decency,' said Mrs Preece-Harvard at once. 'I am sorry if that has happened. The girl will feel that she has no claim on Priscilla. Connie was always independent and rather proud. I never liked her, but I never bore her any ill-will. A thing like that is a shock to a child. I think it a very great shame!'

Mrs Bradley felt herself warming towards Mrs Preece-Harvard. Besides, she had found out from her all that she wanted to know. The depths of Mr Tidson's villainy, she felt, were completely unmasked. She was contemplating these depths when Arthur Preece-Harvard came back with a library book.

'Thank you, darling. And now I shall need my glasses,' said his mother.

'There is just one point, though,' said Mrs Bradley, as soon as Arthur had gone. 'Connie would have been two years old at your marriage. Would she retain any memories of those two years which might lead her to discover the truth for herself, do you think?'

'Oh, she lived with Priscilla until my marriage,' said Mrs Preece-Harvard. 'That is why Priscilla was ready to have her back. She is very fond of Connie. She always has been.'

When tea was cleared, Mrs Bradley suggested that the mother and son might care for a drive in her car before she returned to Winchester. Mrs Preece-Harvard, who had taken an enormous, although, on the whole, an irrational fancy to Mrs Bradley (since she liked and admired her for just those qualities which Mrs Bradley did not possess, but with which she had, with some histrionic ability, endowed herself for the afternoon), accepted on behalf of her son, but excused herself from the outing on the plea of a necessary rest before she dressed for dinner.

Arthur had thawed at the prospect of inspecting the car, and seemed pleased, in a reserved fashion, to go for a drive. He himself selected the route from George's maps, and they drove alongside the River Stour to Blandford St Mary and then to Puddleton, and came back through Bere Regis to Bournemouth.

Arthur sat beside Mrs Bradley for the outward journey, and by George on the return one. He was a well-informed boy, and conversation did not flag. By the time they reached the furthest outward point, and left the car whilst they explored Puddletown, the *Weatherbury* of Thomas Hardy, and went into the church to look at the Norman font, Mrs Bradley and the boy were on terms of considerable mutual confidence.

It was when they came out of the church that he mentioned Connie Carmody, and asked how she was.

'She is pretty well, I think,' said Mrs Bradley.

'Is she – does she – has she forgiven us yet?' asked the boy, with a sidelong glance. He kicked a stone out of his path in an attempt to give a lightness to the question which, it was easy to tell, it did not hold for him.

'I don't know,' Mrs Bradley answered. 'What should you do if you met her suddenly?'

'I don't know. We used to have pretty good times together when we were small. Of course, that was some time ago.'

'Yes, so I understand,' said Mrs Bradley. 'When you do cross-country running, are you always alone?'

'Oh, no, I'm never alone. And, in any case, Connie isn't likely to be about in the winter, is she? Anyway, I don't do much running, you know, except perhaps on a *remedy*. I *mug* pretty hard. One can't do everything in *toy-time*, so I don't have time for *thoking*, although, of course, I play games.'*

'Yes,' said Mrs Bradley. She asked no more questions, and Arthur, at her suggestion, with which he seemed eager to comply, sat beside George in front on the homeward run.

'What do you make of him, George?' she asked, as George put the rug over her knees preparatory to beginning the journey back to Winchester.

'I could not say, madam. He seems a pleasant enough young gentleman, but I couldn't quite make him out.'

'No. I feel like that myself. Poor boy! I do not envy him his mother, his riches, his relatives, or his vocation.'

'He goes to a very fine school, madam.'

'Yes. We will envy him his school, then.'

'Straight back to Winchester, madam?'

'Please, and as quickly as we can.'

'I say,' said Laura, when Mrs Bradley had concluded a very late dinner, 'what do you think of Alice's eye? Take a deck.'

'What am I supposed to think of it?' enquired Mrs Bradley, examining a slight, purplish bruise just above Alice's left cheekbone.

'I chucked the soap at her,' went on Laura, 'and that's the result. We wondered how it compared with the Tidson and Carmody bruises, that's all. Remember? You told us about your piece of soap and young Connie Carmody and the ghost.'

'I remember. But bruises prove very little.'

Laura looked disappointed.

'I thought it might be a jolly good clue,' she argued. 'Not that I meant to hurt her. I suppose it wasn't Connie you hit with the soap that night, by the way?'

'I've wondered that myself,' said Mrs Bradley, untruth-

---

* Italicised words are peculiar, I believe, to Winchester College, and mean respectively *holiday, work, evening preparation, idling.*

fully. 'Incidentally – although I dislike to disconcert you – it was the nailbrush, and not a piece of soap, which struck the ghost. I cannot help feeling that one would bruise more easily from the one than from the other.'

'Oh, I see,' said Laura grinning. 'That experiment of ours washes out, then.'

Mrs Bradley cackled, and the subject was dropped. When she got to her room that night she locked the door, closed up the other entrances, and settled down to re-read George's notes on the Preece-Harvard will. They disclosed nothing that was now new. One way and another, she had learned from other sources all that the will could tell her, and the fact that Connie was young Preece-Harvard's half-sister she had been able to guess and had had the guess confirmed. The important point was that, if Arthur Preece-Harvard died, the entailed estate passed to Mr Tidson, who happened to be the nearest male heir. This was the clue to the whole strange business, Mrs Bradley conjectured, but was not one which could be translated into anything at all suspicious unless Arthur Preece-Harvard should be murdered.

She burnt the notes in the fireplace, scuffled the thin, black, curled-over sheets together, looked out of the window, and then prepared herself for bed. She was almost immediately asleep, and nothing occurred to disturb her.

Next morning she went out early and saw, at the bottom of the High Street, the long-striding, hatless, beautiful figure of Crete Tidson. Mrs Bradley took great care not to catch up with her. She could not help wondering what it was which had tempted Crete out and at such an early hour.

Crete stood on the bridge for a time and watched the passage of the water under the old mill. Then she crossed the road, but, almost immediately she had done so, she seemed to change her mind, and, instead of following the riverside path, she struck eastwards along the main road, and, walking extremely fast, had soon rounded a bend.

Mrs Bradley, abandoning her original project of walking as far as Saint Cross alongside the water, set out in Crete's wake and discovered that she was in for a longish walk – or so she thought at first.

The matter, however, became more mysterious than this. About a mile beyond the town a by-road branched southward from the main road, and then made a right-angle turn to the east, so that, by following it, one could get back into the town.

Crete followed this road. In the bend a car was drawn up. Crete began to whistle the tune of a popular song. Out from the car came a man's hand, and out of the hand fell a letter. The car, which was facing the same way as Crete and the advancing Mrs Bradley, then drove off. Crete stooped, picked up the letter, and walked straight on in the wake of the car.

Greatly intrigued by these manœuvres, Mrs Bradley, who felt that she had seen all there would be to see, turned at once, and returned to Winchester by the way she and Crete had both come. By the time Crete reached the hotel, Mrs Bradley was upstairs, and she descended, as though for the first time that morning, to discover Crete at the vestibule sideboard on which it was Thomas' custom to place the newspapers and the letters of the guests.

Crete looked up and wished Mrs Bradley a very bright good-morning. It was clear she did not know she had been followed. Mrs Bradley responded with suitable enthusiasm, and, immediately after breakfast, rang up Gavin at his hotel. He came round to the *Domus* at a quarter past eleven, so that it looked as though he had merely dropped in for a drink. She outlined to him the provisions of the will, and detailed her conversations with Arthur and Mrs Preece-Harvard.

'But that's what you thought,' said Gavin, referring to all Mrs Bradley's conclusions. Mrs Bradley agreed.

'Have you found the stone with which the dog was killed? And have you found out who moved the dog and when?' she enquired. 'I shall be interested to see the stone when you find it. It will certainly – well, *almost* certainly, let us say – be found at the bottom of the river. To-morrow I shall go fishing.'

'I could come with you.'

'No, no. To-morrow perhaps you had better come nowhere near me at all.'

'Right. Forgive me for asking, but have you ever done any fishing?'

'A little. Enough to know how to make a cast.'

'I'll let you have some of my flies. Do you want to borrow a rod? Tell me what your idea is.'

'I think it is time the murderer realized that I am dangerous, and had the chance to knock me on the head.'

'Oh, but look here, I say, you must be careful! It wouldn't do—'

Mrs Bradley cackled, and poked the young man in the ribs.

'Talking of accidents,' she said, 'you haven't yet told me all about the nymph who caused you to get so wet. You remember? You came to the hotel—'

'And Thomas put me in here, in the smoke-room, and told me not to move out of it because of the hotel carpets! Yes, I remember, of course. Well, you remember that at just after five it came on to rain?'

'Yes, of course I remember. And you went in after the nymph. That, too, I know. But where exactly did you see her?'

'You know that little road which connects the Southampton Road with the new by-pass? It runs past the swimming pool and over a couple of bridges. Well, beside the first bridge there is an old, broken, wooden footbridge under which the stream is fast and a good bit deeper than one imagines, and rather narrow.

'Until the rain came on, it was pleasant there, and I was standing on the wooden bridge, looking fairly aimlessly at the water, when I spotted a sort of commotion. I watched, and the sedgy reeds parted and I saw – I swear it! – a woman's head with fairish hair coloured something between the green of an olive and the yellow of a dead wild-iris leaf. It was gone the next second, but I heard a laugh, and then an exclamation in Greek.'

'In Greek?'

'In ancient Greek, too! "Too cold and chilly," was

the exact exclamation I heard. At least, that would be the translation.'

'It sounds like a quotation from the *Frogs* of Aristophanes, does it not? "Too cold and chilly," is a line in the *Frogs*, I think.'*

'It is most likely. I do know, anyhow, that I agreed with the remark when I had lowered myself into the stream. I hadn't stopped to think before that! I was anxious only to find this naiad who spoke Greek.'

'Did she fly from you as soon as you entered the stream?'

'I don't know, but I didn't find her. The stream was deeper than I thought, and it was running pretty fast, and I was wading against the current. I caught just a glimpse of her, you know, while I was still on the bridge, or perhaps that was only my fancy. Anyway, it was apparent that there was nothing more to see, except old Tidson, who was very calmly fishing from behind a clump of tall reeds. He cast very badly, as a matter of fact, and nearly hooked me. I can easily understand he hooked his hat! I climbed out near to where he was, and told him I'd seen the nymph and had even heard her speak. I asked him whether he'd spotted anything moving, but he said he hadn't seen a thing, except a very impressive trout which he insisted upon describing in far too elaborate detail. He did say that he had heard a voice coming across the water, but that he hadn't really taken any notice. At the time he heard it, he thought that this special trout had taken his fly, and he wasn't in the least interested in anything else in the world.'

'What kind of fly?'

'A hackle caperer, he said. What difference does it make?'

'I should have thought it might have been a sherry spinner at this time of year, that's all. But pray go on with your story.'

'Well, there isn't much more to tell. I felt compelled to apologize to Tidson for walking about where he was fishing, but he seemed to have taken it all in pretty good part, and the last I saw of him was when he began packing up his

---

* Line. 115. Translated by D. W. Lucas and F. J. A. Cruso.

belongings to go home. I came on here to see you, and that was that.'

'Interesting,' said Mrs Bradley. 'I must see what Mr Tidson has to add to it all. It would be a pity if, after all this time, he had lost the chance of seeing his nymph. I should call it quite unbearable, in fact.'

The inspector looked her straight in the eye.

'And, after that masterly display of side-stepping, what do you *really* think?' he demanded. 'I suppose you mean that the nymph I heard and half-saw was Mrs Tidson, but, if so, what was she up to?'

'Trying to work herself up to the point of committing suicide, perhaps,' said Mrs Bradley. Gavin looked at her, but she seemed to be thoroughly in earnest.

'Weave your spells,' he said. 'I am your attentive and open-mouthed listener. Go ahead, please, and be as theoretical as ever you like. After all, the atom bomb began as a theory, I suppose.'

'So, probably, did the conception of good and evil,' Mrs Bradley remarked. 'Light your pipe, then, child, and let us be cosy. First, though, what about the dog?'

Gavin took out his pipe.

'Ah, yes, the dog,' he said. 'I've been asking the local people more about it. They are confident that the wretched carcase was not there at the time, or immediately after, the boy Biggin's body was found, and the vet. says the dog had not been dead as long as that, and that agrees with the post-mortem.'

Before this entrancing subject could develop, Mr Tidson came into the smoke-room.

'I can't find Thomas,' he said.

'Ah,' said Mrs Bradley, not at all taken aback by his sudden appearance, although Gavin wondered how much he had heard from outside the door, 'You are just the person, Mr Tidson! You now have ample confirmation of the presence of your naiad in the Itchen. Mr Gavin has not only seen her, but he has heard her speak.'

'That wasn't the naiad. That was Crete,' said Mr Tidson snappishly. 'I *told* her the water was too cold, and that bathing wasn't permitted. I am really rather cross with Crete. I wish you would speak to her for her good. As a doctor, I mean. She has a high temperature and a cold in the head to-day. I don't care for a snuffling wife. It is most annoying when people sniff, and complain of a headache, and all through their own fault, too! If she *must* bathe, she ought to go to Bournemouth. I won't have her frightening the fish!'

Mrs Bradley said that she was sorry to hear that Mrs Tidson had taken cold, and that the bathing at Bournemouth was enjoyable, but that it seemed a long way to go for a swim, although Connie Carmody had done it.

'At any rate, it will teach her not to make fun of my nymph,' went on Mr Tidson. 'I dislike practical joking, especially on subjects of academic interest.'

'Talking of those,' said Mrs Bradley, 'I am still most intrigued by those contusions you all sustained on the morning after the night when I threw the nail-brush. Do you remember? Not that I intended *that* as a practical joke, but it must have seemed rather like it.'

Mr Tidson looked bewildered.

'When you threw—?' he said, blinking, as though he found her statement too difficult to follow.

'Yes. An intruder or marauder, or even—' She paused and eyed him beadily.

'Or even?' said Mr Tidson boldly.

'Or even a murderer, entered the room I had exchanged for my own, and I threw the soap. It slipped, so I tried the nailbrush. It got home. Next morning Connie, you and your wife, and even poor Miss Carmody, all had bruises on the face. Do you remember?'

'I remember Crete's criminal carelessness,' said Mr Tidson. 'And I remember that we explained to you what had happened. But why did you throw anything at all at the intruder? Would it not have been better to arouse the household? – Perhaps not, though, as it wasn't a private house. Were you much alarmed? I suppose you must have been. And how did you come to be near the nailbrush to throw it?'

'Well, Connie complained of ghosts,' said Mrs Bradley, 'and we exchanged rooms. It occurred to me that she might have been the victim of an intentional intrusion, so I thought I would wait up to find out what happened, or, rather, whether anything *would* happen.'

'And somebody really came in?'

'Yes, by way of the air-raid-precautions passage, which, later, upon my representations, the management kindly blocked up.'

'Really?'

'And next day you all had those bruises.'

'Even Connie!' said Mr Tidson with meaning.

'Yes, even Connie,' Mrs Bradley agreed.

'But only one person entered the room that night?'

'Precisely. Only one person.'

'Coincidence,' said Mr Tidson, with a shrug.

'She must have had a *very* long arm to black four people's eyes on the same morning,' said Gavin. Mr Tidson turned round on him at once.

'In a city which harbours a naiad in a chalk stream, *anything* may happen,' he said in a tone of reproof; but before he could continue he heard Thomas come into the vestibule, and, breaking off his remarks, he darted to the door to waylay him.

'There *is* one more thing,' said Mrs Bradley, when Mr Tidson, having demanded an ABC time-table from Thomas, had gone off to the lounge to peruse it. She described the early-morning walk on which she had followed Crete Tidson out of the town.

'And somebody in a car brought her a letter?' said Gavin. 'What do you make of it? – an assignment? She's a very beautiful woman, and Tidson isn't very exciting, I imagine.'

'Well, whatever I make of it,' said Mrs Bradley, 'this peculiar case is mostly guess-work.'

'Then you *do* make something of it? – Come on! You agreed to put your cards on the table.'

'Right. I should not be at all surprised if the letter did not contain a message from Connie Carmody.'

'But isn't Miss Connie Carmody supposed to dislike and

distrust the Tidsons? I understood that she was afraid of Mr Tidson, in fact.'

'She gave that impression, but their interests in some matters are the same.'

'You mean she is jealous of the boy, young Preece-Harvard, and the Tidsons want his money? I'd like to have a look at that letter.'

'There is no need to trouble about that. I can guess what was in it. You might be able to trace the man who brought the letter, but I don't really think that is necessary. If the letter was what I think, we shall prove it from the Tidsons' reactions, particularly those of Crete. I should not be surprised if she is getting rather tired of the business.'

'She wouldn't give the whole thing away if we pressed her hard, I suppose?'

'I doubt it. It would make her an accessory. Besides, whatever she might tell us, I doubt whether she could prove it. The murderer has made one bad although unavoidable mistake, but I don't think Crete was there, and I don't think she knows how significant it was.'

'How do you mean – a bad mistake?'

'In killing the second boy. I don't think that was part of the original plan.'

'I see. This lad Biggin might have seen the first murder committed, I suppose. He must have been sleeping out, from what we can gather. Is that what you mean?'

'I should say there was little doubt of it. The boy was in hiding, as you say, from the authorities, and may easily have seen what was done. He may even have tried to threaten the murderer on the strength of it.'

'It's a plausible theory, anyway. But why kill the first boy? Why have murdered young Grier?'

'To show how easy it was to kill and not be found out, perhaps!'

'That's not what you really think. There must be a stronger motive.'

'Well, there may be an additional motive, but we've nothing to go on. No obvious motive arises, as far as the evidence goes.'

'You're right there! Nothing adds up. What do you make of the dog?'

'I think Tidson was the first who found it. It was where the second body was found, or near enough—'

'How do you know Tidson found it? That seems to me rather far-fetched.'

'It wouldn't if you had seen him fishing with that old boot to draw a crowd of children to the spot, as Kitty, Laura and Alice did. He wanted the dog to be found and a certain inference to be drawn—'

'Of course! That the dog had been killed by a sadistic lunatic, and that the same person had killed the boy!'

'Exactly!'

'Well, if you're right, I should say the whole thing's in the bag. Tidson himself is the murderer, wicked old man! Somehow, I always thought he was. Now, how are we going to get him? I can ask him how he came to get soaked through that night, but he's sure to have some plausible excuse to give me.'

'He will stick to the story about his nymph,' said Mrs Bradley. 'By the way, I think Connie killed the dog.'

'You do?'

'Yes. A good thing for Mr Tidson, I should say. The dog may have saved his life.'

'Oh, substitution of some sort?'

'Yes, and rationalization. Her hatred of Mr Tidson is dangerously deep.'

'But when did she do it?'

'Since she has been staying in Lewes. You have only to ask at the hotel which night she did not sleep there. Of course, they may not know, but it would be well worth trying.'

'Thanks for the tip. But still, the dog isn't those boys.'

'Nevertheless, *cave canem*,' said Mrs Bradley.

Chapter Seventeen

*'They enquired after Nancy very civilly and
sent Compts. . . . It was an awkward day for
visiting . . .'*
Diary of a Country Parson: the REVEREND
JAMES WOODFORDE, Vol. 3, 1788–1792.
Edited by JOHN BERESFORD

'SO THAT young Connie was telling lies about hating the
Tidsons,' said Laura, when the report from Lewes had
come in, and Connie's messenger had been named by the
police of that ancient and interesting town, who, incidentally, had nothing whatever against him. 'I should never
have thought it!'

'And you need not think it now,' said Mrs Bradley. She
and her secretary were again alone at the *Domus*, for the
Tidsons and Miss Carmody had departed (with the full
complement of luggage, this time) and with them, in the
sense that they had caught the same train and were not due
to return to Winchester that summer, had gone Kitty and
Alice. 'If we could find Connie's letter it might throw some
light upon her relationship with the Tidsons, although not
very much, I imagine, but I still do not believe there is any
love lost. And now I think that you and I, child, should
return to Kensington, calling for Connie first and taking her
with us. A short course of your bracing society will be the
very thing for her, I imagine. We must re-orient her mind.'

Laura looked disappointed.

'Cheer up,' said Mrs Bradley. 'We can do no more here
for the present, so nothing is lost by our return. The rest
lies with the police.'

'But what about those stones? The weapons, you know,' said Laura. Mrs Bradley shrugged.

'The police will find them,' she said. 'But there *is* one more thing we have to do, now that the Tidsons and Miss Carmody have gone. It is something that will interest you, I think. I have arranged that nothing is to be touched in their rooms until to-morrow. Young Mr Gavin is coming this afternoon, whilst most of the guests are out, to blow chalk all over the furniture. You'll like that, won't you?'

'Fingerprints!' said Laura with enthusiasm. 'And then we can compare them with those they're going to find on the stones. By the way – a thing I didn't know before – fingerprints don't wash off, not even in running water. David Gavin was telling me about it. Oh, and talking of David, and to cut short a long and embarrassing story—'

'Dear, dear!' said Mrs Bradley. 'Don't tell me I'm going to lose you! I might have guessed that I was playing a foolish, short-sighted game when I introduced a Scotsman into your life!'

Laura grinned.

'You've guessed it,' she said contentedly. 'Yes, the lad and I have come to a sort of understanding. I'm not to interfere with his career, and he's not to take me away from my job, and we fight all the time in any case, but, apart from that, there seems little reason why the wedding bells, as such, should not peal out in the comparatively near future. Your congratulations are neither solicited nor desired. I think, myself, I'm being a bit of a fool, but you probably know how it is.'

'Well, well!' said Mrs Bradley. 'Dear me! And I never suspected a thing!'

'Call yourself a detective!' said Laura. 'I thought it stuck out a mile! Still, we haven't really seen much of one another yet, you know, and it's a nuisance I shall have to be the one to have the children. It's such a waste of time, and the sort of thing calculated, I should fancy, to drive intelligent females mad, but there it is. Three boys and a girl is my schedule, to be produced within nine years. What do you think? Is that reasonable? I thought I'd get it over, you know, and then take up motor-racing or something. I shall try to get some sort of foster-mother for the offspring – someone like old K., who's good with children.'

Mrs Bradley hooted with respectful amusement, and then said soberly:

'Talking of foster-mothers—'

'Ah, yes, that Grier woman,' said Laura. 'Look here, let's order some of Thomas' champagne cocktails. Do you remember him giving Mr Tidson more brandy in his? I wonder whether he'd do the same for us? Perhaps I had better not suggest it.'

She summoned Thomas, and informed him that she was shortly getting married and required something to drown her sorrows.

'Och, aye,' replied Thomas. He looked at her oddly, shook his head, made a scraping noise in his throat, and then went out.

'Something on his conscience,' said Laura. 'You'd better get him to spill it. There's not very much gets past the Laird o' Cockpen.'

'You may be right in both surmises,' said Mrs Bradley, 'but I don't think we'll trouble him at present. I fancy that he was merely expressing disapproval of lawful matrimony.'

After lunch Gavin arrived, looking pleased with himself. With him came a fingerprint expert, and, assisted (or, as Gavin informed her, hindered and interrupted) by Laura, they tested every article of furniture in the bedrooms of Miss Carmody and the Tidsons for fingerprints. A splendid set of Connie's prints had been taken at Mrs Bradley's Stone House by Laura upon a tumbler. This she now proudly produced, to the amusement of Mrs Bradley and the staggered incredulity of her swain.

'Thought they might come in useful at some time or another,' she observed. 'I've been preserving this exhibit under my tallest hat ever since I brought it back from

Wandles Parva. Don't look so moonstruck, David,' she added to Gavin. 'Stranger things will happen in the future, so you'd better prepare yourself now.'

'You're telling *me!*' said Gavin. 'What's the matter with this room, Buckle?' he suddenly demanded, turning off to address his expert. 'Can't we get cracking?'

'Nothing's the matter, sir, except that every single print has been wiped off everything,' replied the fingerprint expert, straightening himself from a kneeling position beside the wardrobe drawer.

'Have you tried the jerry?' Laura indelicately demanded. Buckle unearthed the repository and carefully tested it, using a dark-tinted powder on its glaze.

'Nothing doing,' he said at last. 'And there isn't another thing, sir. I'll say that whoever used this room last must have had prints on record, sir. Very wily birds, to have covered their tracks as well as this, I reckon.'

'Guilty consciences, too,' said Gavin. 'Cheer up, Buckle! Better luck in the next room, I dare say.' He led the way to the bedroom Miss Carmody had occupied. Here the conditions were vastly different. Miss Carmody's room was practically knee-deep in fingerprints, as Laura chose to express it. The prints, announced Gavin with considerable confidence, belonged to three or four different people. Buckle agreed.

'Miss Carmody, the housemaid, and the porter who brought down the luggage (those on the finger-plate of the door, sir), and a set belonging to some other person who came in.'

'Crete Tidson,' said Gavin, 'very likely.'

'So, if some of these are Crete Tidson's fingerprints, she can't have anything to hide,' suggested Laura.

'If she had anything to hide, her prints wouldn't be in this room at all,' agreed Gavin. 'Even so, it doesn't get us much further. We shan't find Tidson's prints on the stone if he's the murderer. Still, there are other possibilities. Now we'd better do Mrs Tidson's room – she didn't share with her husband – and if she's left prints we may take it she's nothing to hide.'

Crete's room, however, was as bare of prints as the first room which had been tested.

'Damn!' said Gavin. 'Ah, well, these we've got will have to be compared with the prints we've found on our collection. If anything tallies, we may be a step further on, and we may not. Plenty of people pick up stones and heave them into a river, goodness knows!'

'The only thing is,' said Laura, 'that there aren't all that number of biggish stones on the river banks for people to pick up and heave. Can't you get something from that?'

'True for you, we might be able to,' said Gavin. 'Anyway, we have to wait and see.'

Waiting and seeing produced a definite result. One of the inspector's collection of large, heavy stones bore undoubted traces of blood. It also bore Connie Carmody's fingerprints. It was also very neatly labelled *Weir*.

'Oh, Lord!' said Gavin, as much dismayed by this discovery as even Laura could have wished. 'Here's a pretty how-de-do, I don't think! What are we going to do now?'

'We must see whether it's human gore,' said Laura, with vivid recollections of the smell of the very dead dog. Gavin brightened; then he resumed his former lugubrious expression. 'Even if it *is* the dog, it's a bit of a pointer,' he said. 'Mrs Bradley has said several times that practice makes perfect, you know. And someone who knew that Connie had killed the dog moved it to where we found young Biggin.'

'That surely lets Connie out?' said Laura. 'And, anyway, you've still some of your big stones to test.'

'Scores, if not hundreds,' Gavin replied. 'But, before I go any further, I suppose I shall have to interview this Connie – confound her for a red-herring and a nuisance!'

'The sooner the better,' Mrs Bradley agreed when she was asked. 'Let us go to Lewes at once. This ought to be cleared up immediately. We must frighten the life out of Connie, although I hesitate to add "for her good."'

'For the good of the general public, I should have thought,' said Laura. 'Honestly, the girl must be demented.'

'Oh, she is not quite as bad as that! Let us agree that she has become slightly abnormal.'

'Life with Auntie Prissie? Morbid streak emphasized by unsympathetic atmosphere? Persecution mania—?'

Mrs Bradley cackled.

'But not engendered by the aunt,' she said. 'Connie's condition is largely the result of shock. Of two successive shocks, in fact.'

'How come?'

'Connie learned, for the first time, at the dangerous age of thirteen, that her life and that of young Preece-Harvard were destined to flow in very different channels. What she was *not* told – thanks to a streak of un-selfishness oddly mixed in with Mrs Preece-Harvard's character – is that she is young Arthur's half-sister, the illegitimate daughter of his father. There followed for Connie, immediately upon this realization, the further shock of the parting, abrupt and cruel, from this half-brother, whom she loved with a passion deeper than that of a mother.'

'Since then she's turned round on Arthur P-H, though, and would like to kill him,' said Laura. 'Inversions, and so forth, I take it. Ah, yes, I get it all now.'

'I don't know whether you do,' said Mrs Bradley. 'Think it over, and don't be misled. I have had no reason to alter my opinion that Connie would rather die than harm that boy. She does not, of course, feel the same about Mr Tidson.'

'Why are you keeping her more or less of a prisoner? And why have we got to have her with us for a bit?'

'Well, I'm afraid for Connie. She is not, in one sense, completely responsible for her actions.'

'But isn't she going to start a job, or something?'

'I only wish I thought so! Now, before we leave Winchester, there is one thing I would very much like to do.'

'Set that man free. He's bound to be let go, though. They can't pin anything on him.'

'He's a strong-willed fellow,' said Mrs Bradley. 'He's fond of his wife, I think, and doesn't want to hurt her unnecessarily.'

'So he gets himself arrested for murder on the word of that awful Grier woman! Can't see much chivalry in that!'

'I think he may have chosen the lesser of the two evils. But my lawyer is going to try to get at him.'

'Ferguson?'

'Yes. He has had one interview already. It was abortive. Here is Ferguson's report. It is just what I had expected. Never mind! He will try again.'

Laura opened the envelope which Mrs Bradley handed her.

'He won't see me. He won't see anybody,' wrote Mr Ferguson. 'He says he does not wish to be legally represented; that he did not commit the murder, and that the police can fry in hell.'

'Well, that's that,' said Laura, folding up Mr Ferguson and handing him back. 'Now what?'

'Now we do what I have been waiting to do – but we could not do it whilst the Tidsons were here – we interview the young woman who is the cause of all the trouble.'

'The naiad?'

'No. The missing sweetheart. The woman that this stupid, chivalrous Potter really *was* visiting that night.'

'Oh!' said Laura. 'What a hope!'

'Of finding her, do you mean? I have every hope. She has a jealous husband or cruel parents, she is known to Mrs Grier, and she may have left Winchester since the murder of little Grier.'

'How do you know?'

'I *don't* know – in the sense you mean.'

'I think I understand. She was with Potter on the night and at the time of the murder. She has been too scared, because of husband or parents, to come forward and give the chap his alibi, and, because she's a coward (as aforesaid) she's cut and run. Is that it?'

'And very plainly stated, except that she may not have left Winchester.'

'But what about Potter? Isn't he a fool not to name her? Is that where the chivalry comes in?'

'Yes. But there are other points as well. I should think he's been expecting her to come forward, and his despairing reception of Mr Ferguson shows that he no longer thinks she will. He hasn't brought the subject up himself for two reasons: first, he loves his wife, but rather as a son loves his mother. He doesn't want to upset her more than she's been upset already. It has upset her to believe that he was involved with the odious but middle-aged Mrs Grier, but he knows that she doesn't really believe her own wild accusations about that. If it came out, however, that he has been visiting a young and passably good-looking woman, and was with her on the night of the murder—'

'She'd probably rather have him hanged than have him home, poor blighter,' said Laura.

'I suppose,' Mrs Bradley went on, 'that he does not believe for an instant that he, an innocent man, can be condemned.'

'And he may be right, at that,' said Laura. 'Anyway, I suppose it's worth the risk, from his point of view. But suppose he *is* condemned? What then?'

'Well, we'll make up our minds that he won't be.'

'Right. Pity if he'd kept his mouth shut and all for nothing. I do admire people who hope for the best and don't babble. When do we begin this Sherlock stuff to find the missing woman?'

'In the same way that Holmes began his search for the missing racehorse,' said Mrs Bradley, with a cackle. 'We note that the dog gave the game away by not barking in the night. You remember?'

'I like having my leg pulled,' said Laura, with great good-humour, 'and especially by intellects I respect; but there is a limit, and you've reached it. Are you talking of Mr Tidson's dog? I call that a very mysterious animal, you know.'

Mrs Bradley cackled.

'But I am not joking,' she protested. 'Come with me, and you'll see.'

Mrs Bradley went first to Mrs Potter.

'Where did your husband work?' she asked as soon as the front door opened.

'Oh, it's you, mum,' the poor woman said. 'He worked for Mr Rummidge.'

'How do I get there?'

'Have you got anything to go on?'

'I know who the murderer is. The police know, too.'

'Then why don't they let Potter go?'

'They will. You must go on being patient. It won't be for much longer now. Whereabouts is this place? And how long will it take me to get there?'

'It's just over the other side there. Take quarter of an hour, maybe. I don't know 'ow quick you can walk.'

'Right. Thank you. Cheer up, Mrs Potter! This business is very nearly settled and – I don't think you'll have much more trouble to keep your husband at home once you've got him back. How is your little girl? Is she still away?'

'No, poor mite. Her cried to come home, so I had 'er. She knows where her dad is. The other children took care of that!'

'Ah, well, we were all cruel at their age. How are you off for money?'

'I've all I want,' said the woman, flushing.

'You're working, then?'

'What else can I do?'

'What indeed?'

'I don't mind work. I've worked 'ard all my life. It's the worry that kills!'

'Very true. Well, don't worry any more. Everything will turn out all right. You see if it doesn't. Have you been to visit your husband?'

'He won't 'ave no one, Potter won't. E's obstinate.'

'He feels he's been badly treated, and so he has.'

'It's his own silly fault!' said Mrs Potter, her chin shaking. 'He done wrong, and now it's come 'ome to 'im.'

'You'll have to forget all that, and allow him to make a fresh start. Men will be men, you know!'

'They're beasts, the whole lot of 'em, mum! That's what they are! Fair beasts!'

'Attractive beasts, too,' muttered Laura. 'I say,' she added, when they were away from the house, 'what price this Potter finding the kid on his way to work? Does that wash?'

'Not well,' Mrs Bradley agreed. 'I think he was infatuated with this young woman of his, and, like many another Romeo, went out of his way to pass the house where she lived. I hope so, anyway, as I particularly want to find out where that was without asking the natives any questions. Potter has kept his secret, and I shouldn't care to—'

'Blow the gaff on him? Quite right. Where now? Round here to where he found the body?'

Beyond the wide shallow water a narrow road branched off which led vaguely in the direction indicated by Mrs Potter as leading towards Mr Rummidge's works.

Before long they came to some houses, not more than eight of them, an ugly, small, red-brick row with long and narrow front gardens and paved paths up to the front doors.

Mrs Bradley scanned the row for a moment. Then she seemed to make up her mind. Leaving Laura standing in the lane, she walked up to the third house and knocked.

Laura, trying to work out what had led her redoubtable employer to make up her mind to try this particular house, decided that it was because of a very fine geranium, almost a tree, which stood on a small wicker table just inside the parlour window.

Sure enough, as soon as the door was opened, Mrs Bradley pointed to the geranium and asked permission to buy it.

'Buy it?' said the woman who had answered the door.

'I don't know as we can sell it. What would you want it for, like?'

'My sun-parlour,' Mrs Bradley answered. 'I have one or two plants, not nearly as good as yours, and I was told in the city that your daughter would be willing to sell it.'

'My daughter?' She turned, and called loudly, 'Come here, Linda! Just a minute, dear!'

In response to the command, a young woman of about twenty-five appeared. She had a dab of flour on her chin. This drew attention to her beautiful complexion. She had short sleeves which showed well-turned, strong, attractive and shapely arms, and her hair was fair and abundant.

'This is it,' thought Laura, watching. The door closed behind Mrs Bradley. Laura strolled off down the lane, and waited for almost twenty minutes. At the end of that time Mrs Bradley rejoined her.

'Geranium not for sale,' said Laura, grinning, 'but everything else according to plan. Did you bounce the girl into confessing?'

'Oh, that wasn't the girl,' said Mrs Bradley. 'But I've got the girl's name and address. And you're right about the geranium. It isn't for sale.'

'What made you think it might be the right house? – especially if it wasn't.'

'I did not think it was the right house, child. I do know, however, that people with very large geraniums, or aspidistras, or whatever it may be, are often the village newsmongers.'

'How come? – Oh, I see! They take cover. The potted plant acts as a screen.'

'Exactly, child.'

'And did you – er – get what you wanted?'

'In very good measure. Both the mother and the daughter knew that Potter came to visit along here, although they did not know his name and do not connect him with the murder. They do know, however, that he has ceased to come. Most valuable of all, they gave me the name of the girl and the address of the house. There *is* a strict father, and Potter *did* come fairly late at night, and once or twice was not seen to take his departure. I did not press them for dates, and they do not realize how much they told me, still less that I was particularly interested. The geranium remained, so far as they were concerned, the main subject of conversation. I bought half a dozen eggs from the back-garden fowls, and here we are, on the way to get Potter released. The daughter was jealous, by the way. Potter is a desirable fellow, you know.'

'Well, but aren't we walking away from the house you want?'

'I don't want the house, child. I want to interview the girl on *my* ground, not on hers. I shall write her a threatening letter.'

'That should winkle her out of her home and along to the *Domus*, I'll bet!'

'I hope so. If it doesn't, I shall visit the place where she works. I shall threaten, at any rate, to do so. I think that perhaps she'll see reason.'

These bullying tactics succeeded. Potter's young woman turned out to be a weakly-looking creature of about thirty, fair-haired and with insipid pretensions to prettiness. Mrs Bradley made mincemeat of her in no time, and hauled her along from the *Domus*, where they met, to the police station, where they parted, and, having scared her almost to death, left her to the local Superintendent.

Against her evidence, abetted by that of the neighbours – that Potter visited her during licensing hours, whilst her father was at the public house – no case against Potter could stand.

'That ought to frighten old Tidson,' said Laura, who felt rather worried. She confided this emotion to Gavin, who replied:

'That will be taken care of.'

'Sez you!' observed Laura, with more thoughtfulness than these words merit.

'No, really,' Gavin objected. 'Not a word will come out

in the papers about the release of Potter, and he's been advised to say nowt. Of course, plenty of people will know he's cleared, and that's as it should be, after all; but officially no news will leak out, and we're only needing time to get on to Tidson. It needs his hat to turn up. Potter swears he saw it when he picked up the boy—'

'I suppose,' said Laura, struck by a sudden idea, 'he did find the boy where he said he did?'

'Yes. We've found a woman who was on her way into Winchester to pick up a very early bus. She saw him lift the boy up (she didn't know, of course, that the kid was dead), and she wondered whether she ought to stay and help. But she'd got the day off from work to go into Southampton to see whether she could get a pair of shoes, and was late already for the bus she intended to catch, so she didn't wait. She didn't mention the hat, and we didn't feel we could put a leading question. If it *was* there, she hadn't noticed it.'

'Oh, well, then, that's that,' said Laura. 'But you've got to keep an eye on Mrs Croc. I'm not having her scuppered by Tidsons. By the way, was it wise to let him get clean away from Winchester?'

'We're having him tailed all right. The local superintendent – an awfully good chap and a mine of information on dry-fly fishing, by the way – isn't sorry to have Tidson go. He pollutes the air of Winchester, according to the superintendent, and will probably cause Saint Swithun to turn in his grave.'

'He's a horror,' said Laura stoutly. 'You've got to get him, you know.'

'Don't worry. But we haven't found the weapon yet, and when we do it won't have his fingerprints on it. I wonder when he moved Grier's body from the weir? On that early morning trip, I guess. He's been intelligent, you know.'

'Yes,' said Laura. 'No peculiar absences from the *Domus* except the telephone one – he must have been windy about something that night; I don't believe he just wanted Connie's address—'

'He's got frightful cheek,' said Gavin, 'and doesn't mind taking a few risks. He worked out that nobody could connect his absence from the hotel with the murders – or, at any rate, nobody could *prove* it had anything to do with the murders – and he did want something out of Mrs Bradley's room. Connie's address was easily the most likely thing he would be looking for.'

'All right. Granted,' said Laura. 'All the same, if she'd come back and found him—'

'She wouldn't have found him. She'd have found Crete, and Crete would have been ready with some plausible tale.'

'Come to borrow an aspirin tablet. I know. Well, I hope you get him!'

'We'll get him,' said Gavin. 'Only, you see, it takes time.'

'And, but for Mrs Croc., you'd have hanged Potter without a qualm.'

'I shouldn't think so, you know. But she certainly put us on to Tidson. That I'll admit, although I can't see yet where it gets us. We can't prove a thing.'

'I see now why Miss Carmody was so worried about Tidson in the first place.'

'*Was* she worried about Tidson?'

'Well, she called Mrs Croc. in at once to give his reflexes the once-over. And she told Mrs Croc. she was sure he had murdered little Grier.'

'Did she? That's rather interesting. What had she got to go on?'

'Only the naiad. But there must have been something else, surely?'

'Perhaps not, you know, if she knew – as she did know, of course – that Tidson was the next heir to the Preece-Harvard money and estates, and had made an idiotic excuse (the naiad *is* idiotic, isn't it?) to get down to Winchester near the boy who was keeping him out of the inheritance.'

'Yes . . . but considering we admit he's been rather intelligent for a murderer, wasn't it a *suspiciously* silly excuse? He wouldn't want to attract attention, surely, to the fact that he meant to come to Winchester when the boy, when he isn't at school, lives so frightfully near, at Alresford.'

'That point has worried me a bit, but perhaps he's forgotten, living abroad for so long, that English people don't stay at home in August. I should think he expected to find the boy at Alresford, and is keeping his hand in now until he can get at the kid.'

'But – keep his hand in? That's insane!'

'Well, isn't the naiad insane? It's all of a piece!'

─────── Chapter Eighteen───────

*'"Nay, nay, she's none drownded," said Mr
Tulliver. "You've been naughty to her, I doubt,
Tom?"'*
GEORGE ELIOT (*The Mill on the Floss*)

A MONTH later Mrs Bradley and Laura were in London,
and the papers were in possession of a curious story.
A naiad, it was reported, had been seen in the River Itchen
not far from Winchester; this on the apparently unimpeachable evidence of three respectable citizens.

'Crete!' said Laura, handing Mrs Bradley the newspaper.
'They must have gone back to Winchester to kill Arthur
Preece-Harvard. We'd better get down there at once!'

'Do you think so?' Mrs Bradley enquired. 'I am inclined
to agree that the naiad must be Mrs Tidson. It seems a
strange thing for her to have done. One would imagine
that the last thing the Tidsons would want would be to
attract attention to their presence in Winchester if they
mean to kill Arthur Preece-Harvard.'

'Well, the naiad has greenish hair. It says so here,' said
Laura. She stood behind Mrs Bradley's chair and pointed
to the description of the visitant. 'Don't you think we ought
to go down and interview these people who say they saw
her?'

'No doubt your Mr Gavin will do that, but, if you want
to hear their story at first-hand, why don't you go alone
to Winchester to see them? I can't come with you just now.'

'May I? Oh, good. I couldn't—' She glanced at Mrs
Bradley's day book, which was on the consulting-room
table – 'I suppose I couldn't go to-day?'

'Why not?' Mrs Bradley comfortably replied. 'I am called away to Hereford to see what Doctor Watson would call a noble bachelor, and there is no reason for you to stay here by yourself. Henri and Célestine can manage. Off you go, child. There's a train in an hour. You might catch it.'

'A jolly good thing Connie wouldn't come and stay with us,' said Laura, 'or one of us would have had to take her along.'

'She showed the natural repugnance to us,' said Mrs Bradley, 'for which I was prepared. I have warned Miss Carmody to keep a strict eye on her movements, but I confess that I should have felt a good deal easier in my mind if Connie had been under our jurisdiction for a bit. Still, it is always a difficult task to save people from themselves. So much so that I sometimes wonder whether the laws of Providence regard as a supremely immoral action any attempt to do it.'

'Funny that Connie had so much to say about that job, and is still with Miss Carmody,' said Laura. 'I suppose you worked it.'

'I don't think Connie ever had a job,' said Mrs Bradley, not for the first time.

The report on the naiad, by the time that Laura reached Winchester, had not received any additions. The creature had been seen twice, each time in the same stretch of water, once by two city councillors walking together, and once by a District Visitor who reported her at once to the police. Laura went out, accompanied by Gavin, to inspect that part of the Itchen in which she had been seen.

They took the now familiar path at the bottom of College Walk, passed through the white wicket-gate, and slackened their rate of walking as they rounded the grassy space where the river made its bend and the stream on the College side of the path ran straight and shallow beside them. They passed the College playing-fields, and the boggy meadows between the swift streams widened.

Thick cresses, darkly, succulently green, the water-mint,

the purple loosestrife, seemed a fitting border to the grey-bright floods that were said to house the naiad. The lance-leaved, saw-toothed hemp agrimony, crowding its corymbs at the head of its three-foot stems, was dwarfed by the mighty hogweed, coarse and hairy. The handsome, purple-tinged angelica, with hollow stem, set off and did not diminish the water-level charm of the wild forget-me-not, still blooming at the end of its season. Dark crimson self-heal, square-stemmed, longlipped (the carpenter's herb, the curative *Prunella*), reared above purple-edged bracts its dimorphic flowers.

'Queer about Connie Carmody and the dog,' said Gavin suddenly. 'I keep on thinking about it.'

'I suppose,' began Laura; and then, urged by some instinct to protect her own sex from the enemy, she stopped short.

'Go on,' said Gavin encouragingly. 'After all, we know who did the murders. But the dog is just a bit odd. Could Connie Carmody be bats, and is *that* why Mrs Bradley wanted to keep an eye on her and have her in her house for a bit?'

'I don't think it's that,' said Laura. 'It was directly Connie had killed the dog, I think, that she gave up all idea of kidding us. She'd killed old Tidson by proxy, I suppose, and she could put up with him after that. Tidson got her worked up about Arthur, and that's why she ran away from here. She brooded a good bit, and came back and slaughtered his dog.'

'And then came over all regretful?'

'No. Only all sick. She didn't regret what she'd done.'

'Not a dog-lover, you would say?'

'No. Only a Tidson-hater, according to Mrs Croc.'

'But why the dog in that particular spot?'

'Oh, practice makes perfect, and that's what Mrs Croc's afraid of.'

'I don't get it.' Gavin looked at her suspiciously.

'Neither do I,' said Laura lightly.

'You don't think the old lady is leading us up the garden, and that *Connie* killed those boys after all?'

'Good Lord, of course I don't!'

'She could have used the same stone, you see, and that would account for the fact that we've found only one with prints on it,' said Gavin.

'Then what about the absence of prints in Mr Tidson's room?'

'I admit that's a snag. And yet, you see, it's such a pointer, too.'

'The lesser of two evils, I expect. Or, at least, the lesser of two obvious risks.'

'Yes. You know, Laura, this case annoys me a bit. He hasn't really been so very intelligent, has he? And yet he's held us up completely.'

'Comes of having no accomplices, you know. You can get away with most things if you know how to keep your mouth shut and can pick the right time to perform.'

'Crete must be in his confidence.'

'Not entirely. They don't get on too well. But partly, I think. She seems to act as the naiad when he wishes.'

'In any case, she couldn't give evidence against him, so I suppose it wouldn't matter what she did – that is, from one point of view.'

'It would matter if she gave other people ideas!'

'What do you suppose is the idea behind this naiad business? Crete being the naiad, I mean.'

'I don't know, I'm sure.' She chuckled. 'It might be a different idea at different times, don't you think? If I had to make a guess, I should say that this time it's to blackleg old Tidson and give away his presence in the vicinity. I doubt whether Crete is a villain. I think she's just an extravagant cat.'

'Without much conscience, I should say.'

'Well, that goes with extravagance.'

'I don't know that, of the two of them, I don't dislike Crete a bit more than old Tidson himself.'

'Of course you do! Outraged male vanity, because she won't look at you!' said Laura.

'It may interest you to hear,' said Gavin, 'that I had some difficulty in getting her out of my hair in the early stages of our acquaintance. She found me handsome, manly and sunburnt, if you really want to know.'

Laura hooted rudely, and startled a gull which had come inland ahead of a gale which had not yet reached the coast.

'Hush!' said Gavin. 'The next thing you'll frighten is the naiad, and, if you do, we shan't see her.'

'I was the naiad myself once,' said Laura.

'So I've heard. What about a demonstration?'

'After we're married, with pleasure. It was quite fun.'

'It must have been. Rather chilly fun, too, I should have thought. Anyway, here's the stretch of the river where she's supposed to have been seen most recently. Ought we to go to ground, and hide behind the willow trees, do you think?'

'Whatever you say . . . You know, it wouldn't be quite an impossibility, would it?'

'What wouldn't?'

'To see her. In fact—' Laura suddenly caught Gavin's arm – 'what's that? See? Over by the reeds in that carrier.'

'A swan.'

'I don't mean the swan. I mean whatever made the swan angry. There's something or somebody there, and, what's more, she's seen us, I think.'

'Well, we're here to solve mysteries. Good thing I've brought my waders.' Gavin seated himself and pulled on the thigh-high boots. 'Here goes. Remember me to Mrs Bradley if I get pulled under and become a little merman or something, won't you?'

Laura, who had no intention of being left out of any excitement which was being provided, promptly pulled off her shoes, put on a pair of plimsolls and unfastened her skirt. Under it she was wearing shorts. She had no stockings.

'Stay where you are,' said Gavin.

'Rot,' retorted Laura. 'Don't be an oaf.'

Her swain made no rejoinder, and together they entered the water. The stream flowed fast, and it was difficult work to get across it.

'Hope nobody sees us who has fishing rights here,' said Laura.

'Police work,' grunted Gavin. 'Can't help the trout at a time like this. Give me your hand and get a move on.'

'Right. I'll pull.' This was not what Gavin had meant.

She started forward hastily, grabbed at his arm, and fell flat on her face. 'Oh, Lord! That's done it!' she added, as she scrambled to her feet with Gavin's assistance. 'Hullo! Neptune's trident or something!' She came up holding a forked stick cut from a cherry tree. 'That's from no willow bush, cully!'

'Why the deuce can't you look what you're doing?' demanded her companion. 'Whoever it was has had time to sheer off by now.'

'I doubt it,' said Laura, grimly, as she dropped the branch and scrambled up the opposite bank, her plimsolls slithering wildly on the mud. 'I think there's somebody here, and I'm pretty sure—'

She did not finish the sentence. The naked body of Crete Tidson was lying half in and half out of the water in the swiftly-rushing carrier. Her head was under. The two of them dragged her on to the herb-strewn grass, and laid her among the coarse flowers of the lush, late summer.

'Prop open her mouth,' said Laura. Gavin's training had been as thorough as her own. They disposed Crete, glorious in all her pagan loveliness, and then, as the textbooks and not the legends had taught them, they knelt athwart her and took turns at indelicately pumping the river water out of her lungs.

'Coming,' said Gavin at last. 'Hope I'm not bruising her ribs.'

'So long as you don't break them,' said Laura, taking his place and spreading her wide, brown, strong-fingered hands on Crete's white body. 'Glad I don't earn my living doing this!'

'Don't talk. It's waste of strength,' said Gavin briefly.

Both he and Laura, indeed, were almost exhausted by the time their patient was able to be wrapped up in Gavin's jacket and placed with her back against a willow.

'Clothes!' said Laura. 'You go.'

'A car,' said Gavin. 'I told Soames to meet us at the bridge. I thought we might not want to walk back. He'll have rugs and probably an overcoat. I'll go and get him to help me carry her. You keep moving. Don't worry about her. You're soaking wet. I shan't be long, but I don't want a wife with pneumonia.'

'Wife!' said Laura with a shudder. 'The one thing I always swore I'd never be. Oh, well, it hasn't happened yet. All right, I'll run about and keep warm.'

'And, look, think this one over: don't keep holding out on me about Connie. You're not at your girls' school now. Well, so long! See you soon!'

It so soon became evident that Crete either could not or would not give any circumstantial account of her dramatic reappearance in the neighbourhood that, at Mrs Bradley's suggestion, sent by telegram from London (for she had not left for Hereford), Gavin gave up questioning her. He had elicited the statement that Crete had come without her husband, and without Miss Carmody's knowledge, to have a last look for the naiad after what she had read in the papers, but Crete refused to say more.

'Where *is* your husband?' had been Gavin's most persistent question. It was one of those which Crete did not answer.

'I don't *know* any more,' she said. 'It's no use to ask me. I don't *know*. And, anyway, what does it matter? I suppose I got cramp. I think I did. That's all.'

Gavin had to leave it at that, and directed his energies to finding Mr Tidson. This did not prove at all difficult. He was back in Miss Carmody's flat after having been on a short visit to Mrs Preece-Harvard. Arthur had gone to stay with a friend in Cheshire, and was not expected home for a week. Mr Tidson had stayed to lunch, and had heard the news about Crete on his return to London. He could give no information about his wife. She had left him in Alresford, and had said that she was going on to Winchester. He had seen her on to the bus. Apart from this, he knew nothing.

Mrs Preece-Harvard confirmed all this, including the facts that she and Mr Tidson had had lunch together and that he had been in her company until he left for Miss

Carmody's flat. In other words, if he had been suspected of trying to drown his wife, his alibi was perfect, for there seemed no reason why Mrs Preece-Harvard should lie. There was also no reason, as Gavin pointed out moodily to Laura, why Tidson should have wanted to drown his wife, or why she should have wanted to save him by her silence if he had.

'Besides,' said Gavin, 'we should have seen that something was up. He couldn't have got away. We were right on the spot.'

'But that's just what's so extraordinary,' said Laura.

'What is?'

'That we got there in time to save her. It couldn't be just coincidence. She's playing some game.'

'She's got me licked if she is. There's not much doubt she was pretty well finished when we found her.'

'Yes, I know. But she's clever, is Crete Tidson. Artistic, too, I expect, and pretty unscrupulous. She wouldn't spoil the ship for a ha'porth of tar.'

'She's got generous ideas of a ha'porth, then,' said Gavin.

'Granted. We agreed she's extravagant.'

Their eyes met like swords flickering, and then they began to laugh.

'Well, *I'm* not extravagant,' added Laura.

———— Chapter Nineteen————

*'But a green reed, inspired by divine inspiration,
with a gracious tune and melody, spoke to her
and said, "Oh, Psyche, I pray thee not to trouble
or pollute my water by the death of thee."'*
WILLIAM ADLINGTON (*The Golden Ass of
Lucius Apuleius, edited by
F. J. Harvey Darton*)

Mrs BRADLEY, summoned to Winchester by an anxious
secretary immediately she had disposed of her noble
bachelor (whose foible, it seemed, was to keep a young pig
in his bedroom), agreed wholeheartedly with Laura that
the fact of their presence on the spot at the moment of
Crete Tidson's mishap was the most extraordinary point
in the affair. She added that she would be with them as
soon as she could.

'I hope it will be very soon,' said Laura. 'I don't like
this part of the business.'

'I hope she'll come soon, too,' said Gavin, 'and I hope
she'll be able to give us the dope. If it weren't for that hat,
confound it! – and Tidson making that telephone call, and
the pricking of Mrs Bradley's thumbs, I'd have been back
at the Yard by now. But the Assistant Commissioner has
put his shirt on the old lady, so here I'm left kicking my
heels while the locals get through an immense amount of
what must seem to them damned foolish work. If only she
hadn't entirely cleared that chap Potter I'd still be wondering
what bee she had got in her bonnet.'

'It's one that will lay eggs,' said Laura.

'More likely to sting her in the eye,' retorted Gavin.

'However, I haven't any choice, and I like the old girl, so here I stay. Luckily, the superintendent plays a jolly good game of billiards, and, of course, there's always you – when you happen to be here! But think of the fun we could have in London!'

Laura refused to consider the fun they could have in London.

'Don't worry. Mrs Croc. has something up her sleeve all right,' she said. 'I think I know what she's after, and what she's afraid of.'

'Mrs Bradley afraid? A contradiction in terms,' said Gavin, grinning. 'I don't think she knows what fear is. Anyway, if she *has* got something up her sleeve, I think she might tell me what it is. Dash it, it's my case as well as hers, and I've got my living to earn.'

'She can't *prove* anything, duck. That's her trouble. Apparently the psychological proof is there all right, but there's no material proof whatsoever. Of course,' added Laura, eyeing her swain reprovingly, 'you police have made a muck of the thing, don't you think?'

'Honestly,' said Gavin, taking the question with a Scotsman's seriousness, 'I don't know what I think. I don't think we've missed anything, Laura. That's one of the things that makes me believe that Mrs Bradley's right about the murders, and that they haven't been done by a local person, but are part of some special scheme.'

'Planned by a fox,' said Laura. 'One thing, whatever Connie Carmody was supposed to do hasn't come off.'

'I don't think we know that,' said Gavin. 'But I wish we could solve the whole thing. They're so beastly, these murders of kids. I'd like to get Tidson if he did them.'

'He did them all right, if she says so.'

'She doesn't altogether say so, Laura. Mind you, if that young Preece-Harvard had been murdered there wouldn't be very much doubt about Tidson's guilt. But even allowing that she's given us the tip, and that Tidson did kill those two boys, we've hunted in vain for the evidence. A panama hat was mentioned, I believe. Tidson has worn one down here, and there seems no doubt that he has lost it, because he's had to buy himself another, but whether Potter's story is true, and the lost hat was underneath Bob Grier's body and later on disappeared, is another matter. One would have thought that those people who live near the Griers and the Potters would have noticed a man in a panama hat. They're not the usual wear in poorer districts. Well, we've questioned them pretty closely and we can't get a thing. And that's how it's been all the time.'

'I know, But there *must* be some evidence somewhere. Somebody must know something and have seen something. The only thing is – *who?*'

'*Murder Considered as One of the Fine Arts* – well, little Tidson must be an artist, I suppose. You find them in all walks of life and in all professions, and, certainly, the naiad was a poetic conception. I wonder what made him think of her? – Although we don't even know for certain that he *was* the one to think of her. That hasn't been proved, you know.'

'Oh, well, I don't know about that! Connie did make a beeline for that flat on the Great West Road. And, actually, Potter didn't call it a *panama* hat. Think that one over!'

'Yes, I know. But she hated Tidson and he scared her. Flies don't usually make direct for the spider's web.'

'Mrs Croc. says that, psychologically, they do. By the way, I wonder how much Connie likes Crete? She's supposed to hate her as much as she hates old Tidson, but that might not prove to be true.'

'Crete hates Connie, anyway. That's quite certain, I thought.'

'Yes. Well, now: I know we can't get Crete to give evidence against her husband, but, supposing he *is* the murderer, do you think we could get at anything through her?'

'Well, we've saved her life, I suppose. She might be disposed to tell us one or two facts about her movements since she first came to Winchester, and that might implicate her husband.'

'I shouldn't have thought she made many movements. She seemed to do nothing but all that embroidery. And, even if she *could* help us, she won't incriminate herself.'

'No . . . I still think, though, as I have thought ever since I saw both of them, that there can't be any love lost between them. Besides, who would half-drown Crete except her husband—'

'Or Connie Carmody? I agree; although there again—'

'Well, there's Miss Priscilla Carmody, of course, and the Preece-Harvards, mother and son.'

'Oh, but—'

'You can't cut out any of them, or put in any of them. There isn't any evidence either way, any more than there is for the murders. All you can say is that, as the Tidsons have no other English connections—'

'So far as we know. That's the catch. We really know most about them from the Canary Islands end.'

'I don't think it's much of a catch. Thirty-five years is a pretty good long time, and Crete, so far as we know, hasn't been in England before.'

'Even that we can't prove, though, can we, unless Miss Carmody knows, and Crete had an English mother.'

'I shall be glad when Mrs Bradley gets down here. Perhaps *she* can get something out of Crete.'

'Perhaps she can. She can see further through a brick wall than most people, can Mrs Croc. But Crete's a dark horse all right, and as for the drowning—'

'Not a put-up job from her point of view, you know. She was full of nasty unfiltered river water. There was nothing phony about that. I've seen half-drowned people before. It's a habit we have in the police force, and I think I know most of the signs.'

'Then either she was attempting suicide or—'

'Exactly. Or. But we should have spotted the party of the other part. We couldn't have helped it. My own view is that it was an attempt at suicide. I don't think murder comes into it, somehow, you know.'

'Didn't another point strike you?' Laura enquired.

'I can't say it did. What?'

'Well, it's against the suicide theory and very much in favour of murder.'

'Go on.' He looked anxiously at her.

'Where were Crete's clothes? We didn't see any.'

'Well, we didn't look for any. We were more concerned with bundling her up and getting her into the car.'

'Would a suicide undress first? And, if she did, and the clothes are still there, well, you left a policeman on duty to keep off sightseers and avoid—'

'Having people leave extraneous clues,' said Gavin, grinning. 'I did. So we go along and look for Crete's garments. Do you know, so much have I become inoculated in favour of the naiad that I never even thought about clothes. It seemed natural to find Crete naked.'

'It had better not seem natural when you're married to *me*,' said Laura. 'Now, look. Somebody has got to stay here at the *Domus* to meet Mrs Croc. and take her to hear Crete's depositions or whatever you call any information she's likely to give. Any objection if I point out that that is your job, and that the search for Crete's clothes is mine?'

'Go ahead,' said Gavin. 'I'll give you an O.K. for Sandbank.'

'Sandbank?'

'Our P.C. I left him on duty at the spot.'

'Oh, yes. Thanks. All right, then. I'll be back in an hour to report.'

But she was not back in an hour. She made her way quickly to the place on the river bank from which they had first seen Crete. She was aware at once of Police-Constable Sandbank, and went over to him with her written authority from Gavin.

'Very good, miss,' he said, saluting, 'but I don't think you'll find much. I've had a look round myself, but I can't see nothing. It's hard to decide how the poor lady could have come here naked, though. She, or somebody else, may have hidden her clothes away, of course. There's plenty of places to search. But it's queer, to my way of thinking.'

'Yes, it is queer. I'm going across.' She went back to the bridge and crossed it. It was soggy on the opposite bank, but, regardless of mud and water, she searched the ground carefully, exploring the reeds and bushes and squelching hopefully through pasture full of waterlogged hoof-prints.

She came out on to the causeway at last, and explored the banks of the brooks on either side. Nothing could be seen of any clothes, although she went as far as the lasher before she turned back.

'No good going further afield,' thought Laura. 'Nobody could have walked naked all over these fields without being spotted by somebody. What about a raincoat, I wonder? You could easily wear just a raincoat and a pair of shoes. No one would notice that. But what could have been the idea?'

She continued her search, but not even a raincoat could be found. She returned to Police-Constable Sandbank.

'Nothing doing,' she said briefly. 'This means an attempt at murder. Somebody must have brought her and chucked her in. Drugged her first, I should imagine, and the cold water brought her round.'

'Ah, very like,' said the constable. 'Times do change. Times past, we didn't have nothing like this in the city. 'Tis the war, I reckon. Rouses the original in people, war do, so I say.'

Laura considered this opinion.

'One thing, this wasn't a Winchester woman,' she remarked. 'Well, I'd better get back to report. No, I won't! I'll have one more hunt.'

She was bending down poking into reeds when a young voice hailed her from the opposite bank of the river.

'Missus, was you lookin' for the old gentleman's hat?'

'Eh?' said Laura, straightening. Opposite her stood a small boy, another in close attendance. The spokesman held out an object which, in spite of the fact that it had been in the water, she had no difficulty in recognizing as the remains of a white straw panama.

'Yes! Hold on! I'll come round by the bridge!' she shouted. She skirted the stolid policeman and cast at him over her shoulder the tidings that things were moving.

The two boys were standing on the bridge by the time she reached it. She gave them sixpence for the hat and thanked them.

'He'll be looking for that,' she said.

'Not him,' said the youngster who had held it. 'He knowed he dropped it in the water, and he made out to catch it with his stick, but he pretended he couldn't reach it. Us went paddlin' after it, but the water was deep, so us come on out again, and it fetched up in the roots of the old willow tree, so us brought it back, but he'd gone. He run when he seed us coming.'

'Would you know him again?' asked Laura, who had been examining the inside of the hat for traces of an owner's name, but had found none.

'Sure us 'ud know him again,' declared the boy.

Another thought struck Laura, who was fascinated by the story of the hat.

'You said he saw you. Did you speak to him?' she enquired. The youngster shook his head.

'Don't reckon he wanted us to, missus, and he wasn't there when we got back. We seed him running away.'

'Which way did he go from here?'

'Over towards St Cross. Us hollered, but he never took no notice.'

'Well, you'd better give me your names and addresses,' said Laura. 'Then, if he gives the five shillings reward, I'll see that you boys get it. Don't speak to him again. Run like bally rabbits if you see him. He kills little kids like you.'

She hastened towards the hotel with her trophy, the hat, but by the time she had reached College Walk she had been visited by what she considered to be an inspiration. Instead of turning up College Street she continued to follow the river. She walked past the walls of Wolvesey Castle and so to the bridge at the eastern end of the High Street. She then crossed the High Street and was soon walking down the narrow road which led to the offshoot of Winchester where lived the Potters and the Griers.

She stopped the first group of children she met, and asked for Mrs Grier's house. Two of them escorted her to it, and lingered beside her as she knocked on the door.

'All right. That's all, thanks,' said Laura. But her audience had no mind to give up their entertainment, and remained almost within arm's length during the succeeding interview. The door was opened by a grubby little girl of about ten, who was reinforced by an even dirtier child, a boy, a year or two younger.

'Mother in?' Laura enquired. The little girl shook her head.

'Father?'

Another shake of the head.

'Ah,' said Laura, 'then this hat is no good at present, is it?' She was turning away when the younger child began to cry. Laura turned round again, and the little girl, flinching, said anxiously:

'He didn't mean nothing. He didn't like the lady what wore it.'

'What lady?' Laura enquired. 'What was she like?'

But the little girl shut the door. Laura turned to the boys who were standing beside her.

'What does she mean?' she asked.

'Why, the little 'un seen a lady – well, that's what 'e *said* – what took Bobbie Grier away and drownded 'im.'

'He couldn't!' said Laura sharply. The boy was silent. '*Did* he say that?' she demanded. The boy began to whistle a tune. He made a sign to his mate, and the two of them suddenly fled. Laura hesitated. Then she went round to the back of the Grier's house.

The garden was very tiny and was bounded by the river, here very shallow. There was nothing to be seen of the two Grier children. Laura, who had been obliged to walk some distance away from the front door and along the street before she gained the dirty little passage which led to the backs of the houses, had counted the front doors as she passed them, so she knew she had reached the right house.

She stepped over the broken stone wall which separated the garden from a muddy little path beside the river, and walked up to the back door. On this she tapped. She was immediately aware of two small noses pressed against the inside of the kitchen window. She stepped back from the door, smiled at the children and took out a piece of chocolate which she happened to have in her handbag.

Before anything decisive could result from this manœuvre there was the sound of a door being slammed. The children disappeared. Laura disappeared, too, and with considerable celerity, so that by the time the newcomer to the house had encountered the children, the self-invited visitor was out of sight from the back windows.

Doubtful as to the wisdom of her proceedings, but feeling that honour demanded the completion of her programme, Laura returned immediately to the front door and knocked.

This time the door was opened by a woman, the slatternly, unchaste, disreputable Mrs Grier.

'Not to-day, thanks,' said Mrs Grier, 'and you leave my Billy alone! I wonder at you, pesterin' poor children when their mum ain't at 'ome to look after 'em! You 'op it, or I'll call a policeman!'

'I *am* a policeman,' said Laura calmly. She held out the hat. 'And I'm here on official business. What do you know about this?'

It was evident that Mrs Grier was too wary to be caught by so transparent a question. It was equally evident that, where the police were concerned, she had a guilty conscience.

'What I says I says to a uniformed officer,' she replied. ''Ow do I know who you are?'

'Very well,' said Laura. She took out a thin notebook which she used for recording small commissions or memoranda. 'Obstructing the police in the execution of their duty,' she said aloud as she scribbled in the book. 'You'd better come along to the station, then. We thought you'd prefer this, that's all. I didn't come in uniform with good reason.'

'Good reason is you 'aven't got one!' said Mrs Grier with great perspicacity before she slammed the door. She then opened the sitting-room window and shouted out of it, 'Go and tell your — newspaper to —! I'm — sick of — reporters and swine like you!'

Laura departed amid jeers (and a stone or two) from children playing in the street, and walked thoughtfully back to the *Domus*.

'The beginnings of proof against Mr Tidson,' she said, when she met David Gavin and found that Mrs Bradley had arrived and was at Crete's bedside, 'although the little kid thought he was a woman. He *is* a bit effeminate, of course.'

Gavin shook his head, but took the hat.

'Identification by a child of seven or eight isn't good enough when it comes to hanging a man,' he replied. 'We shall need to do better than that. Still, it's a pointer, and gives us something to start from, I'm bound to agree.'

'There is one other point,' said Mrs Bradley, when the matter had been put to her by Laura. 'We do not know for certain that the hat belongs to Mr Tidson. Still, I think you have done very well,' she added, observing that her secretary wore a somewhat crestfallen expression. 'Particularly as I can get nothing out of Crete. Perhaps the hat will help, although I'm not sanguine.'

'She *was* half-drowned, wasn't she?' said Laura.

'There is no doubt of that, child. But she won't say, at present, how she came to be half-drowned.'

'Annoying of her. She could help us a lot, if she liked.'

'She may have some old-fashioned ideas, child.'

'Oh, heavy loyalty to husband, and that sort of tosh,' said Laura scornfully.

'Possibly. I was thinking of self-preservation,' said Mrs Bradley flatly. 'It is one of the primary instincts.'

'In that case, you'd think she'd tell.'

'Do you really think so?' Well, well, time will show. It usually does, if you don't interfere, but are content to sit still and let it pass.'

'Yes, but with that Preece-Harvard boy coming back here to school—'

'True. But events are shaping well, and if there is the slightest chance of getting the hat recognized as Mr Tidson's I am sure your young man will manage it, although, when he does, it won't help him. And now, child, to quiet our minds you and I will visit the Cathedral and gaze upon the remains of Saxon kings. It would be a fascinating and perhaps not impossible task to reassemble the bones correctly,' she added. 'I confess I should like to try.'

'How do you mean, correctly?' Laura enquired.

'Well, the contents of the mortuary chests, which now, as you know, rest on top of the screens of pierced stonework erected by Bishop Fox, were desecrated by Cromwell's soldiers, who, with Puritan frenzy and sadly misdirected zeal, flung the bones of Edred, Edmund, Canute, William Rufus, Emma, Ethelwulf and certain other persons including the Saxon bishops Wina, Alwyn and others, through the stained-glass windows of the Cathedral. The bones were collected and re-housed, but who knows whether correctly? I would give a good deal to be allowed to examine the contents of those chests. However, I don't suppose it will make much difference, in the long run, whether the bones are correctly reassembled or not.'

'I wonder what the odds would be in millions of chances to one that the bones *are* reassembled correctly?' suggested Laura. Discussion of this eminently insoluble exercise in mathematics lasted them until they reached the west front of the Cathedral.

Once inside, Mrs Bradley confined her attention to the mortuary chests, the Early Decorated oak choir stalls and the carved vine of Bishop Langton's chantry chapel. Laura wandered about by herself, chiefly in the north transept, and beside the Chapel of the Holy Sepulchre with its wall-paintings depicting the Passion.

She encountered Mrs Bradley once in the retro-choir, where she found her employer gazing, apparently in abstraction, at the small entrance to the Sanctum Sanctorum and apparently oblivious of her presence. That this was not the case, however, Laura realized as Mrs Bradley addressed her.

'Corpore sanctorum sunt hic in pace sepulto,
Ex meritis quorum fulgent miracula multa.'

quoted Mrs Bradley into her secretary's ear.

'You've been inside!' said Laura. Mrs Bradley, impeccably reverent, did not cackle. She merely nodded confidentially, and fell to a further study of the entrance to the Holy Hole.

'The vault, and not the Feretory, lies within,' she said; and they neither spoke nor met again until they came across one another at Izaak Walton's black marble slab. They left the Cathedral together.

'Well, that has cleared our minds,' said Mrs Bradley. Laura could not agree, but did not say so, and, without more words, they returned to the *Domus* and Crete.

Laura remained downstairs, but Mrs Bradley went up to the bedroom to which Crete had been taken, and, without invitation, drew a chair to the bedside and sat down.

Crete turned her head and looked at her persecutor distastefully. She had recovered as much colour as she usually had, and her greenish hair, now dry, was partly covered by a very charming boudoir cap which gave her the appearance of an exquisite early sixteenth-century portrait.

Her wide, strange eyes were without expression. Her red mouth neither betrayed nor illumined her thoughts. Mrs Bradley produced the panama hat more as one who produces rabbits from toppers than as one who confronts a suspect with Exhibit A, and proffered it for inspection.

'I suppose you recognize this?' she said. Crete smiled.

'Poor Edris! I rated him soundly, the silly old man. He loses his hat when he is fishing, and then goes out very early on the morning that little boy is found dead and brings it back with him. Can you imagine anything so silly? I tell him to lose it again. He does, and the kind English bobbies have found it. Now, I suppose, they will accuse him of murdering the boy. It is incredible, the stupidity of the police!'

'And, in the end, of murderers,' retorted Mrs Bradley. 'Why did you fish with the old boot down by the weir?'

'To amuse the poor children,' said Crete. 'And I do not like to kill fish. I do not like to kill anything. It is just as much fun with a boot. But how do you know about the boot? It was just a game. Why were we spied on? It was a holiday foolishness, that is all.'

Mrs Bradley felt a growing appreciation of this redoubtable foe. She got up.

'By the way,' she said, 'it wasn't you who entered Connie's room and whom I caught on the side of the head with the nailbrush, was it?'

'I entered Connie's room?' exclaimed Crete. 'But why should I do that, please?'

'To pour vitriol into her ear, I imagine. You've had a letter by hand from her since she went to Lewes, haven't you?'

'It is the first time I have heard she is in Lewes.'

'Maybe, but she wrote to you from Lewes, all the same.'

'Yes,' agreed Crete. 'I must not lie. I must not make a denial. But you do not judge jealousy too harshly, I think, do you?'

'I never judge it at all,' said Mrs Bradley. 'When does young Preece-Harvard return to school?'

'Do I know him?'

'By hearsay only, I think. The nephew, you know. Young Arthur.'

'Arthur? Ah, yes, of course. Edris speaks sometimes of Arthur. He is a clever boy, and inherits money, I think.'

'An impeccably-phrased description.'

'Please?'

'Let it go,' said Mrs Bradley, employing a phrase she had learned from Laura Menzies.

'You are intelligent,' said Crete, raising herself from the pillows and giving her tormentor a rare and very sweet smile. 'Sometimes I think devilish. You have sewn me up into a parcel. Isn't that what the English say? Well, I had better come clean. That is an American expression. We had Americans often on Tenerife. I like them because they have energy. I think Connie Carmody tried to ensnare my husband, and, you know, she is younger than I, and Edris is an old man and not quite a good old man sometimes. Therefore I am jealous, and when Edris wishes to learn where Connie has gone, I think I would like to know too. I affect to help him, but really I am helping myself.'

'He put through the telephone call that took me out of my room, and you ransacked my belongings,' said Mrs Bradley. 'Yes, we guessed all that.'

'Then Connie telephoned telling me where to meet her,' Crete went on. 'But it was not Connie. It was a stupid letter, all accusations. A madness.'

'But why should Connie telephone?'

'We advertised. She is a murderer. What do you say about that?'

'I bring murderers to justice,' said Mrs Bradley calmly. 'And sometimes to that travesty of justice, the gallows.'

'You speak in the English way, with humour,' said Crete. 'And the English humour has facets. It is like heaven.'

'Well, the English justice isn't very much like heaven,' said Mrs Bradley, 'although more so, perhaps, than the Greek or the Spanish justice, of which I believe you have some knowledge.'

'I will discuss all three with my husband,' said Crete, 'and meanwhile I would be grateful for his hat.'

'The police will buy him another,' said Mrs Bradley. She walked out, spinning the deplorable wreck of a panama on her hand.

'But how do we get him?' cried Gavin. 'And if she won't say that he pushed her in, we can't do anything about it unless somebody else saw him do it, and that's unlikely. And we can't even call it attempted suicide. Nobody is going to believe that a woman stripped herself naked before trying to drown herself in a respectable river like the Itchen. It doesn't hold water.'

'Crete did, quite a lot,' said Laura, who was listening not particularly sympathetically to this tale of woe. 'What's more, Crete expects to be arrested.'

'How do you know that?' enquired the inspector, looking interested and alert, like a thrush within sight of a worm.

'Just an idea,' said Laura. 'What's more, you'd *better* arrest her,' she added darkly. 'The plot thickens, it seems to me, and, as soon as young Arthur P-H. gets down to Winchester, we shall be pretty near the climax. That's quite certain.'

'I couldn't agree more,' said Gavin. 'But we haven't even

the most superficial circumstantial evidence that any harm
is intended to young Preece-Harvard.'

'Well, you arrest Crete for bathing without a costume,
and see what happens,' said Laura. 'She won't have thought
of that, and it ought to flummox her properly. She wants
to be arrested for attempted suicide, I'd say, and any other
charge will spike her guns.'

'But what about the hat?' demanded Gavin.

'Can't you get one of your experts to tell you how long
it's been in the water? She may be telling the truth about
the hat. If she wanted to accuse her husband of attempted
murder she'd have come across with it, I should think. The
hat is either an accident or a red-herring.'

Gavin chuckled.

'You're an ass,' he said. 'Or are you, perhaps, a genius?'

'Occasionally,' Laura replied. 'And on this occasion definitely not an ass. You think it over, sonny, and get your
hooks on Crete. Then we shall see what we *shall* see.'

'Signs and wonders,' said her swain, 'but nothing that's
any good to a plodding police officer, believe me.'

'All right. What price Mrs Croc. trying to get Crete's
goat, then?'

'Did she?' He looked interested. 'Tell me more.'

'Well, I would if you felt sympathetic, but I'm not here
to waste my sweetness on the desert air.'

'Say on, sweet chuck.'

'All right. From Mrs Croc's account of the interview –
and I will say for the old duck that what she tells you is
gospel and certainly isn't intended to mislead – at least,
not often! – it seems pretty clear that she indicated where
the Tidsons got off. That ought to produce repercussions.
I feel we are on the verge of getting action.'

'Yes,' said Gavin gloomily. 'I feel it, too, and I'm not so
certain I like the idea of it, either. You see the way that
particular cat is likely to jump, I suppose?'

'At Mrs Croc's throat, I suppose you mean. But I think
that's what she intended.'

'Very likely. But, hang it all, she's an old lady and I can't
have her expose herself to such danger. I thought we were

agreed about that. If Tidson and Crete are already responsible for two murders, they are not likely to stick at a third,
particularly if it's a case of shutting somebody's mouth.
They've nothing to lose either way, and they've shut young
Biggin's mouth already, if what we think is true.'

'I know, but there's nothing we can do.'

'Except keep a weather eye lifting. But I don't like it,
Laura. It isn't good enough.'

'That's if we're right about the Tidsons. But, if you
remember, you queried that yourself some weeks ago. And,
after all, what have we to go on? There's Tidson's hat, of
course, but that's a red herring, I think, and, if Crete won't
accuse him, we can't. Besides, he's probably got a water-
tight alibi, anyhow.'

'I know. But we don't want to get him for having a stab
at Crete. We want to get him for those boys.'

'But that's where we're absolutely stuck.'

'Not absolutely, now that child's mentioned the hat. Do
you know what we've got to do? We've got to get Tidson
to the station on some charge or other—'

'American film stuff?'

'Yes, if you like. Spitting on the sidewalk over there;
drunk and disorderly over here.'

'You wouldn't find Mr Tidson drunk and disorderly.
He's far too respectable for that! He wouldn't dream of
getting drunk.'

'I'm afraid not, no.'

'But suppose he did, and the local police pulled him in,
what could you do? He'd only be fined ten bob or something,
wouldn't he?'

'I'd confront him with one or two people – identification parade and all that. They've got a man now at the
station for pestering women. We could line old Tidson up
in the same parade, and see whether any of the witnesses
picked him out; not, of course, for pestering people, but
on any other score. For instance, if only we could show
that he'd ever been anywhere near the Griers' house it might
help us quite a bit.'

'Well, I still say those children I met at the house proved

that, but it's a long shot, isn't it? And a bit unfair, if he's innocent of the murders.'

'I know. But we've got to do something. It's stalemate so far, and I've been down here for several weeks now. My superiors are getting fed up, and an about-to-be-married man can't afford to have his superiors raising their eyebrows because he doesn't get action.'

'I quite agree. All the same—'

'All the same, you don't like a frame-up. Neither do I. On the other hand, I can't have Mrs Bradley getting bashed over the head with a stone, and the body slung into the river. I'm worried, Laura. I feel she's started something which I may not be able to stop.'

'She'll take care of herself,' said Laura. 'And I'll dog her footsteps and so forth. Does it matter if we murder the Tidsons if it stops them murdering us?'

Gavin grinned.

'I shouldn't think so. Ferdinand Lestrange would be called for the defence in that case, I should imagine, and he doesn't very often lose the day. But you be careful. I don't want an idiot wife. Being bashed over the head is apt to produce some effect on the intelligence, you know, and if Tidson were to get busy again with a brickbat—'

'To change the subject,' said Laura, 'don't you think something more could be done from the Bobby Grier end of this business? I believe Mrs Grier is frightened. Couldn't you frighten her a bit more? And those kids who said a man with a panama hat took Bobby away and drowned him – Oh, yes, I *know* the baby one said it was a lady, but that doesn't count for anything.'

Gavin looked dubious.

'I *might* get something,' he agreed, 'but what would it be worth if I did? I can't bring kids into court with a tale like that, and, if I could, I wouldn't want to.'

'Who's asking you to bring them into court? You've only got to get them to recognize Tidson as the man in the panama hat, and then you get on with your proofs. They're bound to be circumstantial, but you can't help that.'

'Not good enough. Haven't you read any witchcraft

trials? Kids will say anything if the idea is put into their heads. And, suppose the kid sticks to his "lady," where is that going to get me?'

'So the hat's no good? And I got all wet and muddy retrieving the beastly thing!'

'I'm not saying the hat's no good. Crete has agreed that it's Tidson's. He'll have to explain how it got there at a time when Crete was half drowned.'

'Which he will like a shot, the same as Crete did. She was much too fly to be caught out over the hat. He'll say it blew off when he was fishing, or else that he took it off, and then, in the excitement of hooking a trout, forgot all about where he'd left it. You'd *have* to believe him. And, if *you* didn't, a jury would. You're right. The hat is a wash-out.'

'I'm going to have a go at him,' said Gavin. 'Drunk and disorderly? I wonder?'

But, as it happened, there was no need for any such charge. Mr Tidson was apprehended, and charged the very next day, for travelling on a train without a ticket.

'There's something damned phony about this,' said Gavin, when he heard of it from the police station; for Mr Tidson had added to his misdeed by striking the ticket collector on the nose. 'What the devil is he up to? He's done this for the purpose, I should guess, and the purpose was *not* to save his railway fare. Something's blowing up. I wonder what?'

'I should say it's blown,' said Laura. 'Crete's told him about her two talks with Mrs Croc. and something about them has scared him. You go and sort him, my lad. This might be a gift from the gods. I wonder what Mrs Croc. has got to say? Oh, and I've got a job to do.'

She picked up an attaché case, opened it, and displayed a transparent light-green waterproof, a wrap-over skirt and a blouse.

'What the hell?' enquired Gavin. Laura grinned and pushed the clothes into the case.

'Three guesses,' she said, 'and you ought to get it first pip.'

'But where did you get them?'

'They're mine, duck. I'm going along to the river to find out how easy it is to sink clothes in some deepish pool. Then I'm going to find exactly where Crete parked hers. That wasn't a suicide attempt. It was some elaborate eyewash. You wait and see what she does next.'

Chapter Twenty

*'He rushed through a long bed of weeds, and
then walloped about distractingly . . .'*
J. W. Hills (*A Summer on the Test*)

CRETE'S next action was somewhat astonishing. Mrs
Bradley remarked that as Arthur Preece-Harvard would
be in Winchester on the morrow, Crete had arranged with
the management of the *Domus* to have a private nurse, or,
rather, two nurses, who would be with her night and day.

'But what's she afraid of?' enquired Gavin. 'It almost
looks as though she's afraid of her husband, after all. Do
you think he *did* push her in? It seems queer if he did,
considering she went prepared to be the nymph, and—'

'No, I don't think he did. And I don't think she's afraid
of him. The nurses will provide her with an alibi, of course,
if young Preece-Harvard comes to any harm in Winchester.
That is partly what the nurses are for, and that, I imagine,
is what the semi-suicide was for. Crete is not going to
involve herself any further in her husband's affairs.'

'But this means she knows an attempt will be made on
the boy, and fairly soon! Who are the nurses? Do you
know?'

'One has been provided by the doctor whom the hotel
called in for Crete, and who usually attends at the *Domus*
if anyone on the staff or among the visitors is suddenly
taken ill, and the other is the sister of Lucy, the chambermaid. This sister is well known to the management, and
has obliged in this way before.'

'I'd better have a look at them, I think, although they
both sound innocent enough. Still, it wouldn't do to take

chances. But, tell me, what do you make of Tidson? I could understand him cheating the railway company, but what about him slugging a ticket collector?'

'I know,' said Mrs Bradley. 'It isn't in character. And what isn't in character is always interesting. Have you interviewed him since he was arrested?'

'No. It's the local beak's job. He's being held on the charge of assault. He paid up the money for the fare, apologized, referred to sudden temptation and said he'd always been honest. I don't suppose the railway company will prosecute, but for the assault he'll get forty shillings or seven days, I should think. It wasn't really a serious case.'

'It's a very curious one. I wonder what Connie Carmody is doing?'

'I don't suppose she's doing anything much. She's with her aunt at the flat in London, isn't she?'

'I'll tell you what,' said Laura to Gavin, a little later on, 'I still say it's a pity we can't prove what was in that letter that was handed to Crete from that car, and I still say it's a pity we don't know a little bit more about that flat on the Great West Road that Connie went to when she fled from the *Domus*.'

'Oh, I don't know. She had nowhere to run to except there or to Miss Carmody's place, and she guessed we should find her if she went back to where she had come from. She knew old Tidson wasn't very likely to turn up, and she couldn't have foreseen that *you* would. The only part of the business that seems suspicious to me is that she had enough sense not to throw the stone into the river, so that the fingerprints and the dog's blood were still on it for us to test. That does look guilty.'

'Yes, it's altogether too clever.'

'I'm going to bounce the secret of that dog-killing out of Connie. It couldn't have been done for revenge. She never even *saw* Tidson with the dog!'

'You'd much better leave her to Mrs Bradley, you know.

You can't possibly hold her for questioning, although I agree she deserves it.'

'Oh, there are ways and means,' said Gavin, easily. 'We can charge her with stealing the dog. I suppose she did steal it, in a way. It will be enough reason for questioning her a bit. We can say that we think the death of the dog may have some bearing on the murders. That won't be untruthful, will it?'

Laura looked doubtful, and said:

'The old lizard told her about the dog, hoping she'd make it a substitute for Tidson, and she did. And I don't believe you could arrest her for stealing it unless Mr Tidson makes a charge, and you know he won't!'

'I don't know anything of the sort!'

'All right, all right. You know your own business best, and I don't need to agree with all you say. To my mind it's a frame-up, and I've said so. Still, if you have to do it, that must be that. I admit that I feel rather sorry for this Connie. She's an under-weather, nervy sort of piece, and I wish you could leave her alone.'

'She's got to come across,' said Gavin briefly. 'We're after a murderer, and a pretty beastly one. Can't spare people's feelings if it means we've got to let him go.'

'I know. But it's beastly, all the same, that the innocent should have their lives spoilt because of nasty old men like Mr Tidson.'

'Talking of Tidson, I wish I knew what he's playing at, to get himself arrested like this. It almost looks as though he has reason to need protection, and, if that's so— Well, I wish I could see through his game.'

It was not at all easy to find out Mr Tidson's game. He was brought up in front of a kindly and puzzled justice of the peace next day, and, having made a bitter little speech to which the bench listened gravely and with great courtesy, he refused to pay a forty-shilling fine. The magistrate, clicking his tongue, was about to proffer the alternative of seven days' imprisonment when an official whispered in his ear. Mr Tidson's fine, it appeared, had already been paid, and Mr Tidson, looking dazed and frightened, was dismissed. He began another speech, but any protest he may have seen fit to make was smothered by the fatherly hand and arm of a gigantic police constable, who removed him almost bodily from the court as the next case came up for hearing.

'Did *you* pay the fine?' enquired Gavin of Mrs Bradley.

'I was about to put the same question to Laura,' she replied. 'We are on the verge of interesting disclosures. The plot thickens to breaking point.'

'I certainly didn't pay it,' said Laura. 'I should think Crete must have sent the money. She'd hardly want her husband in jug.'

Enquiry, set on foot by Gavin, proved that the philanthropist who had paid the two pounds was a young lady. The description, which followed, of her size, appearance and apparent age, certainly would not fit Crete but might have fitted Connie Carmody.

Gavin immediately telephoned to Miss Carmody, and discovered, as he had expected, that Connie was no longer in the flat. Her bed had not been used, and her aunt could not account for her disappearance.

'Well, that beats everything,' said Gavin. 'I suppose she had better be found at once. And now, what about this Tidson?'

'He has gone to see Crete, at the *Domus*,' Mrs Bradley replied. 'Let us both go to see him.'

Mr Tidson, Mrs Bradley was interested to discover, was in a remarkable state of terror. He could not answer any questions. He merely begged them to save him, but omitted to mention from what.

Gavin commented on this.

'That chap,' he said confidentially, 'will cut his own throat before we hang him if we're not mighty careful. What do *you* think?'

'As you do,' Mrs Bradley responded. 'Nevertheless, I am inclined to leave him to his fate.'

'Yes, but why should suicide *be* his fate? What's he been up to? How do you account for the wind-up?'

'Well, I doubt if it means a guilty conscience. I don't believe Mr Tidson is troubled by conscience at all. No, I think we are watching the unfolding of an interesting logical sequence of events.'

'But where the devil is Connie?'

'Here in Winchester, I imagine, lying in wait for the unfortunate Mr Tidson, instead of (as he had hoped and planned) for her half-brother, Arthur Preece-Harvard. I let the boy come back to school here because I knew he was not in danger from Connie, and Mr Tidson, who has such a powerful motive for putting him out of the way, will never dare to touch him while we're here. It is a situation I shall watch with peculiar relish.'

'What are you getting at?' asked Gavin. Mrs Bradley cackled.

'Once upon a time,' she said, 'there was a man who incited another man to murder their mutual enemy. But the second man, victim of the fearful poison engendered by the promptings of the first, killed, not his enemy, but the man who had slain his conscience. What do you think about that?'

'I see the point of it,' Gavin answered. 'You believe he's been inciting Connie Carmody to kill young Preece-Harvard, and has spent his time in Winchester demonstrating to her how easy it is to commit a murder without being found out.'

'Well,' said Mrs Bradley, careful not to express agreement with this, 'I don't know about that. No doubt it would suit Mr Tidson very nicely if Connie (or anyone else) would put Arthur out of the way and leave him to inherit the money. But, of course, he made a mistake if he supposed that Connie entertained feelings of hatred for the boy. Connie, in point of fact, adores him, as she has done from their earliest years.'

'Then why in the name of goodness hasn't she given old Tidson away to us weeks ago? If she'd spilt the beans we could have acted upon her information.'

'Connie, you must remember, is not only young; she is unversed in the ways of the world. She did not think we should believe her. She distrusts people – who can blame her? The world has not treated her too well. Besides, she is intelligent enough to realize that we could scarcely interfere with Mr Tidson's plans until something more than she could tell us was proved against him.

'In other ways she is not a clever girl, and she is also remarkably obstinate. It was not easy to persuade her that her best course was to go away from Winchester for a bit, and she would not have consented (even although she was terrified of Mr Tidson) if Arthur had not been safely tucked away in Bournemouth. I knew she would return to Winchester as soon as the College re-opened after the summer, and I have no doubt that she is here, that she paid Mr Tidson's fine, and has turned the tables on him by making him fear her as much as – in fact, a good deal more than – at one point she feared him.'

'Do you think she led Tidson up the garden, then, and allowed him to believe that she *would* kill Preece-Harvard when the time came?'

'I don't know. She was evidently horrified by him, not only because of his motive for having Arthur murdered, but sexually, of course, as well. I don't think a young man like yourself can begin to fathom the depths of that kind of horror, which is far more than merely physical. She probably allowed him to think that she would act in accordance with his suggestions.'

'Both kinds? Ah, I begin to see daylight. I suppose that accounts for the visit of the "ghost", after which she insisted on changing rooms with you.'

'The "nun" was undoubtedly Mr Tidson.'

'Oh, yes, the apparition that squeaked. Always a very phony story.'

'And it accounts, too, for the visitant at whom I hurled the nailbrush. That was undoubtedly Miss Carmody, who came to find out what was going on.'

'Then why the black eyes of the others?'

'Thereby, I fancy, hangs a tale. Anyhow, that ludicrous situation spiked poor Miss Carmody's guns, as Mr Tidson knew it would. An elderly maiden lady cannot afford to look ridiculous if she values her self-respect. I saved her by taking her off to Bournemouth for the day.'

'Not knowing that the Preece-Harvards were there?'

'Not knowing at that time that the Preece-Harvards were there. It must have given Mr Tidson a shock when he knew where we had been, for I have little doubt he knew where Arthur was.'

'What about that flat on the Great West Road? An address of convenience, no doubt?'

'Yes. The letter about the naiad came from there, and Connie had a key which Mr Tidson may or may not have given her at some time.'

Laura groaned.

'Yes,' said Mrs Bradley, 'quite a horrid person, Mr Tidson, and Connie is—'

'Connie must be a dope,' said Laura roundly. 'The thing is, we ought to find her before she can do Mr Tidson any harm.'

'I'd leave him to it,' said Gavin. 'The wicked old villain!'

'For murdering the boys, hoping that Connie would kill Arthur, or for trying to seduce Connie?' Mrs Bradley ironically enquired.

'The last, of course,' Gavin vigorously and honestly replied. Mrs Bradley and Laura laughed, and the latter observed, as she tucked her strong arm into his and affectionately dug her elbow into his side:

'Spoken like a man and a mutt!'

'Yes, well now,' said Gavin, 'after all that, what about him?'

'I think,' said Mrs Bradley, 'that our best plan might be to await him. He's bound to turn up.'

The person, to everyone's surprise, who turned up first, was young Preece-Harvard. They found him at tea with Crete, with whom he seemed to get on very well. The surprise was partly on Crete's side. It was evident she had not realized that Mrs Bradley already knew the boy. She recovered at once, and said quickly:

'I was very anxious to meet him. We are related, as you know, by marriage.'

Arthur gave his own explanation, which coincided with hers.

'I had leave,' he said, smiling at Crete, 'as Mrs Tidson is my aunt and is going back to Tenerife so soon. I have to be back for chapel, of course. I am disappointed not to see Uncle Edris.'

'Oh, he will be back before you go,' said Crete, with a half-glance at Mrs Bradley. 'He had to visit your Aunt Priscilla in London. I expect him at any moment now.'

But Arthur was obliged to leave without meeting his uncle and heir.

'It is sad,' said Crete, accompanying him to the outer door of the hotel. 'He has missed his train. It is like him. If you met him you would perhaps know him. You must say prayers for me, please, to your saint. You are quite the nicest boy. You must come to Tenerife and stay with me. I shall have a new playfellow for you, and one you will like.'

'A Spaniard?' exclaimed Mrs Bradley. Crete smiled and pressed Arthur's arm into which she had slipped her own.

'Arthur knows that I jest and make fun for him,' she said; but when she had waved farewell to the boy and he had gone striding off down the narrow street with his black gown flying and his long grey-flannelled legs making it look even shorter than it was, she turned to Mrs Bradley and said:

'I think poor Edris is in danger.'

'I think he is,' Mrs Bradley agreed. 'But it's of no use to ask me to help him out of it. I don't even know what help he needs.'

'Nor I. He is with poor Prissie.'

'Is he? I did not know that. He is very lucky not to be in prison.'

'He sent me a telegram.' She produced it. Mrs Bradley took it, seated herself on an oak settle which was against the vestibule wall, and read the telegram.

'In London join you soon,' Mr Tidson had written for transmission.

'He comes this evening, no doubt,' said Crete.

But at ten o'clock that night there was still no sign of Mr Tidson. Crete, shrugging, gave him up and announced her intention of going to bed. At half-past ten Thomas came into the lounge to tell Mrs Bradley that she was wanted on the telephone. It was Gavin.

'So you're still up and about?' he said.

'Yes. The vultures gather,' said Mrs Bradley, cackling mirthlessly into the receiver.

'Is Tidson there?'

'No.'

'Expected?'

'I gather that he is.'

'Crete Tidson isn't with you, is she?'

'She is at the hotel, but she has gone to bed.'

'She has quite recovered, I take it?'

'It seems so.'

'Well, look, I've got a clue to the murder of that second boy. Can't tell you over the telephone. When can I meet you to-morrow?'

'As early as you like.'

'At half-past ten, then. I'll come to the smoke-room and wait there until you turn up. I think we've got him cold. To-morrow, then. Good-night.'

As it happened, this appointment did not materialize at that place and time. Mrs Bradley woke early on a beautiful morning, rose at six, and by seven was walking between the lime trees towards the west front of the Cathedral.

From the riverside path Saint Catherine's Hill showed a long slope interrupted only by the dark shadow of the fosse, which made a sudden sharp dip in the smoothly-flowing contours of the turf. The grove of trees on the summit of the hill looked almost black. The greenish willows along the edges of the river, and marking its brooks and carriers, leaned, heavily foliaged, towards the swift, clear water; and the sedges showed the traces of yellowing autumn.

The air was clear and fairly cold, so that Mrs Bradley, walking, not fast, but faster than she had at first intended to do, did not see Mr Tidson until she was coming back towards the city. Feeling considerably warmer by the time

she had walked up and over the hill, and had come opposite the wooden bridge, she turned and walked up the path
to stand on the bridge and gaze at the water flowing so
deeply below her.

It was then that she saw Mr Tidson. He was lying on
his back with his head on a rolled-up coat. A cowman
stood beside him as though on guard.

'The young lady tried to save him,' said the cowman. 'I
come up as soon as I could, but too late to give her any
help. Her couldn't do nothen for the poor old gentleman,
her said. Her weren't too strong a swimmer, and, in the
end, her had to letten him go. Hers gone off now to get
help. I offered to go, but her wouldn't have none of that,
and seeing how wet she was, I thought maybe the run ud
do her good. I'm afeared there's nothing ee can do, mum.
Us pump-'andled him all us knew. He's gone, I be afraid.
Got his legs all tangled in the weeds, I reckon. Wasn't no
help for him at all. The young lady said she got there too
late to do him any good.'

Mrs Bradley thought it extremely unlikely that the weeds
which she could see in the river were of the kind to twine
round Mr Tidson's legs and drown him, but she did not
say so to the cowman. She knelt beside Mr Tidson, gripped
his nose with a steel thumb and finger, and pressed her
other hand over his mouth.

This unorthodox treatment had on the corpse a most
extraordinary effect. Mr Tidson began to writhe and
struggle.

'Ah,' said Mrs Bradley, in brisk congratulation, 'that's
much better.' She helped Mr Tidson to his feet and regarded
him thoughtfully. 'How wet you are! You had better run
home and change.'

'Well!' said the cowherd admiringly. 'If ever I see the
beat of that there! You'd be a doctor, no doubt, mum?'

'Yes, of course,' agreed Mrs Bradley, gazing benignly
after the rapidly retreating form of Mr Tidson.

'And that ud be the new-fangled treatment, no doubt?'

'Well, the old-fangled treatment, I think,' said Mrs
Bradley. 'Which way did the young lady take?'

'Same as the drownded gentleman, mum. That way. I feel as if I'd seed a meracle.'

'I think perhaps you have,' said Mrs Bradley. She turned and, picking up her skirts, went hastily after Mr Tidson.

Mr Tidson, on the unimpeachable evidence of Thomas, had not returned to the *Domus*. Mrs Bradley rang up Gavin and asked him to meet her without delay under Kings Gate.

'This is where we practise a little mild deception,' she said. 'Your part is to back me up by saying little and wearing a look of deep concern.' She then explained what had happened, and, as she talked, she hurried him along to the *Domus*.

'Well, that finishes the naiad, I presume,' he said, grinning broadly when he had heard all. 'Mrs Tidson will have to be told. Can I leave you to break the news?'

'I shall be glad to do so,' Mrs Bradley replied. 'We must find out first, though, how much she knows already.'

Crete appeared to know nothing. She took the news very calmly.

'So the naiad embraces him at last,' she said, smiling slightly and focusing her large, dark eyes on the window. 'Ah, well, it could be expected, I suppose.' She evidently took it for granted that Mr Tidson was dead, although Mrs Bradley had not said as much.

'Why did he kill those two boys?' asked Mrs Bradley.

'It was experimental, like atom bombs,' said Crete, with a sidelong glance at her and a very slight shrug. 'He wished to show that it could be done. It is dangerous, that mood. But he proved his point. One needs to take pains, that is all.'

'Yes,' said Mrs Bradley. 'One needs to take pains. And what do you think happened to-day?'

'Oh, I think there was a fight with the nephew, perhaps,' answered Crete. 'Or maybe he just tumbled in. Or maybe Connie Carmody killed him. She did not like us. We were displacing her with her aunt. There was jealousy there, do you think?'

'It would be interesting to know,' said Mrs Bradley, even

more interested in Crete's attitude towards Mr Tidson's mishap than in the actual occurrence itself, which, from the cowman's account of the matter, she had little doubt had been brought about by Connie. 'I feel you need more sunshine and less criticism than we have here,' she went on. 'How would you like to return to Tenerife as soon as the inquest is over?'

'I must get my fare from Prissie,' said Crete in cool, business-like tones. 'She will like to get rid of me, no doubt.'

Mrs Bradley agreed with this estimate of Miss Carmody's probable reactions, but did not say so. She merely observed in an offhand way and with her snake-like grin:

'Will you need to borrow your husband's fare, too?'

'Oh, Edris!' said Crete with something very like contempt in her tone. 'He must be buried in England. Here in the city, no doubt. I could not support him on a ship. Suppose perhaps someone should fall in love with me on the vessel? With one's husband dead in the baggage room—'

'Well, one's husband is not dead yet,' said Mrs Bradley. Crete looked at her enquiringly.

'It is a joke?' she asked.

'Oh, no. He was not quite dead when I found him,' said Mrs Bradley. Crete, after taking a minute at least to absorb these obviously unwelcome tidings, took them philosophically, much to Mrs Bradley's appreciative admiration.

'Drowning was too good for him,' she remarked. 'What has been done with him now?'

'He fled from the scene of the *contretemps*, and is now at large. I hardly anticipated that he would return to the *Domus*,' replied Mrs Bradley. 'I expect, though, that Detective-Inspector Gavin will want to find him.'

'For the murders? I am afraid I have given him away. Do you think so? No matter. I take back everything I said, and I will not make any statements.'

'They would be valueless,' said Mrs Bradley calmly. 'The evidence of a wife will not be sought for.'

'So?' Crete smiled. 'Then I think I ask Thomas for champagne. You will pay for me for a bottle and we shall share it?'

'Very well,' Mrs Bradley agreed. Laura came in whilst they were talking. She gave them a glance, caught Mrs Bradley's eye, and went out again, to find Gavin in the hotel vestibule. She buttonholed him at once.

'So it's up to you to look for proof,' said she. 'I rather hope you'll find it.'

'Proof of what?'

'Of the fact that Connie Carmody tried to murder this Tidson.'

'We can't possibly prove it. According to Mrs Bradley the only witness was the cowherd, and *he* was quite certain that Connie did her best to rescue the fellow. There isn't any doubt about that. Besides, you'll find that Tidson won't accuse her.'

'How do you mean – won't accuse her? I'd have thought, for his own safety, that he would.'

'If he does, he will have to explain why she should want to murder him. Still, that might not fickle a downy old bird like Tidson.'

'I don't think he'd risk telling lies, in case Connie should tell the truth about Arthur Preece-Harvard.'

'But there *isn't* any truth about Arthur.'

'So far, no. But if you think Tidson's guns are spiked, you've got another thought coming. He doesn't want to kill the kid himself, but he means to have the fortune, I should say.'

'Guesswork, my sweet. Don't be feminine.'

'I hardly ever am,' returned the Amazonian Laura. 'And that's why I'll make a far better grandmother than wife. Anyhow, I don't see why you want to worry this Connie. Haven't *you* ever said you wanted to murder someone?'

'Rather a lot of difference between saying it and trying to do it, don't you think?'

'Not according to Scripture,' said Laura, 'and, in any case, it's only an academic difference, isn't it? It simply means you haven't got the pluck.'

'I can't allow that. The difference between committing a murder and not committing one is fundamental,' argued Gavin. 'And as for Scripture – well, never mind about that.

You've got something to tell me about Crete's clothes, haven't you?'

'Oh, yes, I got them all right. They were weighted with stones, all small ones.'

'In the river?'

'Yes. I can show you the place.'

—————Chapter Twenty-One—————

*'. . . but I had gained a little sense, dropped my
point, pulled off line and finally hand-lined him
out.'*

J. W. Hills (*A Summer on the Test*)

'OH, YES, your clue,' said Mrs Bradley.

'Well,' said Gavin, 'it's a button off the boy Biggin's shirt.'

'Found where?'

'Do you remember telling Laura about that walk you took with Tidson when you climbed Saint Catherine's Hill?'

'I remember, yes.'

'And how, when you went with Connie, you found what looked like a tramp's lair?'

'Yes.'

'The police, of course, have combed the whole neighbourhood very thoroughly indeed, and among the rubbish at the bottom of that hole they discovered this button which, we can say with certainty, came off Biggin's clothing and has his prints on it. It's really a trouser button, and has taken an identifiable impression of part of the boy's left thumb. And there are other things.'

'Including, of course, one sandal, and a pair of badly-stained gloves,' said Mrs Bradley.

'And another sandal has been seen in Tidson's possession,' said Gavin, looking reproachfully at her. 'Unfortunately, I should not think it can any longer exist. I do wish you'd mentioned it earlier in the enquiry.'

'I should have misled you,' said Mrs Bradley. 'And it was a very well-worn sandal Mr Tidson lodged on the municipal dustcart on the morning after the death of Bobby Grier. I doubt—'

'Yes, well, we must get that sandal,' said Gavin, interrupting her. 'It's got to be found. That and the button should hang Tidson if the sandals match up, as they will. Besides, there are those gloves—'

'The gloves are indeed a master touch, and have been very carefully planted,' said Mrs Bradley. 'As to the sandal, I don't know what you could prove from it. Mr Tidson is not likely to dispute that it was at one time in his possession, since several people actually saw him with it.'

'Yes, that's true,' agreed Gavin.

'Very queer, though, about that sandal,' observed Laura. 'I can't see why he should have brought it with him to the *Domus*. Isn't that a very odd thing?'

'Not particularly odd. It is the sort of thing people do subconsciously,' said Mrs Bradley.

'He made no mystery of it, certainly.'

'Well, of course, we have to remember that it had not been the property of Bobby Grier, and it was Bobby's death which, at that time, and for some time afterwards, occupied our attention.'

'True enough. We didn't know about Biggin then.'

'I do hope you will find the other sandal, if you think it can possibly help you.'

'We shall find it all right, if the municipal authorities have done their job patriotically.'

'Salvage?'

'Yes. I suppose the sandal was made of leather? Of course, he'll be able to explain away the fingerprints, if he made any, but—'

'Oh!' said Laura, who was standing beside him.

'Say on,' said Gavin. 'Or shall I say it for you? If there are *no* prints, *that's* what he'll have to explain, as he says he found the sandal along the river! He wouldn't have had gloves on then!'

'He'll deny that it is the same sandal,' said Laura, 'even though the two make a pair.'

'I know,' said Gavin grimly. 'But I'll break him in halves

if he doesn't come across with what he knows. 'I'm sick of old Tidson. He cumbers the ground. By the way, I thought we'd better play safe where the Preece-Harvard kid was concerned, so I've warned the College authorities.'

'Good heavens! What did they say?' enquired Laura. 'Did they believe you? Didn't they throw you out?'

'No. I saw the Second Master. He listened to the whole thing very patiently, quoted Gilbert Chesterton, reminded me of the College rebellion of 1818, and sent me along to Preece-Harvard's house-master.'

'What did he quote from Chesterton?'

'*The Napoleon of Notting Hill.* It was after I had told him about the naiad. He said, "Yesterday I thought that something next door to a really entertaining miracle might happen to me before I went to amuse the worms." And then he went on to tell me that he had been a student of crime for many years, and had once been guest of the Detection Club. I said I liked Roger Sheringham and Nigel Strangeways much the best of all amateur detectives, and that I wished Father Ronald Knox had written more detective stories. I also invited him to visit our Rogues' Gallery whenever he was in Town. Anyway, they won't let Preece-Harvard out of their sight, although nothing will be said to him about it, so that's a job taken out of our hands.'

'That's that, but what are we going to do about Connie?' asked Laura. 'As I see it, she's the next problem.'

'We've nothing to charge her with, Laura. We don't know officially (and we never shall) that she tried her best to make away with Tidson,' Gavin replied. 'But now to waylay the little man.'

Mr Tidson laughed at the story of the sandal, and said that he had picked it out of the water and had brought it home to tease his wife and Miss Carmody about the naiad. He was plausible, sceptical, non-committal and, when pressed very hard, challenging.

'I don't know why you should think I had anything to

do with these murders,' he protested. 'What could I gain from them? You cannot show that I ever met the two boys. The whole accusation is ridiculous! It is *quite* ridiculous, and you know it!'

'As ridiculous as the naiad, no doubt,' said Gavin. 'You come with me, and I will show you where we found the other sandal.'

'I have no idea why you think the other sandal would interest me in the slightest, my dear Inspector,' said Mr Tidson, waving his hands. 'The sandal I placed on the refuse cart made one of a pair, I have no doubt, but of what pair it would not be easy to say.'

'The gloves make a pair, too,' said Gavin. 'I hope to prove that the pair is yours.'

'Gloves?' said Mr Tidson. He seemed about to say more, but changed his mind.

'Well, be seeing you,' said Gavin, with a cheerfulness he did not feel. 'Give my regards to the naiad.'

'One moment, Inspector,' said Mr Tidson. 'There is one thing I ought to tell you. I admit that the naiad has been a considerable disappointment to me, so I propose to acquire a wireless set and listen to Cathedral choirs as an alternative.'

'No more fishing with old boots?' said Gavin, suspicious of this cheerful attitude.

'I shall not go fishing any more. I am convinced that I shall never see my naiad. Moreover, I am afraid of Connie Carmody. You know, you should question her closely,' said Mr Tidson. 'She did her very best to drown me. She is a very strange girl. I think she is a schizophrenic. She probably killed those poor boys during one of her attacks. Split personality, you know.'

'You old devil!' said Gavin suddenly and with loathing. Mr Tidson looked mildly surprised.

'I am only giving her the benefit of the doubt,' he said, smiling a little. 'She may not be a schizophrenic at all. She may be a werwolf or a vampire, for all I know.'

* * *

The municipal authorities found the sandal that Gavin wanted. It took some time, and the winter had begun to creep across the meadows, the willows were naked whips in the sudden gales, and the river leapt white and full between blackened banks before the case against Mr Tidson was resumed.

Mr Tidson had gone into lodgings. He declared that he dared not stay in the house with Connie. Crete, he observed horrified at the prospect of winter in England, had returned to Tenerife.

Gavin arrived at just after three on a grey and muddy afternoon in early October, and found Mr Tidson alone. Mr Tidson welcomed him, invited him in, and told him that the landlady had gone to the cinema for the afternoon, and that he hoped she would bring him home a kipper or a bloater for his tea.

'You won't need either,' said Gavin. 'You're coming with me. I've a few questions to ask you.'

'Oh?' said Mr Tidson. He went over to his wireless set, and, in the middle of twiddling with knobs, he put his plump hand to his mouth and began to cough.

'Look out, sir!' said the sergeant. 'I think he's swallowing something!'

'Here, you! Spit it out!' shouted Gavin. He and the sergeant leapt upon Mr Tidson like a couple of tomcats on a rabbit. Mr Tidson opened his mouth.

'All gone!' he said, with a childish little giggle of glee. 'It was only a cough sweet, Inspector.'

'Now, look here, Tidson,' said Gavin. A voice from the wireless receiving set interrupted him. There came the announcement of Choral Evensong. The inspector strode across to it to switch it off.

'Oh, you can't be in all that hurry,' said Mr Tidson. 'Do leave it on, my dear Inspector! They are going to do Wesley in E.'

'And now for the truth,' said Mrs Bradley. Mr Tidson looked at her appraisingly.

'You wouldn't believe it,' he said.

'We might,' said Gavin aggressively. Mr Tidson shook his head.

'Nonsense, my dear Inspector,' he said. 'You do not want the truth. You want to find me guilty.'

'Same thing,' said Gavin. Mr Tidson smiled.

'By no means, Inspector,' he said, 'as Mrs Bradley realizes, even if you do not.'

'Go ahead,' said Gavin. 'And keep it short.'

'Well,' said Mr Tidson, 'I came here to look for my naiad. There seemed no reason at all why I should not see her. Besides—' He paused.

'Perhaps,' said Mrs Bradley, 'it falls to me to explain. Correct me, Mr Tidson, if I go wrong.'

'Ah,' said Mr Tidson, in great relief. 'I place myself in your hands with the greatest confidence. At one point I thought you had failed, but I know now that I misjudged you. I should have retained faith, for, without faith, works, as the Scriptures point out, are redundant and dangerous.'

'What Scripture points out,' began Gavin, 'is—'

'Spare me the Biblical knowledge and the spiritual pride of Scotsmen,' said Mr Tidson, raising a small, plump hand. 'Mrs Bradley is about to tell you a bedtime story. Pray silence, Mr Policeman, for the grandmother whom you have been teaching to suck eggs.'

'Mr Tidson,' said Mrs Bradley, speaking mildly, although there was an expression on her face and in her birdlike, unmerciful eye which boded Mr Tidson no good, 'you are waspish. You must forgive him, my dear David,' she added, turning to Gavin. 'You see, since he decided to look for his naiad in Winchester, young men of about your age have twice tried to teach him to mind his own business.'

'You dare!' shouted Mr Tidson, half rising from his chair. Gavin put out a large hand and pushed him back.

'Three's your unlucky number,' he remarked. 'Remain sensible, seated and civil, little man, or I might forget myself.'

'*Parlez doucement, lentement et en français,*' said Mrs Bradley appreciatively. 'The first young man pushed him into the river. That must have been along the slightly gloomy railway walk from the road bridge towards the old weir, where the water is shallow and stony. That accounts for his coming back wet through, and it accounts for his abrasions. You remember?'

'But—' said Gavin, surprised.

'Yes, I am sure there is some young fellow somewhere – and a girl as well, of course – who can testify that this happened on the night of Bobby Grier's death,' Mrs Bradley continued.

'What is this insect, then – a Peeping Tom?' asked Gavin, in deep disgust.

'Very aptly expressed,' said Mrs Bradley, regarding Mr Tidson with benevolent interest. 'His nymphs are many and varied. Another swain at a later date punched him in the eye. He bore the mark of it next morning.'

'Ah, the soap and the nailbrush,' said Gavin. 'But—'

'Mr Tidson was so much annoyed by that particular incident,' went on Mrs Bradley, 'that he even struck his wife, providing her with an injury equal to, and similar to, his own. I don't wonder she does not like you very much,' she continued, turning to the unfortunate Mr Tidson.

'I've spent all my money on her,' he said, with a frightened look. Mrs Bradley nodded.

'So much so,' she said, 'that you've been suspected of having designs on the life of young Arthur Preece-Harvard so that you could inherit his estate.'

Mr Tidson's expression of fright and concern deepened.

'But I don't even know what the boy looks like!' he protested. 'I should not recognize him if I saw him!'

'Mrs Tidson knows him,' said Gavin drily.

'Whether Mr Tidson knows him or not, or has designs on him or not, does not affect our enquiry,' said Mrs Bradley.

'Tidson has no alibi, then, for the death of Bobby Grier, but that doesn't necessarily connect him with the death of young Biggin,' said Gavin, frowning. 'Well, that brings us back to Connie Carmody.'

'Whose motive, as she has informed me several times, was to get me hanged,' said Mr Tidson, plucking up heart and looking a great deal more cheerful.

'And not such a bad idea at that,' said Gavin unkindly. 'However, we're interrupting Mrs Bradley.'

'Connie was the tenant of that flat on the Great West Road,' said Mrs Bradley. 'I knew that she must be. For one thing, we were told that the tenant was a woman. Besides, I knew that Connie would never have risked going there if she had thought there was the slightest chance of running into Mr Tidson.'

'But what about the rent?' asked Gavin.

'Ask Miss Carmody. Connie had a hundred a year of her own from the late Mr Preece-Harvard's private fortune, and her aunt, you will discover, supplemented that. Connie's rather ungracious remarks about charity told me the truth. She did not regard her hundred a year as charity, and there was no earthly reason why she should. Where you went wrong, you know, Mr Tidson,' she added, turning towards the little man, 'was in letting her know that Mr Preece-Harvard was her father. That was very unkind, I thought. Naturally prone to brood and to feel ill-used, those tidings had the worst effect upon Connie. They also brought to her notice the full implication of what it would mean to you if Arthur Preece-Harvard should die. She began to see you as a double enemy – for you are right in supposing that Connie intended you mischief. She saw you first as an interloper, a nuisance and an expense to her aunt. It also became obvious to her that the flat on the Great West Road (which she had so very recently rented) would have to be given up, and, with it, every thought of her independence, if you persisted in living on Miss Carmody's money.'

'I thought Connie did not show Prissie sufficient gratitude, and that was why I told her about her father,' protested Mr Tidson.

'Well, be that as it may, Connie disliked you very much. Her first act of revenge and antagonism was designed to make you look foolish. She wrote the letter to the paper about the naiad. She selected a neighbourhood of which she had some knowledge (she had accompanied her aunt to Winchester during the season of air raids) and it soon became a matter of interesting conjecture whether a stranger (yourself, say) or only someone well acquainted with the neighbourhood, could have staged the two murders so successfully.'

'Now I know it was Connie Carmody,' said Gavin, with an innocent look, 'I can't see why I ever thought it was you, Tidson. Her character, her temperament, that one brick we found with the blood and the fingerprints on it—'

'Yes, she was clever in a way about that,' said Mr Tidson. 'In fact, she was very clever indeed to risk leaving it with *my* dog's blood and *her* prints. I suppose she had washed off the original human blood in the river.'

'That is certainly an idea,' said Mrs Bradley. 'And when one comes to think, she was very slow to enter that grove of trees the day she and I took a walk to the top of Saint Catherine's Hill.'

'You remember that I mentioned repressed spinsters,' said Mr Tidson.

'I do remember. You meant me to think you were referring to Miss Carmody, but, as I realize now, you were really giving me a pointer to Connie,' Mrs Bradley agreed. Mr Tidson began to preen himself a little.

'Well, I knew *I* hadn't killed anyone,' he said. 'And if it *had* to be one of our party, naturally I fastened on Connie. She was out that night alone—'

'Oh, yes! She left her aunt at the west front of the Cathedral and went off by herself, did she not? Of course,' Mrs Bradley added, eyeing Mr Tidson with that expression of kindly curiosity to which she had subjected him before, 'she is so much stronger than you are that I *did* wonder whether you would have been able to transport Biggin's body from the top of the hill to the weir.'

'Oh, I am not so puny!' said Mr Tidson shortly. 'Besides, I could have rolled it down the slope.'

'When did you come across it, by the way?' asked Mrs Bradley?'

'Why, when I was searching for my dog,' replied Mr Tidson. 'I found it in the bushes with the dead animal, and I thought our friend the inspector ought to know what had happened. I therefore pushed it out where I knew it would immediately be seen. I suppose I ought to have reported it, but I thought – well, no doubt even the inspector, prejudiced as he is against me, can understand the feelings of an uncle.'

'Even a wicked uncle, eh?' said Gavin, scowling at the toes of his boots. Mr Tidson sniggered.

'I do like a good loser, Inspector,' he remarked.

'Yes, indeed,' said Mrs Bradley. 'But, since the dog is going to figure largely in the enquiry, it would be interesting to know how you recognized it as your dog. It was in a sorry state when Laura Menzies found it.'

'The dog? Oh, I recognized it by the collar, of course,' said Mr Tidson eagerly. 'That was how I came to connect poor Connie with the second murder. I never thought there was any doubt about the first one.'

'Got an answer to everything, haven't you?' said Gavin, still with his eyes on his boots. Mr Tidson giggled happily.

'And where is this collar now?' Mrs Bradley enquired.

'Ask the inspector,' Mr Tidson replied. 'I have no doubt he has it in safe keeping.'

'You, too, I hope,' said Gavin, touching the bell on his desk. 'Ah, come in, Sergeant. Edris Tidson, I arrest you for the wilful murders of Robert Grier and John Biggin, and it is my duty to warn you that anything you say will be taken down in writing and may be used in evidence.'

'But why, why, *why?*' screamed Mr Tidson. 'I tell you – I tell you—!'

'There, there, sir. Best take it easy,' said the sergeant.

'I want to know *why!*' yelled Mr Tidson.

'In a word, you gave yourself away over the dog-collar,' said Gavin. 'In fact, you've given yourself away over the dog altogether. Mrs Bradley and I have been playing ball, and you've dropped neatly into a trap. – Got his statements down, Sergeant? – You couldn't have seen the body when you were looking for your dog. It had been discovered before you even bought your dog. That's one thing. Then, that sandal you brought to the hotel. Your having retained possession of it was inadvertent; your disposal of it was masterly; but you forgot that if you had really picked it up in all innocence it would have had your fingerprints on it, didn't you? Even *you* do not keep your gloves on when you go fishing!'

'But my fingerprints *are* on it! Of course they're on it!' shrieked Mr Tidson, struggling ineffectually with the sergeant.

'It was Connie who faked all the evidence, of course,' said Mrs Bradley, 'just as it was Connie who wrote the truth to Crete Tidson from Lewes.'

'But it was Tidson who attempted to murder Crete when she taxed him with his crimes! We found the forked branch, you remember, with which he had held her down,' said Gavin, nodding.

'That is what we were meant to find. She got nurses to guard her night and day until she felt fully recovered. I agree about that,' said Mrs Bradley. Laura noted and digested this reply.

'But why didn't we see him?' she asked. 'We looked, you know, didn't we, David?'

'The reeds made sufficient cover for a fisherman, I expect,' said Gavin. 'I know they would for me, and it would not have taken him more than a minute to wriggle away from us there.'

'And did he really kill little Grier because the kid had seen someone push him into the river?' demanded Laura.

'It scarcely seems credible, does it?' said Mrs Bradley. 'But injured vanity is an imponderable factor, and Mr Tidson's vanity had been very sadly injured.'

'Do you think he would ever have harmed Arthur Preece-Harvard?'

'Well, if he had, I'm afraid he would have been suspect at once, unless he could have made it look as though Connie had done it out of jealousy or revenge.'

'Well, I wouldn't put anything past him. One thing puzzles me more than the murders, though, really. Did he truly believe in his nymph?' demanded Gavin.

'Yes, I'd like to know that,' said Laura.

'Who can say? Your thought on that matter is just as good as mine. Look around you. What do you see?' said Mrs Bradley.

Laura obeyed the command, but did not answer the question. Instead she said to Gavin:

'When did *you* know he had done it?'

'As soon as I heard about the first panama hat. I did not see how Potter could have invented that hat which he declared he had seen beneath the boy's body. It is not a usual type of hat in these days, and is, I should say, completely unknown in the district in which Potter lives. I didn't think there was the slightest reason why he should have mentioned it unless he had actually seen it. And as, therefore, I concluded that that part of his story was true, and as Mr Tidson's activities on the night in question were somewhat odd, a field of what Mrs Bradley calls speculation was opened.'

'Wasn't it the sandal which really dished him, then?'

'Not in my opinion. The defence, I think you will find, will challenge us to prove that the two sandals make a pair. They are both so very badly worn that I think such proof would be almost out of the question.'

'Besides,' said Mrs Bradley, 'Mr Tidson's behaviour with the one which he brought to the hotel was not that of a guilty person, and, if he sticks to his story of having found it alongside the river, I doubt whether we can successfully contradict him. Besides, I think you forget—'

'You don't think he stands a chance of getting off, do you?' asked Laura, struck suddenly by this unwelcome thought. Gavin shrugged.

'Stranger things have happened,' he replied. 'It is almost impossible to tell what kind of evidence will convince the general public, and in a case of child murder it will make a difference if there are women on the jury. Well, I must go back now. Some of us work.' He grinned. Laura nodded, a little coolly, and, looking at Mrs Bradley, said:

'I suppose Connie's evidence would dish herself as well as Mr Tidson if she could be got to speak? I mean, she helped to transport the body, didn't you say?'

'No, I didn't say so, and I don't think she did. I don't think Biggin was killed on Saint Catherine's Hill at all. I think the murder took place very close to where he was found. None but a madman would have dreamed of transporting the body that distance and over such difficult ground.'

'How did Connie get hold of Mr Tidson's gloves to be able to plant them in that hole on the hill? And the second sandal – where did that come from?'

'I leave all that to you,' said Mrs Bradley. 'I can only say that they appeared in the hole *after* the police and I had both scrutinized its contents. Does that suggest anything to you?'

'Only that Connie went to some pains to make certain that the sins of her Uncle Edris should find him out.'

'True. Go on from there.'

'I can't.'

'You will. But Mr Tidson did *not* try to murder Crete. He has a perfect alibi, unless Mrs Preece-Harvard is lying.'

'And is she?'

'No, I don't think so, child. The forked stick was Connie again.'

Chapter Twenty-Two

> *'I caught my last Trout with a worm, now I will*
> *put on a minnow and try a quarter of an hour*
> *about yonder trees for another, and so walk*
> *towards our lodgings ... But turn out of the*
> *way a little, good Scholar, towards yonder high*
> *honeysuckle hedge: there we'll sit and sing ...'*
> IZAAK WALTON (*The Compleat Angler*)

THE magistrates remanded Mr Tidson.

'We need further evidence,' said Gavin. 'Where in heaven's name do we get it?'

'We concentrate upon the peculiar and distinctive features of the case,' Mrs Bradley replied. 'Chief among them I rate the obscure movements and extraordinary actions of Connie Carmody. There is also the one inexplicable lapse of Mr Tidson.'

'Of course,' said Gavin, pursuing his own thoughts, 'Tidson has put up a pretty good show. He's declared that the gloves were planted – a point we can hardly dispute – and he's underlined the complete absence of motive. Absence of motive, that is—'

'So far as a jury is concerned. I agree,' said Mrs Bradley placidly. 'A jury wouldn't look at Mr Tidson. Practice makes perfect is such an old-fashioned idea.'

'It isn't only the absence of motive,' said Laura. 'They'll see that if the gloves were planted there was no reason why that hat shouldn't have been planted, too – that is, if they believe Potter. And then there's another thing—'

'Oh, let it all come!' groaned Gavin.

'Well, don't you see what Mrs Croc. means by Mr Tidson's curious lapse? There ought to have been a third victim.'

'Eh?' said Gavin, staring.

'Me,' said Laura. 'If we really think he murdered little Grier because the kid saw him take a ducking, I ought to have been murdered weeks ago. I actually tossed him in.'

'Good Lord, yes, so you did.'

'Well, why hasn't he crept up behind me with his half-brick? It was different with the bloke who threw him in first. I don't suppose their paths have crossed again.'

'It's a point,' said Gavin, rubbing his jaw.

'How do you suppose that Connie got hold of his gloves, and – we'll say for the sake of argument – his hat?' Mrs Bradley enquired.

'Burgled his bedroom, I imagine.'

'I don't think she'd have dared. She was very much afraid of him at that time. She may have wiped out his finger-prints later.'

'He could have left his hat and gloves in the Cathedral at some time,' said Laura. 'But why on earth didn't he say so?'

'He will – at the trial – if it ever comes to the point. And the point is it may sound like the truth. We have to face the fact that Mr Tidson is as clever as Connie is foolish, and the jury may well believe him.'

'And the old villian is not committed for trial,' said Gavin, looking perturbed. 'He'd like to make her the guilty one, and himself right about her motive – she did every-thing she could to get him hanged.'

'And over-did it,' observed Laura. 'But surely Mr Tidson soon found out what she was up to? Why didn't he give her away?'

'I said he was a clever old man,' said Mrs Bradley. 'No doubt it suited him very well to let Connie go all the way in faking the evidence. He depended upon me to save him. He as good as told me so. The deeper Connie involved herself the harder it would be for us to find out the truth. He knew that perfectly well. He must have chuckled when he brought that meaningless sandal to the *Domus*.'

'Not entirely meaningless,' said Laura.

'Meaningless so far as the police were concerned,' admitted Gavin. 'We can't even prove that those sandals ever belonged to young Biggin. There's nothing to show that they did. His parents are not prepared to swear to anything. His father wants to stick to that bit of money, and hates the police like poison. But if Tidson can't be proved guilty, I still don't get what his game was unless—'

'Yes, that's it,' said Mrs Bradley.

'You mean he realised that Connie was doing her best to incriminate him, and that if only he could give her rope enough she would hang *herself* in the end?'

'That is what I think, but of course we shall never prove it. Connie has been criminally foolish, but I think we all knew who the guilty party was. Of course, she had a strong double motive in trying to incriminate him—'

'To get Mr Tidson hanged and so be rid of him out of her aunt's house, and to save for ever young Preece-Harvard,' said Laura.

'But, of course, she gave herself away (as I told you) by placing what she believed to be objects which would incriminate Mr Tidson in that hole in the ground on the top of the hill *after* she had seen me search the hole. That was a childish thing to do. Then – very interesting, this! – she gave herself a black eye that morning when she saw that the others all had one!'

'I wonder what caused a careful person like Mr Tidson to leave his precious gloves in the Cathedral?' said Laura, frowning.

'I have checked the Cathedral services,' Mrs Bradley replied, 'and I think he must have been carried away by the setting of Bairstow in D.'

Mr Tidson was released for lack of evidence, and immediately rejoined his wife in Tenerife – this to her great annoyance, as she informed Miss Priscilla Carmody by letter. Connie Carmody, anticipating trouble in England, went over on the next boat a week later. Miss Priscilla Carmody received news of her safe arrival from Crete Tidson, and almost immediately afterwards there followed from Gavin (who had gone at once to the island) news that her body and that of Mr Tidson had been recovered from deep water at the end of the Mole at Santa Cruz.

They were locked in each other's arms in a grip that was not the clasp of love. The charitable islanders believed that one of them had died in an effort to save the other from drowning. Laura, drawing Mrs Bradley's attention to this report in the English newspapers, remarked:

'Well, I'm glad it didn't happen in Winchester,' and her blue-grey eyes saw in retrospect the grey Cathedral, the hills and the lovely darkening reaches of the river.

The prospect widened and grew as clear as a vision. She saw willows and the tall, green reeds, the patches of weed, the clear and stony shallows, the uncertain deeps; the rough and thick-leaved water-plants by the brink, the blue forget-me-not, the toffee-brown water-dropwort; and in side-stream and carrier, ditch and brook no less than in the broadly-curving river, over the weirs and under the little bridges, the smooth, hard rush of the water.

She saw the mallard in flight and the moorhens' nests built on flotsam; the scuttling dabchicks, the warblers swinging on the sedge; she saw the lithe stoat slinking swiftly back to his home; the swans like galleons for beauty; and, last, a solitary trout in a small deep pool, as he anchored himself against the run of the stream.